Sparks Fly Upward

BOOK 1 of the SUPERSTARS TRILOGY

SIG KRIEBEL

REDEMPTION
PRESS

Published by Redemption Press, PO Box 427, Enumclaw, WA 98022. Toll Free (844) 2REDEEM (273-3336)

Redemption Press is honored to present this title in partnership with the author. The views expressed or implied in this work are those of the author. Redemption Press provides our imprint seal representing design excellence, creative content, and high quality production.

Unless otherwise noted, all Scriptures are taken from the Holy Bible, New International Version, Copyright © 1973, 1978, 1984 by the International Bible Society. Used by permission of Zondervan Publishing House. The "NIV" and "New International Version" trademarks are registered in the United States Patent and Trademark Office by International Bible Society."

This is a work of fiction. All of the characters, names, incidents, organizations, and dialogue in this novel are either the products of the author's imagination or are used fictitiously.

ISBN 13: 978-1-68314-015-3 (Print)
          978-1-68314-016-0 (ePub)
          978-1-68314-017-7 (Mobi)

Library of Congress Catalog Card Number: 2016948740

Stock Photos by:
© Shutterstock / InnervisionArt
© Shutterstock / Alex Malikov
© Shutterstock / Tatiana Koshutina
© Can Stock Photo Inc. / jeka84

*To the greatest Teacher of all and
the students who follow Him*

*... man is born to trouble
as surely as sparks fly upward.*

—Job 5:7

August

1

"WHAT ARE YOU afraid of?"

J. Bradford McCauley smirked at the question but refrained from offering a sarcastic comeback. Why risk insulting one of his students by belittling his bluster on the first day of school? Half the things teenage boys said came from rampant testosterone, and this accusation wrapped in a question was no different. It sprang not from humble, sincere curiosity—which was ironic, considering McCauley's real fears—but from basic adolescent arrogance. Teenage psychology was pretty predictable. The goal of the whole conversation leading up to the kid's question was to confront authority, to mark territory, to test limits.

"Come on!" the kid insisted. "Tell us! What are you so afraid of?"

Entertained, the class waited. In their juvenile mindset, any refusal to answer on McCauley's part, any hesitation, even, would be tantamount to an admission of fear.

As if on cue came the next words: "You're just afraid."

All its disguise now discarded, the question lay exposed in its true colors as a blatant, in-your-face challenge designed to humiliate. The atmosphere tensed with anticipation.

"No, I'm not afraid," McCauley said. He sat down on the varnished desk before the class in a move calculated to impress them with his unflappable control. "I'm just not a gambler."

Chuckles leaked from the students sitting near the burly blond boy with a rosy face and straight flaxen hair who was instigating the ruckus. On top of his desk, his notebook and textbook were not opened. As the students had previewed the course syllabus and policies, the boy, whose name was Matt Rademacher, said, "I'll bet you that I can guess your height within an inch, your weight within five pounds, and your age within two years. If I do, you let me skip class the first week. Okay?"

McCauley had smiled obligingly. These were the kinds of easygoing shenanigans you expected the first day of school. In the long run, playing along might establish valuable rapport with the kids.

"I don't know ..." he had said, and before his last word had died, Matt was condemning him for cowardice.

"All right, then," Matt replied now. "I won't skip class. But you have to let us go early, okay?"

Murmurs of approval spread through the room.

"Be my guest. Make your guess."

Every eye in the class turned to Matt, who closed his eyes tightly and placed his forefingers, dramatically, on his temples.

"Six foot ... one," he said. "Weight: 210 pounds. Age ... age ... age ..."

"Eighteen!" someone shouted, raising a round of laughter.

"Age: Thirty-five years old," Matt finished.

Every face returned to McCauley.

"That's pretty good," he said.

"But is it good enough?" Matt asked. "Let's see your driver's license."

McCauley reached into his hip pocket and felt a ripple of alarm shake his heart. His wallet was not there. It contained no money, it never did, but he could not afford to lose his Visa credit card or even his Riverside University library card, which would cost five bucks to replace.

"My weight is 213 pounds," he said. "My height and age are just as you said."

The students applauded and cheered, and Matt stood up and bowed to his admirers.

"So, B-Mac, when can we leave?"

McCauley held back from censuring Matt for calling him by the fabricated nickname. The kid was just trying to see how far he could push a part-time teacher. More and more, teenagers took it for granted that they could assume informality in their relationships with adult authorities. The trend did not bother McCauley.

He answered, "As soon as we finish the handout." He had no doubt he could use up the final fifteen minutes.

On the wall the red second hand swept its regular tick-tick-tick around the face of the sterile white clock. Most of the twenty-five senior high school history students were darting occasional brazen glances at the clock, wondering how long their teacher might extend his introductory remarks. When he had been their age, McCauley remembered, you went to school only half-days for the first week, which helped you ease your body and mind back into the academic routine after a summer devoid of intellectual exercise. Not anymore. Halfway through the last period of the day, his class had become fidgety. He remembered that feeling, too. Even though winds of change had blown through education during his generation, clocks still looked the same, and he remembered how slowly the second hand moved from one minute mark to the next while you waited for the bell to ring. Sometimes it seemed as if time got stuck there, in between two seconds.

"Everybody look at the paragraph on late work," he said. "My main rule is this: Get your work in on time. Deadlines are crucial to me, because I work on such a tight schedule myself. I don't want to have late work coming in that fouls up my schedule. That's why the penalty is so severe. One letter grade for each day an assignment is late."

Some of the students fell to scribbling notes on the syllabus. First days always amused McCauley: So many students paid teachers and their rules a respect that eroded to contempt or ridicule before the week was out.

In the front row, a pretty brown-haired girl with a baggy gray Riverside T-shirt was gazing out the window, twirling a maple leaf by its stem between her thumb and forefinger, her sandals on the floor, her bare feet resting in the wire basket for books under the forward seat. Looking at her, McCauley remembered a vivid image from a song he loved, a pair of lines about a girl with her shoes kicked off, sitting on top of a car, sipping a drink under a gentle rain.

"As for grading, let me emphasize that the research paper will be the single most important piece of work you do in this class. Your progress on this paper will count for half your grade during the first quarter, and the final product will count for half your grade for the semester. During the first quarter you need to choose a topic, discuss it with me in conference, do the research, and prepare an outline. The second quarter you actually write the paper. If you've prepared well, the writing will be a snap."

To emphasize his meaning he snapped his fingers, which shot a twinge of pain through his wrist.

"Second semester we will build on that paper," he went on, unconsciously flexing his fingers. "For the next few weeks, every Monday I will take a minute to remind you about the research paper and encourage you to get to work. You won't be able to say that you forgot. How many of you have ever done a paper that takes all semester?"

Of the half of the class still listening, about one third raised their hands. "Okay," he continued. "Do *not* wait too long to begin. Choose a topic as soon as you can."

The girl sitting next to the leaf-twirler raised her hand and asked, "Can you give us some ideas, at least?"

McCauley had expected this question and began shaking his head while it was still in the air.

"No, no, no," he said with energy. "Why not? Because I don't know any of you well enough to give you ideas. If I knew what interested you, then I could give you ideas. Look, I want this to be a personally rewarding project, not just a required part of the class. Take something you are really deeply interested in, and study its history. That's all. For me, that would mean studying what the Founding Fathers of this country believed. But you decide for yourself."

The girl said, "Can it be something that doesn't have anything to do with school?"

McCauley's fingers quit flexing and reached up to flatten out his thick black mustache, then ran down his chin, itchy from that morning's dull-bladed shave. Suspecting another attempt to paint him into a corner, he replied, "It can be, yes. But we'll decide that when you meet with me, individually, to talk about the topics."

"How 'bout football?" blurted Matt.

"Football is okay for a general topic, but of course it would have to be narrowed down. You might study the history of certain football rules, for example. Or you might study how equipment has evolved. Get it?"

Matt nodded and whispered something to a buddy. The notion of narrowing a focus seemed to drain his excitement.

"I want you to have a genuine interest in your subject," McCauley resumed, addressing the whole class. "That's why I don't have a list of sample topics. Make up your own topics yourselves. You must learn that everything has a history behind it, and that history has made it what it is. If you ignore the past, you won't understand the present."

He looked down at his wristwatch, which he had set on his desk, as was his custom when teaching. The time was 2:35. He still had ten minutes to go. With a college class, he would have no qualms about dismissing them early, but not here, where the taxpayer was footing the bill one hundred percent, where any indiscretion might elicit a hostile response from parents or other powers that be.

After all, this was Brookstone High School, the state's pride.

"Look at the last page," he said, initiating a flurry of page-turning. "It's about cheating. In a word: Don't."

"Aw, BM, you're no fun," came Matt's voice, trying a new nickname.

"You can try it if you want," McCauley said. "But if you get caught, the penalty is spelled out for you on this page. It's pretty severe, and I doubt if it's worth the risk."

"But Matt is a devoted gambler," came another boy's voice. The back of the room broke into more laughter and clapping. McCauley looked down at his seating chart, its ink barely dry, and determined the comment had come from Cody Summers.

McCauley was puzzled by the push-back against the standard rules against cheating. "I wouldn't advise taking this gamble," he repeated.

"But BM," Matt said, "didn't you ever cheat when you were in school?"

Still raw from Matt's earlier line of questioning, McCauley flinched.

"I *am* in school," he retorted, recovering his composure, and, with a burst of his own bravado, he added, "I can speak from personal experience that it isn't worth the risk."

"Personal experience? So you *have* cheated."

"No, that's not what I said."

"Come on, tell us about your deep, dark secrets."

McCauley tried to keep a straight face. If he smiled, he knew all too well, he would lose control of the class on Day 1 of the school year, and the next 179 would melt into absolute chaos.

"I keep them locked away in a safe," he said.

"Ooooh. So you've cheated *and* you have hidden secrets." The students at the back of the class were laughing uproariously, those in front struggling to quash giggles.

"Why are you all so curious about *cheating*? Why would you want to even think about compromising your integrity? Your integrity, your reputation, your good name—that's the most important thing you'll carry through your life. Don't throw it away. In this class, I expect you to do your own work. If you try to pass off somebody else's work as your own, you're cheating yourself as well as that somebody else." For emphasis, he was about to add "and God," but he checked himself. In a public school, to mention even his unorthodox deity in an ethical context might land him in hot water.

Besides, he had already run into trouble with education officials one time too many. What a hypocrite he was, warning *them* not to cheat.

He settled against the front of the desk and changed the subject, saying, "Let me run through this seating chart."

Sitting in the front desk of the right-hand row was the girl who was still staring out the window. She had filled in her name as Erin Delaney, and when he called it, she jerked to attention.

"That's me," she said. When he called the name of the student behind her, Erin looked outside again and kept twirling the maple leaf.

The girl next to her, who had asked the question about topics, was Jessica Southard. She looked a little like Erin.

Double-checking the seating chart, verifying nicknames and correct pronunciations, took less than ten minutes.

"Well, we still have a few minutes left. Does anyone have any questions about the class, or the syllabus?" McCauley asked. "Or about me?"

A student asked whether he was married. He was accustomed to that sort of thing, from both high schoolers and college undergraduates.

"No, but I'm engaged," he said.

"Where's your ring, then?"

Several students laughed as McCauley held up his left hand.

"I'm not engaged to a woman," he said. This evoked even more laughter. "I'm engaged to my work."

"You're a history teacher," one student said. "You're living in the past."

He smiled as if he had never heard the joke before, and he let his eyes move from face to face. They came to rest on Erin Delaney's, which had rejoined the class, probably to check the time. Her skin looked brown and wholesome, her tan natural, not purchased. A crescent of freckles darkened her face, ear to ear.

"But your future is in my hands," he said. Almost in unison, the class let out a low *ooooh*, and waited for a comeback from the student who had made the crack about living in the past. Erin Delaney made eye contact with McCauley, then quickly turned away.

The red second hand swept across the top of the clock, the 2:45 bell sounded, and students exited the room.

Matt stopped to ask, "How come you didn't let us out early?"

"I never promised to. Hey, you work at an amusement park or something? Guessing ages and weights?"

"No." He smiled defiantly.

"How'd you do it, then?"

"I *cheated*." He tossed a thin wallet onto the desk.

"Where'd you get that? I was worried I had lost it."

"We picked your pocket on the way in."

"*We?* You and who else?"

"Cody mainly. Don't worry, all your money and cards are still there."

"All my *money*? That's a good one. Why did you do it?"

"Some of the girls said we couldn't, so we arranged a little wager."

McCauley grunted, calculating. Too many of Matt's verbal darts had struck near the bull's-eye of his personal past. If Matt could pick his pocket so easily, was it possible that Matt might have also … no, McCauley decided, no way. Still, he wished that when he had referred to his safe, he had also been studying Matt's face, searching it for any sign of understanding.

"A wager with the girls," he said. "I should have guessed. What do you win?"

Matt winked and said, "You don't want to know. After all, you're already married."

McCauley nodded, pocketing his well-worn billfold. This Rademacher kid was clever with words.

"Just kidding," Matt continued. "All I win is a can of Pringles. Some new flavor. They have about a hundred now."

After the last student was out the door, McCauley swept his bare hand across the whiteboard to erase his name, then wiped his hand on his loose blue corduroy slacks, leaving a dark smudge of marker powder. He collected the papers off his desk, packed them into his green canvas backpack, and retrieved his motorcycle helmet from its safe haven under his desk. Almost ready to leave, he spotted the flotsam and jetsam of first-day trash in the back of the room, and when he went to clean up the mess, he found a note, addressed to nobody and signed by nobody, that said: DID YOU HEAR MATT WON $50K? Nearby he picked up a folded paper on which someone had drawn a crude hangman scaffold with a completed stick-figure corpse, its head cocked in death to one side, above five blanks with only one letter filled in, an *E* in the middle slot.

Outside the door to his classroom he listened to the familiar sounds of a dawning semester—the rumble of hundreds of feet on stairways and in hallways, the metallic squeak and slam of lockers opening and shutting, the chatter of voices mingling in recognition and reunion. Every autumn marked a new beginning, as fresh as each morning. McCauley strapped his watch back onto his wrist and flexed his hand a few more times, wondering what new problem had arisen in his aging body.

In the hallway he stopped to watch the students, their faces bright with rest and the excitement of the summer that had crested a few weeks earlier. At that age, he remembered, seeing old friends in new settings brought an avid rush to your blood. School seemed so new and promising and romantic those first few days, bursting with so many dreams, so many hopes, and so many resolutions to study harder, pay more attention in class, goof off less, and impress teachers and coaches and parents and peers—especially the opposite sex. He remembered so well, for he had played that game so well. In fact, he was still playing it at a level where the stakes were higher and the dreams more ambitious.

Academically, Brookstone High School boasted the best players in the state of Indiana. Two years earlier the school had been honored as the best in its classification (between 500 and 999 students) by a governor's educational panel. Its reputation was unshakeable and growing. Its SAT scores averaged among the top two percent nationally, and the president of the United States himself had mentioned its remarkable achievements during an education speech in Indianapolis the previous year. Recent graduates had gone on to prestigious schools such as Harvard, Yale, Princeton, MIT, Northwestern, Duke, Stanford, and UC-Berkeley. This record was quite significant for a school that less than a decade before had consolidated from seven smaller high schools with colorful rural names like Corbin Creek, Orange Stone, and Tipton.

J. Bradford McCauley did not put much stock in these tidbits of trivia, however, for he was just a part-time secondary teacher whose real interest and investment lay twelve miles south, at Riverside University, and—as the teenage wisecracker had truly pointed out—two centuries in the past. The only reason he knew about Brookstone's blue-ribbon achievements was that they were emblazoned for everyone to read about in two-inch letters on posters in the school's Wall of Fame, where administrators overseeing a staff of student assistants scurried to keep up with the accomplishments of the school.

On his way out of the building, McCauley paused in the Atrium that housed the "Hall." The principal, William LaGrange, and the guidance director, Tolan Myers, were leading a tour for a cluster of elderly visitors who were no doubt educators from Indianapolis or Chicago or Washington, taking a taxpayer-financed trip to find out what made Brookstone tick. LaGrange was speaking, and, because the Atrium was at that moment relatively empty, his voice came to McCauley in layers of echoes. Myers stood to the side, his hands clasped behind his back, his balding crown glistening in the muted sunshine that fell softly from the skylight overhead.

McCauley's own high school and high school experience had been only average. He had never breathed an atmosphere of serious academia until college, and he regretted this deficiency once he saw how better college preparation would have served as a springboard to the success he still sought, saving him perhaps five years of his quest. He was thirty-five now, and the superstardom he pursued and hoped to claim with his doctoral dissertation was almost within his reach. Expecting to finish his Ph.D. within the year, he could already taste the satisfied thrill of reputation that awaited him when his contribution to the field would be hailed as a landmark of avant-garde scholarship.

McCauley daydreamed a while longer beneath the black-and-white faces of past Brookstone valedictorians and other award winners looking down from on high, their photographs intentionally and symbolically situated above eye level so that visitors and succeeding generations of students would have to look up to see them.

He heard his name called. LaGrange was waving for him to join the group.

"This young man is an example of what I mean by taking advantage of our natural resources," the principal said, placing his hand on McCauley's shoulder. "When you have a Riverside University a stone's throw south, you figure out ways to benefit from it. Brad McCauley is a Ph.D. candidate at Riverside, and we have been privileged to have him teach U.S. history for the past four semesters. Each semester we have up to ten part-time faculty from Riverside. Of course this cuts our costs because we don't have to pay for their full benefits"—here McCauley noticed Myers smiling from the fringe of the group—"and at the same time we get top-flight teachers."

One of the visitors asked whether McCauley was certified.

"He is," LaGrange answered quickly. "He taught a few years in Ohio public schools before coming to Riverside for graduate school. Not every one of our part-time faculty is as formally qualified."

Another visitor asked, "Why would someone in Mr. McCauley's position want to teach in a public school?"

McCauley paused until he knew LaGrange had no answer for him. Then he said, "It's partly economics and partly for career purposes. A graduate student can always use a few extra dollars. And I believe that the scholar of the future owes a debt to the generations who will follow, even to those students who will not study history past high school."

He opened his mouth to add to his explanation, then checked himself. There *was* a third part to his answer—he longed for a past that he could never recover, to walk back through a door forever shut to him—but why dredge up that piece of history?

Nodding, the questioner said, "Do you also teach classes at Riverside?"

"I do."

"And which do you prefer?"

He shrugged and answered, "The highest bidder." These days, that was the plain truth. "Actually, my answer would depend on where you are from."

After the chuckles died down, LaGrange said, "Thank you, Brad. I know you're on a strict schedule, and so are we." He said to the group: "If you'll follow me on into the library ..."

McCauley loved his phrase "the scholar of the future." His eyes surveyed the pantheon of academic stars looking down from the heavens and wondered whether among them might not be a rival with whom he would lock horns in the years to come. He relished the prospect of pitting his learning and rhetorical skills against those of other experts, other scholars.

By and by, the click of a woman's shoes echoed into his ears from across the hardwood floor, and he turned to see the petite form of perky Robin Hillis, the English teacher.

She called hello to him and waved, and a glitter of gold from her wrist also waved.

"Welcome back, Mr. McCauley," she said. She stopped at a door leading out of the Atrium to give him a chance to reply.

"Thank you," he said. "Did you have a good summer? Did you teach?"

"Not me. Summer is for family." He thought the words sounded mechanical, possibly remorseful.

He nodded.

"Are you teaching just the one class again?"

"Just the one," he said. "I wouldn't have time for more."

He could see that she felt awkward. Should she go on through the door, or keep talking from a distance, or walk over to him? McCauley decided to help her out. He looked at his watch and said, "I hardly have time for *this*. I have a class at Riverside at four o'clock." Robin waved again and went through the door, her long dress swishing.

Outdoors a flood of sunlight poured down from a cloudless sky. Bees buzzed among the sappy tree boughs hanging over the nearest parked cars. Students milled about in pockets that were either rowdy or secretive. McCauley put on his sunglasses. Behind their dark cover he could see that many eyes were watching him, sizing him up as a teacher, regarding him as the unknown quantity that he was. Though this was his third year, he had taught only four classes total, all senior-level, so every student he had taught before was now gone. He was a perpetual question mark.

McCauley put on his helmet but immediately removed it to clean off a smudge from the faceguard. To inspect his work, he held it up and turned it at different angles, and in so doing he saw a distorted convex reflection of the ornate Brookstone High School building—its tall marble columns, its wide portico and steps, the arches above the doors and windows, the detailed decorative brickwork, the ivy climbing the brown stone walls. Even in the puffed-up image it looked impressive. It really was pretty fabulous for what was basically just a small-town school, he had to admit.

He started his motorcycle and pulled out of the parking lot as the first of the fleet of yellow buses pulled in. A Frisbee sailing across his path momentarily eclipsed the brilliant disk of the sun and he jumped at the brief flash. Matt Rademacher's question came back to him—"What are you afraid of?"

A block farther he slowed down to cross the bumpy railroad tracks. Then he sped south.

2

TRY AS SHE might, Robin Hillis found it hard to regard Brad McCauley as anything other than a comic figure. Her information was admittedly sketchy, coming almost entirely from Lydia Knowles, an art teacher whose son was a history student at Riverside University. According to these sources, McCauley was entirely caught up with himself and his private notions about what a couple of dozen philosophers and statesmen thought about God a couple of centuries before. The poor, deluded man really believed he was going to shake the foundations of humanities scholarship.

So yes, he was a comic figure—but her world was sadly short on mirth nowadays, so as she tidied up her own classroom and toyed with different arrangements of desktop items such as her pencil holder and crystal Christmas tree and precious "Birdie" card, she permitted herself also to toy with thoughts about McCauley, for her amusement.

Tall tinted windows spanned the outside wall of her second-story classroom. She paused to look out over the playground and parking lot, both awash in August glare. Across the street from the school stood a Methodist church, built in 1846 with stunning architecture now defaced by crumbling walls; behind it rose the too-flashy sign of the First Fidelity Bank on the next block. When the bank had been built five years before, it had impoverished the skyline, distracting from the church's magnificent steeple. Now, whenever Robin gazed out the window, her eye went first to the bank sign. What a pity. At least it was the bank where she and her husband, Zeb, did business.

Her eyes fell to the foreground, where an ugly mass of twisted metal marred the otherwise pretty landscape between the parking lot and the road. Some ten years earlier an ambitious art student had created the post-modern sculpture that even won a statewide contest. Nevertheless, when the school board first considered displaying it on school grounds, a controversy ensued regarding the wisdom of exhibiting a piece of art that seemed to glamorize chaos and lack of direction in front of a school whose reputation and vision were exactly the opposite. The sculpture melded random discarded junk such as a refrigerator, rebar, computer monitors, mangled bicycle wheels, and concrete blocks—all surmounted by a bent steering wheel on a shaft tilted at an angle that suggested, remotely, the famous flag over Iwo Jima.

Robin turned away. A smudge on a side whiteboard that had resisted her previous efforts at erasing drew her attention. The new markers she was using did not come off the surface very easily. No matter how heavily she threw her minuscule weight behind the eraser, ugly streaks and shadows remained. The new brand of markers probably had a corresponding type of eraser she was supposed to use. Whatever, her boards looked sloppier now than before she had tried to erase them. She would have to ask Bragley and his custodial crew, who were fiercely secretive and almost territorial when it came to their special chemical sprays, to give every board a thorough cleaning. Even then, until she got the right markers or erasers, the problem would keep reappearing, minor, perhaps, but annoying.

In the teachers' lounge, Robin settled into a molded plastic seat at a round table. Following a generation of petitions and political infighting eventually made moot by state law, cigarettes were at last banned in the lounge; still, the smell of smoke lingered, clinging to curtains and the fabric of the couches and stamped into the carpet through the years. Never a smoker, she had not used the lounge often during her teaching career, instead developing the habit of grading papers in her classroom or at home and eating lunch in her car or outdoors or even in the cafeteria.

And, because she so seldom came to the designated work room for teachers, she had never talked face-to-face with McCauley. He *did* use the lounge—and he was, coincidentally, a smoker, according to breathless journal entries from students, mostly girls, in Robin's classes, girls who bemoaned the cruel trick of fate by which McCauley's part-time schedule brought him to school only one period per day. Like second-hand smoke, all of Robin's filtered information about McCauley did not seem very noticeable or harmful, but she wondered about him and his impact on students, because his name came up more often than you would expect for a man who was on campus so little.

Her mailbox yielded up the usual first-day junk. Another copy of the student handbook, with changes highlighted in yellow. A one-page listing of faculty and staff addresses and phone numbers with a request stapled to it, asking for everyone to verify that *their*—the pronoun disagreement standard for administrative material—information was correct. Tomorrow's announcements, which she was to read to her home room, already printed. Finally, a blue half-page announcing that on November 5 after school in the library all faculty and staff were required to attend a one-hour "Awareness Workshop" on sexual harassment.

Robin went back to her table. She was in no hurry to go home: Zeb was a thousand miles away for the next three days, again. She had no papers to grade, no lesson plans to prepare, and no dinner to make. She felt guilty sitting on her little island of potential leisure—there must be something to do. Across the lounge, another teacher was bending over the copy machine, consternation wrinkling his brow.

Tolan Myers walked in and looked around, mild disapproval registering on his features. Once school was in full swing, Brookstone's full-time faculty would be required to stay on campus until at least four o'clock. Many were involved in extra-curricular activities that kept them until much later, but even those who were finished for the day at 2:45 were expected to remain.

Myers said, "Hello, Robin. How was your first day?" He was a little chubbier than last spring, she thought. Too many Dairy Queen Blizzards.

"Day number one was fine," she said, "but it's only a cover page, and everyone knows you can't judge a book by its cover."

"What do you mean?"

"I don't know." She laughed at herself. "I was just trying to be metaphorical."

"Did Erin Delaney talk to you today?"

"No."

"Do you know who she is?"

"No."

"She's the younger sister of Patricia Delaney and Sarah Delaney."

"Oh." The older Delaneys were past valedictorians whose father, a local rags-to-riches story, was one of Brookstone High's major supporters. "Sarah was one of my students, but not Patricia."

"Erin Delaney wants to switch classes and have you for English instead of Butch Young. She said she'd feel more comfortable with a woman teacher."

"Oh. And you're asking my permission?"

"It's an extra student, I know, but this is a special family." His voice sank to a whisper and he added, "It's partly my fault, too. She made this request last spring when she registered, and I put a note in her file. But things got real hectic this summer at Dairy Queen, when we had to get ready for the inspection—well, I shouldn't make excuses. But Erin's request got lost in the shuffle. So if you would say yes, it would help me out as well as Erin."

"Oh. Okay." Though she harbored no reservations about letting someone new into the class, she liked to hear Myers rationalize his mistakes. He taught two classes of mathematics and spent the rest of the day directing guidance counselors. Plus he owned the town's Dairy Queen, which was supposed to give students (those few who might not be college-bound) experience in running a business and working with people.

By the time Robin reached the school parking lot, it was almost empty. She rolled down her windows and opened the sun roof, diluting the baked air of her car's maroon interior. After starting her engine, she tilted down the rearview mirror to check her appearance. Any day now she expected to see the first signs of sagging skin from her cheekbones or jaws to complement the first gray hairs that had sprung up over the summer, less a discouragement than a novelty—seeing them, she had stood before the mirror for five minutes in utter surprise.

Now forty-six, she could no longer remember the last time anyone had mistaken her for a sister of her own daughter, a mistake hilariously common during Anyssa's teenage years. Even Zeb used to come up behind her on the porch or in the garden and ask, "What's up, 'Nyss?" Those were the days! How fun to put on jeans and a sweatshirt and go the Bridgebury Mall with Anyssa and revel in the truth that their delicate bodies were proportioned and shaped almost identically, their skin equally smooth and soft. Ah, yes, those were the days!

Robin drove home. She lived only a few blocks away, and in a few days she would resume her routine of walking to and from school in decent weather. She didn't feel old, not really. Just … abandoned. Discarded. With the kids and Zeb around she had been more active and felt more alive. But now Anyssa and Trevor were home almost as much as their father, even though Trevor was working in Detroit and Anyssa was in college in Kentucky. Zeb, bucking for a promotion at Key-Comm, had quit apologizing for his long hours on the road, which had become a way of life during the last two years. Both of them realized that every time he expressed any sorrow it had the unwanted effect of calling attention to his increasing absence. But Zeb believed he would be rewarded with a promotion by Christmas.

Robin lightly tapped her horn turning into her driveway, and across the street five faces popped up and a couple of paintbrushes waved. The Roosts were painting their quaint little picket fence.

She went over to say hello.

"Who are *you*?" Howard Roost asked in mock ignorance. "You look like the lady who used to live across the street from us—what was her name, honey?" He looked at his wife, a spot of white highlighting her chin, then up to the sky, grasping at an elusive name, "Willis, Wills, Hills, something like that. But we haven't seen her in many moons."

Robin blushed with a quiver of guilt. She had not been a good neighbor recently. In fact, she could not even remember her last good visit with Howard and Jerri.

"I guess I haven't seen much of you lately, have I?" she began.

"Honey, don't we have another brush somewhere?" Howard Roost asked Jerri. Robin laughed. Lena Roost, always the picture of health, said,

"At least *ask* her first, Dad!" Lena's son Philip, five or six years old, was also helping, along with Jack Kitchell, one of Robin's former students and Lena's "boyfriend" for too many years to count.

Jerri agreed, "It has been too long, Robin! But it's our fault, I guess."

"Everyone's so busy. I hardly ever see Zeb anymore, either!"

Howard's brush stopped midstroke. Sensing his scrutiny, Robin hurried on, "All he does is travel, travel, travel, it seems like."

Jerri asked, "How was the first day of school?"

"They're always the same. Everyone is so excited to be back that they forget how much hard work is ahead. Lena, your name came up today when some teachers were talking about the brightest students they ever had. Your brother got a vote, too."

Lena brushed a drooping blond bang from her face and said, "Wait till you get Philip."

The boy piped, "Where's Mr. Hillis?"

"He's in Dallas this week," she replied. "How long is it going to take to finish this job?"

All eyes turned to Jack, a certified public accountant in Bridgebury. "My estimate is three more hours," he said. "But with another helper we could cut that by at least ten percent."

"I could help …"

"No, we're just kidding you," Howard said, looking up. "I'm sure you have plenty of work of your own."

Not really, Robin thought.

Howard had the most appealing eyes, small and deep-set, surrounded by wrinkles and circles so that it looked like someone had dug into his sockets to put his eyes in place. The eyes of Jesus must have looked like that, she often thought. Compassionate and exuberant and knowing and brimming with life.

She turned to cross the street back to her house—then something checked her, some involuntary impulse that at first hovered just beyond her consciousness but soon resolved into a simple longing for the past, a wish to recover even a whisper of the joy she remembered from many magical hours spent with the Roost family, hours that always transported her deeper into everything that mattered, everything that was real about her life and all of life.

"What were you all talking about?" she asked, awkwardly. "Before I came over, I mean. You all looked so animated!"

As soon as she asked, a pang of embarrassment swept through her. Howard's eyes studied her face, penetrating, searching.

Almost in defense, she blurted out another sentence, straight from her heart: "Oh! I just miss talking to you, all of you!"

Howard shifted his attention back to the fence. She could tell that he was weighing how to answer her, or perhaps whether to answer at all.

She could read him like a poem! She knew his mannerisms from all those shared times, the fun multi-family dinners whose desserts turned into timeless, stimulating conversations, the impromptu summer-night get-togethers on the Roosts' exquisitely trellised back patio, the cooler autumn evenings around the patio's glowing fire pit, the Sunday brunches the Roosts used to throw, opening their home to anyone from their church or neighborhood …

"Sparks fly upward," she heard Howard say.

"What?"

"We were talking about how sparks fly upward. In the Book of Job, one of his comforters says, 'Man is born to trouble as surely as sparks fly upward.'"

"Oh."

Why had she spoken up? She had intruded where she did not belong, trespassed on sacred ground. The last thing she wanted was to talk about *her* sparks, *her* trouble.

"That's not very … uplifting," she remarked, unable to stay silent.

"Well, it's the truth," Howard said. "And you know the story gets better."

"But it gets worse first, right?"

Why couldn't she shut up? An unwelcome suspicion stole over her, a sensation of danger, of venturing too close to a fire, of edging too near the brink of a bleak abyss that would overcome her with vertigo and suck her into its dark, deathly embrace. Yet she felt powerless to resist—her questions kept forcing themselves through her lips, energized with a life of their own, leaving her a mere spectator, watching and waiting for answers that she knew would not come from her wonderful neighbor or from across the street, but from someone and someplace far more wonderful.

"Right." Howard glanced at the fence again. The others were painting but obviously listening. "Are you sure you don't want to help us?"

"I can't," she said firmly. "You said it yourself: I have plenty of my own work to do."

She said good-bye and retreated into her century-old home, all alone. From the lovely bay window in her living room, which Howard Roost had built five years ago, she watched his family whitewash the fence with as much fun as you could find in any Mark Twain scene. Only Jack seemed to treat it as a job—but then he was always different. Why he had never married Lena was one of the town's enduring mysteries. Jerri had told her once that Jack didn't understand the needs of women or the ways of women, and now, as Robin Hillis recalled that conversation, her mind drifted uneasily to Zeb.

3

"JESS, I JUST don't like men teachers," Erin Delaney said. "That's all."

A gum bubble the color of watermelon green grew from Jessica's lips, expanding to the size of a cantaloupe before its thinning surface burst and her tongue and fingers peeled it off her chin.

"Why? I mean, it's not like you have to *sleep* with him."

"Everything is always *sex* with you," Erin said. "You're acting just like a guy." They both laughed, and Jess rolled up her pant legs and dipped her toes into the water. "There aren't any women history teachers left," she said.

"I know."

"I'm sort of glad Matt's in that class, but I'm sort of not glad. Know what I mean?" Jess's voice pleaded for affirmation.

"I think you're better off without him, if you want my opinion."

"Are you better off without Nathan?"

Erin untucked her long shirttails from her blue jeans. Before she could answer, Jess said, "You're right: This isn't too cold at all."

The two cousins waded out to the middle of the river, which during the rain-starved summer had never been more than waist-deep. Large boulders broke the surface of the lazy current like dozens of islands. The girls sat on stones and dangled their shiny legs in the water.

"McCauley is good-looking, you have to admit," Jess said, kicking her feet. A canoe appeared around the bend.

"I still can't believe you made me sit in the front, though."

"But I couldn't sit in the back, not with Matt back there!"

"We could have sat in the middle."

The canoe slowed down to steer through the rocks. Erin heard its metal bottom scrape against sand in an especially shallow channel. The two shirtless men in the canoe, their bandanas soaking up sweat around their foreheads, were so engrossed in their tricky navigation that they did not even look up.

"It should be a cinch A," Jess said. "Matt's brother had him last year and said it was a cinch A." Jess had evidently become infatuated with the word *cinch*.

"How come he only teaches one class, I wonder?"

"Because he's still in college. He teaches at Riverside too, and he's finishing up his doctorate."

"How do you know so much about him? Did you find a Facebook page?"

"Erin, it's common knowledge. You would know if you were a little more sociable."

Erin basically ignored social media. Most of her school information came from her cousin, the closest thing she had to a friend.

"So tell me what else you know," she prodded.

Jess was eager to comply: "He's not married—except to his research—he rides a motorcycle because it's cheaper, he lives in an apartment somewhere north of West Bridgebury, he loves pizza, and he smokes but he wants to quit. Plus he's good-looking."

"I wish we were in more classes together."

"Me too."

"What's Matt going to do with all that money he won?"

"Cody said Matt's dad said he could use twenty percent of it to buy a car. Twenty or twenty-five percent, I forget. It works out to $10,000. But Sheena Straley says Matt's going to get a van."

"A van? Why a van?"

"It will be more fun for a bunch of guys to cruise around in a van, I guess. God, I wish we were still going together. I mean, now that he's rich he could really treat me right."

"Have you seen Grandpa Dee lately?"

"No."

"Me either. I think I'll go see him one of these nights."

Not far downstream, Highway 22 spanned the Orange River on its splendid white concrete-and-steel bridge. Every few moments the girls heard the hum of a vehicle passing overhead, its pitch rising while it crossed the bridge and dropping again when it reached solid ground.

"I miss Nathan," Erin said. She looked to shore and saw nothing but white and yellow butterflies; then she unbuttoned her shirt as far as her bra. "I really miss him."

"Why? You never did anything."

"Yes we did, Jess."

"You did? You never told me."

"Just forget it," Erin said, exasperated. In Jess's one-track lexicon, *doing things* meant going to bed with a guy. Poor cousin, would she ever learn that there was more to life than following the crowd?

Even as she mentally criticized Jess, however, Erin cringed at her own hypocrisy, aware that she was no less guilty of following the crowd, or at least knuckling under to the wishes of others. Her inability to resist pressure might look more acceptable, even respectable, since it involved her future career and meant giving in to her parents rather than to friends. Yet what was the difference, really?

Her frank self-assessment brought to mind her first assignment of the school year, a writing prompt asking her to outline an agenda for self-improvement during her senior year. At first she had rolled her eyes at the condescending question. Mrs. Hillis was well-known for her love of student journals, a blessing for the many students who reveled in self-absorption but a burden for the few not given to introspection. The general view of former students was united on two points: First, the prompts, or some of the options at least, tended to pry into student privacy, and second, Mrs. Hillis never betrayed secrets. She was safe.

Although Erin had not yet written her journal entry, she knew how she would answer the prompt, the past hour with Jess having only cemented her certainty. She would write about her need to grow a spine, to quit letting other people walk all over her—even Mom and Dad—to take steps to live her own life instead of the life everybody else wanted her to live. Just imagining her new self, envisioning the change, thrilled her heart.

At the same time, though, her spirit slumped. What good was *writing* about how she would change? Unless she truly changed, the writing would stand as one more monument to her hateful tendency to shrink from the truth of who she really was ...

"The first time Matt ever kissed me was under the bridge," Jess sighed. "Did I ever tell you that?"

What was Jess talking about now? Annoyed, Erin changed the subject: "Did I ever tell you about the whirlwind I saw here? The waterspout?"

"Waterspout?"

"Yes. The waterspout." Erin had never told anyone. She had stored up the memory as a treasure that her only real god or goddess—nature—had provided for her alone.

"I don't remember if you did."

"You know what I miss about Nate? With him I felt no pressure at all. I never had to go to a party, or drink, or come here, or go to a football game." She began flapping her shirt to ventilate her sweaty skin underneath. "Now I don't know what to do. Mom and Dad keep telling me to go out and find someone better than Nate. *They're* pressuring me. Which is weird in a way, since they never liked Nate."

"Nobody at school ever understood what you saw in him," Jess scoffed. Erin looked away, so Jess tried to soften her reproach. "I mean, I know you like him, and that's okay, but you could have about anyone you want."

That day at lunch some high-strung idiot classmate had taken a single green bean from the cafeteria, placed it between two pages of Erin's biology textbook, and slammed the book shut. The image of the squeezed, squashed bean rose now in her mind.

"Everybody tells me what I should do," she snapped, buoyed to boldness by the idea of standing tall for herself. If she couldn't withstand Jess's subtle pressure, how would she ever realize her budding senior-year resolution? "I mean everybody: Mom and Dad, people at school, Matt, and now you. It's really nobody else's business." Erin felt better having thrown up some defense against the unrelenting intrusions on her will.

"Excuse me for living."

"Oh, Jess, it's not that …"

A leaf floated nearby and Erin plucked it from the surface with a deft swipe of her hand, dabbing it dry on her shirt.

"Cottonwood," she said. "Shaped like a heart, upside-down."

"It seems weird with nobody else here," said Jess. "Doesn't it seem weird?"

"I guess. I never came here much with lots of people."

The Junction, everybody called it—where the river met the road. That clever clause wasn't altogether accurate, since the magnificent bridge crossing the river was exactly eighty-eight feet higher than the river's average level. Erin knew that detail and many more from listening to Cody Summers recall his memories of watching his dad, a construction manager for a Bridgebury company, help build the bridge when Cody was a toddler easily wowed by a summer full of cranes, earth movers, and other heavy equipment, steel beams and welding sparks, the echoing pounding of pile drivers, and concrete and asphalt trucks rumbling in and out by the hour. As a more mature Cody—who planned to study engineering in college—explained it, the Junction Bridge was the culmination of a joint venture in which federal and state agencies poured several million dollars of funding into the Civil Engineering School at Riverside University as part of a research project studying the decay of materials in bridges. The whole structure of the bridge, as well as much of the surrounding highway, was imbedded with a network of ultra-keen sensors that monitored a range of chemical and physical changes, everything from the effects of rain and salt to minuscule geological shifts caused by tiny tremors half a continent away. How and why Riverside's researchers had chosen such a humble, obscure location for their bridge was a mystery to Harrison County. The river ran through a sloping valley—but the completed bridge looked more like what you would find over a deep gorge in Arizona or Colorado. "The Absolute Overkill Bridge," Cody said his dad called it. Indeed, the entire stretch of rebuilt highway leading up to the bridge from east and west was more than a mile long, and the large central arch of the bridge appeared more fitting for a harbor where tall ships would pass beneath, even though nothing bigger than a motorboat ever navigated the Orange River's stony shallows through the Junction.

Where the river met the road. Along either bank was a stretch of about fifty yards of small smooth stones. For Erin, the riverbank was nicer than the beaches at Lake Pritchard, where she lived, because you could come here at times and not feel crowded. Not on Friday and Saturday nights, of course, when fifty Brookstone students usually showed up with the trappings of modernity that filled Erin with discomfort—blasting car stereos, arrogant attitudes, cigarettes and drugs, filthy language, alcohol, childish contests and fights. The Junction was a laboratory, she had written once in an essay for psychology class, a social laboratory for curious teenagers to experiment with their minds and bodies. The more timid students kept watch for cops as the more daring dove or dropped from the overpass. The bridge was like a shrine, a landmark in their lives. They drank under it, smoked dope under it, made friends under it, made love under it, fought under it, laughed under it, cried under it. As for details, since she seldom stayed long when the Junction weekend parties cranked up, Erin depended on Jess, who was now swimming in her own memories.

"In the spring we had the best party," she mused. "I remember Matt and Steve—"

She stopped abruptly, and shook her head sadly.

"Matt knew Steve better than anybody," she murmured. "All summer he kept saying—"

"Let's don't talk about Steve," Erin interrupted. The mention of his name, like a conjuror's trick, called up the sickening sight of his body dangling from the flagpole on top of the school building. The counselors had come and herded the students like cattle into small groups just to tell them that suicide is no answer, and that if they had problems they must find someone to talk to.

"But he kept saying it was Myers's fault."

"Please!" Erin shouted. She splashed back down off her stone and waded to shore.

4

THE LAST DAY of August was also the last day of the first week of school, with seventh period cancelled for the annual back-to-school convocation. More than six hundred Brookstone students and about forty faculty and staff filed into the auditorium hung with red and gold bunting and filled with the stirring sound of trumpets blaring variations on the school song.

Robin Hillis, the first teacher to arrive, took a seat in the section reserved for faculty. Twirled around her fingers was a strand of twine sprouting a gold, helium-filled balloon. Everyone coming into the convo was being handed a balloon, either red or gold, and already in defiance of spoken instructions two balloons had been released and floated to the ceiling fifty feet overhead.

On stage sat three trumpeters, two boys and a girl, also decked out in school colors. From their gleaming instruments small flags fell, emblazoned with the Brookstone letter *B*. In back of the musicians, seven chairs arranged in a semi-circle awaited local dignitaries like the mayor and the school superintendent. Two podiums flanked the seats, and behind everything rose dense, gaudy arrangements of flowers and tall floor plants whose foliage was shiny, possibly plastic.

Robin heard the distinctive voice of Tyler Batta, the boisterous broadcaster-wannabe who practiced his future craft at various school events.

"... Some say the governor is planning a spring trip to Brookstone as well. And the latest rumors suggest that one of Indiana's two senators may also visit the school this year. In any case, folks, we will keep you treasured listeners up to date on who's who among the famous faces coming to BHS this year. Seniors in our listening audience, don't forget to cast your vote for this year's senior class song. You can pick up your ballot from any Student Council member, or look for it in the first issue of *The Clause*, our award-winning school newspaper ..."

Slowly the auditorium filled. Once, such a display of pride and accomplishment would have been unthinkable. Nobody cared. Nearly two decades earlier, school spirit had ebbed to its lowest point; since then the resurgence had been astounding. The consolidation had brought in new faculty and student blood, true enough, but that infusion alone could not account for the drastic transformation of Brookstone High from a run-of-the-mill small-town school into a nationally acclaimed model. Robin was proud to teach here, and her heart swelled with satisfaction as students entered quietly and took their seats with a palpable reverence. There was a living tradition at work now, which everyone understood and respected. Not every individual student was academically gifted, but they were all part of a tradition that encouraged and demanded that they give their best. Parents, alumni, community civic and business leaders, and university personnel all contributed to this proud Brookstone heritage. It was not a perfect place—no place in the world was—but she was pleased to have found a niche here.

Teachers began taking their seats. Robin nodded greetings to Butch Young, another English teacher, wearing his usual white shirt and black bow tie. Doreen Ralston, the FACS teacher, sat down with a purse the size of an overnight bag. Behind her was Allan Kontis, the physics teacher. Allan was tall and had the longest face she had ever seen—though his receding hairline was to blame for most of that effect. Bob Hostetter and Michelle Newman, young and single math teachers, sat together. All week, rumors had been flying about their summer romance. A trace of Indian blood had intermingled at some point in Michelle's family lineage, bequeathing to her a dark skin, dark hair, and dark eyes. Bob, on the other hand, was fair-skinned, and some of the coarser gossip in the air speculated on the appearance of their future offspring. Mark Heath (sociology) and Bill St. Clair (U.S. history) also came in side by side, St. Clair with a briefcase, and sat in front of Robin. Mr. Heath—it was hard to call him Mark—was the veteran on the faculty, with more than three decades of teaching experience and six children now in college. How could he afford that? The other St. Clair, Maria, a Spanish teacher who was not related to Bill, sat with Carla Leeka, a health and girls P.E. teacher. Latecomers included Mitch Adams, Sherwin Ray, and Philip Noonan. Noonan was the world history teacher and baseball coach, his teeth permanently stained from years of chewing tobacco as a minor-league ballplayer.

The trumpeters marched off the stage to the right just as William LaGrange climbed the steps on the left in choreographed synchrony and motioned for his guests to seat themselves. Robin felt a nudge and heard Lydia Knowles whisper, "It's the governor." No one knew he would be attending, but in this election year you could hardly expect him to pass up a chance to pat himself on the back for his education initiatives. After all, there were several hundred future voters in attendance.

The other VIPs included Walter Patingale, the school corporation superintendent with his robust shock of blond-gray hair; Marilyn Byrd-Fritts, the dean of the Education School at Riverside; Laura Kearns, last year's valedictorian who was now a freshman at UCLA; and Tolan Myers. Robin leaned toward Lydia and asked, "How does Myers rate? You'd think that man was lieutenant governor, from the company he keeps. And what's with his ears?"

Lydia had no time to answer. As soon as the audience saw the governor, applause began, and LaGrange stood back from one of the lecterns and also clapped for a long while. Then he stepped forward and said thank you about five times, when once would have sufficed.

"Before we begin today," he said, "I want to make an important announcement. I see a few of you have released your balloons prematurely. In a moment members of the Student Council will come down the aisles and pass markers down each row. What we would like you to do is write your name on your balloon. We're going to have a contest, sponsored by Tony's Tux & Bridal Shoppe in Bridgebury. As you might guess, the contest has to do with the Senior Prom. After your name is on the balloon, let go of it and let it fly up to the ceiling. Over the next few days, the helium will seep out and the balloons will come back down. Whichever balloon is the last one on the ceiling—with a name on it—will be the winner. If the winner does not attend the prom, he or she will have the option of taking a cash prize. Don't let go of your balloon until you've put your name on it! You can't win if your balloon is already gone."

LaGrange then introduced the guests, who stood and smiled and waved. Myers was introduced last, and Robin giggled when she heard a few catcalls rise above the polite applause from the students. In her view, Myers was one of the imperfect parts about Brookstone High School.

The convo proceeded as she expected. The governor congratulated the school on its continuing success and its recent selection as one of a hundred national "A-Plus" schools. A plaque was presented to LaGrange bearing a letter signed by the president and his education secretary. Marilyn Bird-Fritts, speaking on behalf of Riverside President Keith C. DeMoss, said the university was proud to have forty-one Brookstone grads among its freshman class this fall. She also announced that beginning in the spring, the two schools would collaborate on a teacher-education program that would match Riverside education seniors with Brookstone faculty for a semester of mentoring. Laura Kearns, who had won the school's prestigious Gold CUPP the year before, spent a few moments encouraging the students to recognize their good fortune at BHS, where they had advantages in terms of parent support, counseling, teaching and tradition that most high school students in the nation would give anything to share. Laura mentioned that she had been flown in, expenses paid, from Los Angeles for this convo. Hearing this, Robin and Lydia stared at each other with raised eyebrows.

Myers was the last to speak. Robin stifled a giggle—for some reason the lower part of his ears looked powdery white. He rose, adjusted the microphone, and brought the student body and faculty up to date on the "placement" of last year's class. Of 162 graduates, 118 were now beginning four-year colleges, 21 were starting two-year colleges, 20 had landed full-time jobs or made a commitment to military service, and two had still not made definite plans for the future. Adding the figures, Robin came up with 161, and she bowed her head. How could you classify Steve Gutierrez and his posthumous, honorary diploma?

"No school in the state, perhaps in America, can match these numbers," Myers bragged. "I know I speak for all of the counseling staff and faculty when I say that we are honored to serve students with such bright careers ahead of them. You make our lives easy."

Robin's long fingers toyed absently with her necklace, and she thought that tonight she would paint her nails red. Zeb was supposed to fly home tomorrow evening from Dallas. Maybe she would have time tomorrow to have her hair done, too, although she had not made an appointment. Her hair was losing its bounce. The curls in front were flattening out.

Myers droned on, spouting Brookstone academic trivia and propaganda. He boasted about the phenomenal growth of the College/University Preparation Program, or CUPP, the joint effort between Riverside and Brookstone begun in the early 1990s to introduce higher-level mathematics, science, humanities, computer, and foreign language classes for college-bound students starting their sophomore year. Now almost two-thirds of Brookstone's juniors were in CUPP, he claimed. This year he expected the Gold CUPP scholarship award to top $10,000. Why, he himself had dropped a $250 check into the cup that very morning, and he knew that area businesses were pledging to hike their support as the Brookstone academic momentum grew more formidable and famous.

Robin looked from face to face behind Myers. The governor sat in rapt attention, nodding with each new fact Myers produced. Patingale rocked up and down with his legs crossed, hands locked over one knee, beaming through the chiseled lines and angles of his distinguished face. LaGrange was taking notes. Only Laura Kearns looked disinterested, distracted, staring up at the rafters, where, LaGrange's cautions notwithstanding, another half dozen errant balloons bobbed against the ceiling.

Sparks fly upward, Robin thought.

5

RARELY DID J. Bradford McCauley find himself confused, adhering so rigidly to a schedule that allocated distinct blocks of time for research, writing, preparing lessons, grading homework, and pursuing his minimal social life. As for sleeping—never one of his strengths—and eating, he squeezed those in whenever he could. Time management was critical to his survival.

Once in a while a mistake in his planning wreaked havoc with his inflexible life, and Friday, August 31, marked one such occasion. It completely slipped his mind that his high school U.S. history class at Brookstone was cancelled for a school-wide assembly.

Making matters worse, he had reached the outskirts of Brookstone, rumbling north on Highway 53, by the time he remembered the convo. Behind his dark faceguard he cussed, downshifted roughly, and sorted through damage control plans. Was there any other reason he needed to be at Brookstone? If so, he might still salvage the trip.

But no reason occurred to him. The ride was wasted.

McCauley turned around in the entrance to the Brookstone Lawn & Racquet Club and waited to re-enter the traffic heading south to West Bridgebury. Then his stomach growled, and his brain drafted a plan that would make the trip at least partly worthwhile. He accelerated on into Brookstone, stopped at the school to check his mailbox and pop his head into the auditorium, then left to eat at the town's Dairy Queen.

He placed his order with a girl whose name tag said SHEENA, who handed him a numbered tag and read it for him, as if he were number-illiterate. Setting his helmet on the table, he slid into a booth. Sheena pulled a squeaky microphone to her mouth and called his order to the back, where other teenagers began to fill it, presumably.

The restaurant was dirty. Above several tables, flies were buzzing about scraps of food on trays that neither the customers nor employees had bothered to empty. The floor was strewn with bits of paper and napkins and many tray liners and packets of ketchup and salt; even more trash was poking out from the swinging doors above the recessed, hidden trash cans. Next to the menu board the Dr Pepper clock read 2:02, well past any lunch-hour rush that might excuse the filth.

While McCauley was shaking his head, he heard his name called.

"Mr. McCauley! B-Mac!"

Matt Rademacher stood at his booth, wearing the brown shirt with the Dairy Queen emblem on the front and a paper chef's hat on his head. At the back of the classroom, Matt did not seem so physically imposing; up close he gave a different impression. About McCauley's height, he weighed probably twenty pounds more—and his biceps were as big around as McCauley's calves. A summer-long regimen of weightlifting had erased the lines of his neck, and his fingers looked as thick as the broom handle they were wrapped around.

"Hello, Matt."

"What are you doing here?"

"I completely forgot about the convo, that's what."

"Ahh! You mean you came all the way up here for nothing?"

"If I get a good double-burger then it won't be for nothing."

"*Double*-burger? Is that what you ordered?" He called to Sheena, "Hey, did he order a *double*-burger or a single?" Sheena looked at the order pad, and said, "A double."

"When you called it back you said a *single*!"

"No, I didn't!"

"Yes, you did." He said to McCauley, "I'll put another patty on. Sorry." Quickly he disappeared behind the counter.

When the order was ready, Matt delivered it personally and apologized again. "I gave you some fries for free, too," he said. He lingered for a moment, as if expecting a tip, then went back to sweeping the floor.

"What are you doing working here?" McCauley asked between bites. "Don't you have football every day after school?"

"Yeah, almost every day. But we have a game tonight."

"What position do you play?"

"Linebacker. I like to punish people." Matt laughed.

"The way I've heard it, it's mostly students who work here. Is that right?"

"*All* students. Myers owns the store, did you know that? When he bought it he wanted to have a place where students could work, save up money for college, learn how a business operates, all that. At least that's what he always says."

Matt did not even try to mask his skepticism. McCauley stopped chewing. His mind skipped back to the note he had found on the classroom floor, and the hangman scrap.

"Why are you working here, then?"

"My mom and dad said it would be good experience."

McCauley nodded.

Matt went on, "This store brings in a ton of business. It's the only decent fast-food place between Riverside and Lake Pritchard."

"How did you get out of the convocation? Isn't it required attendance?"

"Yeah, but Myers always has to excuse somebody to work here. He does everybody's schedules, and he always fixes it so that every hour there's at least three students free to work here. More at lunch."

"But you aren't free last period."

"No. Just today." Matt had swept around to the door, which he opened; with a powerful shove of the broom he sent all the dust and litter outside to be tracked right back in with the next customers.

"I guess Myers—Mr. Myers—is a good person to know," McCauley said. "Counselor, teacher, restaurant owner, employer."

"He's okay," Matt said grudgingly. He looked out the window, across the street to the computer store. "Some people can't stand him, though. Did you like that sandwich?"

"It was great. Can I get another one?"

"Sure! Another double?"

He checked his wallet and replied, "No, just a single this time."

"Are you a little short? I'll give you a double for the price of a single."

"It's a deal." Embarrassed at his poverty, he remembered how Matt had grilled him about the issue of cheating on the first day of class: *Haven't you ever cheated?* Here was a perfect chance to answer honestly, in private, to get that burdensome bit of his personal history off his chest. If he wanted, he could even spin the story to minimize his guilt. Plus, his conscience argued, if he were a really dedicated teacher whose primary concern was preparing students for life, he should tell Matt the truth, that the real reason he was practically penniless in this filthy fast-food restaurant was his own academic dishonesty. Sadly, though, the tower of his idealistic dedication to the profession had been razed years before, in Ohio, in that unfortunate incident that was *not* his fault but for which he would pay for years to come. His secrets at times seemed to torment him from opposite directions with the same result—scaring him to silence.

McCauley also remembered Matt's lottery windfall, which offered him a second opening for conversation, and he chose the path of least resistance by asking, "Did you win a big prize or something?"

"Yeah! Me and Cody bought rub-off lotto tickets at the Amoco station. His was a dud but mine won $50,000."

"Wow! You could afford to buy me a lot of doubles with that."

Waiting for the new order, McCauley took several deep breaths to check for the pain in his ribs that had bugged him for weeks. Once he had heard a cell researcher say that our bodies are programmed to die after so many years, that longevity is as uncontrollable as eye color or skeletal frame, that from the moment the DNA recombine to make us unique, the cellular clocks begin to tick, and they keep ticking until something in their inscrutable programming tells them to stop. Some cells run down faster than others, some organs shut down earlier than others, and some systems quit performing sooner than others. When enough cells and organs and systems die, your midnight hour strikes. Because this notion of internal genetic clocks weaved together so seamlessly with his view of the physical universe, McCauley adopted it, uncritically.

In fact, he believed that certain of his cells and organs and systems were already sputtering. A few years before, he had first noticed a pain in his left knee that felt most acute when he squatted or when he straightened the knee after it had been bent for a long time. Next his teeth began to fail him: Within the space of eighteen months he had to get two crowns, which left the top of his mouth so sensitive to cold that he could not eat ice cream or even salads or refrigerated fruit comfortably. When his knee began to hurt, he quit jogging, and even though he had curtailed his smoking, he could feel his breath growing shorter year by year. Now, whenever he climbed more than a flight of stairs, he was huffing when he reached the top.

There was more. His posture was slowly conforming to that of a fern; a hump was developing in his back from years of bending over a keyboard. Had he learned to type properly, without looking at the keyboard, he might have avoided this curse of scholarship, but he was too old to re-train himself. He battled frequent headaches, always low and on the right side, blaming them on his posture and the eye strain from hours spent in front of a computer screen. Sometimes lower back pain prevented him from standing long in one place or from taking even short walks. His intestines were wasting away, he feared, because he had problems with gas that only five years before he would have laughed at. His fingers were already starting to curl away from his thumbs, a process that would keep going until he was an arthritic old man. Already those fingers ached after a lot of typing. All this activity was proceeding as relentlessly as the ticking of a clock, he thought. The Universal Clock.

Two other considerations colored his thinking about his health. The first was that brain cells, according to the researcher, were exempt from the laws of genetic clockwork. Brain cells never died, an awesome fact that underpinned his limitless hope for the future. The second fact was that among his systems, his sex drive had been the first to noticeably wither. He had not had a steady girlfriend since long before coming to Riverside, and his confidence had ebbed to a level he would never have believed, especially since he had once taken pride in his virility. Tick-tick-tick. Thank God the brain cells didn't die.

As Matt brought out a new tray with a new burger and another complimentary order of fries, the glass door of the restaurant swung open and Robin Hillis stepped in. The click-click of her heels sounded so much like the tick-tick in McCauley's mind that he smiled at the ironic sympathy. Seeing him, Robin waved and then turned to say hello to Sheena. After placing her order, she settled into the booth opposite his.

"The famous J. Bradford McCauley," she said with lighthearted mockery. "Why are you here?"

Her use of his extended name irked him. Years earlier he had gone by "Jim" but had intentionally changed the designation to enhance his image as a scholar when he arrived at Riverside. Now Robin seemed to be looking right through him.

"Fate," he said. "Because the ticking clock of the universe would have it no other way."

"So I am fated to be here too, that means?"

McCauley shrugged and explained how he had messed up his schedule.

"So now," he concluded, "I actually have some time to kill, which is rare for me."

"My husband works with important clients who are in big cities all over the country," she began. Her fingers reached up to adjust the golden earring, shaped like a heart, that dangled from her left ear. McCauley had never talked much to Robin Hillis, who seldom visited the teachers' lounge. He tried to estimate her age, wondering whether her genetic clock was ticking faster or slower than his. She continued, "This last year he has been gone more than he's been home, and I have had plenty of time to kill. And today, with the convo, I didn't need to stay after school, so …"

"So you're an expert?" he asked. "On killing time?"

"No. But like everything else, time can be killed."

"How long have you taught English?"

"My whole life. Ever since I started teaching, it's been English, and it's been at Brookstone."

The skin on Robin's face was clear as a teenager's. Thin lines curled cutely around the corners of her mouth, and her eyebrows arched high and gave her an alert, merry expression. He estimated that she was in her late thirties.

"Do you have any children?"

"We have two. The youngest is a junior in college."

"In college where?"

"Asbury College in Kentucky."

"Asbury. Isn't that a church school? A seminary?"

Robin nodded. McCauley's mind flew to Asbury Park, New Jersey, a place he had never visited but felt familiar with from an early, obscure Bruce Springsteen album.

"Hmm. What about the oldest?"

"He works just outside Detroit."

"How old is he?"

"*I'm* forty-six," she said, smiling.

"That's not what I was getting at," he said, surprised at her intuition.

"Well, now you know."

"I'm thirty-five."

"I know. You are a popular subject on one of my character sketch assignments. It's a descriptive writing exercise. I have the students describe somebody at school, a student or a teacher or a staff member. You'd be surprised how many girls write about you."

He looked down at his fries and said, "What can I say? You probably know a lot about me."

"Not really. They all spend about ninety percent of their papers describing your looks, and the rest about your driving ambition to be a history researcher and teacher."

Robin's order number was called, and she came back with a chili dog, onion rings, and drink.

"They messed up my order," she said. "It was supposed to be a cheese dog."

"When you grade papers," McCauley asked, straining for an intelligent question that indicated his interest, "what is the biggest problem in the writing?"

"Logic is a big weakness. Consistency of thought—or integrity might be a better word. Consistency between what they say and what they do."

"What they *do*? How do you take that into account when you grade papers?"

"I can't. But if you're writing and believing lies, the first place it shows up is in your behavior. The things you do show what you really think and feel. That's how I know that a lot of students write lies. And"—she paused for a long swig of soft drink—"the lies are hard to maintain. They unravel, even in the writing. So the papers are poorer, on the whole, than the papers that are honest."

A few other customers came and went, and McCauley noticed that some of the trash Matt had swept out earlier was now scattered along the floor in front of the counter. The door opened again, and Myers blew in, went behind the counter, poured himself a drink, and looked around the restaurant. Then he disappeared back to the grill area, where his voice rose in some criticism—probably about the dirty store, McCauley thought, and he's giving Matt hell. But a moment later he left by the glass door, and neither Matt nor Sheena nor the other boys in the back came out to clean the tables.

"It is true that I want to be a researcher," McCauley said. "I've spent the last six years working on what has turned into my dissertation. Sometimes I tell the students—the Brookstone students—that I'm married to my work."

"At least your work is always there for you," she said reflectively. "What exactly is your research?"

McCauley warmed to his subject. Every genuine scholar longs for a truly interested audience, even an audience of one. His second burger was deep in his stomach, the last fries were halfway down his esophagus, and Robin Hillis was just starting her meal. The circumstances had supplied a perfect chance to explain his thesis, and he dove into the task with relish.

Robin listened politely. She stopped him only once, to say that she had heard of deism when she took part in a team project with a social studies teacher focusing on American literature from the time of the Revolution. But mostly she just let him ramble along until finally he was dying to know what she thought.

"I think you're a revisionist," she said, and the thin lines curled around the margins of her smile. "But thank you for taking the time to tell me all about it. If we ever have a chance, I'd love to talk to you about it more."

September

6

DENSE AND BRILLIANT, the monarch butterflies covered the trees across the river, transforming them with surreal color. Erin Delaney remembered a nature documentary about migrating monarchs descending by the millions in great clouds of orange along their route through the Americas. Here there were not that many, but thousands for sure.

In the west, beyond the quiet bridge, the oval sun hovered near the tree line. Erin never wore a watch, but she knew it must be around 7:30. Within an hour of sunset on this Friday night the Junction would turn into a completely different place. Rowdy kids would assemble after the football game against South Jasper. There would be noise, and trash, and loud music, and screaming, and splashing. In the shadows under the bridge, boys and girls would whisper and touch and kiss, and farther back, in the woods, they would buy drugs from dealers operating out of Bridgebury whose networks reached into the towns and rural areas of northern counties.

Erin planned to be gone by then.

Mesmerized by the monarchs fluttering above the beans, she recalled the childish prank Matt Rademacher had played on her a week or so earlier. Right after lunch, when she opened her biology textbook to the second chapter, she found a wet clot of dark green—someone had smashed a green bean between the pages. Later as Matt had walked behind her at her locker, she heard him ask his friends in an intentionally loud voice, "Boy those *beans* were sure good at lunch, weren't they?" And they had all laughed and not looked back.

Erin walked barefoot along the riverbank opposite the butterflies. She could not figure out why there were none on her side of the water.

She wished it were spring, when the masses of lilac bushes along the paths beneath the bridge wafted their sweet fragrance for miles, it seemed. By next spring, where might she be? Probably far away from the river and butterflies and lilacs ...

Early September had brought late summer rain, although the farmers complained that it was too late to rescue their corn crop from a disappointing harvest. The river had risen a couple of feet, enough to hide many of the boulders in the middle as its current flowed along, gurgling, splashing against the rocks. It was a serene evening.

Like the monarchs, Erin's mind was fluttering from one idea to another. She spent some time fretting over a topic for her history research paper, because her appointment with Mr. McCauley was coming up fast. She had no clue what to do. He kept saying to pick a subject you liked. Butterflies? Water sports? Waterspouts? Bare feet? Honestly, she had no real academic interests.

She tried to think about something else, to avoid piling more pressure on herself. Her stress level was already high enough. In early August when she had told her parents she was quitting volleyball, they had automatically assumed she intended to dive headlong into studies—which was the farthest thing from her mind. Erin was not like her sisters. They had brains and grand ambitions and the spirited support of Mom and Dad; she lacked all three ingredients of success. For the previous two years her parents had believed that Erin's avenue of accomplishment ran through athletics. She was taller than her sisters, physically stronger. Her sophomore year she progressed vastly as a volleyball player, but last year she had not improved at all, and during the summer her coach had admitted bluntly that Erin should not expect to play much on this year's team. So her quitting was not a terrific shock to anyone. Still, in her achievement-oriented family, her decision underscored the anxious question of what Erin intended to do with her life.

Some kids Erin's age, including many of her classmates, escaped academic pressure by stepping into their social lives. Not Erin. Her mother and father had never much cared for Nathan Dyer, so they were pleased when he broke up with her shortly after he graduated. Now living in a freshman dorm at Riverside, he had not called her once since school started. She missed him but hid her feelings from her parents. Still, which was worse, their harping about her studies or her athletics or her boyfriends? It was all the same. The football cheer for the Brookstone defense summed it up perfectly: *Pressure here! Pressure there! Pressure, pressure everywhere!* Now Mom and Dad were hinting that she should go out with Matt, whose phone calls she had evaded so far. His bean trick was probably supposed to be some sort of come-on.

Dusk gathered around her. Erin sat down on the smooth bank, aware that her time was short. She reached up inside her loose flannel shirt and scratched the skin over her ribs, her fingers cool, the sensation ticklish. She looked forward to the changing colors of the trees and their falling leaves.

A passing car's horn wailed, but Erin did not look up.

During a partly cloudy afternoon three months earlier, all alone, looking for pretty leaves, she had seen the most beautiful thing. Facing the sun with her eyes closed, she heard a loud high rustling beyond the bridge. Upon opening her eyes, she saw wind whirling through the branches and leaves of one tree whose boughs bent over the water, then the rustling ceased and a stream of water began climbing the sky, like a cobra rising to the sound of pipe music! Higher and higher it went, at least a hundred feet up, and as it moved along the bank toward her, Erin rose to her feet with a rush of adrenaline. A little tornado! She looked both ways along the bank and across the river—in vain, for there was no one else to see the sight. The waterspout reached the bridge, which truncated its top third and splashed river rain down on the concrete. Somehow, the bottom half emerged from under the bridge and shot up again, just like before. Erin kept watching with her mouth open, wishing she had a camera. About thirty yards away, the waterspout changed course and angled across the river to the opposite bank, where it began shooting water in all directions. Its shape grew more defined and visible as it sucked up leaves and dust. At last it disappeared over the bean fields. Afterward, tracing the whirlwind's path along the bank on her side of the river in hopes it might reappear, she was awestruck by its cleansing power—a swath of the hard dirt along the bank had been swept clear, every piece of debris sucked violently into the sky.

Another car horn sounded, this one behind her. She stood up, wiping the sand off her rear end. The car honked again, and she heard her name called.

It was Matt. She didn't answer him but started climbing back up to her own car.

"I knew you'd be here," he called. "Jess told me."

Jess, who had dated Matt for a year before he dumped her. Jess, who kept saying how much she wanted to be back together with Matt. Jess, her cousin, who now seemed to be in a league with her parents to force her to go out with Matt. If only she were a year older! Then she could have gone off to Riverside with Nathan …

"Hiya, Erin," he said when she reached the gravelly area that the kids used as a parking lot. He was munching on Pringles, his trademark snack, and tilted the can toward her. She shook her head no.

"How long have you been here?" he asked.

"I don't know."

"I've tried to call you about a million times. You're never home."

She was about to plead volleyball practice, but her tongue twisted at the lie, and she just stammered that she was sorry, then asked, "What are you doing here? What time's your game?"

"It's a late start because they're giving awards to all the academic winners from last year."

"But don't you have to be in uniform by a certain time?"

"Yeah. I'm on my way now. You'll be here later, won't you? Everybody will be here. We'll have a cookout at the fire pit, and Gordie will set up his speakers and blast away the music."

"I don't much care for big crowds," she said. Then, not exactly sure what prompted her, she added, "Jess must have told you that."

"What's Jess got to do with it? I'm through with her, you know."

Erin took a deep breath, hoping to convey her irritation, but Matt stared at her chest and said in a low voice, "You're not wearing a bra, are you?"

No, for she had removed it and stuffed it in the glove compartment before walking down to the river. She had left her shoes in her car, too. She hated shoes, except for sandals. She hated all tight clothing.

"So what?"

"Nothing. It's … great!" A sheepish smile crept across his face, and he continued to stare at her flannel shirt, as if somewhere she showed through.

"I have to go," she said sharply. She half expected his strong hand to block her way, but he stood aside.

"Yeah, me too."

Following her, he asked, "So, are you coming back later? What's wrong, anyway?" He came to the passenger's window of her car. "Are you all right?"

"I'm fine," she said. "Why shouldn't I be fine?"

"But why are you acting so upset?"

"Nothing, Matt. It's not you, it's just … everything."

"Do you always come down here all by yourself?"

"Not always. Sometimes with Jess. But all alone sometimes."

"But why?"

"Just to think about things."

"Like what?"

"School and things."

"Oh. Sorry about squeezing that bean in your book. It was Jarrett's idea."

"Right."

"Really, I swear!"

"It's okay."

"I had my conference with McCauley today. I think I have a topic for the research paper."

"What is it?"

"The history of football strings."

"*Strings*? You mean like first and second string?"

"No! The seams on the football, where you hold it to throw a pass."

"Right," she said dubiously. "He's going to let you do that?"

"Yes!" Glee filled Matt's voice. "It'll be a piece of cake. I can make up the whole thing; he'll never know. I've got it all figured out. I already told him a bunch of lies and he believed me. I told him that there's a history behind how many seams there are, and how thick, and what color. He was nodding his head like he wished he'd thought of it. I'll make up magazines and books and quotes, the whole works."

"I bet he catches you."

"How much?"

"I was just ..."

"No, really. I'll bet you he *doesn't* catch me. I'll bet you a steak dinner at the Top Notch."

"I don't like steak."

"Okay, if you win the bet you choose the place. Deal?"

Erin shook her head and squinted as a pair of bright-beam headlights screamed into her eyes. She heard and felt the strong bass throb of drumbeat pounding from the new arrival. It was time to go, and she turned the key in her ignition.

"Are you coming to the game?" he asked. Driving away, she heard him call out, "Is it okay if I call you, or not?"

7

TO THE REVVING engine of a chainsaw shrieking through her open bedroom window, Robin Hillis opened her eyes in a flood of yellow sunlight. Next to her bed the digital clock read 10:05. She spent a moment trying to recall what had kept her awake so late the night before—then she remembered, with a plummeting spasm of emptiness, the nausea she had felt upon identifying with the ironically named Constance in a DVD of *Lady Chatterley's Lover*.

She had rented it while picking up her groceries at Sam's, the culmination of her semi-regular Friday excursion into Bridgebury. Even as she punched the Redbox button to finalize her purchase, her heart questioned its own motives. As an English teacher, she liked to keep up to date on the dramatizations of the classics for possible use in the classroom. Of course, she would never teach *Lady Chatterley*, not at Brookstone, not in any high school. And she had never placed any of the works of D. H. Lawrence in the "classics" category. Nevertheless, she reasoned, it might be entertaining for her until Zeb called from San Francisco.

He had never called. Around two in the morning she finished the movie, surprised at her stamina, yet hypnotized by the story of Lady Chatterley's drive for fulfillment, which seemed so familiar, in a dreadful way. Not the sex—the story might have been told better without being so graphic. What Connie really longed for was intimacy of a simpler sort, the kind that paid you respect and admiration by presence and by words. It seemed so contrived that Lady Chatterley's husband was an invalid … Afterward, Robin watched a few minutes of the round-the-clock news on CNN, then plodded to bed. This was a three-day weekend, so it didn't matter if she stayed up late one night. Monday there was no school thanks to a special act of the State Legislature to Brookstone High School as a reward for its previous year's special achievements. Zeb would get back home Sunday night.

She reached for her glasses next to the clock and sat up in bed. The chainsaw was running right outside the window, in Mr. Floyd's yard. Finally he was taking down that walnut tree, which was such a nuisance to clean up after each fall. Robin pulled on a pair of sweatpants and a shirt, gave her hair a dozen firm strokes with a brush, and went to the kitchen.

Minutes later she took a cup of coffee to the front porch. As she suspected, Howard Roost was doing Mr. Floyd's work. Lena was there helping, and Philip. Howard was evidently explaining to the boy how to fell a tree. He had cut one wedge out of the trunk and was pointing to another spot and gesturing about how the tree would come down. Philip's eyes, however, were torn between the trunk and the chainsaw, so Howard's lesson got lost in the boy's fascination with a piece of machinery that could produce such prodigious racket. Philip stepped back with Lena while Howard cut the second wedge and the walnut tree slammed to the earth with a crack of timber and a mighty whoosh, slowed only by its buffer of leaves and breaking branches. Philip jumped up and down and shouted. Robin heard him say they should cut down all the trees. Lena saw her on the porch and waved.

The Bridgebury *Courier*, rolled up and stuffed into a plastic bag, lay on the porch, but Robin let it sit. Watching the Roost family was better than whatever news she would find on the pages of the paper. Howard started cutting off the bigger branches from the trunk, and Lena dragged them away to give him more room to operate. Jerri Roost arrived on the scene and began to help, too. Philip moved along picking up walnuts and dropping them—*thump! thump! thump!*—into a plastic garbage bin.

Soon Howard turned off the saw, went to his garage, and came back wheeling a curious contraption of metal, silver and red, with a funnel like a megaphone sticking out one side. He tinkered with some controls, then pulled a cord that brought its engine to life with a volume twice as loud as the chainsaw's. Philip threw his hands to his ears and stood motionless, staring at the machine. Jerri stepped back, and spotting Robin, came up to her porch.

"What is that thing?" Robin shouted.

"A chipper-shredder!"

Robin nodded. Howard fed long thin branches into the funnel, and inside the machine, rapidly rotating blades snarled and bit and chewed and reduced the wood and leaves into tiny bits of mulch that fell out the bottom into a conical pile of green and brown. The noise drowned out any attempt to talk, so Robin merely watched. Jerri sat down on the long concrete wall across the front of the porch, her legs scratched from her helping with the branches and brush.

When Howard waved to both of them, the joy on his sweating face pierced Robin with poignant awareness that she did not belong in this picture. She felt like an alien, an outsider, even though these were her best friends and favorite neighbors. Her own children were gone, and Zeb was gone, and even the glorious brilliance of this Saturday morning could not fill up her emptiness. How badly she wanted to cry just now—to let Jerri know how lonely she was, to say that she could not stand another day of Zeb's absence! Why hadn't he called last night, to save her from that dark movie with its sorry, adulterous wife?

The chipping process continued for twenty ear-splitting minutes. Jerri went back to help pull more branches over to the machine. Adjusting to the decibels, Philip went back to collecting walnuts, though now when he tossed them into the bin, Robin could not hear them rattle.

What a terrible, terrible hollowness! Was her marriage really disintegrating like Mr. Floyd's walnut tree? Was it dying, to use Eliot's famous phrase, not with a bang, but with a whimper? Deep in her stomach, that pressing grief, was that the whimper of her soul?

When Zeb comes home, she told herself, we have to talk. We *have* to talk. It can't wait.

To break her obsession she withdrew inside for another cup of coffee. The engine of the chipper-shredder shut off, leaving a yawning silence in her ears. Thankfully, the happy voices of Howard and his family began to patch up the stark stillness.

She returned to the front porch. What had been a walnut tree thirty-five feet high, its branches drooping under the burden of their freight, now was a stump, a short stack of logs less than a foot in diameter, and four ragged pyramids of mulch.

The Roosts joined her on the porch again.

"You do great work, Howard," said Robin. "And Philip, I should have hired you years ago to clean Mr. Floyd's walnuts out of my yard."

"Don't tell me you're just waking up," Jerri said, a hint of friendly accusation in her voice.

"Last night I was up really late," she answered. "Studying."

Howard Roost seemed to study her reply, then asked, "Isn't it just amazing how little volume is actually in a tree? Just look at that! All that tree turns out to be a few bags full of mulch. Plus the logs. Which, by the way, Wayne Floyd said you are welcome to have."

"I'll have to have him over for a fire this winter."

Philip was throwing up a walnut and swinging at it with the newspaper, using it as a bat, and Lena grabbed it away.

"Philip, use the broom," Robin said, pointing to the corner of the porch. "I think you can even unscrew the handle."

Instead, Philip's short attention fled toward a motorcycle jetting past. The rider's faceguard flashed as he looked their way; then he was gone. Philip jumped up and down, imagining a ride.

The conversation settled into typical lazy, late-summer weekend small talk. Howard asked how his mantel was holding up. He had designed and built a number of items of oak furniture for the Hillis home over the years. "If you hadn't bought this house," he often said to Zeb and Robin, "we would have, sooner or later."

Indeed, it was a grand home, but not magnificent by the standards of Brookstone, where dozens of nineteenth century houses survived. It had two full stories and an attic tall enough to stand in. On the outside, the Hillises had recently put on a new roof and gray vinyl siding. Then they had painted all the shutters—sixteen pairs—a darker blue. Howard had installed a bay window, and they had replaced a couple of the house's original windows every year for the past ten years. Inside, they had decided to keep the plaster walls until they crumbled, but to enhance the appearance of each room they were adding fancy oak baseboard or wainscoting and crown molding where the ceiling met the walls. Year by year, their home was turning into a masterpiece of restoration.

Once the grown-ups got talking about the house, Philip begged his way into a tour. Even though he already knew the layout by heart, his young mind never tired of the unique features hidden upstairs. From the bathroom a narrow door opened into a walk-through closet and came out in a bedroom. The entrance to the attic was a constricted chute that everyone except Philip had to squeeze to enter. A short door led into a little crawlspace under one stairwell, and the other stairway—well, it was a spiral affair with a sturdy, shiny wooden banister that Philip loved to polish by sliding down.

With Robin's permission, Lena took Philip—or vice versa—inside. A moment later, Howard excused himself to clean up his mess.

When they were alone, Jerri brought up the one subject Robin wished to keep at a safe distance: "Zeb sure has been traveling a lot lately, hasn't he?"

All the frustration and sorrow she had been holding down burst into her eyes, and Jerri, stunned, reached over and took her hand. "Robin! Robin, what's wrong?"

"Oh, Jerri!" she sobbed. "I'm so sad!"

8

"A REVISIONIST," J. Bradford McCauley muttered as he shifted into a semi-bearable position at his work desk, a card table sagging from the weight of the bulky computer resting on top. "A historical revisionist." But that's what he had come to expect from fundamentalists like Robin Hillis. At least she had listened politely while he explained his thesis; she had not objected to every other sentence as many of his naïve, closed-minded, middle-class college students did.

He flexed his fingers instinctively above the keyboard, a habit he had fallen into during the long months of painstaking composition. Whenever he sat down at his computer, he envisioned himself as a virtuoso musician seating himself to thunderous applause at a piano on a stage, flipping back his tails with the customary flourish, setting the hearts of his audience quivering in expectation of the magic about to fall from his fingertips. Indeed, he too was producing a work of art. McCauley believed that his dissertation would break new ground not only in constitutional historical studies but also in the writing style of academic treatises.

On top of his computer monitor he had duct-taped a digital clock, the colon between the hour and minutes flashing on and off, on and off, every half-second, on and off, never stopping, a consciously symbolic prop as he pecked away at his supreme academic endeavor, which bore the proud title "Clockwork and the Constitution: How Deism Defined the Founding Fathers."

Any time his research dragged him through valleys of discouragement, McCauley drew strength from that stable, consistent clock, whose colon kept flashing, pulling him forward into the future, where inevitably he would make a great name for himself. His fame was as certain as his birth. The magnificent plan that the Maker of the universe had set in motion eons in the past was working out perfectly—with a special place for him, J. Bradford McCauley, and the truths he would reveal.

There was a downside to the great plan, too, as his aching joints reminded him. His body was dying, each atom hurtling relentlessly toward a final oblivion that would somehow pour his spirit back to God. And there was pain in that process, and worry, and fear. That was all right, though. Even those emotions and feelings were part of the plan, ordained from the beginning. Above those feelings, superior to them and interpreting them, was something that rested in a timeless peace.

His telephone rang, and a girl's shaky voice at the other end said, "Professor McCauley? This is Janet King from the History 220 class."

His mind muddy, McCauley answered "Yes" while trying to match the name to his rosters from Brookstone High and Riverside University. History 220 meant college, but he could not put a face to the girl's last name; it was still too early in the semester for him to have learned everyone's names.

"I wanted to talk to you about my grade on that first quiz."

"The first quiz? Janet, I haven't even graded them yet."

"Okay. Okay. Well, do you think ... would it be asking too much to grade mine now?"

He rustled among some papers in his teacher's edition of the textbook for History 220.

"I guess I could," he said, suspicious. "Why are you in such a hurry?"

"Because I think I bombed it, so I was wanting to start on something for extra credit this weekend if I did."

McCauley laughed.

"Janet, we're only in the second week of the semester."

"But I have to get an A in every class or I can't stay in school. So I can't wait until it's too late."

He found her paper and said, "Okay, I'll grade it and you call me back later."

The trouble with today's students, he thought as he hung up, was that they had no balance to their lives. They were either bookworms or socialites. It was an era of extremism—like calling his ideas and work "revisionist."

The image of Robin Hillis's thin face passed through his consciousness, her orange sunglasses, high cheekbones, and alert eyebrows. He wondered what her husband sold, that they could live in such a dazzling house, and he wondered what it looked like on the inside, through the tall old-fashioned windows that winked at him whenever he rode past on his motorcycle.

He graded Janet's paper: She missed just one out of ten. He wrote a nine, circled it, and added a whimsical message that he underlined twice: STUDY HARDER!!

Half an hour later his doorbell rang. He peeked through the peephole and saw a red-headed girl, backpack slung over her right shoulder. Janet! He froze, adrenaline surging and falling in an ephemeral rush. There was nothing to do but open the door.

"I thought you were going to call me back," he said. "You didn't have to come all the way up here. And how did you know where—"

"I was out anyway, so I thought ... did I screw up on the quiz?"

He cringed at her word choice and answered, "No, you didn't *screw* up. You got nine out of ten right. If everybody screwed up like that it would be a happy world."

She stood motionless until he said, "Come on in. You wanna sit down?" An old wound compelled him to behave as kindly as possible. "Do you drink coffee?"

Declining the drink, she set her pack on the carpet and dropped into a reclining chair, her eyes scanning the one-room apartment, passing over the many open books, the cluttered closet, the unmade hideaway bed, the dishes on the counter by the sink.

"I'm your typical bachelor," McCauley said apologetically. Then he regretted volunteering the information.

"What do you have *that* for?" She pointed to a gray, eighteen-inch-square safe nestled beneath an end table next to the bed.

"I keep personal valuables in it."

"Why don't you put it in a closet or something? Hide it in a wall, behind a picture or something?"

"I don't know."

"Is ninety percent an A in your class?"

McCauley sighed. Janet was genuinely worried.

"Can I give you some advice? Don't worry about what grade you're going to get. It will just drive you crazy. Not everybody is an A student. Some people are C students, and no matter how hard they try they will always be C students. Some people don't even belong in college. And some people can snore their way to an A."

He wanted to declare that everything was pre-determined, but fear checked him—fear of getting bogged down in a philosophical argument that would do nothing except siphon away precious time from his dissertation.

"But you don't understand my parents," Janet insisted. "If I don't have perfect grades, then I won't be able to stay in school."

"*Perfect* grades? Why?"

"Because of my scholarship. They can't afford to pay for my college, and if I don't get all As I might not be able to keep my scholarship."

"Don't worry," he said. "All I can say is, everything will work out. It always has, and it always will."

Janet said, "I don't want to be a worry-wart, but I can't help it."

Maybe she *can't* help it, McCauley thought. Maybe that's her role in the great universal scheme. But he said, "Look, I don't want you to worry yourself to death. Grades aren't that important. Did you know I teach high school up the road here?"

"I know. My brother goes there. Jim King."

"Oh, so you went to Brookstone?"

She nodded.

"Then you know that last year a kid killed himself over grades. Hanged himself from the flagpole."

Janet rubbed her nose.

"But I have to get all As."

"So far you have an A."

"But I'm borderline B, aren't I? If I missed one more question, I'm a B student."

"If you got one more right, you were perfect."

"But I didn't get one more right."

In frustration, he cried, "What are you getting at?"

She stood up, looking around his apartment. "Nothing," she sighed. At the door she stopped and said, "I just have to get all As, that's all. And I'm not off to a good start. What happened there?"

She indicated a hole in the wall from which a crooked light switch hung, detached, its wiring dangerously exposed.

"You wouldn't believe me if I told you," he said, his hand throbbing with phantom pain.

Even as he shut the door behind Janet's bobbing red hair, McCauley knew that his mental preparation for the day's work on his dissertation had wilted beyond any hope for revival. Janet could not have bothered him more if she had tried. Her unexpected and unwanted appearance at his apartment, her casual use of the word *screw*, her questions about his safe—they all collaborated to undermine his purpose, sending a torrent of rage coursing through him.

The roads called to him. Hopefully, he thought, a half hour of riding would put him back into a frame of mind to write. But he was mistaken: The late summer day was tinged with its own regret that simply magnified his own. Each mile seemed to thrust him deeper into the heart of his emotions until he began to exult in the feel of the wind, the road, and the yellow sunshine and to hum a tune that went with Springsteen lyrics he loved, lyrics about the thrill of music and muscles and the pulsing, exploding magic of the roads.

One of the oldest, tritest truths occurred to him—he couldn't run away from his problems, or drive away from them, not even at a hundred miles an hour. If anybody in the history of the world had ever screwed up, he had. The first time was excusable, for he had been innocent, no matter what Mary Ann Childress and her greedy, finagling lawyers claimed. But then he had screwed up disastrously. On his dissertation, no less. On his ticket to glory and security. And unlike Janet King, there was no way for him to compensate for his dire error.

9

EVERYONE KNEW HOW to do it. You needed a programmable calculator to be safe, but acquiring one was easy if you reminded your parents how both math and science classes these days depended on calculators. Besides, many parents didn't even ask questions anymore: When it came to academics at Brookstone, they flashed their cash and credit cards with a proud disdain for potential excesses.

Once you had a good calculator, then came the only really dangerous part. Somebody had to steal the test, physically or electronically, or buy it. Erin had heard Matt say that with Myers you could sometimes buy a test direct, but she had her doubts about that, since Matt was always bragging about what he had done or was going to do but ninety percent of his words turned out to be just hot air.

When somebody came up with a copy of the test, usually from a student in an earlier class, then you had several options. Sometimes the copy already had the answers on it, so all you had to do was figure out the intermediate steps, provided the teacher "required" you to show your work. Usually you could get the class brain (Cody Summers or Lance Tracer or Cara Eberle) to do the steps that led to the right answer. Or maybe the test copy also showed the steps, in which case you were home free. All you had to do was program the figures into the calculator. Then when you hit the F1-ENTER key, the first step would appear on the calculator. F2-ENTER provided the next step, and so on all the way to the calculator's limit, which was usually 99,999. Lance had figured out that you could cheat on a quarter million different tests of twenty-five questions each, using one calculator.

Once in a while a pilfered test had no answers at all, which was a pain, because then Lance or somebody would have to actually take the time to do each problem, step by step, and check it, before anybody else could benefit.

During the test itself, if you were smart, you would make your effort more believable by missing a problem or a step here and there, and by erasing a lot, or scribbling out figures. Even if you didn't have a calculator, you could usually "borrow" one during the test, with all your answers a few buttons away.

Erin Delaney had never cheated on a test in her life. She knew all the secrets, though, and she knew that all around her at that very moment her classmates were taking the shortcut to success, to the honor roll and reputation and scholarships and first-rate colleges and high-paying jobs. She let her eyes wander from seat to seat. For tests, Mr. Myers always made the class arrange their desks in a circle facing inward, and he paced the floor inside that circle.

What a joke.

For the first time this year she was aware of the effects of the new dress code. The joint PTA-school board task force that developed and dictated such policies had prohibited words or letters on clothing, unless those words related to education. Therefore all Erin saw as she looked around the circle were the names of schools: Virginia, Florida, Illinois, Stanford. And Riverside, of course, which brought a fleeting melancholy thought of Nathan Dyer. There were also a couple of football jerseys, which evidently passed muster. Maybe the numerals qualified for being math-related. But no more free advertising for Aeropostale, Old Navy, Foot Locker, Limited, Hollister, Gap, or any other store from the parade of mall retailers.

Erin finished the last problem. She was sure she had eight of the twelve questions answered correctly, and she was fairly sure about two others. That left two more, and she was stumped on those. No strategy came to mind. Had she missed a day of class? No. Her mind was simply blank about how to proceed. Rather than worry herself any more, she turned her paper over and stared out the window. You never liked to be the first person to turn in your test because then everybody watched you walk back to your seat.

Why didn't she jump on the cheating bandwagon? That would solve the pressing problem of her nagging parents. Nag, nag, nag. Do this. Don't do that. Be more like your sisters. Ever since she quit volleyball they had been harping about her grades, reminding her that she would never be able to follow in the footsteps of Patti and Sarah. Even thinking about it now, Erin's eyes rolled.

Asking Jess for answers to tests would be easy. Jess was into cheating almost as deeply as she was into boys, or (as she would say, mischievously) boys were into her. And Jess never grew weary of asking—pressuring— Erin to join in. She never came right out and said, "Everybody else is doing it" but that was the foundation from which all her persuasion rose.

Matt, too, would be more than willing to help her. But the moment she went to him, he would probably read it as a sign of her acquiescence to his romantic interest. He was calling her house about every other day, and the one time she had been home she told him she couldn't talk because she didn't feel well. Which was true—all the pressures were squeezing her head, and his call just added one more worry.

Sometimes all the pressure forced into her mind the image of pincers slowly tightening around her temples, crushing her thoughts and feelings into nothing.

Erin looked across at bleach-blond Terri Harlow, who was tapping calculator keys and copying the results onto her page. She always stuck her tongue out the left side of her mouth when she was writing. Next to her, Bill Frost was erasing furiously, hoping Mr. Myers saw his effort. Bill was one of the football players in the class, wearing jersey number 84.

The last time Jess and Erin had gone alone to the Junction, Erin had sensed a rift deepening between them. Jess said she didn't mind if Matt wanted to go out with Erin: "It's none of my business, I guess." That was all false indifference, though, and Erin saw more clearly than ever that she could not win. If she rebuffed Matt, her parents would be angry and Matt would keep hovering too close for comfort. If she went out with him, Jess would probably stop talking to her, which would be unbearable because without Nate, her cousin was the closest thing to a friend that she knew.

"Just suppose I did let him take me out, just once," Erin said. "Then would you be mad? Even if it was just to get him off my back?"

"Like I said, it's not up to me," Jess said. She seemed afraid that Erin might actually like Matt—how could anybody *not* like Matt, with his rock-hard muscles and dimpled grin and sharp sense of humor?—but she wouldn't admit this.

"Come on Jess. Tell me the truth, would you be mad?"

"No. I never get mad at you, do I? Like when I keep asking you if you want answers on tests and quizzes, and you always say no. I never get mad, do I?"

"No, I guess not."

"Have you *ever* cheated?"

Erin recoiled from answering. Like so many issues in her young life, this one was pregnant with pressure. To say *yes*—to lie—would open the door to more entreaties from Jess, but to say *no* would label her in Jess's mind as a self-righteous saint.

Erin heard a gentle tap on her desk, which yanked her attention back from nowhere-land. Mr. Myers was standing in front of her desk, a couple of other students smiling at her.

"Finished?" he asked in a whisper. Erin nodded, and he took her pages and stapled them.

Erin watched him walk on in a circle around the class, collecting papers. In any classroom, the effect of the first person handing in a test was like that of a faucet turning on, leading to a stream of people suddenly finishing in the space of about a minute.

Why were Mr. Myers's ears always chalky white? There were only a few chalkboards left in the building; almost every classroom had whiteboards now. But Mr. Myers was old-fashioned. Erin had caught a glimpse once into the back office where he and Mr. LaGrange often retreated together, and she remembered the large chalkboard in one corner, always looking freshly erased but never clean.

The class waited for the bell to ring, respectfully silent while the last few students scurried to finish. Erin did not know how many people in the class cheated. She knew there must be others who tried to earn their own honest grades, but if she had been called to give sworn testimony about who they were, she would have pleaded ignorance, or pleaded the Fifth Amendment.

Sometimes when she refused her cousin's offers, Jess would say, "Why not, Erin? I don't see why you make such a big deal out of it. There's nothing wrong with it."

Involuntarily, her fingers went to her blouse buttons. Then she realized that she was already unbuttoned as far as classroom decorum, let alone the stricter dress code, allowed. Her feet felt smothered, too, even though her tennis shoes were untied and her bare heels outside her shoes.

Erin Delaney believed there was something wrong with the cheating, and something very wrong with Brookstone High School. But every time Jess challenged her on that point, she recognized that her own defenses and justifications were only a fuzzy cloud. This frightened her. She felt a huge void opening up beneath her heart, a gaping chasm of nothingness that could swallow her at any moment. The situation reminded her of pictures she had seen of sinkholes in Florida that sucked in land and pavement and cars and houses. Somehow she had not fallen into the psychic sinkhole she perceived; however, the mystery of what preserved her only added to her fright.

The bell rang. Mr. Myers asked all of them to rearrange the desks in straight rows on their way out, and the room filled with sounds of the metal feet of the desks and chairs grating across the room's tile floors. Erin saw Cody hand Mr. Myers an envelope on his way out of class, and she thought she detected a wave of anger redden the teacher's face. Quickly he stuffed the envelope in his inside coat pocket.

At lunchtime, Erin headed straight for the cafeteria. The senior class song, "I'll Take My Chances," by some country singer named Carpenter, was pouring from the loudspeakers, as it did during passing periods several times a week. Crossing the Atrium floor, Erin heard Matt's deep jovial voice call her name. He was leaning with feigned leisure against a pillar, talking to Cody, but as soon as Matt turned his attention to her, Cody walked away.

Matt waved for her to come nearer, and he asked, "Wanna have lunch with me?"

"I guess so. Let me go to my locker first."

He walked with her back across the Atrium, under the bright-faced photographs of hundreds of students who had forged the Brookstone tradition.

10

SPILLING HER GUTS to Jerri Roost lightened Robin Hillis's emotional burden, even though Zeb came and went again without Robin broaching the subject of his neglect.

Each minute in her spacious, empty house seemed like an hour in her lonely, forlorn soul.

School became a more bearable place, largely because Robin now ate lunch and spent her free period in the teachers' lounge, attending to small talk, or shop talk, or any other kind of talk. Naturally there was always a chance that someone's offhand remark or unwitting question might direct her mind to Zeb, but thankfully this seldom occurred.

One kind of talk that Robin anticipated each day was her running discussion with Brad McCauley about his Riverside doctoral dissertation. Their casual, polite exchange at Dairy Queen had, over subsequent weeks, assumed a life of its own. Brad typically arrived fifteen to twenty minutes before his last-period class, which began at two o'clock, and when he found Robin in the teachers' lounge the Monday after their initial conversation, he asked with affected offense, "Have you made a revision of your evaluation of me yet?" Robin had blushed and stammered a quick apology—"I never meant to hurt your feelings!"—then, seeing the wide smile break out under Brad's bushy mustache, she knew he was needling her. He sat down and they kept talking about the Founding Fathers and the religious currents of the 1700s, with Robin mostly asking questions and Brad going to greater and greater lengths to answer. The next day he came even earlier; soon he was there waiting for her when her free period began at 1:10 each day, a full period before he taught his class.

On a grey Wednesday in late September, Robin left her sophomore literature class with a buoyant step. Yesterday Brad had offered a selection of quotations from Thomas Jefferson in an attempt to persuade her that the third president's view of God was at the opposite end of the spectrum from what the modern-day political far right wing wished everyone to believe. Believing Brad's argument to be incomplete, Robin went home and dug up some quotes of her own that implied Jefferson's God was as personal as Jefferson. Today she would spring them on Brad to see his reaction.

As she clicked along the congested corridor, weaving among students—*wham!* A careless boy, running and yelling over his shoulder, smashed into her broadside, sending her sprawling, her glasses knocked crooked on her nose, her books skidding along the polished floor, her purse staying attached to her only because its long straps happened to be looped over her shoulder. The student fared no better—he fell face-first and slid several feet, his own papers scattering in front of him. Their collision would have brought riotous laughter had a teacher not been involved. Instead, the many witnesses stared first at Mrs. Hillis in her undignified position, then at the boy, who stood up, his face blushing, his lips muttering an embarrassed apology. He picked up her books as she straightened her glasses and uttered the obligatory, "Slow down a little," and he said yes, yes, he knew he should, and then he walked away stiffly. The onlookers went on their way, leaving Robin to clean up the papers. But the nearest waste can was at the end of the hall, and before she reached it her eyes fixed on the trash she carried. Each page was part of a blank test from the freshman biology class. Someone had written a note on the first page: "JIMBO, GOOD LUCK, AND DONT TELL ANYONE WHERE YOU GOT THIS! L." ANYONE was not only capitalized, but underlined three times. The writer's contraction lacked its apostrophe—no surprise there—and the mysterious "L" had surrounded her lone initial with a circle of valentines.

In the lounge, Brad sat at their accustomed table, sipping coffee. Robin had always wondered what it was like to drink with a mustache. Could you feel it on your lip, or was it like hair on your head, something you never noticed? Brad looked like he had not slept well.

"Hello, Mrs. English Teacher," he said, but she replied in a high whimper, "Look what just fell into my lap." She slid the test across the table.

"Where'd you get this?" Brad asked. It was hard to tell when he was being serious, because his low gentle voice sounded the same when he was telling a joke, expounding his mangled history, or asking a question.

"In the hallway. A student ... dropped it."

"What are you going to do?"

"There's not much I *can* do. I didn't get a close look at the kid. There are a lot of *Jims* here, and even more *L*'s."

"Who's the teacher?"

"Ninth grade biology would be Jeannette Frye."

"Let her handle it. Or better yet, take it to LaGrange."

Robin sat down.

"What's wrong?" Brad asked.

The gentleness in his voice was reassuring; though still a stranger in her life, he was present, and he was not silent. She looked into his eyes with pleading in her heart and said brokenly, "This is—this is a lot bigger deal than you think."

"This?" He pointed to the pages. "Why?"

"Because a lot of this sort of thing goes on here. More than most of us, or at least some of us, care to admit."

"Here? At Brookstone?" His smile broke out again, as though he thought she was trying to fool him.

"Yes."

"Well, I guess that's not such a surprise. It's a high school, and kids are kids. All the surveys show that more than half of them cheat."

"No, you don't understand." Robin licked her dry lips, troubled, wondering whether Brad was really safe to talk to, already feeling tugged toward him, lulled into trusting him—personally.

"Why are you so upset about it?" he whispered with animation. "If kids cheat, I say turn 'em in!"

Robin closed her eyes in a futile wish to turn back the clock. Other faculty had come into the lounge, and she feared other ears were straining to overhear.

"Let's talk about it somewhere else," she said, leaning close to him. "Come to the parking lot, but not till I've been gone a few minutes."

The afternoon was partly overcast, a whisper of autumn colliding with the blast of humidity in portent of thunderstorms gathering in the west. Bees were buzzing among cars where trees had dripped their sweet sap. It was comfortable in a nostalgic way, Robin thought, these first hints of the end of summer. She paced back and forth in front of the parked bicycles.

"Why did you ever quit teaching high school in Ohio?" she asked when McCauley joined her. Suddenly she felt uncomfortable being with him, not so much because of *him* as because of *them*. Who might be watching? He placed a cigarette in his mouth but did not light it. As he talked it dangled from his lips.

"I wasn't stimulated enough by the level of learning."

"We're too stupid for you, is that it?"

"No, no," he said, the cigarette drooping. "That's not what I meant at all. I just don't like to talk about Ohio."

Robin laughed, and Brad saw that she was joking.

"Now we're even," she said.

"Why couldn't you talk in the lounge?"

"Oh, Brad. Where do I begin?" They went along the sidewalk, and she gazed to the north, over the school building, and tried to gather her thoughts. The clouds seemed so utterly peaceful—yet so far away. "This is a great school, with a lot of really bright kids and dedicated teachers, but it has some serious problems. You wouldn't know. You're only here an hour every day, and … everybody knows you won't be around forever."

"Right. So what?"

Having reached the part of the parking lot reserved for motorcycles, he sat down on his. Robin fixed her eyes on his cowboy boots, brown, with pointed toes.

"I don't know if I should tell you," she said. A light breath of wind from the northwest swept over the lot, rustling a few early fallen leaves, blowing her yellow hair into her eyes. She looked at the pavement. "Maybe it's better if you don't know."

"Either tell me or don't," he said. "So what if there are students who cheat here? It doesn't reflect badly on the school, or on its faculty. Every school has bad apples. No matter how much you try to stop people from doing what's wrong, they will keep finding new ways to do it."

That sounded sensible enough, sane enough. She thought of Lena Roost, her neighbor, a previous valedictorian whose photo was one of dozens on the Wall of Fame in the Atrium. Was it possible that Lena was a cheater?

"But doesn't it bother you?" she asked.

"Yes, it bothers me. I believe strongly in academic integrity." The firmness of his answer felt reassuring and made her look up to his face, only to find that Brad was looking down now, studying a crack snaking along the pavement, evidently.

"For yourself, yes," she said. "But what about for your students?"

"For myself, yes," he repeated slowly. He paused and looked across the parking lot to the sculpture at the entrance, where a prankster had wrapped ribbons of toilet paper around the steering wheel, ribbons now streaming in the breeze. "For my students, too. If I catch anybody cheating I won't look the other way. But I can't spend all my energy trying to catch every violation. Sooner or later they'll get what's coming to them. That's how history works. It's a rule as dependable as clockwork."

Robin shook her hair back in place with a sideways flick of her head. *Clockwork, schmockwork*, she wanted to say, but this was no time to change the subject. She saw Bragley, the head custodian, picking up trash that had collected against a fence, and she made a mental note to ask him to help with that stubborn smudge on her whiteboard.

"I try to tell myself that it's not my business," she said to Brad. "I ran up against some cheating about ten years ago, and I don't know if I handled it right. I changed the way I teach the class to make it harder for anybody to cheat. It's more work for me, but at least I know I'm not tempting the kids."

"What do you do that's different?" Brad's cigarette bobbed up and down as his lips formed the words. The wind was playing with his hair, too.

"I mostly avoid simple quizzes with multiple-choice answers. I make most of the kids' grades depend on writing assignments, in-class, usually unannounced. They hate it, but I grade leniently. On literature tests I give them options on which questions to answer. I make different versions of the same test so that students sitting next to each other aren't answering the same questions. And for their final exam each year, I make it an oral test, partly."

"I bet they *really* hate that." He chuckled around the cigarette. "It sounds like a dissertation defense."

"Oh, they have time to prepare. And for most of them who prepare, it goes like"—she allowed a calculated pause to pass—"like clockwork."

When Brad looked up from his motorcycle seat, Robin caught the gleam in his eye and felt warm, exhilarated, appreciated—encouraged, almost, to toss her prior restraint aside and tell him what she really thought and *felt* about the school's cheating, how its growth over the years had been so slow as to not arouse alarm or suspicion, how what had started perhaps as a single tiny bad seed had sprouted and sent runners and roots in many directions, like certain wicked weeds, spawning ugly new growth not only among other students but also among teachers, parents, business supporters, even school board members, how the once-clean culture of the school had been poisoned by the passionate pursuit of academic glory, how that infection, whose broad contours everyone recognized but whose depth nobody really could fathom, had become a taboo subject, forbidden, as jealously guarded as any family secret, how she wanted more than anything to rip away the veil, reveal the falsehood, and restore goodness even at the expense of the glory, and how his tacit reinforcement, his own words of righteous condemnation, were nudging her toward the brink of action.

Still, Brad McCauley was an outsider. She did not dare tell him the worst things about Brookstone High, Indiana's pride.

11

EVERY TIME HIS phone jarred him awake before nine o'clock in the morning, J. Bradford McCauley felt a call to arms as adrenaline poured through his bloodstream. Too many times the wakeup calls came from Gregory Travis, the retired Riverside history professor, the fossil whose chance discovery while picking through the strata laid down by deceased historians had cast an ominous shadow of extinction over McCauley's thesis and future. He should have booted Travis from his Ph.D. committee when the old man retired. Instead, he had let him stay, and like an old geezer with rolled-up pants waving a metal detector over a beach, hoping to uncover a precious hunk of forgotten treasure, Travis had dug up something terrible. One day he had called McCauley to "talk about it," and once per month since then McCauley had gotten an unwelcome note in his mailbox, or an early morning phone call.

This time, however, it was the voice of Tolan Myers at Brookstone High School that greeted McCauley, requesting that Brad meet with him fifteen minutes before his last-period class to discuss "a student issue."

At 1:45 sharp, according to the school clocks, McCauley knocked on Myers's mathematics office door and heard a muffled "Come in!" Myers kept another office next to LaGrange's, a second office, a nicer office, reputedly oak-paneled with plush carpet, so when Myers had directed him to meet at the math office, McCauley felt mildly disappointed. As a part-timer, he didn't rate.

Myers was leaning forward at his desk, and a girl wearing a long, loose dress was gathering up papers to leave.

"If you can do the first five problems by tomorrow, Becky, that will be a good beginning."

"Thanks," she said, and squeezed past McCauley with a hurried, "Excuse me."

Myers motioned to her seat and said, "Extra help." He smiled in a superior way that made McCauley feel like he was being analyzed. On Myers's desk was a folder with B. MCCAULEY written in terse, slanted letters on the tab—a folder plainly meant for him to see.

"I had a visit with Tory Johnson yesterday," Myers began, leaning back. His collar was tight, and he wiggled two fingers between his neck and tie and pulled outward. Why didn't he just loosen the tie and undo the top button?

McCauley glanced at the desk. There was no folder for Johnson in view.

"He said he was upset with a grade on a quiz in your class."

"Yes, that's right," McCauley said. "He talked to me about it."

"What was the disagreement, exactly?"

"There were several short answer questions worth five points each, and he thought he deserved more points on some of them."

"So it was a matter of judgment on your part?"

McCauley nodded.

Myers reached down to the floor in back of his desk and brought up a large plastic Dairy Queen cup, its bottom half wet with condensation. He took a drink and set the cup on his desk. The largest drops of water trickled down the side.

"Grading short-answer questions is tricky," Myers said transparently. McCauley wondered what a math teacher would know about it. "You have to be careful you treat everyone equally."

"I know that."

"Tory's problem isn't the quiz *per se,* "Myers said, pausing to assess the impact of his Latin, "but his grade point average. He has a chance to become a Foursquare."

"A Foursquare?"

"Somebody who makes the All-A honor roll every quarter for four years. Sixteen times—four squared. It had never been done until 1986. Now there are a few students who finish a career as a Foursquare each year. He has a chance."

McCauley decided to wait and let Myers have his say.

"So that's why he's so concerned."

Still, McCauley didn't take the bait.

"Maybe with that in mind," Myers went on," you could find it in your heart to be a little lenient on this quiz."

"I was lenient on the *first* quiz. For everyone. Now that they know the kinds of questions to expect and the kinds of answers I'm looking for, I'm more demanding."

"Couldn't you phase in the demandingness, set the bar higher, more gradually?"

"I could, but after the first quiz we spent half an hour discussing my expectations. Nobody has any excuse."

Myers pulled at his collar again and thrust his lower jaw forward. His face seemed to be turning red, or was the fluorescent lighting tricking McCauley's eyes?

"Let's take a walk," Myers said. "Have you had lunch?"

"Yes, hours ago."

"Dessert?" He opened a miniature refrigerator, the kind college undergraduates keep in their dorm rooms for drinks, and pulled out a Dilly Bar from the tiny freezer.

"No thanks."

"I shouldn't either, but I missed lunch," Myers explained.

Locking his office door behind him, he led McCauley down the corridor and into the Atrium. In five minutes its stillness would be overrun by a stampede of students en route to last-period classes. Myers plopped down on a bench and McCauley followed his example.

"Do you mind if I ask you a question?" McCauley asked.

"Be my guest."

"Why are you, as the school's guidance counselor, discussing Tory Johnson's quiz with me? I would think that fell under the jurisdiction of the principal or academic dean." He resisted adding that guidance counselors ought to guide and counsel students, not teachers.

"Hmm," Myers said. "I wouldn't have expected you to ask that. Your psychological profile doesn't portray you as confrontational."

"Confrontational? Since when is asking a question confrontational?" McCauley was unable to smother a laugh, which turned into a cough. In fact, he was *not* by nature one of those annoying people who seem to relish and thrive on conflict. But in this environment, where he had so little real investment and so little to lose, he was a little more willing to risk stirring a pot. "What profile are you talking about?"

"Remember when you first applied here, we had you take a test?"

"Yeah, I remember."

"We make heavy use of those tests. They help us in guidance, scheduling, and so on. We know which students ought not to be in classes together, and which teachers can handle larger classes. We know what extra-curricular assignments are best for which teachers. We know how different students will respond to different forms of motivation or discipline. We use the test results to assign students to tutors, and so on."

McCauley had regarded that test as just another employment-process requirement to satisfy, rushing through it in order to return to Riverside for an appointment. Nobody had told him how important the test was.

He asked, "Are you going to answer my question?"

"Why am I going to bat for Tory? Because he asked me to, basically. He hasn't officially appealed his grade. Usually when a student wants to appeal, the situation can be taken care of informally. Hopefully that's the case here."

"Let him appeal," McCauley said, unsure how the process worked or where his show of boldness came from. In calling Myers's bluff he was taking a chance that would make Matt Rademacher proud. "I can defend the score I gave him."

"He's not going to appeal," Myers said offhandedly. "Look at this, would you?" He indicated the hallowed trappings of the Atrium. "You know, Brad, it's incredible what has happened at this school in the past decade. It used to be a place for farmers' kids to get their diplomas before going to work in gas stations or grain elevators. It was about eighty percent hicks. Now we have education experts from all over the U.S. of A. coming here to learn how to run a high school."

Atop classical columns spaced evenly about the Atrium, bronze busts of six famous educators of the twentieth century faced inward as though deliberating in perpetual judgment over whatever students and faculty might be milling about below. Beneath each statue was a panel bearing a quote about the relationships among learning, freedom, and happiness. Between the busts were photographs of Brookstone's academic elite. The intended effect of juxtaposing the students with the luminaries was to exalt Brookstone. Maybe someday the students would have statues, too.

Hanging from the ceiling, laminated vertical banners proclaimed the accumulation of national recognition for the school. Three green banners with white letters—PRESIDENT'S CHOICE—represented the White House's tribute each of the past three years. A nearby pennant, flapping in the breeze of a vent, came from the National Education Association and called Brookstone SCHOOL OF THE YEAR—INDIANA. The American Federation of Teachers weighed in with a pair of ensigns from consecutive years citing Brookstone as a GOLD MEDAL WINNER. An array of Education Department honors included a Secretary's Award for Indiana and three straight Excellence in Education Awards.

All the words of honor ran together in a blob of meaningless praise after a while, McCauley thought. Maybe the professional fame he sought would leave him feeling the same way.

His eyes drifted to a large section of wall featuring parallel rows of photos under a bold title: PYRAMID OF EXCELLENCE. Across the top row were the nation's president, vice president, and education secretary. The next row down featured a triumvirate of state leaders: the Indiana governor, lieutenant governor, and secretary of education and various state senators and representatives. Below them were local leaders, school board members, and captains of area industry who had established themselves as friends of education. A fourth row showed the school principal, assistant principal, guidance director, and faculty. Across the bottom ran a panoramic photo of the previous year's student body. McCauley could not help but notice that the structure of the pyramid implied that the foundation for Brookstone's excellence was the student body.

"Tory Johnson's father," Myers said, "is one of this school's biggest supporters. He donated about a hundred grand for the library annex."

McCauley realized that this comment was supposed to persuade him to relent on Tory's grade. Maybe, McCauley wanted to say, Tory ought to take advantage of that library to study for history quizzes.

"I guess what I wanted to emphasize to you is that at Brookstone, the solid tradition comes from the way faculty and students and parents and community work together. I know you have to teach in a few minutes, or I could tell you story after story. I just hope you'll do all you can to help Tory."

"If he's willing to work hard, I'm willing to work hard with him."

"Good. That's good. I know you won't let us down."

Let *us* down? What did that mean? Before McCauley could phrase a new question to "confront" Myers, the bell rang, doors at opposite ends of the Atrium swung open, and teenagers trickled and then streamed into the area, leaving Myers tugging again at his tight collar, the top of his bald head as red as a cherry on a Dairy Queen sundae.

October

12

WHEN HER SISTER Sarah left home for college in the East, Erin inherited the large bedroom at the back of the Delaney home, a room that had passed down from daughter to envious daughter, a room with its own bathroom, a spacious walk-in closet, and a large square bay window facing west. With Sarah and Patricia both gone, there were now two empty bedrooms between Erin's and the rest of the house, and Erin grew to treasure the insulation from her parents, though her father was in the process of converting one of the empty rooms into a den. The other now contained all of Sarah's belongings. In her second year at Princeton, Sarah still came home several times a year. Patti no longer had her own bedroom.

On an early Wednesday evening the first week of October, Erin retired to her room after a hasty microwave dinner of spaghetti and tomato sauce. Neither of her parents was home: Her father had a business meeting, and her mother was catering a Chamber of Commerce function. Even on nights when she was all alone in the house, Erin liked to isolate herself in her bedroom, lie back on her bed, and try to escape from the troubles that most days piled upon her. Tonight the sun was setting in back of long streams of clouds, painting them pink. The weather was cooling, the forecasts calling for temperatures to drop into the high thirties that night. Erin shivered. She was wearing a Riverside sweatshirt and maroon sweat pants, both oversized, plus droopy white tube socks. As soon as she had come home from school she had sat in the shower under nearly scalding water for twenty minutes. Afterward she powdered her body heavily, ate dinner in a loose bathrobe, and then changed to the sweats in case anyone stopped by. The furry cottony lining inside the sweatshirt and pants felt cozy. She had no underwear or bra on.

Now she lay on her bed, one knee up and the other leg hanging over the side, her arms crossed behind her neck, the tall boxed speakers of her sound system, set on either side of her room, pouring out the pretty piano music from a CD called *Autumn*, filling Erin's mind with images of the glorious fall colors that would begin to explode during the next few weeks. Years before, in grade school, she and her classmates had learned to press fallen leaves between sheets of wax paper to preserve their colors. She had never forgotten the process, never tired of the game. The most beautiful leaves she had ever found were pressed and framed and hung on her wall. Except for a few favorites, Erin did not know one kind of leaf from another. If a Riverside professor had explained to her how and why leaves turn yellow and red and gold and brown, she might have paid polite attention but would not have cared. Those details did not interest her as much as the beauty itself. She poured her energy into appreciation and near-worship of nature, which seduced her anew day by day, year by year. She would never outgrow her fascination with its splendor.

The telephone rang. Ordinarily she would not have answered, but sometimes when Mom worked she called Erin in an emergency—bring two dozen more of the punch glasses with the etched swans, or an extra box of the green napkins, or this or that. Over time, Erin and her sisters had bailed her mother out of many catering jams.

But when she answered the phone, her one fear materialized. It was Matt.

"Erin?" he asked, unsure. This was the first time she had ever answered the phone when he called, so he was surprised. "Whatcha doing?"

"Not much," she said automatically and with immediate regret. She tried to amend her answer with a fib about working on her research paper for Mr. McCauley's class. Already she was way behind—she had not chosen a topic, and the young teacher was beginning to pressure her.

"Some of us are going to Riverside for research one of these nights," Matt said. "You wanna go too?"

"Riverside?" She thought of Nathan. "Yeah, maybe I will."

Now that he knew she was not busy, he invited her to take a drive with him. She tried to wiggle out of it, saying she needed to be near the phone until at least eight o'clock in case Mom called—but Matt would not let that hinder their getting together. He would pick her up at quarter after eight.

The previous Saturday night she had surrendered to the will of her parents and Matt and many classmates and gone out with him to see a movie. Not a single one of her many fears—which grew out of Jess's many stories—was fulfilled. Matt had hardly touched her except to help her out of the van and once when their buttery, salty fingers brushed in their shared popcorn. All evening she expected his arm to cross behind her and rest on her shoulder, and she thought he might expect a good-night kiss when he brought her home, but no, his behavior was *impeccable*, to use an English vocabulary word. Monday she stayed with him at lunch, and Tuesday she deigned to talk with him in the parking lot after school. Everything had been comfortable so far—which worried Erin all the more.

At 8:15 sharp, hearing a honk, she flipped on the porch light and ran out to his van. She had put on more proper clothing and brushed her hair, and when she climbed into the car he was looking at her house and said, "Isn't anybody here?"

"No."

"Just you?"

"Dad will be home in half an hour," she said. "He has some hospital meeting once a month in Riverside."

"My mom and dad won't let my sister stay alone by herself," he said. "But she's only a sophomore. Maybe next year they will."

They went to Dairy Queen and sat in a booth for forty-five minutes, drinking Cokes from tall plastic cups and eating a huge tray of french fries provided gratis by the kids working that night. Matt loved salt; he emptied five of the small double-barrel packets into a grainy white mound on his corner of the tray, and no fry made it to his mouth without being mashed first into the salt. At the other end of the tray, Erin squeezed out several packets of ketchup.

"So what does Jess tell you about me?" Matt asked. "I always wonder what she tells you."

"Nothing. Do you think we just talk about *you* all the time?"

"She hasn't told you anything?"

"Why don't you ask her?"

"Did she say we ever did anything?"

"Maybe. Quit trying to make me say what she said. I'm not going to get her in trouble with you."

"I'm not trying to get her in trouble. I just want to know if she's been telling lies about me."

"Why don't *you* tell me about the two of you, since you seem so hot on her still?"

"I'm not hot on her still," Matt laughed. It was hard to rile him, because he took everything in such a good-natured way. The only time she had ever seen him upset was after Steve Gutierrez died.

Erin said, "But since she's already told me things, now you have a chance to tell me too. So what's your side of it?"

His fingers, loaded with salted fries, stopped halfway to his mouth. "You mean did we ever do anything?"

"Yeah."

"Why do you want to know that?"

"Why do you want to know what Jess said?"

"Okay, okay, okay," he said defensively. "Never mind."

"But I'm really interested."

"Don't worry, Erin. I didn't do anything with Jess that I wouldn't do with you."

"Oh, I suppose that's supposed to make me feel better. You're just afraid to say. Why?"

"I'm not afraid. It's just not the kind of thing you talk about with a girl. If you're a guy, that is."

Erin yawned and stretched and shut her eyes, well aware that Matt was staring at her chest again.

Trent Fox came out from behind the counter and began filling the salt and pepper shakers at the tables. When he reached their booth, he began talking to Matt.

"Cody says you lucked out the other night," he said.

"Phhssst," Matt answered in derision. "I can roll sixes like that whenever I have to."

"He said you would be afraid for double-or-nothing."

"A rematch? With just him? Any day."

"A short game?"

"Short or long, it don't make no difference to me. I can't believe he said I lucked out. I'll see if he says that to my face."

Trent left and Matt shook his head for a long time, for effect.

"That Cody loves to lose money," he said. "Do you ever play Risk?"

"No. I've never heard of it."

"Never? Well, it's like a war game. You have armies and countries, and you try to take over the world. Me and Cody and Trent and some other guys started playing it this summer. Maybe I can teach you how to play sometime."

"Do you ever play dominoes?"

"Dominoes? That's for old farts."

Erin giggled. "That's who I play with—Grandpa Dee. He loves dominoes. He taught me to play."

From Dairy Queen they traveled out Highway 22.

"Let's don't go to the Junction," Erin said. "It's too cold."

Matt turned on the van's heater, whose warm air flowed out the dusty vents and poured down onto their feet.

"That feels good," she said. "It might get in the thirties tonight."

"Great football weather." Matt honked at a car coming from the other direction that refused to dim its high beams. "Steve loved cold weather for games," he added, then fell silent for a moment. "I always think of him on Highway 22 because he's buried right up here in Green Ridge Cemetery."

"Do you want to go there?" Erin asked. Even though she had not known Steve Gutierrez very well, she knew he had been well liked by nearly everyone.

Matt flicked on his bright headlights until they flashed on the sign for the cemetery. A gravel road wound around and among the graves; the car's headlights swept across the land and out into a flat field, ragged with corn stubble. Reaching over, Matt pulled a flashlight from the glove compartment.

"Do you know which one is his?" Erin asked.

"I come here about every other day."

"Oh." Erin felt a pang of sorrow for asking. "I didn't know." Powerful emotions were swirling in Matt, far deeper than the superficial urges that produced his day-to-day arrogant, easygoing temperament—far deeper, and far more frightening to Erin, unsure how to react, paralyzed by uncertainty. When he put his hand on her shoulder, she let him guide her. They picked their way among the tombstones. Steve's was easy to spot: It was so new that it still stood straight up.

In the flashlight beam they read the simple words on the tombstone. Matt's arm did not leave Erin's shoulder, and she felt him pull her gently against him. It was true, what Jess had said, his body was solid as rock, solid as the tombstones.

"It's just hard to believe," Matt said. "Hard to believe."

"I'm sorry, Matt. Maybe we shouldn't have come here."

"No, it's okay. You have to go on living. Just like the counselors said … after he died."

"But if you come here every other day, maybe you aren't … you know. Maybe you haven't gone on living."

"Erin, if only you knew. Every day I see that bastard Myers I can't forget Steve. He did it. Myers did it."

"Myers? What do you mean?"

"Myers made him do it. He killed himself, but Myers made him do it."

"How?"

"I don't know, exactly. But I do know that he has ways."

Although Jess often talked about Matt's ravings over Steve's death, Erin had never paid much attention. After all, Matt had a reputation for embellishing what truths he told, usually in pursuit of humor, and, through the humor, attention. In the few weeks they had been hanging out together, Erin had noticed how Matt ironically used humor as a shield against people. Tonight his behavior only solidified her judgment. Over many hours with Matt, she had been mentally noting what she liked and disliked about him, assessing his quirks and qualities, forming a mental debit and credit column, preparing for what she regarded as the inevitable day when she would dump him, rejecting everything her friends and family wanted—and finally, triumphantly, taking a strong step on her own. She felt proud of her growing commitment to herself.

Still, what about Matt's sadness over Steve? Up to now, she had not figured on that. It messed up her calculations.

"Come on, Matt, let's go." She started off, but he did not move. The light bouncing back off the white tombstone barely lit his face, his lower lip extended, his eyes dazed. Erin reached back and took his hand, which seemed to break his concentration, but his fingers tightened on hers.

"Ouch, Matt!" She did not really feel any pain; still she slapped his arm with her free hand. Matt relaxed his grip but did not let go of her hand. His skin felt rough on her fingers, rough but warm.

"Come on," she said again. "Can we please go now?"

Matt flipped off the flashlight.

"Are you afraid of dying?" he asked. His fingers began to caress hers.

"I don't know, Matt." She thought of her Grandpa Dee in the retirement home. "I think it would be terrible to die *all alone*—or to die *young*."

"Me too."

Erin heard the thump of the flashlight hitting the ground. Matt swung her around in front of him and their free hands clasped. He brought their four hands together between them, as though they were praying. Then he let go and she felt his hands cradling her head. He kissed her, and just like their first date at the movie, none of her worst fears came true. It was a gentle kiss; she did not even think of pushing him away.

Afterward, she was no more attracted to him or put off by him than before.

13

ROBIN HILLIS SAT cross-legged on a large round pillow at the living room coffee table, grading papers, her television tuned to a college football game with the volume low, so low that the words of the announcers were barely audible, mostly obscured by gusts of whistling wind outdoors. Whenever the cheers of the crowd rose, Robin looked up at the screen automatically. She was no sports fan—but anything was better than the maddening solitude of the house when Zeb was away.

A week earlier, before leaving on his latest business trip, which on this night placed him in Toronto, Zeb had told her, "If I can just hold out until Christmas, I think it's in the bag. I really believe that."

"It" was the promotion he had been pursuing for more than a year. His hopeful words had climaxed a gracious four-day interlude in his frenzied coast-to-coast travel schedule. During her husband's time at home, two feelings jostled within Robin: gratitude and a determination to talk to him about his schedule, to beg him to cut back, even if it meant jeopardizing the promotion. Yet she was loath to bring up the topic while he was with her. Why spoil a good thing?

At the end of the first week of October he left again, and the evening before, as they sat across from each other at dinner, apprehension gnawed at Robin's soul. This was the perfect opportunity to talk about *them*, but she struggled for the right words. Was it really that important? Couldn't she hold out for a few more months? But the last time she had postponed raising her objections, she had paid a steep emotional price. This time she had to say something to let him know how much she missed him. So she spoke, trembling inside, and at her first tentative words, he said, "I know, I know. Honey, I really do understand. But listen: If I can just hold out until Christmas, I think it's in the bag."

She felt … dismissed.

Okay, okay, she told herself. I tried.

The papers Robin was scoring were expository essays on a poem from the students' literature anthology. Grading essays was always enjoyable for Robin because they gave her the best insights into how her teenage students thought. She liked adding comments of praise and encouragement at the end of each paper. And she liked seeing boys struggle with poetry—not struggling to *understand* it, necessarily, but struggling to *enjoy* it.

At nine o'clock Zeb called from his hotel, keeping his promise, but their conversation was short and dull. He sounded tired, preoccupied. Tomorrow would be a big day, he said, which Robin interpreted as, "I need to get off the phone so I can get some work done and get to bed." So they did not talk long.

She adjusted herself on the pillow. Half an hour passed.

Then she heard a series of firm raps on the front door. No doorbell, just knocking.

She crossed the carpet in her bare feet, admiring her red toenails. The stones in the foyer were cold on her soles and the tips of her toes as she stood on them to peek out through the door-hole.

Her heart jumped—one hand went to her mouth.

She turned the knob and opened the door a crack, looking around and asking with fake surprise, "Oh, hi! What are you doing here?"

Brad McCauley's hands were clasped behind his back. The porch lamps on both sides of the door lit up his facial features. His hair had its usual severe blown-back look.

"I was having trouble concentrating," he began, haltingly, as if that explained everything. "On my dissertation."

"Oh," she nodded, waiting for him to say more.

"Can I come in?"

"I suppose you know my husband is not at home?"

He looked down. "Yes, I know."

Robin's mouth dried up, her tongue running roughly along her lips, cold air sweeping in around her feet and ankles, creeping up her blue-jeaned legs.

"I don't know what to say," she said. "I can't let you in."

What was that she felt—disappointment? Where had *that* come from? She had said the right thing....

"Okay."

He looked down again.

"What do you want?" she asked.

"I couldn't work. I needed a fresh perspective on the dissertation. I thought maybe I could talk to you about it."

"Okay," she said slowly, her voice sliding upward as if inviting him to amplify, or promising to do so herself. "But I can't let you in." The hesitancy in her voice, in her heart, took her by surprise. She tried to look past him, to the houses of the neighbors, to see whether anybody was watching. Beyond the porch, everything looked dark except for the street lamps.

"Wait here," she said, flipping off the porch light, closing the door, her heart pounding. Somehow she had stumbled into a crossroads— somehow, yet in her bewilderment she really believed it had happened without any forewarning. If she let him in, she might be opening the door to the kinds of domestic horrors her less fortunate students sometimes wrote about. She ought to send him away, yet she could never do something so heartless and face him the next day.

She bounded up the stairs and pulled a pair of tennis shoes over the red toenails and white feet. Back at the front door, she took a jacket off the coat tree and turned off the foyer light.

Then she stepped outside.

Brad was sitting on the porch swing, visible only in silhouette, framed by the fuzzy gold light of the street lamps, a cigarette drooping off his lower lip, unlit, evidently. She laughed.

"Why don't you just light up?" she whispered.

"What? Oh, this." Clearly, he was nervous. "I don't smoke anymore, but this is the last stage in quitting, and I can't get past it."

"So," she said. "You're working on your dissertation, and ..."

"I'll be entirely honest, Robin"—had he ever spoken her name before?—"I haven't been able to ignore the things you showed me from Jefferson and some of the others."

"I'm sorry if I ruined everything." She felt smug, triumphant; at the same time, she doubted that she had brought to his attention any objections he hadn't long ago overcome.

"No, it's not that. Everyone knows the Founding Fathers said those things, publicly. That's never been the issue. In their private writings they were more liberal, and I believe more honest. My whole thesis is based on that premise and that kind of evidence."

Robin sat on the porch rail and listened. As Brad spoke, he began to sway on the swing.

"I just don't know how well I can prove my point, which is that the sayings and writings that appear orthodox come from the Founders' immersion in the mainstream, even though they personally were more free-thinking."

"So you are *assuming* they are free-thinking. That's your starting point, your real premise."

Brad shifted on the swing, the sole of one of his boots scraping on the concrete. "Well, not exactly."

He sounded like one of her students squirming under a severe cross-examination. She sympathized: It was surely agonizing to undergo the kind of scrutiny he would soon have to face from his committee, who would be far less gracious than she. Robin herself had defended a master's thesis, but her work was hardly on the cutting edge of controversy. Still, maybe she could help him.

"Just keep talking," she said. "If you talk it out, maybe that will help clarify it."

"Okay. I don't believe the Founders were grounded so securely in traditional Christian faith as is commonly supposed."

"Is it okay if I ask questions, or do you just want to run with it for a while?"

"Let me run with it for now."

"All right. I'll try to remember my questions."

"I think the predominant philosophy in most of their lives was deism, but they couldn't help but speak—at least in public—in more orthodox terms because that was the consensus opinion among the common people. So I've found this dichotomy in their lives. In some of their correspondence among themselves, and in their diaries, they let their deepest beliefs run free, but in their public pronouncements they had to be more conservative."

Across the street the Roosts' lights went out.

"That's it in a nutshell," Brad said.

"That's it? Oh, I was waiting for a full lecture."

"That's not my whole thesis, no. But that's the answer to your question, which is a necessary part of my dissertation—a refutation of the prevailing mainstream notion about the faith of the Founders."

"Did any of them ever *say* they were afraid to trot out their real views, into the public spotlight?"

"No," he said with resignation. "That's a real weakness in my work, maybe. Then again, if they had said that, there wouldn't be any dispute for me to write about."

Robin imagined a smile, pregnant with mischief, lengthening under Brad's mustache in the darkness. She nodded in deep thought. She was not able to concentrate fully on the subject, though. A vague fear began to steal over her that someone might be watching them. Leaving the porch light off was a mistake, but at least she hadn't let him in. The metal parts of his motorcycle gave off a gleam; she wished he had parked it in a less conspicuous place.

"I don't know," Brad continued. "I have genuine doubts sometimes, because the so-called orthodox Christian sayings are so clear-cut. That's what got me started on the topic—they're *too* clear-cut. If they were said today, whoever said them would get hammered for being too political. It's like they were trying to please somebody."

Robin considered this. There was another good possibility. Maybe the Founders were devoted Christians who were experiencing the same spasms of doubt as everyone. She was about to say so, when Brad asked, "You want to take a spin with me? I do my clearest thinking when I'm riding."

"Oh, no," she said, mostly out of reflex. Then she stammered, "It wouldn't be safe."

"Oh, you can wear the helmet. I don't always wear it anyway. I didn't coming up here."

If she had left the porch light on, she thought, she would be able to see his face now. In the grays it was impossible to read him. What was he really asking?

"Well, I guess not," he said, rising. "Maybe ..." The sentence trailed off into a hollowness that penetrated Robin's heart. She did not really want to go back inside, grade papers before a mute TV screen, crawl into her bed alone, and whine a prayer to God that her husband would come back. She had been crying herself to sleep for weeks now, if not physically then spiritually. The emptiness was expanding in her life, inflating, crowding out everything else in her soul. What could she do to fill it? Just tonight it would be so nice to have someone talking to her.

"No, no," she said quietly, firmly, jumping off the porch rail and standing in his path. "I'll go with you. I think it would be fun."

"You're sure?"

She nodded quickly.

With the helmet on she could hardly see a thing. When Brad started the engine, she feared the racket might trigger the whole block's porch lights to come on.

He called back over his shoulder: "Put your hands around my stomach if you want. Don't be embarrassed. Or you can hold the bar at the back of the seat. But hold tight. I would feel terrible if you fell off."

Robin felt the cold bar behind her, pressing into her hips: "This is okay back here," she said.

How long had it been, she wondered, since she had been on a motorcycle? At least twenty years. This one was so much bigger and more powerful. She felt like she was on top of a horse, the seat was so wide.

They motored up the street. At the first stop sign they had to wait for several cars, and her fear of being seen rose sharply, but died. Nobody would know her inside the helmet. People would think a man was taking his child for a ride. She wished she had put on socks, though. The night air was cold. But the skin of her ankles also felt the heat radiating from the engine, or the muffler, she didn't know which. She knew nothing about mechanics. Neither did Zeb—they both depended on friends like Howard Roost for so much.

Soon they reached the open highway. The first burst of acceleration nearly toppled her off the back, and involuntarily she let out a short scream.

"Hold tight!" she heard Brad call. She leaned forward against his back, shielding herself from the wind.

What a shame that there were no stars! That was the first thing she thought of as they shot south on Highway 53. How strange to be here! The rumbling of the engine and the rocking of the motorcycle underneath her—so strange! So very, very strange! Yet exhilarating, too.

They closed rapidly on the taillights of an automobile, but then a new explosion of speed carried them past it, Robin's heart freezing with fright as their single headlamp's bright beam flashed off a triangular NO PASSING ZONE sign.

Robin called into the wind, "Can't you read?" She tried to sound enthusiastic about his risk-taking, though she really regarded it as foolish.

"Those signs aren't for us," she heard him call back. "Just for the cars!"

After a few minutes she began to make out the lights at the edge of West Bridgebury, where the campus spread over the north half of the city. He must live along here somewhere, she thought.

"Any place you want to go?" Brad called back.

"No!"

"You drink coffee?"

Why was he asking? He already knew she did, from the lounge.

"Not tonight," she replied, fearful of going anywhere she might be recognized, aware that on campus she might easily run into former students.

Brad slowed and turned off to a side road. Soon he came to a parking lot, where he brought the machine to a stop but kept the engine running.

"This is where I live." He pointed to a door on the lower floor of a two-story apartment building, one of several arranged in a square. "Just a dinky bachelor pad."

"If you need more room," she began, then stopped, reluctant to say anything that could be taken as an invitation.

"If what?" he asked.

"Nothing," she replied. "I was thinking of something else."

"Want to ride around campus? Or should I take you home?"

"Didn't you want to talk anymore about your thesis?"

"Okay. I'll always talk about that."

She didn't want to ask where, not while they sat in his parking lot.

"There's a little courtyard around back," he said. "Let's go there. It's still not too cold, is it?"

"No, I'm fine."

The courtyard was enclosed by the apartments, illuminated by white safety lights that shone inward. The last moths and insects of the departed summer were flitting about the lights in small arcs, seeking heat as well as light.

Robin and Brad sat across from each other at a picnic table. Nearby an elderly couple in cast iron chairs bent over the orange and red embers of a fire, feeding it occasional twigs that created crackles and sent sparks swirling into the sky.

"Are there a lot of students living here?" Robin asked.

"No, not many at all." Brad's cigarette was gone and his hair looked even more beaten down by the wind. "There are a lot of older folks. It's a perfect environment for study, to be honest."

They talked for almost two hours. Once again, the fairest description was that Brad talked and Robin listened; once in a while she asked a question or made an observation about his argument. At the end Brad began to yawn, and Robin, who had not even thought about the time, said: "It *is* getting late. I probably have to start tomorrow earlier than you do." Then she thought, *Why?*

Going back to Brookstone, Robin wrapped her arms around Brad's belly. He seemed so firm there, not like Zeb—but who could say what the next fifteen years would do to Brad? Look at what the last ten had done to her! The wind was driving from the west, to their left, chilling her neck and fingers and the outside of her legs. She leaned close to Brad, resting her cheek on his back, facing east, her feet numbing with the cold. She couldn't wait to get home and curl her hands around a cup of hot tea or cocoa. Again she marveled at how wide the motorcycle was, and she tried not to think about her legs straddling Brad's hips, squeezing him, comforted by his warmth.

When they came to Dogwood Street, she redirected him to the back alley, where he plodded along till she said, "Here. This is it."

Brad turned off the engine and helped her remove the helmet.

"I can't ask you in," she said. "You do understand, don't you?"

"Of course I do."

"I'll see you tomorrow, then."

"Thanks for listening so well. You really are a great help."

"Oh, it's nothing. Thanks for talking to me."

14

CONSPICUOUSLY DISPLAYED IN the Brookstone High School lobby was an art student's colored pencil caricature of the school building composed of about thirty rectangular bricks. Inside each brick was a single word or short phrase expressing part of the school tradition. The drawing bore a title printed in italics underneath: *Building Blocks of Success.*

One of the blocks said FACULTY. Another said PARENTS. A third said TIME MANAGEMENT. And so on. Some were general, some specific. Some were clearly *ingredients* of success; others might more accurately be called *areas* of success.

One block contained three simple letters: SAT.

During the previous decade, when Brookstone had leapt into the national spotlight, its SAT performance had attracted notice sooner than anything else. At the beginning of that time, the average scores of Brookstone students languished near the 45th percentile in the state. Within six years Brookstone had become the state's leading school on the same tests. The previous year, Brookstone's valedictorian, Jamie Batta, had recorded a perfect score on the test—800 verbal, 800 math—one of just five students nationwide who could make such a claim. The school's uncanny improvement had been chronicled in articles in the *Wall Street*

Journal, Newsweek and *People*, and both CNN and Fox News had sent reporters and camera crews to record footage and conduct interviews that aired as part of their perennial coverage of the education crisis in America. Even Brookstone students who were not college-bound often paid for and took the test, simply because SAT success had turned into part of the school's culture.

Twice a year, every October and April, the SATs were administered on site in Brookstone's cafeteria or library to juniors and seniors. During the summer, the test was also offered at Riverside University, and many students heading into their junior year took the summer version, fully intending to try again in the fall. The Riverside test was a warm-up, according to that strategy. You learned what kinds of questions to anticipate and what kinds of reasoning were being tested, and you got some practice on questions about verbal relationships. Then when you retook the test, everything was easier. Students who wanted even higher scores for college admissions took the test a third time sometime their senior year.

Such was Erin's situation. Because her family had been in Florida on vacation for two straight summers, Erin had never taken the Riverside test. She was happy to miss any standardized tests, of course, but there was a trade-off: Now her parents expected her to do well on the October test, to improve her junior-year scores significantly. They talked about purchasing special software to help her prepare, but she dissuaded them; when they asked her about a private tutor, she declined. Every time that she assured them such steps were unnecessary, she felt the vise of their pressure tighten another turn of the handle.

The current version of the test had three parts: reading, math, and reasoning. Expecting to have most difficulty with the math section, Erin was glad to get it first. After sixty minutes of anxious fussing and figuring, she finished. Between sections the students got a short break, and Erin headed into the restroom.

She could not believe what she found there.

Five or six students were bunched around another student, talking at once, agitated, hurried, hysterical, leading Erin to wonder whether someone was injured, bleeding to death in their midst—murdered by SAT Math. Then she saw that each student, armed with a pocket dictionary, was looking up words the old-fashioned way, their phones having been confiscated in the test room.

The center student had smuggled a copy of the verbal section out of the test hall.

"What did you have, Erin?" She felt a tug on her sweatshirt and turned to face Jess, who had not spoken to her since learning that Matt had kissed her.

"Math," she said, still stunned by the definition feeding frenzy.

"Oh, I need to find somebody who had the thinking part. The reasoning. That's what I have next." She raised her voice: "Anybody have the *thinking* part yet?"

"Erin!" came another voice, from a girl she didn't even know. "Erin! You had math? Here, help me do this one." She thrust forward a copy of the math section, the same questions Erin had just answered.

"Where did you get this?"

"Ryan brought it out."

"I can't help—" then she changed her refusal to "I didn't know how to do that one." The girl's face fell.

At last Erin clambered safely into a stall, where she hunkered down until the intermission ended. She should tell one of the test monitors. But why? She would be putting up her lone word of accusation against the denials of dozens, for indeed everybody in the restroom seemed to be involved. She did not want to get mixed up in the matter. Only by pure accident had she stumbled into their nest, their orgy of cheating. The restroom was obviously a pre-arranged meeting point.

She heard a shrill whistle followed by frantic rustling and whispered, urgent exclamations, tearing pages, toilets flushing, and faucets turning on and off.

"Everything all right in here, girls?" came an adult's voice. "Let's get back! The next section starts in one minute!"

Thinking this was a safe time to emerge, Erin left the stall and the restroom. In the hallway Mrs. Frye was walking ahead of her, alone. If she told her, what would Mrs. Frye do? Return and check the waste can in the bathroom? Even if some scraps had missed the toilets, what would they prove?

There really was no use raising a fuss.

That night she went with Matt to the Junction. The football team had no game this weekend, and part of the tradition at Brookstone was the SAT bonfire, a cookout and outdoor bash to celebrate the conclusion of the October test. For a change, Erin felt like participating—she was confident she had done well enough to please Mom and Dad—but after the restroom episode she imagined that she might be the only one with an honest reason to celebrate.

Worse still, she dreaded seeing Jess, who had not yet seen her cousin together with her old boyfriend.

Matt was surprisingly subdued at the wheel as he turned into the Junction. Erin didn't ask why. She still didn't know him well enough to be demanding information. Their relationship was creeping forward, surprisingly. If he ever pressured her, though, she would "turn tail and run," to use an expression of Grandpa Dee's.

Matt's buddy Cody had spent most of the summer in Australia, where he learned to bungee jump. Everyone at school was talking about his unofficial (and probably illegal) bungee set-up at the Junction. Erin was looking forward to seeing it, and when she and Matt drove up, a cluster of students already occupied the bridge. Using a bathroom scale, football players were weighing heavy rocks. Jess was there, writing down the weights. Tyler Batta flitted among his classmates along the bridge, "broadcasting" into a hand-held recorder.

"What are you doing?" Matt asked. Far below them, on the west bank, Lance Tracer backed his pickup down to where the bonfire would burn. He and some friends started unloading brush and scrap boards for fuel.

Cody said, "G' day Matt, mate." He had the Australian accent down pat. Everybody laughed.

"What we got here," Cody continued, "is your good old-fashioned experiment. Basic R and D. Research and development, you know what I mean? Take this fellow here"—he stepped on a basketball-sized piece of granite—"he weighs in at 85 pounds. So we take a cord and strap that rock into our net, and let her drop. Then we see how far down she goes. And we just keep testing and learn what the cord can hold. Let's say it can handle 120 pounds. Then if somebody who weighs 120 pounds wants to jump, we know which cord to use."

Cody was hailed all around for his scientific acumen.

The slender fingers of Jess's right hand were curled around the neck of a bottle of beer, her jaws smacking noisily on a wad of gum, her eyes coolly regarding Matt and Erin, who imagined Jess was sizing her up for a cord around the neck.

"We already have these five cords tested," Cody said. "If you weigh in their ranges, we can drop you tonight."

"What are the ranges?" Matt asked amid a stir of anticipation. He popped the plastic lid off another cylinder of Pringles—cheddar barbeque—and shook about twenty of the molded chips between his thumb and forefinger, where they created an inch-thick plug.

"Let's see." Cody took a notebook from Jess. "Our strongest cord is rated 220-pound. What are you?"

"Two-ten."

"You're okay, then, mate."

"What do I do?"

The murmurs started again. Erin said, "You're not serious?"

"I'll try it," Matt said, underscoring his commitment by stuffing the chips into his mouth and crunching them, the intoxication of admiration already warming his blood. Swallowing, he said, "I'll try anything."

Below, doused by gasoline, the bonfire fuel blazed to life, though the sun would not set for another half hour. Walter Patingale, the school superintendent himself, appeared to deliver a load of scrap lumber from his construction business—his standard donation to the event. Beyond that, the nearby woods contained enough dead wood to keep the fire burning past midnight, and many kids would stay that late. This was, after all, not a school night.

Cody explained how the cord wrapped around your ankles.

"You go head first?" someone asked.

"They make chest harnesses too, but these are more daring," said Cody, abandoning his Down Under accent.

"So the cord snaps me back when I get close to the water, right?"

Jess taunted, "Suddenly you're not so brave."

Matt smirked and said to Cody, "Just remember if something goes wrong, you owe me ten bucks on that bet. You have to pay Erin."

That brought laughter from everyone except Jess.

"Nothing's going wrong, mate," Cody said. "I wouldn't want anything to happen to the easiest Risk opponent this side of the Big Pond." He added, "That's the Pacific Ocean, for you geography illiterates."

Matt stood on the concrete ledge of the bridge, humming and mouthing the words to "I'll Take My Chances." The top end of the cord was wrapped several times around the steel bar that acted as a safety rail on the bridge. There were a couple of hooks, too. The whole arrangement looked very strong—unless Matt was too heavy for the concrete and steel.

"Should I jump like a diver?" he asked. There was more uneasy laughter at his procrastination.

"Don't really matter, mate," Cody said. "When you get to the bottom, if your head's not down, it will snap down."

"The cord doesn't look very long."

"It'll get a lot longer."

"Like a certain part of your body," Jess volunteered.

The other kids giggled, and Erin, feeling strangely protective, looked for a stinging comeback to throttle her cousin. Matt was quicker with his reply: "Like *you* would know!"

All eyes turned to Jess, who raised the beer to her lips.

"Okay," Matt said. "Here goes."

He shut his eyes and gritted his teeth behind a smile, as if getting set to dive into an ice-cold pool.

Tyler Batta thrust his recorder into Matt's face and asked, "Any thoughts as you prepare to take your dive?"

Matt glared at the device.

"Tyler, don't you ever shut up?" someone called.

"Hurry, somebody's coming," Jess said anxiously. A car rounded the bend to the northwest, less than fifteen seconds from the bridge.

Matt jumped with a scream of *Whooaaaa* that stretched out like the cord. All eyes on the bridge peered down and all eyes on the bank of the river looked up as Matt's weight plummeted to within a yard of the water's rippling surface, paused for the briefest point of time, then snapped upward. Applause broke out. As soon as the upside-down Matt knew he was safe, he clenched his fists and cried: "Yes! Yes!" The car slowed, passed the kids on the bridge, and sped on toward Delphi. Once Matt's diminishing up-and-down motion stopped, Cody and the other boys on top pulled him back to safety on the bridge.

"That's fun!" Matt shouted victoriously. "You guys gotta try it!"

"Not me," Jess said. "I already took one too many plunges."

Erin shot her a swift, angry glance. Even if she wasn't yet sure about her own feelings for Matt, she knew that Jess was being unfair.

Matt said, "Come on, Erin, let's go down."

Soon the hot dogs and coat hangers arrived, and stray six-packs emerged from car trunks and coolers. Over the years an unwritten division of labor had evolved and passed down from generation to generation, class to class, for the bonfires. Male athletes always brought the drinks and meat for grilling; girls brought hot dog and hamburger buns, paper supplies, plastic ware, and garbage bags; if you didn't fall into either category, or if you weren't sure what to bring, you brought chips or dip or some snack or dessert. Whoever happened to be working at Dairy Queen sent over packets of condiments—ketchup, mustard, mayo, onions, and relish.

Erin wondered whether her experience during the SAT intermission had been a hallucination. Nobody was talking about the test. A few other kids tried bungee jumping—Jess did, after all her cute talk, and her lie about her weight resulted in her being dipped in the river. There was plenty of talk about football and the Thanksgiving dance. Cody and Matt, always dreaming up new ways to compete, staged a contest to see who could heave a concrete block the farthest. The girls broke off into separate groups and talked about clothes and hairstyles. Erin stood on their fringe waiting for somebody to say something about the SATs.

Night settled slowly. The stars emerged in frosty October brilliance. It grew too dark to try more jumps, too cool to risk getting drenched. The fire burned steadily, and kids who had wandered away in small groups or couples came back to its warmth. The pile of crushed beer cans grew higher; the alcohol and laughter flowed with less inhibition. Erin herself was not drinking. Matt had drunk a couple of beers, but he was okay.

Then, during a lull in the talk, Jess announced: "I think I aced the verbals."

Lance Tracer, the quickest wit among them all, retorted, "Excuse me, I must be having trouble hearing tonight. I thought you said you *aced* the verbals. Aren't you the same Jessica Southard who once told Mrs. Tice that you thought a *puissant* was a kind of ant that was attracted to urine?"

Uproarious laughter erupted all around the fire. Even Jess could not help but join in—the story was true, and when it came to English skills she was much like the conjectural monkeys set at typewriters to peck randomly until they produced a reasonable version of *Hamlet*. Before entering high school, she had twice flunked English. Her rise from the language arts ash heap was just another Brookstone success story.

The silence now broken, other kids loosened up and shared their stories about the test. Looking around at the fire-lit faces, Erin felt uneasy. Some of the girls she had seen in the restroom were here. What did they think of her? She yanked on Matt's sweatshirt—and for the first time she noticed the blank expression that clouded his features.

"Let's take a walk," she said.

They went down to the river and walked along its bank, under the bridge, past the place where she had watched the waterspout rise in its whirling crystal splendor. Matt's hold on her hand seemed mechanical.

"Is something wrong?" she asked tentatively. "Did you do okay on the tests?"

He said moodily, "Who cares about the stupid tests?"

"What's wrong, then?"

"Oh, Erin, I'm in trouble," he said sadly. "Big trouble."

Even as she debated with herself whether she wanted to know more, she heard herself asking, automatically, "How?"

"It's Myers. I owe him a lot of money."

"Mr. Myers? Why do you owe him money?"

"Promise you won't tell anybody, not even Jess."

"I promise I won't."

"It's because of Steve. Steve owed Myers money for getting him into this Navy program."

"What? What are you talking about?"

"Myers filled out a false grade report for him."

"Mr. Myers lied for him, you mean?"

"Don't sound so surprised. The bastard does it all the time. But he keeps asking for more and more in payment. So, I owed Steve $150 from that car stereo he sold me, remember?"

"No. How should I know about that?"

"Never mind. But I owed him $150, and I guess right before Steve … died, he told Myers he could pay me as soon as I paid him. So now Myers has been bugging me."

"That's not fair! Why don't you go to Mr. LaGrange?"

"What's he going to do? You don't understand how Myers works, Erin. He's so careful, nobody can pin anything on him. It would just be my word against his."

"But Matt, how did you get involved in this in the first place?"

"What do you mean, how did I get involved? Just by being a student here, that's how. Don't act so surprised. You know how it is. That bastard controls everyone's grades."

Erin's head spun with confusion. In the space of a few hours she had walked into a den of academic thieves and now she was hearing that even the school's guidance counselor wasn't honest. She didn't know what to believe.

"But how can he expect you to pay? And what if you don't? What can he do?"

"He can see to it that I can't be in sports, for one thing. He can lower my grades to keep me out of whatever college I apply to."

"I didn't know you wanted to go to college."

"Of course I do. Don't you?"

"Not really. Mom and Dad will make me, though. I'm supposed to follow Sarah to Princeton." If she was forced to go anywhere, she wanted to follow Nathan to Riverside.

"Today during the last part of the tests he was walking through the room, and he dropped me a note that said he expected fifty bucks by next week. Or he would suddenly discover a past error in my transcripts that would make me ineligible for football."

"I can't believe it!" Looking over her shoulder at the bonfire, she calculated. "You have the note. Isn't that proof against him?"

"What—do you think he signed it and put it on school stationery?" Matt said sarcastically.

Erin fell silent.

"I thought of stealing the money from the cash at Dairy Queen, but it would be so obvious if it disappeared one day and I paid him the next. He does the books for the store himself, so I couldn't get away with it."

A new insight struck Erin.

"Oh," she said. "Oh."

"Oh, what?"

"You feel guilty for Steve because you couldn't pay him and—do you think he killed himself because he couldn't pay Mr. Myers?"

"That bastard," Matt said, and began to sob. "He did it, as far as I'm concerned."

Later they ascended back to the road, circled around to the parking lot, and drove off without saying good-bye to their classmates. Matt said he wanted to be alone, away from them all, except for her. Although he had been drinking, Erin judged he was fit to drive, and he had no problems. Passing the cemetery, Matt muttered, "That bastard" once more. Erin reached across and touched his hand.

In Orange Stone they drove to the lookout point above the west end of Lake Pritchard and sat in the van listening to the low, heavy-beat music from the stereo—the $150 stereo that was causing so much trouble.

"There's so much pressure, you know?" Matt said. For the first time in their weeks together, Erin felt like he understood her, and when he pulled her closer to him on the car seat, she did not resist.

He kissed her, and she smelled the alcohol faintly.

"So what do you think, Erin?" he asked, kissing her neck. An uncomfortable sensation spread through her. Matt moved closer, his strong large body pressing her, squeezing her against the bottom of the seat. His hand moved under her sweatshirt now, cool on the warm skin of her stomach.

She slapped it away.

"No, Matt," she said. "I think no!"

He sighed, acted offended, and started the van.

15

THE BLACK SECOND hand sweeping over the Dr Pepper logo on the Dairy Queen clock got stuck for a few seconds between the cola-colored numerals 4 and 5 every time around. Watching it from his booth, J. Bradford McCauley wondered whether the regular delay also affected the minute hand, and the hour hand. No, he decided. The time—5:35—was accurate; therefore, the sticking sweep hand was not connected to the minute and hour hands.

He did not know how clocks worked. All he knew was that they worked.

Quite naturally, for him, pondering the clock sparked thoughts about clockwork, and also quite naturally for him, those thoughts slid into musings about his own life. If a man's life measured threescore and ten years, then his had reached its midpoint—high noon on a 24-hour scale. At that age Dante had (according to Robin) produced his masterpiece, which began:

> *In the middle of the journey of our life*
> *I came to my senses in a dark forest*
> *for I had lost the straight path.*

Positive that his own masterpiece was imminent, McCauley figured that if one hour on a clock equaled about three years of his life, then his

117

fame was about a quarter of an hour away. A smile curled the corners of his mouth but just as quickly passed away. The midpoint was certainly not the prime—his body already felt ragged, spent, defeated. Fatigue had hounded him for weeks because of his late nights composing at the computer screen, and his sleep, never sufficient, had lately become acutely unsatisfying. Often he fell asleep watching TV and awoke with a start from violent dreams to see the humming test pattern of the university station, whose broadcast hours ended sometime after midnight. His elbow might be bruised, or his head, or his ankle, from his spasmodic jerking and turning in his sleep. His sleep—or lack of it—had always been a problem. He blamed it for driving away two girlfriends.

He held out his hands. His index fingers kept curling outward, like an old man's. When he flexed his fingers, joints cracked, and pain flared in the knuckle of his left little finger. Many parts of his body were running down, but the deterioration of his fingers bothered him most because they were the real voice for his intellect. If he could not write, he would shrivel into a professional cipher. But what could you do? You couldn't reverse the process: The Universal Clock ran one way only. Even his worry was somehow a programmed response he had no control over.

How strange, though, what the clockwork of the mighty universe had swept into his life these last few months. He never imagined spending so much time away from his dissertation, away from Riverside University, and so much time loitering in the teachers' lounge at Brookstone High School, or at the town's sorry Dairy Queen, waiting for its Dr Pepper clock to reach 5:45, when he would go to meet Robin near the railroad tracks on the west side of Highway 53, south of town.

The kids running the restaurant this afternoon were all strangers to him, sophomores and juniors, probably. Maybe next year—but no, he would be long gone by then, climbing the lowest rungs of the ladder toward tenure at a big-name university whose identity lay hidden in the incomprehensible workings of the Universal Clock.

These kids were laughable, really, in their ignorant disregard for professionalism. He had been sitting for only ten minutes, but already he had watched them foul up a simple order by dipping a vanilla cone in butterscotch instead of chocolate. Another high school kid had come in and gossiped across the counter with the cashier while an elderly couple waited, and waited, and waited to place their order. Behind him he had heard a mom with a little boy say to him, "Boy, they put enough mayonnaise on your burger to float a boat!" To which the kid complained, "I said *no* mayonnaise."

The elderly couple finally received some service, and their order had been filled, more or less. The sandwiches were wrapped in foil and the drinks had been poured and capped, but none of the food had been given to them. The sandwiches sat in the silver metal slots where the unseen cook at the hidden grill had dropped them; the drinks stood separately, next to the ice cream toppings, virtually forgotten. The old folks whispered to each other; McCauley knew they were wondering where the cashier had gone. Nobody was at the counter. The old man craned his neck to look to the back of the store. It was a good three minutes before one of the brown-shirted kids came out and handed them their order, without offering any apology for the delay.

McCauley shook his head.

At 5:43 he dumped his two remaining onion rings and their greasy paper bag into the trash and left the restaurant. Against the cloudless sky, the sun hung low near the horizon, still brilliant: The side of every building dazzled, the pavement gleamed, the windshields and chrome of autos flashed as they passed. McCauley squinted until he pulled his dark helmet on and rode away.

Robin had designated a meeting point that lay just half a mile from her home but far enough outside of town that she would not be seen. He thought her precautions too severe: He was never going to pursue anything dishonorable with her, anything illegitimate, though she was attractive to him in a fresh way. In fact, he wondered whether he was using her in a non-physical way. Should she receive mention in the acknowledgments to his thesis? No, she would insist that he keep her anonymous. McCauley waited in the colorful shelter of oak and maple trees that edged a gravel road off the highway just north of the Lawn & Racquet Club. Robin liked to take walks after school; she would follow the rails and meet him where the tracks intersected the gravel road.

McCauley spotted her long before she knew he was watching. She looked less like a child and more like a woman here, away from the hundreds of students, many bigger than she was. He had not thought of her as petite until now—but surely she was petite and deliciously proportioned, he decided while she stepped from one railroad tie to the next, wearing plain white tennis shoes and no socks, tight jeans, a sweater of many colors, and a jacket tied by its arms around her waist. Her attention shifted to the tracks as she began to walk on the rail, her feet conforming perfectly to its width. For a long time she kept her balance, until she looked ahead, saw him, and slipped off the rail with a happy squeal.

"You're not a teacher, you're a gymnast," said McCauley. He was relieved that she did not seem nervous today. In a small town like Brookstone, she probably often ran into friends during her walks, so this was a perfect arrangement for her.

Robin tilted her head, their eyes making contact, holding it for a stirring instant.

"If I had not grown up so fast, I might have *been* a gymnast. But I was this big by the time I was twelve."

"This is not big," McCauley said, holding out his hands in mock appraisal.

"Are you ready?"

"Are you absolutely sure this is okay?"

"Believe me, Brad, I don't have any problem helping you as long as it's not under my roof, our roof. But if you have any second thoughts, it's okay. I can just turn around and finish my walk."

The sun lit Robin's fair, squinting, smiling face.

"It was *my* idea," he said.

"Then let's go."

His idea was for them to order a pizza from Yippy's, the campus favorite, and share it at his apartment while refining his manuscript. Previously, Robin had only heard him talk about it; now he was ready to let her see it in print. He asked her to promise to critique it gently, secretly expecting that she would find little to criticize except for grammatical and style issues. Every content question she had raised in their prior discussions was already addressed in his dissertation, so he looked forward to hearing her praise, effusive and effulgent.

Once they stepped inside his apartment, however, the Universal Clock ticked out a different course. McCauley went straight to the phone to place the pizza order and was put on hold for several minutes, as if he had been at Dairy Queen. Meanwhile, Robin toured the small apartment, which he had cleaned the day before.

While he waited on the phone, he heard her ask, "What in God's name is this?" She was standing before a tattered shirt, framed behind glass and hung on the wall beneath a printed identification card suggestive of a museum display—Harlan's Last Night—with a second line giving a date from thirteen years earlier.

McCauley explained: "That is a relic of my undergraduate days. Harlan was a roommate. We shared a bedroom. Sometimes I do crazy things in my sleep, and one night I tried to put on his shirt in my sleep. He was a really scrawny guy, and his shirt was way too small. That's what happened. He was awake and saw the whole thing, and he freaked out. He tried to talk to me, but I wouldn't wake up. He watched me tear his shirt to shreds trying to pull it on. Afterwards he decided it wasn't safe to live with me, so he moved out. We didn't speak to each other for a while, then things cooled off and we treated it as a big joke, and he sent me the shirt as a Christmas gift."

"It seems like a silly thing to hang on your wall."

"Well, give me a break. I'm a bachelor. It wouldn't stick out so much if I had a bedroom to hide it in."

"This is the littlest TV I've ever seen." Robin pointed to the four-inch diagonal set next to the couch, which was also his hideaway bed. "Do you actually *watch* this?"

"It's all a struggling doctoral candidate can afford. Even on that four-figure Brookstone teacher's salary."

"You must have to hold it awfully close to your eyes. It's a wonder you aren't blind, Brad."

"Well, the fact is, I do have pretty bad eyesight." He thought of his genetic clock tick-tick-ticking. His vision was the first of his senses to begin winding down. "I wear contact lenses when you see me, and I wear glasses most of the time around here."

Robin sat down on the couch in her snug jeans, crossed her legs, and interlocked her fingers in her lap. The telephone receiver cradled between his neck and shoulder, he washed his hands, noticing that she was looking at the safe under the end table.

"I didn't order any drinks," he said. "I have coke and diet coke and some sun tea."

"Diet for me."

"Actually, it's not *official* Coke. It's a cheaper cola."

He poured the drinks into plastic Riverside cups.

Robin remarked, "I can't imagine you with glasses. Do you have any pictures?"

"I have a photo album. Under the other table there, where the lamp is." Robin hopped up and went to get it. His eyes followed her, admiring her lightness, her spunk. She looked fresh, invigorated—but she was forty-six! How had she stayed so trim? What an injustice, what a shame that the clock ticked so generously slowly for some people. She sat on the floor, one leg curled under her and the other straight out on the carpet, turning the pages of the album.

"What are these? Family?"

"Some of them," he said. "An assortment of my favorites, really."

"Who's *this* girl? Oops! I guess I should have asked first: Is there anything in here you don't want me to see?"

"No, that's okay. There's nothing too personal in there."

In a moment he joined her and started telling the stories that went with some of the pictures. His manuscript, "Clockwork and the Constitution," lay open next to the computer on the card table.

Once the pizza arrived, he set out paper plates and napkins stamped with the logo of another fast-food establishment, and spread a campus newspaper over the carpet. They ate on the floor.

"This sure beats the cardboard pizza they serve at the cafeteria," she said. "No wonder kids have food fights sometimes."

"Food fights at Brookstone, Indiana's pride?"

Her eyes beamed at his sarcasm, and after she swallowed she said, "Kids are kids."

"You'll get no argument from me. In a lot of ways the kids I teach at Riverside are worse than the ones at Brookstone."

"I've been teaching twelve years—I didn't start until Anyssa was in fourth grade. In my opinion, kids are less mature as juniors and seniors today than they were even ten years ago. Something's happening. I always blame families. And when I hear our next-door neighbor talk about what teaching was like forty, fifty years ago, it makes me sick."

"How?"

"He was a shop teacher who retired twenty-five years ago, at least. Sometimes when we get to talking, he remembers how the discipline was stricter then, and kids were so polite and well-behaved. You know. The usual stuff you hear from older folks."

When she said that, Brad smiled. "Older folks," he repeated. "I already feel like I am one of them."

Robin's eyes beamed again while she chewed. She was so prim. Her wrists looked so slender and fragile coming out of the heavy cotton of her sweater. McCauley's eye fell to her gold bracelet, then noticed a matching necklace and even an anklet on the bare, white skin above her tennis shoe.

"You wouldn't say that if you could read what some of the teenage girls say about you."

"Don't mock me. It's only their hormones."

Robin looked around the apartment again. Her hair was cut short, revealing most of the back of her neck, but she let a few strands hang in front of her ears.

Spotting several stacks of cassette tapes and CDs on a bookshelf, she rose and said mischievously, "Let's see what kind of music a history scholar listens to."

McCauley watched her cross the room.

"Bruce Springsteen," she said. "I've heard of him."

"I should hope so."

Robin chuckled. "Kids are always writing about pop music. They think it's the answer to every problem they have. What is it you like about Bruce Springsteen?" She read aloud the titles of some of the tapes.

"I like his earlier stuff best. He seems to be very honest about what he thinks. I like that. Do you know any of his music?"

"No."

"Borrow something. Then you can tell me what you think."

"It's a deal." She laughed. "Kids are always asking me to listen to their stuff. Most of it I can't make heads or tails of."

"Take the one with the handwriting all over it. Those are my favorites. I put them all on one tape."

"I don't see the one you mean."

"Oh," he said, remembering. "I'll get it. It's in the bathroom."

"Why do you have so many clocks?" she called.

"I just like clocks."

Returning, he handed her the tape, apologizing for being so old school.

"You do have a tape player, I take it?"

"I think I can find one. In the attic, maybe."

Her hand swept an arc around the room.

"One room, basically, and three clocks," she observed. "Four, if you count the one on your computer. Five, counting your watch."

McCauley went into the kitchen for a drink refill.

"What are you going to do when you finish your Ph.D.?" she called to him.

Thinking about the Universal Clock, thinking of himself as a part of a pre-planned universe, he said: "I have no control over that."

"Of course you do. What do you *want* to do?"

"Does that really matter?"

"Of course it matters. I can't believe you're saying this."

"I have a lot of unorthodox ideas," he admitted. "For instance, I believe free will is an illusion."

Robin drew up her knees and wrapped her arms around them. "Why?" she asked. There was no judgment in her voice, no disagreement, only curiosity.

"If we really had free will, we could change things. And I don't think we can change things."

She looked past him, deep in thought. Usually people—even in the free-thinking academic milieu—dismissed his ideas about free will as careless extremism. Her equable reaction encouraged him. "What are you thinking?" he asked.

"I'm just wondering how that would apply to *my* life." After a short time, she said, "It makes life meaningless, in my opinion."

"No," he said gently. "It means you have to find the meaning somewhere besides yourself."

"I agree with *that*," she said. "Do you believe in God?"

"Yes, I do. But ... would you be shocked if I said I was a deist, just like the men I've spent years studying?"

She shrugged. "I don't know. My understanding is probably pretty basic compared to yours."

"Want me to explain it? It won't take long; it's not very difficult."

"Let me get some more pop first." She sprang to her feet. Calling it *pop* sounded quaint to him.

"Deists believe God made the world but doesn't interfere with it in history. They believe you can learn all about God from studying the natural world. You don't need a revelation like sacred writings to know who God is. That's it in a nutshell. So there is no free will, because everything we are and do is already predetermined."

"So ... what? We're all just puppets in a show? Where do you get a sense of purpose in all this?"

"I get it from the magnificence of the universe in time and space. And in my own life I see that. There's a plan. I can't change it even if I want to. In fact, even my desires and thoughts are part of that plan. I get a lot of meaning out of knowing that."

"But is there any right and wrong? If everything is predetermined, then how can there be right and wrong?"

"You have to think of it on a higher level. You have to believe that when something happens that seems wrong, it really is part of the plan of the universe."

"That means it makes no difference what I do with my life," said Robin. "Maybe I just don't understand it, deism."

"It's not that different from mainstream historic Christianity," he said. "Really, it's not."

"I guess I just don't understand it. Do you worship or pray?"

"In a sense I do. I think about the world, and how it works out, and what I'm doing in it. I'm thankful for who I am, and where I'm going."

"You said you don't *know* where you're going."

"That's true, I did say that. I can't ever be sure until I get there. But I know that God, whoever or whatever he or she or it is—and I do think of God as a *He*, with a capital letter—has made the universe so that I am a history scholar, and I hope He makes it so that I am a good one."

He ran his hand over his face and felt the day's itchy stubble. "You see, even my goals and ambitions are part of the plan. I can't explain it much better, but I know it's true. Everything is determined. Everything. Every last detail. Nothing is by chance, like the evolutionists say, because they don't believe there's a God in control. In deism, there is a God in control. He's in control through the machinery of the universe, through space and time. Everything that happens is part of what He built into the universe at the beginning. Maybe it was a big bang like the scientists say, or maybe just 'Let there be light.' I don't know. Either way, everything proceeds from that. And everything is determined, from the way atoms and chemicals behave to the way people behave. And our lives are determined—our sicknesses, our talents, all of it. Each detail is part of the machinery. For me to teach at Brookstone for a few years isn't just one option of what might have happened. It's the only option. It's the way the universe is planned. I might think I chose it, but that's just the illusion. We always think we choose what we do, because our mental perceptions and processes are part of the universal machinery, too. It's all determined. When that kid ran into you in the hallway, it was determined. For you to have picked up the nickname 'Birdie' was determined."

"Wait! How do you know about that?"

"I saw the card you keep on your desk."

Her eyes flashed anger, briefly, then softened.

He continued, "For you to ask about the clocks was determined. For us to be here is determined. Am I making it any clearer?"

Robin lowered her knees and crossed her legs, the red fingernails of her left hand scratching her ankle, making a scraping noise, leaving dry white lines on her skin.

"I'm still trying to see how it applies to me."

"Just think about it for a few days," he said with enthusiasm. "It's a very comfortable system of belief. I think so, anyway."

"But ..." and she raised another question, which brought forth another spirited reply. More questions and more answers followed, and before they knew it, the hands on McCauley's kitchen clock had merged at 10:55 P.M.

All the way back to Brookstone, with her hands clasped tightly around his waist, he wondered how to tell her good-night. At the door that opened into a dark screened-in porch, she lingered and said, "I want you to know that I really hope you realize all your ambitions." The words struck him as odd, as conveying a palpable urgency he did not feel. It was too dark to see her face. He reached out and his hand rested on her hip.

"Robin, is something wrong?"

"No," she said, brushing his hand away. "If there is, it's all determined, right?" Her question rose in a collision of defiance and despair. McCauley's heart fell. Her voice went on, cracking, "Maybe we can talk about it some other time."

McCauley rode home in turmoil, dismayed that nobody understood him.

16

GEORGE DELANEY, GRANDPA Dee, fixed his dominoes with a military stare and murmured, "Six and a deuce, six and a deuce." He played a double-deuce, a spinner, and rapped the table with his knuckles. Erin recorded his ten points with a precise X, then without hesitating played a deuce-four, knocked the table, and said, "Dime."

"Six and a four, six and a four," Grandpa repeated. He had such a limitless stock of nervous habits that Erin played less for the fun of the game than for the chance to watch her lovable grandfather's mannerisms. Sometimes he rubbed his thumbs against his forefingers, creating a squeaky friction that brought a smile to her face. When he was in a corner or had no play, he liked to repeat, "Hmm, hmm, hmm" in a sliding musical scale. Always three times, with each *hmm* a little lower in pitch. At least twice a game he would reach out with his domino, pause with his hand hovering over the table, and announce—as if his play required an explanation—"I'll *tell* you what I'm gonna do." Then he would put down his domino so you could *see* what he was gonna do.

George was eighty-eight now. Cancer had eaten away hunks of skin and tissue around his right eye, a bee sting had led to the removal of part of his left ear, and the merciless iron fingers of Alzheimer's were closing on his brain. One day Erin and her father had stopped to see Grandpa Dee and he had cried, "Good Lord, Sam, look at how much you've grown!" Later her father had explained that sometimes Grandpa Dee's mind played tricks, remembering his son as a little boy rather than a grown man. That was scary enough, but what made it worse was its unpredictable nature. Once while she was visiting, he flew out of his chair during *Jeopardy* and cried out, "Surround him, I say! Surround him, and make him pay! Make him look at himself and see what he's done!" Her father had explained that one, too: Grandpa Dee had been in the war, in Europe, and often his mind, triggered by a sound or a word, flashed him backward into discussions on how to finish off Hitler.

For their game, Erin had washed a cluster of grapes and put them on a plate next to the draw pile, but she was the only one eating them. Next to the table, a sliding glass door opened onto a concrete patio, ten feet square. Erin's mom had bought a couple of tall plants to jazz up the patio, but the first frost a few days before had killed them both. Grandpa Dee never even thought to bring them in.

The residents here lived pretty comfortable lives, she thought. The grounds were spacious and rolling, thickly wooded toward the lake, and the individual apartments were kept in good shape. Grandpa Dee lived in a two-bedroom unit, but his lease would expire at the end of December. Since Grandma Dee had died, he would not be able to remain in such a large unit. If there were two of you, they let you have a spare bedroom. Erin didn't understand the policy, but Grandpa Dee didn't object to having to move. The single units were just as nice, he said.

Grandpa Dee won the game by blocking the board and recording a 105-point domino on the last hand. As Erin added up all the black dots and confirmed his victory, Grandpa Dee said, "It's time." For *Wheel of Fortune*, he meant. Erin flicked on the TV.

"Did you know a guy at Brookstone won $50,000?" she asked.

"Aw, go on." That was another of his favorite expressions, conveying amazement or disbelief.

"Really," she said. "He won on a scratch-off lottery ticket at the Amoco station."

"Oh, you mean the Rademacher kid. Yeah, I did hear about that. Your mom and dad told me."

"Oh." Erin frowned. "Did they say I was … dating him?"

"No. My little Erin a gold-digger?"

Erin tossed a pillow at him, and after it struck him squarely in the chest, Grandpa Dee ducked.

"I'm *not* dating him," she said. "But they want me to."

"Why don't you? Isn't he rich enough?"

Erin pelted him with a second pillow.

They watched *Wheel of Fortune*, Grandpa Dee's favorite show, which in addition to its regular weeknight rerun slot had also started airing on Sunday afternoons. For his birthday the previous year, his grandkids had sent him five different posters of Vanna White that were now pinned up around the apartment. One poster showed Vanna in a short skirt and plunging neckline holding up a blank square, and the kids had written in the square, I'D LIKE TO BUY A "D" FOR GRANDPA DEE!

She loved Grandpa Dee more than anybody in her family, her memory teeming with a procession of rich images from her earliest years. As a toddler he would sit her on a workbench a safe distance away from the whirring grinder as he sharpened mower blades, sparks shooting and dancing and bouncing, like the sparklers from their Fourth of July celebrations. As she grew, so did her adventures with him, fishing, hiking, hunting, and hanging out with him every August at the Harrison County Fair, the highlight of her summers, the fair where he knew everybody and his brother, even that scar-faced blacksmith who let her put on the monstrous gloves and use the long tongs to dip the red-hot horseshoes into the water. Once, coming home from the fair under threatening skies, he pointed toward the horizon and said, "Tornado," with no more alarm than he might have identified a toad in the garden. He was such fun.

As the credits rolled at the end of the show, Erin suggested they take a walk.

Somewhere somebody was burning leaves. The smell of the smoke spread over the area. Erin breathed in deeply: This was pure autumn, the crisp air, the rustling, brittle vividness covering the land and clinging to the trees, falling leaf by leaf, red and orange and yellow and brown, the sun brighter than at any time during the year, but for all its blazing not burning your face. They walked to the crown of the hill that sloped down moderately to the west end of Lake Pritchard, and as the sun rested for a few seconds in line with the slope, balancing on the visible horizon, their shadows stretched all the way to the water, then disappeared in the day's last shade. Far out in the lake the sun caught the white triangles of a line of boat sails.

Erin sat down on the leaves, Grandpa Dee on one of the sturdy cast-iron benches strung along the ridge. They were the only people out.

"You still collect leaves?" Grandpa Dee asked.

"Yes. But only really special ones."

"You gonna be a tree doctor or something, when you go to college?"

Even here, bathing in the open grandeur of an autumn evening, the family pressure was not far off.

"I could never be a doctor," she said. "I'm not as smart as Patti."

"Ah, that doesn't matter."

Erin let loose a long sigh. "Mom and Dad don't understand that."

"They ought to. Your dad ought to, at least." Grandpa Dee chuckled.

"What's so funny?"

"Ah, I just always remember your dad telling me he was going to college, and how surprised we all were. Nobody had ever went to college in our family before your dad. Did you know that?"

"Oh, yeah," she replied. "He's reminded us a million times."

"Yeah, I remember it well," he went on, but Erin wondered about the accuracy of his recollection. "I was out by the water pump working on that blasted tractor. It was always broke. The same dad-gum belt kept coming off. Jerry and Chuck were helping me; I don't know where Hank was at. But we asked Sam to give us a hand, and he kind of huffed and helped, and then he said, 'I think I should tell you guys that I'm going to college to be a doctor.'

"We all stopped dead. All eyes were on him, and he felt the heat. He just said it again, 'That's right, I'm going to study to be a doctor.' Then he walked off. Nobody had done nothing but farm in our family for three generations."

"I never thought of that," Erin said. "Uncle Chuck, Uncle Jerry, and Uncle Hank. They're all three of them farmers."

"But no, your dad, he had to be different." Erin detected a resentment in Grandpa Dee's voice, and for a curious change she felt herself identifying with her own father. She lay back in the cool cushion of the leaves and stared up into the jagged oak branches dripping brown leaves like slow-falling drizzle.

"You wanted him to be a farmer?"

"You're blasted right I wanted him to be a farmer. Just like the rest of us. He said that wasn't good enough for him."

"I can't picture dad ever being a farmer."

"Well, I couldn't picture him being no doctor, neither." He chuckled again. "When push come to shove, he says to me, 'The Good Lord didn't make everyone to be a farmer.' That was it. We never argued about it anymore after that. He made a good doctor, everything said and done. But I wonder if I'd be living here if he was a farmer."

Erin suddenly realized, with a mild shock of insight, why Grandpa's bitterness about his son defying him had deepened so dramatically since Grandma Dee had passed away.

She sat up and faced him. "Grandpa, do you like living here?"

"Naw, I hate it," he said, spitting and rubbing his face, near his bad eye. "I'd rather die on a farm, where I belong."

She started to ask how he could not like this place, but another insight stifled her. Everyone is different, she thought—Dad and Grandpa, and Grandpa and me. Wouldn't it be great if you could just switch places with people? She would love to live here in the surreal wooded wonderland, a peaceful paradise compared to her rough-and-tumble existence.

"Does Dad know you don't want to stay here? Couldn't you go live with Uncle Hank or Uncle Jerry?"

"Sure, he knows. But he has his brothers tied around his little finger. Sam always gets his way. Always has and always will. When I let him go to college, that was like opening the barn door to him always getting his way."

A wave of new discouragement flooded Erin's heart. Dad would have his way. Whether she liked it or not, she would go to the college and succeed in the field he chose. Her education, her social life, her career—her whole existence would be forever smothered by his suffocating expectations. She felt squeezed between him and Matt and Jess and even her teachers. Tomorrow she had to meet with Mr. McCauley and present to him her research paper topic and outline. She was as far from choosing her topic as she was from the sweet days of country drives with Nathan, or the carefree hours traipsing alongside Grandpa Dee at the County Fair, or reveling alone under the wild, swirling freedom of the Junction waterspout.

November

※

17

"HAVE YOU EVER been in LaGrange's office?" Brad McCauley whispered to Robin in the teachers' lounge. Although she had become more adept at sensing his moods from the subtly different inflections of his baritone voice, she could not immediately read any emotion into his question.

"I've never seen anything like it!" he babbled on. "It's more like the office of the president of a university. Oak paneling on the walls, oak chairs, an oak desk as big as a CEO's, thick carpet, a chandelier. They really treat him right."

Everything he said about the majestic trappings of the principal's office was true. Robin had been in it only a few times, but she had listened to Bragley, the veteran janitor, rave about its magnificence once when she had stayed long after hours to grade papers. A source of mystery among many teachers was LaGrange's second office, really a back room shared with Tolan Myers's next-door administrative office. Except for LaGrange, Myers, and Walter Patingale, nobody made regular visits into that inner sanctum; in fact, Robin questioned how McCauley had rated the privilege of an invitation to LaGrange's primary office.

Nevertheless, she felt that his fascination was mostly affected. He was hiding something.

Teasing the truth from him would have to wait, however. The teachers' lounge was almost full, and in front a woman dressed in a sharp blue professional outfit—a long skirt, a blazer, a loose-fitting white blouse—was efficiently removing packets of printed material from a briefcase and arranging them in separate stacks. Her hair was brown, cropped to a mannish shortness, its only decoration a basic white barrette. She looked "all business," Robin thought, questioning the fiscal wisdom of bringing in an expert on sexual harassment from the corporate world to make a presentation to teachers. Couldn't they find a qualified school official?

Once the materials were distributed and the audience busy giving them the requisite courtesy consideration, Tolan Myers introduced the guest speaker as Priscilla Verhoven, from the Office of the Dean of the Riverside School of Business. The compromise between business and education backgrounds satisfied Robin.

Her name still sinking into the brains of her audience, Ms. Verhoven launched into her presentation: "Sexual harassment is any person's conduct which unreasonably interferes with another employee or student's status or performance by creating an intimidating, hostile, or offensive working or educational environment. Now, we don't pretend that it's possible to specifically indicate every kind of prohibited behavior. Today we will look at certain cases that will help you understand what constitutes sexual harassment, especially in an education context."

She instructed everyone to look at the first handout, printed on goldenrod paper. Fifty hands reached simultaneously for the colored sheet. At once Robin's practiced editing eyes spotted dozens of slash marks in the text, and she rolled her eyes at the clutter of *he/she*s.

Her attention drifted. Two years earlier on a summer evening, she and Zeb had crossed the street for a cookout on the Roosts' back porch. A member of Howard's church—a man who worked with Howard as a counselor—was facing a lawsuit for sexual harassment, and the four of them began talking about it around the placid sizzle of the steaks on the grill. Jerri said, "All these new laws and initiatives to teach everyone about sexual harassment aren't worth a penny, if you ask me. I know all the businesses are trying to educate their personnel about it, but it's so silly. If people haven't learned any common decency through twenty or thirty years of living, no half-hour seminar or fancy full-color brochure is going to make any difference." As usual, Howard summed it up best by saying, "Unless our hearts change, nothing else will change either. And no amount of education can change your heart." Zeb quickly said, "But we won't close down all our schools," which sparked nervous laughter. The Roosts had homeschooled their two children until high school, with undeniable success. Lena had been a Brookstone valedictorian and Gold CUPP winner, and Scotty had finished second in his class to win the Silver CUPP.

"... may consist of a variety of behaviors including, but not limited to, subtle pressure for sexual activity, inappropriate touching and language, demands for sexual favors, and physical assault." As Robin tuned back in to Ms. Verhoven, her blood began to seethe. This woman was basically reading from the page, word for word, as though Brookstone's teachers could not understand simple English. Didn't she know where she was? This was Brookstone High, home of seven faculty who had won Indiana Golden Apple awards, whose CUPP program was the envy of the nation!

Her eyes climbed to Brad's face. He was in rapt attention, his eyebrows scrunched and his head tilted slightly to one side. Never having seen him look so thoroughly engrossed in anything, not even his beloved misguided dissertation, she was amused.

Did he know she was staring at him?

Below the table her blue shoe inched toward his boot, and then stopped. She forced a cough and shuffled her position, crossing her legs, looking around the room as discreetly as she could. Coach Tom Batta, wearing his letter *B* jacket as always, was sitting with his assistant coaches, Sherwin Ray and Phil Noonan. None of the three had opened the handout—yet every year Batta could be counted on to open his mouth two or three times in shrill denunciation of the "dumb jock" stereotype he believed was leveled against his players. The meaty forearms of Damon Browne, the industrial arts instructor, were bared to his rolled-up sleeves and crossed defiantly. Ed Sojka was doodling, drawing what looked like molecular diagrams on the table top, hypnotizing Robin's eyes with his pencil work until its eraser end rose to his glasses and nudged them higher on his nose. The women faculty were more attentive. Doreen Ralston was actually taking notes, and Barb Rector's eyes were sneaking ahead to later pages in the handout. Michelle Newman, the geometry teacher, looked like she might be analyzing the angle between Ms. Verhoven's mouth and the clock, calculating its cosine or sine or tangent or whatever, as her eyes kept flitting back and forth between those objects.

Ms. Verhoven made a reference to "creating a threatening atmosphere," and Brad's fingers went to his chin. Robin had grown acquainted with this gesture and interpreted it as a signal that his interest had risen another degree. What could he possibly find so intriguing about this subject?

Then the thought occurred to her that Brad was attracted not to the speech but to the speaker, so she fell to studying Ms. Verhoven's figure, dress, and makeup. She appeared altogether too trim and businesslike for Brad. Her flat shoes were boring black, her outfit hid every square inch of her flesh except her hands and face, and even her baggy blouse seemed stiff as a clerical collar around her neck. Many times Robin had felt Brad's eyes admiring her own legs, and she felt gratified by his attention. Compared to her, what did Ms. Verhoven have to show? It was impossible to tell, because her ankle-length, deep-pleated skirt hung too loose to reveal even a hint of the shape underneath. Both women had short hair, but Robin judged that her red earrings added a dash of color to her face that her rival lacked. In fact, Ms. Verhoven wore no makeup at all except for a light lipstick.

Robin breathed in and out through her nose, but the noise failed to catch Brad's attention.

The "seminar" was supposed to run a full hour. Above Ms. Verhoven, the lounge clock's minute hand clicked into the due south position, 3:30, the presentation only one quarter finished. Maybe Brad was staring at the clock, the symbolic muse for his dissertation.

Shifting in discomfort, Robin entered into an exercise she used with her students to prepare them for descriptive writing. She let her imagination drift, visualizing herself in Brad's apartment, standing in front of his rickety computer table, its dissertation open in its black three-ring binder, half a dozen open books arranged in an arc on the floor, snatches of text highlighted in neon yellow or orange or pink, scores of photocopied journal articles, stapled together, scattered depending on their most recent usage or stacked if they had fallen out of favor. Gradually Brad's brain was collecting, considering, analyzing, correlating, interpreting, assessing, evaluating, discarding, sorting, and rearranging the information into fresh furrows of thought in the field of constitutional studies. Each newly refined version of his proud product he tucked away, not encoding it electronically on his computer's unreliable hard drive but instead storing it on a flash drive secured to a lanyard that when not in use he looped several times around the handle on his safe or deposited inside the safe.

Her mind's eye kept wandering. It fell on the avocado-colored telephone, the back of its receiver handle bisected by a crack, and she pictured him cradling the receiver between his shoulder and ear in the strained position that no doubt contributed to his on-and-off neck pain. Then she pictured his tiny television, smaller than a toaster, and the counter in the kitchen, always littered with Yippy's Pizza boxes and bread stick bags. His refrigerator had a dozen magnetic hearts from the blood center, lined up in two rows of six; he was a regular donor. She saw the framed shredded shirt, the hand-sized hole through the drywall, and his gray cubic safe "hidden" beneath an end table, the safe whose existence he had never explained. By degrees her meandering fancy flitted into the bathroom, filthy by her family standards but appropriate for him—iron drip-stains in the sink, the uncapped shaving cream can, the shower curtain streaked by mildew. The scene was too unsavory even for her imagination.... Back in the living room, she envisioned his hideaway bed pulled open—had she ever seen it that way?—the covers rustled messily, as if he had risen haggardly at three in the morning to record fresh insights delivered to his brain by some nocturnal muse or dream messenger.

In the teachers' lounge, Robin's eyes closed as she imagined Brad clad in only boxers climbing back into bed, and anyone watching her rather than Ms. Verhoven would have seen a smile rise almost imperceptibly to her lips. With a gentle shudder of surprise, pleasant surprise, Robin realized for the first time that an evening was approaching when Brad would knock at her door and she would let him inside. Their fledgling relationship was carrying them toward such a tryst, a tryst whose very idea had frightened her at first—but no longer. She was ready to cross the threshold. Ready and … willing.

When it happened, would it be a matter of irresistible fate, as Brad believed? She looked at the clock once more, trying to reconcile his impersonal view of God and man with her own life. Truly, God did seem very far away from her just then. As far away as Zeb, as far away as the end of the weary seminar. That was only a feeling, though, and feelings would always come and go. It was preposterous as well as blasphemous to imagine that her marriage to Zeb had been destined to slide into this deepening rut. What happened to free will? Hadn't Zeb chosen to spend more and more time living in airplanes and the hotel rooms of distant cities? Hadn't she chosen to climb aboard Brad's motorcycle? Of course! Regret—guilt, really—wrestled with something else in her soul, something that cried out for attention and understanding and acceptance, just as the teenagers cried out. The guilt produced another sudden fantasy in which she and Brad, barreling down Highway 53, smashed head-on with a wayward semi and died in agony.

That bizarre thought, in turn, reminded her of the hallway collision with the student several weeks earlier. That accident could not have been fated, in Brad's scheme of the universe, considering its obvious moral implications. How silly to believe that the universe works itself toward goodness all by itself!

The evidence of cheating she had come upon, or that had come upon her, continued to vex her, imbedded in her thinking like a bee's stinger in her skin. Seldom did a day pass without some minor event in her classroom reminding her that she must remain ever vigilant with her own students. She suspected no one in particular, but Brad's attempt to trivialize the matter with those noxious words "they all do it" had produced the opposite conviction in Robin, for now she believed that whatever she knew about cheating at Brookstone might be just the tip of an awful iceberg.

Over the years she had been involved in a handful of incidents, a number she thought was about average for a high school teacher. Many more times she had heard rumors but never wasted time or energy to confirm or refute them. In the first place, it was none of her business. Secondly, she wanted to trust the integrity of the other teachers and administrators. They were all respectable role models and responsible professionals, as far as she could tell. But some of the rumors involved teachers who were still on the faculty.

Still warm from its earlier dalliance, Robin loosed her fancy further. Her eyes roamed the lounge, and she wondered which of her colleagues might bend the rules, and why. *Why?*—that was the real issue. To maintain Brookstone's lofty reputation? Or to line their own pockets, too empty even after decades of fruitless collective bargaining at the local or state level? Either reason was understandable, but most teachers were like herself, laboring in two-income marriages, having chosen their profession out of love for children, not for money.

She forced her attention back to the business at hand, where the seminar shifted into question-and-answer gear. A number of hands went up, mostly belonging to men. Ms. Verhoven kept hammering home what seemed to be the seminar's keynote phrases, "threatening environment" and "atmosphere of intimidation." Each of her answers to men led to whispering in the audience. Several teachers, men and women, asked questions about harassment *from* students, and when Ms. Verhoven took the position that female teachers might be so threatened but that men really faced no comparable danger, Brad's hand shot up and he declared, "That's as discriminatory a statement as I've ever heard, either here or at Riverside." The room sat stunned, momentarily, at the accusation. Robin felt an odd impulse to rise, to protect Brad, to vindicate him, her heart convinced that he was simply expressing earnest protest, perhaps too harshly, too aggressively, but with no hostility. However, his outburst released tension in the lounge. Several male teachers applauded lightly, and even Ms. Verhoven's apparent sense of offense transformed into a simpering smile.

"Perhaps I overstated my point," she conceded. "Let me try again, without sounding too stereotypical. Teenage boys are often physically bigger and stronger than their women teachers. They are going through a time in their development when they are most likely to be antagonistic and least likely to want to control their urges. You can see where that might lead to problems with women teachers, especially younger teachers who have less experience in dealing with it.

"But with you"—she looked at McCauley—"there is less danger of a teenage girl being tempted to try to overpower you, or being *able* to."

"But ma'am," Brad replied. "You're not trying to tell the men in this room that the only way to overpower them is by *force*, are you?"

"I'm not sure what you're driving at."

"It's pretty basic, really. I think that you've turned this seminar into a—" he stopped. Robin felt embarrassed for him because he clearly realized he had become the focus of attention. "You have defined sexual harassment in a way that excludes the possibility that male teachers can be victimized by female students, when every man in here knows that's not true."

Robin heard a several grunts of approval. Unwittingly, Brad had become a mouthpiece for more widespread skepticism.

"Has this happened to you?" Ms. Verhoven asked with concern that Robin could tell was not genuine. She was manipulating Brad, reflecting his heat back to him.

"No," Brad started, and now the women were laughing. "But I always know it could."

"Why?"

"Because I'm a normal human male," Brad said, in mounting frustration.

"And the girls in the school? Do you find them attractive? Tempting?"

"Of course they are attractive."

"Tempting?"

"I'm not sure …"

"Have they ever harassed you in the ways we have talked about today? Have they offered you favors for giving them higher grades?"

"No, but can't you see that it *might* happen?"

"Yes, it might happen. But the truth is, we see a lot more pressure applied against women faculty from their male peers and male students than we see applied to males."

"Depending on your definition of pressure," Brad responded evenly, "I can accept that, but I think you're making a mistake when you say men aren't equally likely to be victimized."

Light gleamed from the smooth crown of Tolan Myers as he walked to the front of the lounge and stood next to Ms. Verhoven.

"I'm sorry to have to interrupt," he said. "But we all agreed to finish by 4:15. Maybe, Brad, you and Ms. Verhoven could continue your discussion some other time? You are both on campus at Riverside every day."

Ms. Verhoven was already packing her materials. She said to Brad, "Please call me. My office is in the Gearhart Building. Really, I'd love to talk about this further. And any one of you—my phone number and email address are in the handouts. Please call me with any feedback or questions."

Once she was gone, the lounge emptied. Myers stood in the same spot, waiting for Robin to leave so he could talk to Brad, but she felt responsible to defend him if needed, so she stayed next to him. Finally Myers sat down across from them.

"Everything you're saying is true, Brad, on an abstract level. But I have to warn you. The courts at this time are siding mostly with women, and with girls, in these kinds of cases. It may seem unfair, but that's the way things stand right now."

"I know," Brad said. "Believe me, I'm the last one you have to explain *that* to." Robin detected the resignation in his voice, which he tried to hide by adding, "I just enjoy a spirited debate, you know?"

Myers smiled. His eyes were large and brown, like a puppy dog's, yet in addition to his role as guidance director he was the chief disciplinarian of the school. Robin often marveled that he was able to rule with such an iron hand when his eyes were so soft.

"If anything does happen with the girls in your class," Myers said, "you let me know. We've handled a few cases in the past. So just let me know, and I'll take care of it."

When he walked out, Robin whispered—for there were still a few other teachers loitering in other parts of the lounge—"You can be sure he won't take care of it the way you want."

"What?"

"He said that if you take it to him, he would take care of it. Brad, that's exactly—let's go somewhere we don't have to whisper."

Their best choice was the parking lot, with most students gone and faculty leaving. Robin slid into her car seat and turned the ignition to roll back the sunroof window; she left the door open and let one foot rest outside on the pavement. Brad sat sideways on the wide black vinyl seat of his motorcycle, his boots resting on the chrome exhaust pipe.

"Remember when that boy ran into me a few weeks ago?"

"The one you keep calling the little cheater?"

"Yes. That wasn't my first brush with students cheating here. About seven or eight years ago I had a case of pure plagiarism, and I took it to Myers, because he had always said he would take care of those things when they came up. But he didn't. He let the kid off scot-free. He said I hadn't made it clear in my class guidelines what constituted plagiarism. The kid copied verbatim two whole paragraphs from *Sports Illustrated*, for God's sake! Now I take care of things myself. But that's not always enough. Once I lowered a girl's quarter grade from a B to a C when I caught her with a cheat sheet on a pop quiz. She appealed to the administration, and Myers changed it back to a B, and he never told me until the end of the year."

"How did he explain that one?"

"He said my penalty was too harsh. But it was written into the class rules from day one, and besides, who is he to overrule me in a situation like that? That's when I changed my whole style of teaching to discourage cheating. I haven't had any problems since then, but I don't trust Myers. There he is now." The tone of her voice did not waver. From behind her windshield and sunglasses she watched him skip down the steps and stroll across the grass toward the parking lot, his briefcase swinging at his side. Looking up, he saw her and Brad, and Robin thought she glimpsed a pause of surprise cloud his face.

Brad said, "I never told you yet why I was in LaGrange's office."

"I know. I was waiting."

"Most of the meeting was so they could tell me they were 'concerned' about how I dress."

"Oh, give me a break." Her left forefinger traced along the top of the steering wheel, and her gold bracelet sparkled.

"Really. They handed me a copy of the dress code and asked me to read it. I figured I was being too lax, letting somebody get away with something that violated the rules. So I read it slowly. It took five minutes.

Then Myers and LaGrange said they had noticed there were some days when I looked a little too laid back, even for a college grad student. Can you believe that? They clamped down on *me*!"

"Oh, Brad, don't let it worry you. We all go out of bounds on their standards now and then. I had a note in my box once that I was leaving campus too early, which probably meant I left one day at 3:59. They feel like they have to guard their reputation for excellence and professionalism."

"They said I shouldn't wear these boots."

"Surely you have something else."

"Sure I do."

"You can always quit the job," Robin said. Both their faces followed Myers's Volvo as it passed them on its way out of the parking lot.

"Not really. I do need the money. If I were twenty-five years old I could always ask my folks to help support me. But not at thirty-five. I've already waited too long to start my career, the way they look at it."

"Did they say anything else? Myers or LaGrange?"

"Funny you should ask. I was in there twenty minutes, and the first eighteen had to do with the dress code. Then finally, they asked me to raise a kid's grade. They sort of tacked it on at the end, as if it was of no consequence. Oh-yeah-by-the-way."

"What did you tell them?"

"I said I'd consider it. I'm supposed to come back tomorrow. But it wasn't even a borderline grade, Robin. The kid's been goofing off all year, and I've warned him. There's no way I'm going to change it."

"Who is it?"

"Tory Johnson."

"Oh," Robin nodded knowingly.

"Oh, *what*?"

"Nothing. There have been disputes about his grades before, I think. What did you give him?"

"I gave him a C."

"Oh. That will keep him off the honor roll."

"That's *his* problem. What bugs me most is that a couple of weeks ago they asked me to raise his grade on a quiz. It's like Myers and LaGrange are this kid's advocates, his lawyers. And I *hate* lawyers."

"Is something else wrong?" Robin ventured, emboldened by the shield of her sunglasses. "It seems to me like something else is on your mind. Did that seminar speaker get under your skin?"

"Not really."

She knew he was lying. To show support she flung out a compliment: "I could tell you were just sparring with her over the philosophy in back of it all."

He nodded deliberately, longer than needed, evidently weighing his next words with great caution.

"She doesn't know the first thing about real sexual harassment," he finally said firmly. "She's just a feminist warrior blowing new hot air into an issue that's already been so distorted that justice is next to impossible. I beg your pardon if I'm stepping on your toes. I'm for equal opportunities and rights, but it gets out of hand."

"Has it gotten out of hand for you?" She could hardly believe she was prying so flagrantly.

"No, that's not it," he said. "Like you said, I just get drawn into the battles of ideas."

He was gazing at the pavement, perhaps at her foot and ankle, which she flexed so the tendons stood out.

Once more, she knew that he was lying, hiding something, concealing something from his history, but weakening in his resolve to keep it from her.

Sooner or later she would know his secret.

18

ERIN DELANEY'S BARE feet padded along the plush carpet of the hallway, stopping only long enough for her to peek into Patti's former bedroom, now morphing into a den for her dad. On the floor sat two large cardboard boxes, their top flaps opened but their contents, a computer tower and monitor, not yet unpacked from their molded cushion of snug Styrofoam bars. Her father's actual desktop was likewise incomplete. It featured prominent wood-framed photos of Patti and Sarah but none of Erin, who knew that in the spring her senior portrait would join those of her sisters but nonetheless felt that her exclusion so far intimated her relative unworthiness. Her feet carried her on toward the kitchen and the sharp transition from the carpet to the cold linoleum floor.

On the refrigerator door was a message scratched in haste upon the note board Sarah had toted home with other mementos from her first year at college. Around the margin of the board, a rainbow of fruit—pears, plums, apples, bananas, grapes—streamed from a less realistically drawn wicker cornucopia in the upper right-hand corner. Her mom's message said:

> *E—*
> *Cold cuts and cheese in fridge.*

> *Sorry, no wheat bread!*
> *Have a good time with Matt tonight.*
> *—Love, Mom & Dad*

Erin groaned and muttered, "'Have a good time?' Jeez, mom, we're going to the *library*. You make everything sound like a date."

The refrigerator yielded up the promised sandwich meats but no cheese, so for dinner Erin simply rolled slices of turkey and ham into tubes shaped like cigarettes, which made her think of Mr. McCauley, whom she had seen talking to Mrs. Hillis in the school parking lot twice now, each time with a cigarette dangling from his mouth.

She did not know where Dad was.

Staring at Mom's message, she thought of Sarah, whose latest letter from college had sickened her with its sugary descriptions of her new boyfriend, who was coming home with her for Thanksgiving. His name was George ("gorgeous George"), he was a senior ("I never imagined falling for an older man"), and he was a painter ("an artist.") The boring truth was that George worked for a company that employed students to paint houses and apartments over summer vacations. That was how Sarah had met him ("One morning I opened my window and there he was on a ladder, wearing only shorts and shoes. I asked him if he did interiors too, and we sort of hit it off right then.")

For Christmas, Patti was also bringing home her boyfriend, Douglas. Everyone in the Delaney household, Erin included, expected that Patti would hear a marriage proposal during the holidays. Anything that kept the spotlight off her (and Matt) was okay with Erin. She dreaded the prospect of her proud sisters parading their successes under the same roof, underscoring Erin's own lack of commitment to a career or a boy.

At 5:30 sharp on the kitchen clock, Erin retreated to her room, plopped down on the bed, and nervously punched the seven digits of Nathan Dyer's dorm room phone number at Riverside University. He should be back from his 4:30 class, she thought—she hoped—unless he went straight to the cafeteria. With each unanswered ring her spirits sagged. Finally the voice of Nate's roommate asked her to please leave her name, the time, and the purpose for her call, and someone would get back to her. Erin stuttered that she would be in the Riverside library for a few hours that evening, and she hoped Nate would be able to come by and say hi to her. Then she hung up and fell back onto the bed, drained, alarmed at how hard her heart was beating.

Matt was unusually silent, even when Erin strained to pay him a compliment about how nice the van looked. It was fine with her if he didn't want to talk. She relaxed, lulled by the low rumble of the vehicle speeding along Highway 22 and the drowsing warmth of the heat blowing from the vents below the dashboard. When they passed the cemetery, though, Matt revived.

"Did I tell you what I'm doing for my art project?"

"No."

"A sculpture."

"Oh. A sculpture of what?"

"I'm not sure yet. But it's going to have something to do with money. How come you didn't take art? It's a fun class."

"I wanted a study hall."

Erin felt the pressure mounting again, the pressure of not having chosen a topic for Mr. McCauley's paper. The last time she had met with him, she agreed to try to squeeze her focus to something narrower than simply *trees*—he had rejected *clouds* and *whirlwinds* outright—and to come up with a historical angle. But she had done neither, which she confessed to Matt.

"I have a topic for you," he said, and waited until she asked what it was.

"The history of lotteries."

"Right."

"No, I'm serious. Or the history of any kind of gambling." His voice trailed off, and he slid back into the morose mood that had dominated their short drive. "Or blackmail," he said.

"You're not any help, you know," Erin said. "It's supposed to be a topic *I'm* interested in, not *you*. What's *blackmail* got to do with it?"

"Nothing," Matt answered evasively. "I was just daydreaming."

Erin ran the back of her fingernail along the spiral binding of her notebook, making it buzz. The van's humming wheels rose in pitch at the Junction Bridge, and Erin, gazing out her window at the half-bare trees on the bank, felt her heart caught up in the ecstatic swirl of the whirlwind. She wondered if whirlwinds were like meteors—if you watched long enough in one spot, were you virtually certain to see one? Or was her experience a special, once-in-a-lifetime gift from nature?

How much she missed Nathan! With him there was always a pleasant island of freedom in her life. Otherwise, each day was an ocean of pressure, expectation, obligation, too many things to do, too many people to please. Nathan never demanded anything. He didn't mind if she wanted to walk out of a movie after thirty boring minutes, or if she wanted to wear jeans and a T-shirt instead of a dress. He never compared her to Patti or Sarah, or to Jessica.

"We just need more space," he said when he broke up with her. "You need more space, more distance from me. And this is the best time, with me going to college. It will be the best for us, you'll see." And then—the words that Erin clung to like a lifeline—"And if later we find we can't live without each other, then we won't."

Since that day Erin had not seen him. Perhaps a few months of college life had changed him. What if he let his hair grow long? What if he started smoking, or got a tattoo? Worst of all, what if he had a new girlfriend?

"Can you believe that about Mora?" Matt asked suddenly.

"What about her?"

"Didn't you hear? She made honor roll."

"Who did *her* work?" Erin said, her bluntness surprising her. Mora Partridge had been her volleyball teammate the previous season—or part of the season, until her low grades earned her a swift removal from the team. That quarter she had received one D and the rest Fs. Mora loved volleyball but little else about school. When she had become ineligible, everyone expected her to transfer to a school in Bridgebury with lower academic standards. But her parents refused to grant her that wish, insisting that she stick it out and learn to study. No one believed she had made any progress, however. Mora was a likeable girl but a first-class ditz—if the school had a Hall of Shame, then Mora would be a unanimous selection for induction.

"I saw her in the hallway today," Matt remarked. "She acted like it was nothing."

"She's the stupidest person I know," Erin replied. "I remember once she got a zero on a twenty-question quiz that was all multiple choice. Cody said even if she guessed on all twenty, she should get five right. He figured the odds of her getting a zero were like one in fifty million, something like that. There's no way she's legit honor roll. I bet her tutors will take all the credit."

A dozen specialized libraries dotted Riverside University's far-flung campus, including a pharmacy library, an engineering library, a management library, an agricultural library, even a family science library. The largest collection was housed in the humanities library, and when Erin agreed to accompany Matt and placed her call to Nate, this was the library she had in mind, since it was the only one she had ever visited. However, following Matt and the jangling keys in his pocket down the stairs and out of the parking garage, she realized that Nathan would have no way of knowing which library she would be using. She could only hope he would assume the humanities library, the largest, the one used most by the public.

To Erin's sensitive spirit the cool dusk vibrated with a latent excitement, a humming expectancy hidden in every detail of campus life. The graceful rollerbladers with their neon-colored gear looked like masters of time and space, executing splendid pirouettes, gliding along the wide brick-paved walkways like carefree campus phantasms. On the cool grassy lawns in front of residence halls, their leaves freshly raked or blown away, girls gabbed and giggled while boys flung footballs and Frisbees to show off their athletic skills. The sidewalks bore masking-tape messages wishing happy birthdays and announcing club callouts and meetings. In one of the malls a speaker at a podium was exhorting a small audience to vote for a certain candidate in the student elections. Everywhere Erin looked, Riverside beckoned to her, promising rest from the wearying life that was trampling her in the town of Orange Stone and at Brookstone High School.

When the wide concrete steps and pillars of the library came into view, Matt threw Erin another unexpected disappointment by veering away toward the new undergraduate library that Erin had heard about but never seen.

"I thought we were going to the humanities library," she said, not hiding her disappointment. But Matt said, "This one is better. It's easier to do searches. They even let you print out lists."

The new facility was underground: All that showed above the surface was a one-story room that served as an entrance with a painted portrait of somebody named Lux, a pop machine, and twin spiral staircases descending to the library itself. Erin did a double take at the portrait—Lux looked so much like Grandpa Dee.

Passing through the metal anti-theft columns, Matt and Erin came to six rows of computers.

"Let me show you how these work," Matt said. He was a bit of a computer whiz, Erin knew from Jess, because one of his brothers had a programming degree from Riverside. He instructed Erin on how to select a search mode (TITLE, AUTHOR, SUBJECT) and choose a keyword. Erin tried *trees*, which brought forth a message that the library holdings included 1,936 titles that contained the word *trees*. Did she wish to see the complete list?

"Hit *Y* for yes or *N* for no," Matt said.

The *Y* option produced a screen full of titles and call numbers.

"Hit the right arrow for the next screen, and so on," Matt explained. "Control-*P* prints the whole list."

Matt moved away to work at another terminal; Erin continued to experiment. She tried a title search combining the keywords *trees* and *history*, but found no titles. This setback depressed her and set her eyes wandering through the library. Everyone looked so casual, so relaxed. Lots of students had kicked off their shoes to sit barefoot at the tables, and girls weren't caked with makeup or squirming to move in impossibly tight pants and shirts. There were lots of flannel shirts, which Erin liked, and long, loose swishing dresses. She wondered why she was suddenly so interested in college life, but she knew why—this was Nate's home now.

"I'm going to go get a pop," she whispered to Matt. "You want one?"

"You can't bring it in here."

"Oh. Well, I have to go to the restroom anyway. I'll be back in a minute. Watch my notebook and jacket, okay?"

She backtracked up the stairs, past Grandpa Dee's lookalike, and outside, where the first November stars were twinkling into view. Their sharp light mixed with the sounds of distant music to comfort Erin's thumping heart as she crossed a shadowed mall to the humanities library. How long should she wait for Nathan? Matt would come looking for her before too long; she should not have mentioned the humanities library earlier.

She found a table with an unobstructed view of the entrance. After a few minutes she took a book from a nearby cart in order to look like she belonged there. Unfortunately, the book was titled *Fresh Faces: A Reconsideration of Revolutionary War Heroes*, which immediately jerked her thoughts back to her struggles to please Mr. McCauley. If she did poorly in his class only, her overall grade point average still might stay high enough to satisfy her parents. But she didn't want to risk it. She had escaped with a B for the first quarter, but her work on her semester project was lagging far behind, and she could not forget McCauley's ominous words on the first day of class as he stared straight into her eyes: "Your future is in my hands."

Erin returned the history book to its cart, wedging it between two others and grimacing at the imagery of the tight squeeze. She found a copy of the Bridgebury *Courier* and began skimming through its less troublesome content. A front-page article by Pete Doty, the education reporter, compared the previous school year's test scores from the high schools within the newspaper's circulation area—no surprise, Brookstone stood head and shoulders above the other schools. There was a photograph of Mr. Patingale, the superintendent, his hair in disarray as always, with a quotation about how pleased he was that "the school's formula for success seems to have no shelf life." Whatever that means, Erin grumbled to herself. She didn't have a clue what a school superintendent did, anyway.

The time ticked to 7:30, 7:45, and 8:00. Nate must not have gotten my message, she thought, unwilling to entertain the possibility that he had chosen to ignore her. As for Matt, he was probably quite upset by her disappearance. She decided to wait till 8:10. When that deadline arrived she granted Nate another indefinite extension, then another. It was too far—and too chilly with no jacket—to walk to his dorm. At 8:30 she gave up.

Bernard Lux smiled from his brass frame as Erin took the first steps back down to the undergraduate library. She should go see Grandpa Dee again soon, she thought. Then a wonderful idea occurred to her, sudden and *serendipitous*—a vocab word she remembered—an idea that nearly drove away her dejection at not seeing Nate. Why not do a research report on the history of the care of elderly people? That surely fit Mr. McCauley's requirements. It was probably narrow enough for a topic, and Erin's interest was genuine and personal. Plus, it might give her an excuse for more visits to Grandpa Dee!

"Jeez, Erin! I've been looking all over for you!" Matt fumed. "Where were you?"

"I took a little walk. I'm sorry, I should have told you. I just wanted to take a walk."

"You shouldn't walk alone on campus. Don't you know how many rapes and assaults there are? Last year that girl disappeared and no one's heard from her since. She's probably dead."

She thought Matt's reaction was overblown, and said so.

"Just remember that this is a dangerous place for a girl all alone at night."

"Yes, Dad." Actually, his concern pleased her, even if his picture of the campus as a treacherous land of hidden dangers was difficult to swallow.

"Did you get any work done?" she asked.

Matt held up a stack of printouts with titles and authors crossed out and modified in his choppy handwriting.

"What?" Erin asked. "What's this?"

"It's my Works Cited list."

"What? You just make up sources? I can't believe you, Matt. You're sure to get caught."

"No way. McCauley doesn't have time to check everything. If it sounds real, he'll believe it. The hardest part is making up quotes. They have to sound professional. But Cody will help me."

"Jeez, Matt. You're putting more work into a fake paper than it would take to do it fair."

Matt flashed his wide smile.

"It's more fun to take the risk," he said. "I love to take the risk, to live on the edge. That's how I got to be such a good linebacker, Coach Batta says."

"This is not football, Matt. The penalties are a lot worse if you get caught. Jeez. Do you ever think about what you're doing?"

"I like to take chances, Erin. Life is no fun unless you take chances."

"Well, you're taking a big one."

"I won't get caught. You'll see. Are you going to do any work, or are you ready to go?"

She spent a few moments explaining her new idea for a project.

"Let me see if there are any books or periodicals about nursing homes," she said. "Then we can go."

"Okay."

While she worked at the keyboard, Matt said, "Guess who I saw while you were gone—Connor St. James."

"Really? I forgot he was going to Riverside. How's he doing?"

"Fine. When I told him why I was here, he told me about his paper for McCauley last year. He did it on windmills. He said he found one article in a magazine and invented everything else. He got an A."

"I'm impressed," she said sarcastically.

"He's in engineering, did you know that? You know what else he told me that I didn't know? Guess how Carolyn Whitlock won that balloon contest at school? She sneaked in a different kind of balloon, made of rubber that wouldn't leak as quickly. A guy in materials engineering here gave it to her."

"Now I'm *really* impressed. Does anybody do things by the rules anymore?"

"Aw, don't get all bent out of shape."

Her sophomore year, the school newspaper, *The Clause*, had planned to publish an exposé on student cheating, but when the administration got wind of it, Mr. LaGrange squelched the report despite cries of suppressed freedom of the press and censorship. That led to the rise of an underground paper printed off campus—*Independent Clause*—that students loved and the administration tolerated.

The printer next to Erin's terminal buzzed lightly, spitting out a list of the library's resources on care of the elderly. It was a short list, but that did not bother her because Grandpa Dee or other people at his retirement home would probably be more helpful than any published material, and Mr. McCauley had given his blessing to the use of personal sources.

"Okay, I'm done," she said. "Let's go."

Outside, he asked, "Are you hungry? We could split a Subway sub."

"That sounds good." Erin's stomach had not recovered from its skimpy dinner or the butterflies that had made their home there as she waited, wondering about Nathan.

While they ate, Erin noticed Matt's eyes staring out the window and across the street to ¿Que Pasa?, which was so crowded that clusters of young patrons were spilling outside, standing on the sidewalk or sitting on the curb, sharing bags of yellow popcorn and waving bottles of beer in the unconsciously relaxed fashion of college students.

"Have you ever been in there?" Erin asked.

"Yeah, lots of times." His voice was matter-of-fact. "I have a fake ID."

"Is anything about you legit?" Her tongue pulled a stray strand of lettuce back to her lips.

"Jess never gave me any trouble like you are," he replied.

Fruitlessly, she labored to think of a comeback involving Nate.

"Why don't you just go back to Jess, then?"

"You're prettier."

"Right."

"You are. You have that little crinkle over your lip—nothing Jess has can top that."

Erin had to smile. For all Matt's faults, he occasionally did or said something that overwhelmed her every objection.

"Nothing?"

"What are you getting at?"

"Nothing."

He looked across to ¿Que Pasa? "You want to go over there? I can get us in, I think."

"Why would I want to go there?"

"It's a wild place. There's all kinds of crazy characters from all over campus. In the summer it's nice to sit on the decks looking over the river. They're closed now, I bet."

"Do you want to go there?"

He shrugged. "Only if you do."

"I don't. Not really."

"So are you going to college, or what?"

"I don't have much choice," she said glumly.

Matt ignored her implied plea for sympathy and asked, "Where will you go?"

She blew a long sigh through her lips.

"I don't know. I mean, I'd like to stay here, but that would be too close to my parents. But if I go away, it will be to a college like Sarah or Patti went to, and that would put all kinds of pressure on me. It's like I can't win."

"I've heard people say you're going to be a doctor."

"That's what my mom and dad want."

Her personal pledge from earlier in the semester rose and taunted her—that promise to herself to start standing up for what *she* wanted. Except for rebuffing Matt that one time, she had not taken even a small step in that direction since writing about it in the journal entry for Mrs. Hillis way back in August. Her inaction exasperated her.

"I think I'm going to be able to get a football scholarship somewhere. It won't be as big a school as Riverside, but still D-1 maybe."

"What's D-1?"

"Division One. The bigger schools, that means."

"What if you get caught cheating and flunk out of high school?"

"Erin, you're so naive. Even if you get caught, you can work things out. Myers takes care of everybody."

"Like you said he took care of Steve?" Matt's face contorted and she stammered, "Oh, I'm so sorry. I know I shouldn't bring that up. Come on, let's go now."

The drive back to Orange Stone was quiet. Erin reflected on not seeing Nate and sank into a sulky, sleepy despondency. Then, at the first flicker of lights from the outskirts of the town, Matt said, "You really had me worried tonight when you didn't come back."

"I told you I was sorry."

"I know. I wasn't only *worried*. I was also a little *angry*."

"Why?"

"Because I didn't want to come to the library just to work on my paper. I also wanted to be with you."

Her mind still fixed on Nathan, she did not want to encourage him. "You mind if I ask you a question?"

"Sure," she said, trying to mask her apprehension.

"Will you go with me to the Homecoming Dance? I just assumed you would, but I haven't asked, officially."

She felt as lonely and out-of-place as she had felt in the humanities library, waiting for Nathan Dyer, who had never come.

"Okay, I'll go."

19

BACK AND FORTH Robin rocked on the front porch swing, half hypnotized by its regular creak, so predictable and comfortable. A few years ago, Lena Roost used to bring over her baby Philip to swing, the boy always turning his head to study the chain, trying to discover the source of the noise. Frequently the strain of the search put him to sleep, so frequently that when he was especially fussy, Lena came to the porch as a last resort.

Robin's eyes crossed the street to the Roosts' cleanly raked yard and freshly painted white picket fence: The scene could have come off a postcard, unreal, too colorful, too bright, too … pure. In one of the windows Robin could make out the form of Grandma Jane waving her cane, probably cheering for her team or expressing her amazement at some mispronounced word on a radio broadcast. What a wonderful bunch of characters, those Roosts. What a family.

Autumn always spread a cozy lethargy through Robin's spirit, and she luxuriated in its placid indolence today. When she came to the porch she had brought a gradebook stuffed with about a dozen papers, planning to mark them before she left to watch the football game and chaperone the Homecoming Dance, but after setting them on the wide porch rail, she neglected them. To even reach for them demanded too much effort. Later her eyes, returning from the Roosts, fell on the papers and filled her mind with diverse images of scholarship from Brad McCauley's apartment.

There were tall, leaning towers of books that an earthquake would topple. From each book, dozens of strips of paper protruded haphazardly, with varied lengths and widths and colors, marking important passages. She had opened one book to one such marker and found two paragraphs highlighted in yellow with a penciled annotation in the margin, undecipherable, written in Brad's private shorthand. Many of the authors were unfamiliar—names like Matthew Tindal, Thomas Woolston, and Samuel Clarke were thrown into stacks with heavyweights like Voltaire, Montesquieu, Descartes, Locke, Jefferson, Franklin, Madison, Hamilton, and Washington. A solitary volume of poetry by Alexander Pope occupied an evidently privileged position, segregated from the stacks; Pope was supposed to be one of those deists, too, she recalled.

Books, however, represented only a fraction of the material Brad had amassed in pursuit of his grand production. Just as important were literally hundreds of photocopied journal articles, all stapled together, all highlighted in neon green and pink and yellow (probably in accordance with some code), all annotated in pencil. Plus he had crammed dozens of spiral-ring notebooks full of ideas and rough versions of parts of the dissertation. Next to the computer lay an expensive-looking volume of the *Encyclopedia of Philosophy* and a facsimile of the U.S. Constitution, printed on yellowed parchment, with passages highlighted in pink. Finally, solid and square, the safe sat mute and mysterious under the end table. Giving in (sort of) to her relentless curiosity, Brad had admitted that he kept his rarest, most valuable documents there.

Using all those resources, he had both constructed a monolithic argument about the beliefs of America's forefathers and molded his own faith. But what a terrible faith, Robin thought, a hollow, comfortless faith with a God so far away that His ears never heard your prayers and so uninterested in His creation that He was sort of like a machine Himself. Everything we thought, said, and did was inevitable, normal, and good. There was no divine intervention possible—Jefferson had gone through his New Testament with a pair of scissors and snipped out every miracle story, Brad had told her, adding wistfully, "And you thought *I* was a revisionist!"

Robin let her eyes wander over to the Roost house again, up the walk to their front porch. She wondered what someone like Howard Roost would reply to Brad's heresy.

What different worlds they lived in, she and Brad! His revolved almost entirely around abstract ideas, hers around the concrete realities of day-to-day living such as a home, and property, and family, and job, and town. Breathing the air of his world had rejuvenated her, like pure oxygen, but she didn't dare breathe too deeply, or too long. He was out of touch with the important actualities that brought real meaning to life, or were supposed to. True, he was breathing *her* air by teaching at Brookstone, but it was foreign air to him, and he breathed it only out of financial necessity. *Necessity*—she chuckled at the double meaning.

I know all about what he *thinks*, she sighed. I wonder what he *feels*. Doesn't it sicken him that his world has no meaning? Is there anything he likes besides his intoxicating philosophy? Does he get angry at the government? Does he fall in love every spring with some attractive new co-ed?

She knew only half of him.

Ironically, that made him like her husband, who this week was on the East Coast.

By the time she arrived at the football field, the second half had already started. Brookstone led East Bridgebury 13-7. Robin ran into Lydia Knowles at the concession booth, and they stood behind one end zone and talked for the rest of the game, keeping their hands warm around cups of coffee and cocoa. Like Robin, Lydia was chaperoning the dance, so a long night loomed ahead.

In the fourth quarter, with the score tied, Matt Rademacher intercepted a pass and ran sixty yards down the sideline for a go-ahead touchdown. Lydia screamed wildly, her coffee spilling in all directions as she jumped up and down.

"He's one of my students," she said when the cheering died down. "I only have four on the team. They avoid art like they avoid my classes."

"I don't know Matt," Robin said. "But the girl he's taking to the dance, Erin Delaney, is one of my students. A really sensitive and gentle girl."

The night air growing cooler, their words trailed away in white wisps.

"Matt's sensitive, too. He's working on a wonderful sculpture for his semester project," Lydia said. "He calls it a memorial to Steve Gutierrez."

"That's so sad," Robin said. "Kids this age shouldn't have to face that kind of pain. When I was in high school nothing like that ever happened."

"Me neither."

An hour later the game was over (Brookstone winning 19-13), and the players, freshly showered and dressed, began arriving at the gymnasium, where their dates waited with cheers and congratulations. How spiffy all the boys looked in their tuxes or three-piece suits! And the girls, so fabulous in a dazzling array of colorful dresses!

On stage a band called "Bread and Jam" warmed up with slow, percussion-heavy melodies ("That's our speed," Lydia said to Robin) until the dance floor began to fill up, then it launched into more ambitious guitar-driven tunes beginning with the senior song "I'll Take My Chances," a folk-country tune that Robin was getting to like. Around a hundred couples were attending; however, only half the basketball floor had been covered in canvas in preparation for the dance, meaning that not everyone could dance at once.

At the opposite end of the gym from the band, half a dozen tables were linked end to end, decorated with school-colored paper and laden with punch, dessert trays, paper plates, napkins, and plastic ware. Lydia and Robin took turns nibbling at cookies and ladling punch into clear plastic cups. Each crystal bowl had a ring of ice, formed by a gelatin or cake mold, that swirled and bobbed as they stirred the contents.

Other chaperones were less inclined to service. Coach Tom Batta was talking football with a circle of mostly boys. Not having bothered to change clothes, he stood out in his cap and nylon letter B jacket. Leona Tice, a music teacher, had separated herself as far from the band as possible. Tolan Myers's bald head was changing colors with the lights from the stage as he made small talk with Damon Browne, the wood shop teacher who had come to evaluate his handiwork, the stage, which featured several giant wooden slices of bread slathered with painted jam.

After half an hour of informal punch duty, Robin excused herself to use the ladies room. Instead of coming directly back, she went up the steps to the balcony to watch the dance from the shadows. The sight of so many young, happy couples, their hearts alive with the excitement of the moment and the promise of the future, suffocated her with profound sadness.

She and Zeb had once been so close.

Rosie Osborn and Laurie Fritz were wearing reverse costumes according to a study hall pact they had made in a fit of teenage hilarity. Rosie's taffeta dress was teal-colored with a wide swath of white looping from her bulging, pregnant stomach over one shoulder and matching white shoes and white bow accenting her short-cut black hair; Laurie's dress was white and the swath, bow and shoes were teal. Molly Traxton had spent who knows how much money on a perm at an upper-echelon salon in Indianapolis, with stunning results. Her hair actually glittered, and she was spending more time thanking people for compliments than she was dancing with her date, Bob St. George, who had not seen Molly until he picked her up an hour earlier and still seemed dazed at her beauty. Jarrett Batta, the coach's son, and his date Lauren Lancaster had come dressed in turn-of-the-century style. Lauren wore a wide yellow dress puffed outward by miles of slip-sheer fabric; the highlight of Jarrett's outfit was a gold pocket watch he loved to click open and shut. Every ten minutes or so, Lauren asked for the time, to give him a chance to show off the timepiece.

Sheena Straley had bought (the rumor) or borrowed (the truth) a striking black dress with white point-down triangles; it had wide shoulders and grew tighter toward her hips and legs, endowing her with the shape also of an inverted triangle. She danced closely with her date, Jimmie Heaton, resting her head on his shoulder and whispering comments that kept him nodding and smiling. One of the best dancers among the students was tiny Kelly Bennett, a sophomore gymnastics and volleyball star. She was matched with another athlete, Steve Stark, and it was evident that they had taken lessons together. Steve wore a black and red tuxedo with a cream-colored flower pinned to his lapel, and his quick-moving shoes, reflecting the shifting lights, truly seemed to give off sparks. Kelly's silk dress, red with a white floral pattern, hung loosely on her supple body as she whirled, twisted, leapt, and swung with Steve.

Without question, the event's least ostentatious apparel hung from the slender shoulders of Erin Delaney, but this did not surprise Robin. Erin wore a brownish, modestly cut, overly baggy dress with flat white shoes—an outfit whose plainness belied the fact that it was certainly the most comfortable clothing on the floor. Erin seemed only half-interested in dancing with Matt, possibly because neither of them was an accomplished dancer and Matt kept being interrupted by pats on the back or handshakes for his earlier football heroics.

Robin shrank further into the shadows as she watched. Next to the refreshment tables the photographer, an overweight man with a face scrubbed to shiny cleanness, had set up his booth and was taking his first customers. When Mary Ann Cadwallader kissed J. J. Weaver as the flashbulb exploded, Robin could not help feeling a twinge of loss. Twenty-six years ago she and Zeb had posed for a photo at a college dance, and his fingers around her waist tickled her in perfect timing with the camera's click. That was still their favorite picture from their days of romance.

Back then he was impossible to evade—how different from now! He would toss messages tied to stones through her open dorm window, or, if the window was closed, hurl his keys noisily against the glass to wake her or attract her attention. Every day she could count on some communication in her mailbox. A chocolate kiss with a note, a card, a fresh-plucked flower, even a poem. How many times had one of them fallen asleep when they talked too late on the phone at night? And now he wouldn't call but once every few days, and then to talk for only five minutes.

The magic in their early relationship had long ago drained away, but sadly so had the something-comfortable-and-stable that had replaced it for the first twenty years of their marriage. Once the children left, Robin had noticed the change. Now she asked herself for the first time whether it might not have been true years before then.

Soon she heard voices close by, on the balcony level. Even though the roar and echo of the band made it impossible for her to distinguish what the voices were saying, in the short intervals between crashing cymbals and singing screams Robin could tell they were arguing. One voice did most of the talking, and after a while she identified it as belonging to Tolan Myers. She hoped to hear more when the song ended, but by the time the last note quavered and died, the voices were also gone.

Soon she heard footsteps, and a different voice said, "Oh, Mrs. Hillis. It's you. You scared me."

"What are you doing up here, Erin?"

"I thought I saw Matt come up here, and I was following him. But I can't find him. Did you see him?"

"No."

"Is Mr. McCauley up here too?"

"Mr. McCauley?" she asked through a ripple of adrenaline.

"Yes. He was looking for you."

"No. I'm the only one up here." She was about to add, "You should go back down," but why? Erin didn't need a mother.

"Why are *you* up here?" Erin asked.

"I got tired of being down there."

"Yeah, I get tired of being around people sometimes, too."

"That's okay. Not everybody is a people person. Are you having a good time?"

"I guess so."

Robin smiled and said, "That's not very convincing."

"Well, I didn't really want to come."

"Why not?"

"I don't know." Her voice spread out into a whine. "I just felt pressured to come."

"Oh."

"I mean, when somebody asks you to a dance, you can't say no. Know what I mean?"

"I think I know."

"Matt didn't really pressure me. But I knew if I didn't go with him, then my parents would be mad, too."

"Why would *they* be mad?"

"I don't know. They expect me to be just like my sisters."

"Oh. Sarah and Patti. They *were* a pretty impressive pair. You should be—" she clipped off the word *proud* just in time, and held her tongue until something else came to mind. "How do you feel about having to follow in their footsteps?"

"It's impossible. I'm not as smart as either one of them. I'm not as athletic, either. You probably heard I quit volleyball, right?"

"Yes, I knew that."

"It was too much pressure, too. I'm just not as good a player as Sarah and Patti were. I'm not as ambitious as they are, and not as pretty as they are."

"Oh, Erin, that's just not true! You're as beautiful as any girl down on that floor! You just don't show it off the way they do. And that's all right. But there is one thing you could do that would always make you even prettier."

"What?"

"Smile more."

"There's nothing to smile about."

"I know how that feels, Erin. Sometimes life makes me want to quit smiling"— she felt smothered by her colossal hypocrisy—"but you can't let circumstances control your happiness."

"I know," Erin answered, and the last word drew out into a sob. Her arms reached for Robin, whose mother's soul melted with pity. She threw her arms around Erin's shoulders and said, "Oh, Erin. What can I do? Tell me whatever's bothering you." Erin's body shook with spasms and sniffles, and her arms, clenched about Robin's neck, would not let go.

"Everybody's happy except me," she sniveled, relaxing her tight hold.

"Why aren't you happy?"

"Because nobody will let me be myself! Everybody expects me to be like my sisters, or like Jessica."

"Jessica? Southard?"

Erin nodded, and her thick, smooth hair slid over Robin's hands. With a smile and a twenty-dollar perm, Erin would be a shoo-in for Homecoming Queen—if she wanted.

"Oh." Robin put two and two together using the sage and subtle formula learned from years of mothering, teaching, and listening. "Matt expects you to be like Jess?"

Erin sobbed and nodded.

"So that's why you feel pressured?"

"If he liked Jess so much, why doesn't he just go back to her? She'd do whatever he asks ..."

"Oh, Erin. What kind of pressure is he putting on you?"

"He wants me to ... you know ..."

"Oh. Say no more." Two thoughts clamored in Robin's head—that Jess probably had not gone as far with Matt as Erin believed, and that Erin should be encouraged to resist Matt. But in the wake of those thoughts came a third.

"What do *you* want to do?" she asked.

"I don't know. I mean, I do know what I *want* to do, but I don't know what I'm *going* to do. It seems like I never do what I want to do."

What a perfect teenage translation of the seventh chapter of Romans, Robin thought. And how ironic that *this* thought brought a wave of happiness—deeper and more serene than the surprised excitement that had tingled her on hearing that Brad had asked after her.

"I know, I know."

"I mean, I don't want to sleep with him, because I think it's wrong. Don't you?" Before Robin could answer, though, Erin plunged onward: "But when I'm all alone and think about it, I can't think of any *reason* not to, except that I just don't want to."

"Have you talked to your mom?"

"No. I hardly ever see her, and even if I did I know what she would say—the same thing she told Patti and Sarah—'If you're going to play around, just make sure you're protected.'"

"What about your dad?"

"I hardly ever see him, either."

"So you don't see them or talk to them very much?"

"No," Erin mumbled. "I'm used to it, I guess."

"Does it make you mad, or sad?"

"I don't know. They were there for Patti and Sarah a lot more than me. But I'm the one who needs them most. I'm the one who doesn't know what to do with my life."

"Are you—do you want to go to college?"

"Not really. At least, not where Mom and Dad want. Riverside would be fine for me."

"Not for them?"

"I doubt it. It would be such a come-down after Patti and Sarah."

"Have you ever told them what you just told me, about Riverside?"

"No, I hardly ever see them." Her voice rose in the adolescent frustration of having to repeat something to an uncomprehending adult. "But my grades aren't going to be good enough to go anyplace special."

"Oh. Are you having trouble in some classes? You're doing fine in English."

"My big problem is history. We have a major project for the end of the semester, and I'm already so far behind ..."

"Is Brad your teacher? Mr. McCauley?"

"Yes."

"What about your other classes? How are you doing in them?"

"In math I'm getting a B right now. In French probably an A. In chemistry I don't know, an A or a B."

"That sounds pretty good to me."

"But Mrs. Hillis, you don't understand. In my family, if I get anything less than an A, I'm a black sheep. I'm letting everyone down."

"Oh, Erin. It's not that difficult. You're a smart girl. You're a Delaney. You're a hard worker. You'll do just fine. If I can do anything to help, I want you to feel free to ask me, okay?"

"Okay. Thanks, Mrs. Hillis."

Her advice hung incomplete, though, until she added, "Whatever happens, don't cheat. There's too much of that going on around here."

"Yeah."

Erin's resigned tone betrayed that Robin's comment had struck a raw nerve, so she pressed deeper: "Yeah? You haven't been—"

"No, no, I would never do that. But ..."

"But?"

Erin sniffled, looked toward the gym floor, cleared her throat, and said, "I hear things all the time."

"Oh, yes, so do I."

She waited for more, wanted more—but no, Erin was finished.

"Do you want to go find Matt now?"

"Yeah. He's probably wondering what happened to me, again. Are you coming down?"

"Not yet."

Erin walked to the stairs, and Robin emerged from the shadows. She ran her white fingers along the railing and looked down at the thinning dance floor then up at the gymnasium clock, its north-and-south hands reading 12:30 in the morning. About twenty students waited in line for photographs, and a like number congregated around the drink-and-dessert tables, where Tyler Batta was conducting "interviews" with his phone recorder and Lydia Knowles had stopped spooning up pink punch while Tolan Myers emptied a two-liter plastic bottle of Sprite into the bowl. Steve Stark and Kelly Bennett had separated and were teaching special dance moves to new temporary partners.

Finally Robin spotted Brad and realized at once that he had been watching her for some time. When their eyes met he waved and made a gesture to say, "Stay there; I'll find my way up."

She debated whether to retreat into the shadows again or remain visible against the rail. Erin had mentioned Brad's looking for her so matter-of-factly! Was their friendship really so obvious? Did he miss her?

"Hi, stranger," she greeted him when he joined her. "You sure vanished this week."

"Yeah, sorry. I've had conferences at Riverside every day with students, plus two meetings with my advisory committee. They all come in bunches. And I found out about another hoop I have to jump through in March before I ever do my dissertation defense."

"What do you mean?"

"It's nothing major, just more busywork and a preliminary interview. But I thought I would be able to skip the step altogether."

After a short pause, she said, "You know, I think you and I are becoming an item."

Then he said the last thing she expected: "How does that make you feel?"

"Oh, students are always getting the wrong ideas about their teachers."

He laughed in that bellowing manner she admired.

"That's not what I asked."

Robin sat down and crossed her legs, smoothing her dress over the top of her thigh. She didn't dare give him an honest reply—that she felt renewed and flattered not only by his attention but also by the students' recognition. Carefully, so as not to seem too blatant, she folded her hands in her lap so that her wedding ring was covered, but her conscience screamed in protest. She scrambled to justify herself. The Homecoming atmosphere was heavy with desire and fantasy and spontaneity and frivolity, she reasoned. Why couldn't she take part?

"Do you really want to talk about how I *feel?*" she asked, testing him. "Why should I dump all my burdens on you?"

"Okay. What should we talk about, then?"

"How about your clothes? Didn't anyone tell you this was a formal affair?" Why did she care what he was wearing? She felt a pang of guilt for running from herself and from Brad's first convicting question.

"I was a little worried when I ran into Myers down there. But he didn't say much. After all, I'm just a visitor, not a chaperone. I thought you liked my jeans-and-boots ensemble."

"You can't help it, I know. When they called you on the carpet over your clothes, did you explain to them how little money they pay you? It would have been the perfect chance to ask for a raise."

"I could never do that. They might fire me, then I'd be in worse shape than before."

He sat down on the other side of the aisle.

"Well?" she asked.

"Well, what?"

"I'm still waiting for you to tell me about your latest meeting with Myers and LaGrange. There were some rumors in the teachers' lounge about your … courage. People were surprised."

"News travels fast, I guess."

"Well?"

"Well, I requested a meeting as soon as I heard that Tory Johnson had been restored to the honor roll."

"Restored?"

"That's right. I gave him a C for the first quarter, and I understood that nobody with a grade below B could make the honor roll. When the list was first posted, he was not on it. Now he is."

"What happened?"

"Myers and LaGrange said they had reviewed Tory's work and scores in my gradebook and thought he should get the benefit of the doubt. I always wondered why they made you turn in your gradebooks every quarter."

"So they changed his grade?"

Brad nodded.

"When I objected, they told me it was their prerogative to intervene and overrule me. I said okay, but at least they should have contacted me first."

"What did they say to that?"

"They said they *had* contacted me. Which was true, I suppose. This has been going on for weeks."

"But they never told you they were changing his grade?"

"No! They said they hadn't gotten around to it yet."

"That's terrible!"

"It's out of my hands," Brad said. "I gave the kid the grade he deserved, the grade he earned. Myers tried to explain this grading method he had applied. He called it *borrowing*. Have you ever heard of it?"

"No."

"Essentially he said he was applying some of the points the kid will earn next quarter to this quarter's grade. So he gives Tory a higher grade now, but he'll have to earn the points back next quarter. He basically starts off with negative points the next quarter."

"Seriously?"

Brad warmed to his protest.

"I've never heard of anything so outlandish!" he went on. "It sounds like the way the government shifts debts to the next fiscal year to make the current deficit look smaller. I wonder: Does the kid have to pay interest on the borrowed credit? And who gets the interest?"

He shot her a mischievous stare.

Robin asked, "What happens if he doesn't earn it back in the second quarter?"

"If he's like the government, he just gets to keep borrowing from the future."

"Yep, I suppose that's what's next."

"Myers said it was simple math. What a joke! Anyway, I'm trying not to worry about it. I've got more important worries."

Robin called his bluff: "I can tell you *are* worrying about it."

"It shows that clearly, huh? Let me ask you something. Do you grade on a curve or by percentage?"

"Oh, it varies. Both at times."

"I grade by strict percentages. *Simple math*, Myers would say."

"That doesn't surprise me. You are so structured."

"Tory's percentage was 76.3 percent. That's about as solid a C as you can get. But once this mess started, I also figured his grade on a curve, just to make sure I was being fair. He actually would have gotten a C-*minus* with a curve. That was one of his complaints, I think, when he went to Myers. He said I should have used a curve. But my method worked out better for him!"

They sat in silence. Then Brad coughed, leaned toward her, and murmured, "They raised it to an A."

"An A? Are you kidding me?"

"I just figured it out. The first time I talked to Myers, he mentioned that Tory was getting a B in calculus. I didn't think anything more until this morning. The new honor roll lists him under five As and one B. Well, the B wasn't mine—it was his calculus class. My grade turned into an A!"

"Oh, that's ridiculous! I could accept them raising it to a B. They could justify it, even though I would disagree. They could claim you are not an experienced teacher, or something like that."

"But I *am* experienced. Why would they have hired me back this year if they weren't happy with my work?"

"They are, they are," Robin said soothingly, reaching across and patting his arm. "I just meant that they could find some defensible reason to raise a kid's grade *one* letter. But not *two*. That just shows they want to control the whole process. Which they are."

"*But why would they do it?*" He stood up, agitated. "What's to be gained? I feel like I'm missing something big here. Am I?"

"Oh, I don't know. It's mostly politics, and money. They probably want to keep Tory happy because his parents have been so supportive over the years."

"Do you think I should do anything else?"

"You've objected. I don't think there's much else you can do, unless you have other teachers on your side. Right now I guess you have only one."

She looked at him until he looked back, and then she smiled.

His eyes returned to the dance floor.

"Are you a dancer, Robin?"

"Oh, not that kind of a dancer."

Steve and Kelly were performing alone now, encircled by admirers.

"You know, I don't regret being in the field of education and scholarship," Brad said. His eyes were on the dancers but his attention seemed farther away, fixed on some rueful memory. "But I do regret that the pay is so lousy. I've been living on a shoestring for five years now. And it bothers me that it might not change much the rest of my life."

"If you're going to teach, it has to be a labor of love. I got married early, so I never had a financial burden because of low pay. But even if I had, I would have taught, because for me it's a calling. I like knowing that I'm making a difference in lives."

"You do make a difference in lives," Brad said. "I speak from first-hand experience. And I don't mean the dissertation only."

"That's a nice thing to say." How careful, how gentle he was trying to be! Just like one of those mortally nervous boys awash in their false bravado on the gym floor. And yet—cutting across her charitable appraisal of Brad came another shot of shame for her deliberate phrasing: *I got married,* she had said, instead of *Zeb and I got married.*

Earlier that evening she had listened to the Bruce Springsteen songs Brad had let her borrow, songs with titles like "Thunder Road" and "Born to Run." His music reminded her of the stuff her students brought her—emotionally explosive but spiritually barren noise from the world of adolescence, mostly bereft of any sensible message. Through its soaring exhilaration and profound sorrow, contemporary pop music was mostly banal—no different from the music her own generation of teenagers had loved but which she now conceded was equally pointless. Brad's songs were juvenile, although many of the lyrics were decent as poetry. What a depressing atmosphere the music created! What a sad life it portrayed! Everything was dark and depressed and not even love could rise above it except in a false, existential way for illusory, ephemeral moments. The lovers in the songs were forever chasing an elusive joy they seemed to know was destined to remain just beyond their reach—like the boy pursuing the girl on the Grecian urn in Keats's famous ode that she taught. Was that how Brad felt about his life?

Perhaps he was just jittery in his own manner, like many of the dancing boys below. She began to pity him, but her conscience kept her from asking how else she was making a difference. Hopefully, he would volunteer the answer.

At last she said, "It works both ways."

He stretched and groaned.

"Are you in pain?" she asked. Her hands came unclasped and she leaned toward him.

"It's my neck. I twisted it in my sleep."

"I guess you can't afford to go see a chiropractor."

"Not even a regular doctor."

"A chiropractor could help you more. It might not even cost much. Are you on insurance at Riverside?"

"Yeah, but I doubt if it covers something like that."

"Quit talking about it like it's voodoo. You just don't understand it. You're terrible about that—judging things you don't understand. Why don't you at least give it a try?"

"I might if I thought I could pay for it."

"Brad, if it comes down to that, *I'll* pay for it." He laughed again, and Robin wished she had never made the offer. Not that she wouldn't help pay a friend's bill, but what did it mean that she so brazenly said so?

Brad said, "It's not just my neck. My whole body is … running down. I keep noticing new problems."

"Tell me about it when you're my age!"

"I'll be dead by then, at this rate."

"Oh, and you'll die penniless and be buried in a pauper's grave."

"No, because you'll pay for my funeral, right?"

"Does anyone other than me ever complain about you being cheap?"

"I'm not cheap!" he insisted vehemently. Then, in a calmer voice, he explained, "I just have … obligations you don't know about. I'm trying to make ends meet until I can get out of school and land a real job."

"What don't I know about?"

"Maybe someday I'll tell you, if you're nice."

"Nice, *schmice*. Face it, dear, you're cheap." *Dear?* Where had that come from?

"Does that bother you?"

"Well, since you asked, it does bother me some."

"Why? You know I can't help it."

"There we go again—claiming you have no choice."

"I *can't* help it! What am I supposed to do?"

"Anything to show me you aren't cheap." A bewitching sense of intrigue was stirring her, challenging her. Aroused, empowered, and startled by her forwardness, she said, "Next time I come over, instead of generic cola in cans, get a bottle of Chardonnay and wine glasses."

"Are you serious?"

"Think of it as a challenge. Prove you aren't cheap." Thinking of the hormonal Springsteen lyrics, she smiled. "Prove your manhood."

"It might be easier under a different roof."

"Ohhhh." Her voice rose in understanding. "I see. *Touché*."

For the first time, they had climbed over the cold, imposing walls of his dissertation, philosophy, and their day-to-day work. And despite the intrusions of her conscience during the evening, intrusions that grew progressively more annoying and aggravating, intrusions that she now regarded as interference that she was right to ignore—despite all of those intrusions, her heart throbbed with delight at one undeniable truth.

For the first time, she and Brad were sharing their feelings.

20

McCAULEY SLAMMED DOWN the telephone receiver and whispered a one-syllable curse that felt so good that he whispered it again and again and finally yanked the phone cord from its socket.

"Call me now, you S.O.B!" he shouted. Raising the phone to throw it against the wall, however, his eye fell on the hole next to the door, so he relented. His violence had already caused enough damage to the apartment, damage that eventually he would have to pay for. One thing he definitely did *not* need was another expense.

Muttering a series of colorful new epithets against Gregory Travis, he pulled out his safe and loosened the lanyard around its handle. In his agitation, it took him three tries to twirl the combination accurately and jerk open the heavy door, his hand going in empty and coming out with two manila envelopes.

Turning the first one upside down, shaking its contents onto the carpet, he skimmed the fateful letter from Travis, a chain-smoking, weak-hearted retired professor, one of three members of the Ph.D. committee that officially had guided and advised him during the three-plus years of his project. Travis was threatening to turn those years of scholarly sweat into a wasteland and pinch the hopeful flame of McCauley's ambition—and the old prof had the power and means to do so. For the past year he had been blackmailing McCauley to the tune of $200 a month, a sum that bought his promise to withhold proof that McCauley's brilliant thesis was in fact a masterpiece of pilfered thought and expression. Now he was doubling the stakes, demanding $400 a month, claiming the hike was justified because he had impending medical bills. Where was McCauley supposed to find that kind of money? His rent and utilities alone came to about $400 a month. How was he supposed to pay for the equivalent of a second apartment?

"That's your problem," Travis had said. "You got yourself into this mess. I'm willing to let you take credit for your dissertation, but I know the truth, and this truth isn't free."

McCauley had never claimed innocence when Travis first confronted him. At first he feared that he might be kicked out of the graduate program, or at least have to scrap his thesis and start from scratch. Travis himself had suggested the alternative: McCauley could call the work his own and realize the benefits that would flow from it—job, prestige, even royalties—but he would continue to pay Travis for his silence about what the prof referred to as an "ethical lapse."

"It's a great thesis," Travis said whenever McCauley voiced second thoughts about their agreement. "It's worthy of the attention of the community of scholars. Your reputation will skyrocket when it's published." Perhaps he knew how soothingly those promising words massaged McCauley's brittle ego. "It's a phenomenal thesis. It's an idea whose time has come."

There was only problem: The idea wasn't McCauley's. Not exactly, anyway. Not purely. By some minuscule quirk of fate, Travis had known about James West, an obscure Southern historian who had written before the Civil War about the Founding Fathers' religious heresies. Eight months into his Ph.D. work, during a summer vacation, McCauley had stumbled into a dim, dusty closet of an antique book shop in Kentucky and found West's self-published monograph, *Faith of the Founders*. Between its crumbling covers slumbered the same ideas McCauley had begun to shape and sharpen for his dissertation, and his heart plummeted when he realized that his concepts were as yellowed as the pages of West's book. How unfair that after thousands of hours of trailblazing he should discover that he was no pioneer!

Who was James West? In vain McCauley searched every catalog and index he could find. Whoever West was, his splash in the puddle of historical research was inconsequential. There were simply no references since 1930 to any work West had ever published. As far as history scholars were concerned, West was a nonentity.

Armed with that conviction, McCauley made a conscious decision to appropriate West's work. There was really no other way for him to proceed unless he wanted to shift his focus from primary to secondary sources, from the Founders to West himself, which would have been academic folly. Every step McCauley had taken in his preliminary work he now saw that West had taken before. Even McCauley's principal metaphor of clockwork was not original: The same analogy was woven into the warp and woof of West's treatment. West dealt with the same historical figures and proposed the same theory for their public silence regarding their deism. Each page of West's book turned McCauley more despondent. It was as though someone had taken his completed dissertation and sent it through a time machine to 1840, where West used it as a basis for his book. But West's bones were decaying in some Georgia cemetery, and if he had any descendants, they hadn't followed in his footsteps. His voice had evidently been solitary in his day; unheeded, it had quit echoing a century ago.

Nobody knew West.

Nobody would know West's voice in McCauley's work today.

Or so McCauley had concluded—in a severe if not fatal miscalculation, it turned out, for Gregory Travis knew of West, even if he might be the only other living historian in the United States who knew of West.

"Nobody knows but us," Travis said when he and McCauley first discussed the obvious plagiarism. He laid out his plan for McCauley's "salvation" and asked his student to think it over. Two days later in the mail, McCauley received the most damning piece of evidence that Travis might use against him—a photocopied chapter from the 150-year-old book, with portions highlighted in yellow that McCauley had lifted and used in drafts of the early chapters of his thesis.

As far as McCauley could determine, the other two professors on his committee never suspected their star student's malfeasance. Only Travis knew. He was an extortionist, but at least he was an honest extortionist. So far he had not broken his promise to keep his discovery between the two of them.

"Four hundred dollars," McCauley mumbled. "Am I supposed to rob a bank?"

He leafed through the other papers on the carpet. One page had a handwritten record of his payments to Travis, who insisted on cash, "to protect myself," he said. If Travis ever talked, there wouldn't be any paper trail convicting him of blackmail. But McCauley expected Travis to keep quiet. Once he died, which couldn't be far off, nobody would ever be able to link McCauley to James West again. In the sky of McCauley's sunny future, Travis was just an unwelcome storm cloud that would blow over. Adding up the numbers, McCauley sighed. Already he had shelled out $2,800 to Travis—more than a semester's graduate tuition, more than a semester's pay as a Riverside teaching assistant.

He glanced at the second envelope. At least the court order was set in stone, he thought. They can't double my payment like Travis can. His thick hand swept the first papers to one side and emptied the other envelope, labeled CHILDRESS SETTLEMENT. Onto the floor tumbled a thick legal document, tri-folded and wrapped in gold rubber bands, plus a newspaper clipping with a photograph of a girl.

"Mary Ann Childress," McCauley sighed. "Where are you now?" It was a rhetorical question, for McCauley knew she was in Baton Rouge, Louisiana. At least, that was the address of the post office box where he mailed her a $250 check each month. In five years that obligation would be paid in full. Most students pile up loan debts in college, McCauley thought. For me it's payments for legal settlements and secret blackmail.

The Childress affair—he thought of it in the terse, distant language of his profession—had shattered his life. Falsely accused, abandoned by his peers, and rejected by his family, he had been denied justice. In the ten years since, he sometimes thought he had compromised too readily to avoid a trial. He should have fought the girl's lies. With the benefit of hindsight, he saw that his case had been much stronger, or the accusations against him much weaker, than he ever comprehended.

He had been young, frightened, dazzled and dazed by the fast-tongued lawyers. At the time, he had gladly embraced the out-of-court settlement in which he agreed to pay his accuser $45,000 over fifteen years. In retrospect, compared to the current private furor over his dissertation, the "Childress settlement" seemed trivial.

He put everything back in the safe.

To mull over his various dilemmas, he stepped into the shower. If his professional and financial worries weren't enough, now he felt a sore spot forming in the back of his throat. Hot water caressed his back and shoulders as he imagined what his life would be like had the irresistible pendulum of the Universal Clock swung him into a medical career. His name was perfect for a doctor as well as a scholar. Whenever he got sick, his thoughts took flight and landed him in medical school, where his dissertation might cover the common cold.

He had become an expert on colds, which were becoming more frequent with age. The first lump in his throat signaled infection, and he knew precisely what stages to expect. First, a day or two when his throat swelled with soreness that made swallowing hurt. Next, a deceptive cessation while the invading germs relocated to his sinuses to plague him with the misery of congestion. Third—and worst—the descent of the infection to his lungs, heavily, generating gobs of green and yellow mucous that he spat out, imparting to his breath the disagreeable flavor of pus. Sometimes his hacking cough became so severe that he felt his sternum would rip in two. Cough drops and nasal spray became dear companions, but they too seemed part of the inescapable cycle, offering psychological but no physical relief. Once he had heeded a friend's advice to fill his system with water—"Drink till you pee like a racehorse" were the exact words—to shorten any illness. That seemed to work. He whipped the cold in two days flat. But on the next invasion of microbes, that soak-'em strategy had no effect at all.

He reached around the mildewed shower curtain and flipped the PLAY button on the cassette player next to the sink. It hissed impotently. Robin Hillis still had his Springsteen mix, he remembered.

Perhaps that was a legitimate pretense for calling her. Since the delightful night of the Homecoming Dance, more Riverside business had kept him from seeing her at Brookstone. He wondered whether she noticed, as he did, that their tentative relationship had turned a corner that night. They had talked together in the balcony long after the janitor, Bragley, had turned out the lights. Alone in the dark, unable to see her face, he had imagined her in the various poses and outfits he had come to know from working with her and watching her for ten weeks.

Dear, she had called him. *Dear*. That word nearly blotted Gregory Travis and Mary Ann Childress from his mind.

He and Robin had covered acres of their personal lives in those wonderful shadowed hours. But even in that promising intimacy he had not confessed the true content of his "dress code" meeting with Myers and LaGrange, even when Robin unwittingly offered him a perfect opportunity by joshing him about his clothing. Something kept him from telling her, and now he was thankful, because her knowing would have shut a window of financial opportunity that now seemed precious.

Myers had frankly declared that if McCauley "played ball" with them on Tory Johnson's grade, he could expect to be rewarded. Moreover, Myers had hinted that he would be rewarded to the degree that his students were rewarded. *Students*, plural.

McCauley hadn't agreed to their offer on the spot, but they meant business. Suppose he did accept their proposal. He might be able to wring $200 a month out of it, enough to offset Travis's higher bills. Or suppose he threatened to blow the whistle on the whole affair. Maybe he could extort a lump sum from Myers and LaGrange to appease Travis. What a neat solution!

Or—what enormous foolishness? As a part-time teacher, he could no more topple Myers and LaGrange than as a doctoral student he could topple his Ph.D. committee. Besides, Myers had explicitly warned him that if he tried to accuse them, he would have no evidence.

"We're very careful," he said, his fingertips touching in front of his mouth. To one side LaGrange listened with a bored attitude. Obviously, Myers was the brains of the operation, the prime mover.

"We'll take care of you," he said. "We know money is tight, and we're willing to help. All you have to do is help us when we make a request."

"Inflating grades so students can stay on the honor roll? I can't believe I'm hearing this."

"Helping them get into the colleges they want," LaGrange said. "These kids are good kids, and it would be a shame to ruin their careers before they ever begin." *College.* That sounded noble, almost.

Myers nodded. "Exactly."

Afterward, there was no hint that they had talked about perpetrating academic fraud in the same rational tones they might have discussed the merits of different seating charts or assessed a fire drill. LaGrange crossed paths with him twice the next day and each time pestered him with small talk about the weather or Riverside athletics. And a mailbox note had summoned him to Myers's office three days later, but only to sign a vacation form for a student. Everything was business as usual.

Toweling off in the steamy bathroom, McCauley thought of two options. He could at least ask Myers and LaGrange how much was in it for him. Or he could tell Robin. Then another question occurred to him: How were Myers and LaGrange able to pay off faculty who participated in the scheme? The scam as he understood it hardly seemed profitable, since students with at best minimum-wage jobs were the beneficiaries. But no teachers would take part without a decent reward. Who bankrolled the enterprise? A mystery began to take shape, tipping the scales in favor of his telling Robin, for he doubted he would get answers from the others, and knowledge seemed more valuable than money.

Once he was dressed, he sat down at his computer and opened a new file, which he named CHEAT. For the next hour he keyed in every shred of pertinent information he could think of—conversations with Robin and other teachers, incidents of shady student behavior in his own class, and the details of his meetings with LaGrange and Myers. The sheer volume of data impressed him, although he realized that every word was officially, technically, legally hearsay.

Today was Thursday, so his Brookstone class was his only teaching obligation, although he did have two late-afternoon meetings with Riverside students, which meant that once again he would not be able to talk long with Robin. With a cold setting in, he didn't relish the windy twenty-minute motorcycle ride to Brookstone, or the strain that lecturing might put on his throat. He considered taking a sick day. He wanted to see Robin, though, for many reasons.

In the teachers' lounge he found her chatting with Lydia Knowles. Rather than interrupt, he went to the mailboxes and tried to behave casually, all the while feeling the scrutiny of many eyes. Myers and LaGrange had seen him come in. Word of his late Homecoming loitering with Robin had probably reached the ears of most of the faculty in the room, plus everyone knew he had challenged the administrators on a grade change. What were they thinking? And Robin, too, must be watching him. Feeling dreadfully out of place, he went to his classroom.

Robin was waiting at the door when the class dismissed.

"I feel like I haven't seen you in years," she said. "Don't tell me you have to run again."

"I do. I'm sorry. I have meetings with students in half an hour. But I have to talk to you about something important."

"I'll call you after dinner."

"Are you sure?"

"Zeb's in Detroit again. He gets back late tonight."

When she called, all she said was, "I just wanted to make sure you're home. I'm coming over."

He figured he had time to either clean up the apartment or dash to the convenience store for a bottle of wine—but not both. Lacking wine glasses, he chose to tidy up, making his hideaway bed and tucking it away to the complaint of the seldom-used springs, clearing two days' worth of paper plates and dirty cups. As he stacked journals and article copies squarely on top of his computer table, he heard Robin's footsteps on the landing and her knuckles against the door.

He pulled open the door. They both paused for an instant, frozen by uncertainty, by expectancy. Their eyes locked, and Brad felt a deep surge of anticipation wash through him. Robin stepped inside as Brad began to say "Come in," and as she brushed past him his nostrils caught a draft of her earthy perfume. He took off her jacket.

"What's wrong?" she asked.

"Nothing. Why?"

"You just seem so … I don't know. It feels different. Is it all right for me to be here?"

"Yes. Everything's fine. I'm starting to feel a bit under the weather. Maybe I seem a little beat."

"Oh. Maybe that's it." Her eyes studied his face.

"Sit down, sit down. You sounded excited on the phone. What did you need to talk about?"

"Oh, nothing really. Nothing in particular. I don't know. Did you clean up this place?"

Brad swept his arm around the room.

"Oh. It looks great. It looks roomier."

"Robin—"

"Brad, I don't know how to say this without sounding like a teenager, so I'll just say it. It seems like you've been avoiding me."

"No, I haven't. I've just had commitments on campus all this week."

"Are you sure?"

He nodded.

"Because I really appreciated Saturday night. I could have sat and talked twice as long. I suppose I should feel guilty, but so far I don't. What do you think's happening to us?"

"To *us?* I don't know, Robin." He wondered what she *wanted* to happen, but he couldn't summon the courage to ask.

"Listen," he said. "I'm trying to drink lots of liquids to beat this cold. You want something to drink?"

Robin declined, and Brad excused himself to the kitchen. Twisting a few ice cubes from the blue plastic tray and pouring a tall cup of grapefruit juice, he admired Robin sitting in profile on the sofa. He thought of words to describe her, and *demure* floated to the surface. One leg was bent, its ankle tucked under her other thigh; her light blue jeans fit crisply, appropriate for an autumn day. Instead of dutifully attending his meetings that afternoon, he should have stayed with her, kicking through fallen leaves, he in his boots, she in her perky white sneakers. As he watched, her fingers picked at a loose thread in her wool sweater, white with a band of red and blue teddy bears marching around her bust line.

"Excuse me again," Brad said when he returned. "I need to take a couple of aspirin."

"Maybe I should leave, if you aren't feeling well."

"Oh, no, don't leave. I have headaches all the time."

"Don't take aspirin."

"Don't?"

"No. Come here." She unfolded her leg and patted the front of the couch between her knees. "Sit down. I'll give you a massage."

"You don't have to do that ..." But he was already moving toward her, dropping to the carpet, and, fighting to think of a graceful way to accept, he felt the inviting pressure of her knees tightening against his arms. There was nothing he could say.

Eyes closed, breathing through his nose, he felt her hands resting on his shoulders, light with promise.

Her voice asked, "Where is it hurting?"

"On the lower right side."

"Is it throbbing, or just a constant ache?"

"Throbbing. For the last hour or so, getting worse. You sound like a doctor."

"Sorry. A mom *is* a doctor. Sorry, I shouldn't have said that."

The apology perplexed him. It sounded too serious, too self-conscious—like a string of gibberish from a scientist or a computer nerd, something from a wholly alien world.

Even through his shirt, Robin's fingers were much harder, much stronger than he would have imagined. For weeks he had watched them perform routine tasks, touching up her hair, surrounding a coffee cup, writing a note, or feeding a dollar bill into a vending machine in the teachers' lounge. They had never touched him before—even when she rode with him, she wrapped her arms around his waist and clasped her hands together. He had always thought her touch would be feathery soft, like her hair uplifted in the breeze, so the firmness of her fingers surprised him.

They rubbed in small circles from his neck along his shoulders, then began to knead his thick shoulder muscles, their pressure growing deeper, more penetrating, more invigorating.

"Does that hurt?" she asked. He mumbled that it was okay. "You seem so tight through here. That's stress. No wonder you have headaches. Can you loosen your shirt a little?"

He unfastened the top two buttons.

"There, that's better," she said. He felt her breath, close and warm on his neck, and he felt her fingers directly, skin on skin, pressing around the lower vertebrae of his neck and digging into the flesh on either side.

"What was it you wanted to talk to me about?" Robin asked.

"It can wait," he said. "It's pretty complicated, and ..." He shrugged. This was no time to talk of something that serious. "Just wait."

"I have to leave at eight. I have to pick up Zeb at the airport."

"Zeb is a fool to travel so much."

Robin did not answer. Her thumbs were pressing along the base of his shoulder blades.

"At first it wasn't so bad. When we were first married, before Trevor was born, I used to go on the shorter trips with him. They were so much fun."

Her touch lightened.

"Living out of suitcases. The cities, the hotels, swimming at midnight, restaurants on tops of skyscrapers. I'd go sightseeing during the days while Zeb did his business.

"Then it all changed after Trevor arrived. I remember the turning point. We took him on a three-day trip to Philadelphia. He was fifteen months old. It was an absolute disaster."

She laughed, plainly distracted, and paused from her massage.

"Our room smelled mildewy and the carpet was sandy, even though there wasn't any beach within fifty miles of the hotel. In the bathroom there was a piece of wood on the wall, holding up the towel rack. The board was not painted and it had a carpenter's measurement written on it in pencil—33¼. The ice maker was at the far end of the hallway, and when you got to it you found out you had to pay a quarter. The cable TV went off one day, and there were so many flies they put a flyswatter behind the door. One lamp had a burnt-out bulb so I couldn't read at night. Across the street was a restaurant with *daiquiri* misspelled two different ways, once on each side of the sign. The worst part was that Trevor got a tick in his hair. I was so afraid he would get Lyme disease. After that, I never went on a business trip again."

"You could go now, couldn't you?"

"In the summer. Or on weekends. But it's been more than twenty years. It wouldn't be the same now."

What did it mean, McCauley wondered, that Robin was talking about her relationship with Zeb? Or that she was emphasizing the disappointment? He had never been involved with a married woman before. Or an older woman—though that issue never rose in his thinking.

Robin's fingers climbed his spine to the base of his skull, then ran up and down the muscles at the back of his neck, squeezing out the tension. His shoulders actually relaxed, tingling from the relief.

"That's outstanding," he mumbled. "You get an A-plus. And you didn't have to cheat."

She stopped abruptly.

He tried to get up but her hands held him down. She was not finished.

Her fingers massaged his temples with rapid back-and-forth motion; then her thumbs took up the same movement under his ears. Finally, her hands traced along his neck, caressed his collarbones, and rested.

McCauley lifted his head and turned it left and right. Once again he smelled Robin's perfume.

"Now it's your turn," he said, getting up.

"Okay." She slid smoothly off the sofa and crossed her legs in front of her.

Up to now, the closest they had been, physically, had come on their motorcycle rides, Robin always in back, clinging to him with each burst of acceleration. Now she was seated in front of him, her tiny back and close-cut blond hair between his knees, and he marveled at how small her body really was.

Eyes shut again, he let his fingers caress Robin's shoulders, but they found the sweater's thickness and rough texture difficult to feel through.

"You should have worn something lighter," he said.

"Here."

As she pulled the sweater over her head, his heart began to race—until he realized that she had a turtleneck on underneath. She threw the sweater to the side, where it landed in a lump. Brad set his hands on her shoulders again and immediately felt a necklace under the turtleneck. His eyes dropped from Robin's pearl earrings to the line of her bra, and he began to rub, closing his eyes.

"Mmm."

"Sorry, I forgot the wine," he said.

"Oh, never mind. This is better than wine. Wouldn't you say?"

"I think so."

Evening was falling, flooding the apartment with cool gray light, besieging him with a horde of regrets—he should have turned off some lamps, drawn the patio curtain, put on music. To do any of those things now would mean breaking off from touching her and jeopardizing the ambience.

"You have no buttons to undo," he said, wincing with the risk. "That's hardly fair."

"Mmm."

His eyes still closed, his hands slipped around to her prominent, delicate collarbones, ready to let his fingers creep further, when Robin reached up and took them, pulling them away from her and over her head, never letting go. She turned and rose to her knees, facing Brad, pulling him forward. They embraced, and he spread his fingers over her hair and surrounded her tiny skull, drawing it to his thumping breast.

"Robin," he said.

"Shhh. Don't say anything."

She pushed him back on the sofa and lay against his chest. He caressed her back, resting his chin on her hair, breathing in its sweet scent.

A few minutes later, when one of his many clocks sounded its eight o'clock bell, Robin rose.

"I have to go."

"Okay."

"Don't avoid me, okay?" Her voice, somehow, was both pleading and level. "Whatever happens, don't avoid me. I couldn't bear that."

"I promise."

"*Whatever happens.*"

Why did she repeat that?

At the door he hoped to kiss her, but as he leaned down she turned away and said, "See you tomorrow," leaving him to watch her bounce down the steps, disappearing in stages—shoes, jeans, jacket, earrings and hair.

He ordered delivery pizza from Yippy's but after a few slices felt full. The lump in his throat was growing, magnified by his every swallow and by his attention, but his headache was almost gone.

For twenty minutes he sat at his computer before giving up on his plan to finish a stretch of his dissertation. Distractions assailed him from every mental quarter—the biggest being the conversation with Travis, who with one phone call could transform McCauley's work into a footnote to oblivion.

However, hours later, when he unfolded his hideaway bed to its harsh metallic creak and lay down to sleep, he was struck by how little Travis's threat bothered him. Neither did the disturbing offer of Myers and LaGrange seem as serious as it should have. He kept thinking of Robin's strong fingers massaging his stress-tight flesh, and wishing she were lying with him.

21

BETWEEN GUM BUBBLES, Jessica Southard was growing increasingly fond of alluding to Erin's shortcomings on the school social scene, trying variations on that theme, landing sarcastic jabs at every opportunity, even though such opportunities were dwindling as their senior year wore on, their friendship drifting apart, strained by Matt's rejection of one and pursuit of the other.

Jess's criticisms of her cousin, for all their mean spirit, were on target, at least partway. Erin didn't talk much, that was true, but she listened well—very well. She heard bits and pieces of hundreds of conversations whispered behind upright books at library tables and shouted over the much-maligned food in the cafeteria. She was intimately familiar with the daily banter that passed back and forth among students in the hallways, even though she seldom contributed to it. In the showers and P.E. locker rooms she listened to the other girls trade secrets and chart their courses for romance and adventure. And at the Junction she heard her classmates spell out their dreams and fears while warming themselves around bonfires, or wading in the river, or hiding in the shadows of the bridge.

Like Jess, most of Erin's peers believed that her infrequent speech indicated her ignorance about their lives.

In fact, she knew very much.

She knew, for instance, that Lauren Lancaster had become pregnant from a midsummer Junction tryst with Dan Foster, leading to a hushed-up abortion in West Bridgebury. She knew that if she ever wanted to try cocaine, sharp-dressing Eric Hillman would be able to help her through his "contacts" at Riverside and possibly even among the "meth element" rumored to be creeping into the smaller towns north of the university. She knew that Tory Johnson was responsible for the vandalism to the playground's basketball backboard, and that Sally Richards, her face seemingly more gaunt every day, had been quietly but clinically diagnosed as anorexic.

She also knew about all the underhanded ways that some Brookstone students maintained their lofty grade point averages, kept their names on the quarterly honor rolls, and won lucrative financial aid packages to prestigious universities from New York to California. Not every academic whiz was a genius or even a hard worker. Some of the superstars had not propelled themselves into the Brookstone High School firmament by their own natural gifts or dedication—no, they had been lifted from mediocrity and set in the sky by helpful teachers and administrators.

A teacher might "accidentally" leave a copy of an upcoming test on his or her desk after school, for instance, and a student who needed to make a high grade might run into the teacher in the library or Atrium, where the teacher would happen to remember something else left in class, a book or a pair of glasses, and send the student on an errand to retrieve the "something else" from the room. "Look first on my desk," the teacher might say. "If it's not there, try the cabinet by the window." The next morning, as planned, the teacher would find an empty desk. The student would ace the test.

Sometimes the process was less elaborate. Jess claimed—but Erin never knew which stories to believe among those that flowed from her cousin's acid tongue—that as a sophomore she had privately taken a poorly written English essay to Mr. Adams, promised him about fifty dollars' worth of fresh produce, and watched him burn the paper, drop the ashes into the trash can, and change the D to an A in his gradebook.

Where had Jess come up with the produce? From her mom, she said. From Erin's Aunt Jen.

Many teachers had "soft spots." The boys said you could bribe Mr. Ray with tickets to professional sporting events in Indianapolis or Chicago. Mr. Sojka, the chemistry teacher, was an avid photographer, and students had reportedly raised grades in his class with gifts of camera accessories, photography books, or photo editing software—or in one case, by posing in his home studio. It was said that Mr. Gallmeyer, a bachelor, could be influenced with gift certificates (in amounts suitable for two) to fine restaurants in Bridgebury, and that Joanne Harman was easily swayed by sufficient gifts of flowers to plant in her garden, famous throughout the colorful streets of Corbin Creek.

Everyone knew that if you could persuade the top CUPP students, Cody Summers or Lance Tracer or Cara Eberle, to help you with a paper or project, teachers would mostly look the other way. Although Matt was just an average student who didn't belong in the same classroom with someone as brainy as Cody, several seasons as athletic teammates had cemented their friendship, and now Matt was riding Cody's coattails into a region of academic respectability he could never achieve on his own. Matt was actually taking a top-level CUPP math class, and—sitting next to Cody—succeeding. Surely Mr. McGrew knew that Matt was no math whiz, that Cody did most of his friend's homework and funneled him correct answers on tests. But McGrew continued to dole out As and Bs to Matt on quizzes and tests and to credit him fully for homework assignments.

The year before, Cara Eberle's role in a computer class project had caused a flap. She had been matched with mostly non-CUPP students, for whom graduation from high school would guarantee decent jobs. That was all the success they sought. Under Cara's "leadership," however, they wrote a detailed program to monitor materials flow through a fictitious auto plant. The teacher had devised the complex problem to challenge Cara, the designated group leader, but when she turned in her reports on the other group members, she credited them with contributions more appropriate to Riverside engineering undergraduates. A student from a team with a less generous leader complained, first to the teacher and later to Mr. Myers, about inequities in the grading of the assignment. Myers "investigated," determining there was no evidence of wrongdoing on the part of Cara or her team members. Of course the team members had done no wrong, Erin remembered thinking, because they hadn't done anything *period*, except to somehow buy off Cara and the teacher.

According to one story Erin had overhead, Mary Nokes, a graduate from the previous year, had needed a 3.90 grade point average to qualify for a particular scholarship. After her final grades were figured, her GPA stood at 3.83. But her parents disputed that figure and met with Mr. Myers the day before graduation, helping him "uncover" an error from Mary's sophomore transcripts, when she had moved to Brookstone from southern Illinois. The error conveniently nudged Mary's GPA past the 3.90 mark—and now she was attending Duke University.

True or false, most of the stories involved Mr. Tolan Myers in some way. That was understandable. The school's guidance director and registrar, he had complete control of every student's academic record. It was said that he accepted bribes directly from parents who wanted their children to land scholarships and grants. How often had Erin heard her own sisters say, "Dad will take care of it"? Perhaps he was propping up her own GPA, behind the scenes, and she did not even know it. After all, Dad always seemed to be friendly with Mr. Myers when they crossed paths at school academic or athletic events.

Monday of Thanksgiving week Erin came to school with a headache. The first item on her schedule was her spring registration meeting, for which she was called out of the last half of her first-period class.

Mr. Myers sat behind his desk and scrutinized her record as if it were a resume and she a job applicant. For someone who was supposed to be a friendly adviser and counselor, he had a way of making you feel uncomfortable. His eyes were friendly but his manner usually made you nervous. His right hand lightly grazed his shining head, as though it were running over hair, and he yawned deeply.

"Well, Erin," he said, leaning back in his chair, "you seem to be surviving this semester."

"Yes, sir."

"I've talked to your teachers, and they all say you're doing well ... except for Mr. McCauley."

She nodded.

"I'm a little behind on the semester project."

"A *little* behind? He says you're two stages behind, and that unless you bear down it will be too late to turn in an adequate project on time."

"I know. I *am* bearing down. It just took me a long time to choose my topic."

"I see." He leaned forward and studied her records again. "You're hoping to go to Princeton, is that right? To be with Patti?"

"That's what *Dad* wants," she said automatically. "I don't think I can get in there." Even if she could, she didn't want to.

"Your index is 3.50 coming into this year. Your SATs were a little low for Princeton, perhaps, but their admissions people will look especially closely at how you do this year. They're willing to forgive a few low grades early in your high school career if you can show them you've straightened out by the time you graduate.

"Your father and I have talked a couple of times. I told him I'd keep a close eye on you. He really wants the best for you, Erin."

"I know," she said with resignation. "I'm doing the best I can."

"Good, good. I think if you can pull your history grade up to an A, then you should be able to improve on your 3.50 for this year. Your spring classes look easier."

He looked up, fixed her with his kind brown eyes, and nodded. Then he leaned back again.

"I'll tell you what I'm going to do." Erin thought of Grandpa Dee and his dominoes and she nearly burst out laughing. "I'll put in a good word for you with Mr. McCauley. I'll ask him to give you any special help you need to catch up on your project. Then if you give it your best shot, I guarantee you'll get the grade you need. Okay?"

"All right. Can I ask you a question?"

"Sure. That's why I'm here."

"Are my grades good enough for Riverside?"

"Riverside? Of course! You could not lift a pencil the rest of the year and they'd let you into Riverside. They're dying to get our students—it's good for *their* reputation! But Erin, why do you care about Riverside?"

"I just wondered."

"Sure, sure. You always have Riverside to fall back on. But you're destined for bigger and better things."

At that point, Mr. Myers began to recount the Delaney family's celebrated history at Brookstone. He recalled how Sarah had written the blue-ribbon essay (worth $3,000) in the statewide competition. He repeated inspiring snippets of her valedictorian speech verbatim. He looked at the ceiling as if to heaven and remembered how deflated Sarah had become at learning her SAT math score was *only* 760, utterly crestfallen, for she had left the test site certain she had not missed a single question. He talked about Patti's legendary science project—ignoring the little detail that college students had done most of the work, for pay—which had drawn the raves of judges and earned spots on *ABC News* and *CNN Headline News*. He remembered that Patti had taken three courses at Riverside as a high school senior and aced all three. He called her the first and only trilingual Brookstone graduate. He could go on and on, he said, but he did have other appointments that morning, and besides, he knew that Erin already understood his point—she was part of a very special family, so very special things were expected of her.

In chemistry class she feigned note-taking and instead doodled. Maybe she was worrying over nothing. Maybe her father *was* taking care of everything.

But if he sent her to Princeton, she would die.

Matt always talked about how powerful Mr. Myers was. If he could convince Mr. McCauley to be lenient, that was fine with her. What Mr. Myers had said was true—she was almost too far behind on the history project to have any hope of finishing on time, which meant an automatic penalty of one letter grade. If she got a C in history, she could kiss Princeton good-bye. How would her father react? She didn't even want to think about that. Her head was already aching enough.

At lunch the aching had worsened to pounding, so she sat by herself and picked at her country fried steak and soupy mashed potatoes. About halfway through the period, Mrs. Hillis set down a tray across from her.

"Mind if I join you?"

"No."

"I didn't think so. You don't care a whole lot about what other people think. A lot of students would be embarrassed if I sat down with them in the cafeteria. I knew you wouldn't be."

Strangely, Erin felt her heart lifting.

Mrs. Hillis took the lid off her milkshake and spooned some into her mouth.

"Am I right?"

"Yes," Erin said. "That's how I am. How did you know?"

"From reading your journals and papers. And I've learned a lot about you from the times we've talked."

"That's wild."

"Do you have any plans for vacation?"

"No, my family's not going anywhere. What about you?"

"I'm not going anywhere either. But my husband will be home for a change. He's been travelling so much this semester that I've hardly seen him."

Erin said, "That's how I feel sometimes. I mean, well ..." She felt reluctant to mention Nathan by name. Recalling Mrs. Hillis's assessment of her personality, though, she blurted out in a spasm of vague defiance, "I haven't seen my old boyfriend, from last year, ever since he went to Riverside in August. And I miss him a lot."

Mrs. Hillis swallowed a bite and answered tenderly, "I'm sorry. I didn't know that. I thought you and Matt were going together."

Erin began bouncing in her seat.

"But I don't really *like* him. I mean, I don't *dis*like him, but ... it's just to keep my parents off my back."

"Oh. Do you ever talk to *them* about it?" Then she added, "No, I remember now. They're never around for you to talk to." After a short pause, she added, "Like my husband." They both smiled.

"Why is it you haven't seen your old boyfriend? You can go visit him, can't you?"

"I've tried to call him a few times, but he's never there. I don't think I should go unless he knows I'm coming. When we broke up, he said we needed to be apart and all that."

"Oh. And you're taking his words literally."

"I guess so."

"Maybe you can see him over Thanksgiving."

"I wish I could. I don't know."

"Does Matt know how you feel?"

Erin slid her tray aside and leaned forward.

"I could never tell him I still like Nathan," she said softly but energetically. "That would be mean. When we first started going together, I thought maybe I would forget Nathan, but no. Matt makes me wish I was still with Nathan even more."

"Let me ask you a tough question."

"Okay." Erin crossed her hands and offered complete attention at the challenge.

"Whom do you want to please in your life?"

"*Whom*? You mean it's not *who*?"

"Never mind that."

"Who do I want to please? *Whom*, I mean. Hmm. I never thought about it."

"Remember when I talked to you at the dance? You were worried about grades, because of your parents. Then last week you told me you felt pressure because they expect you to go to college somewhere you'd rather not go. And now you say you're staying with Matt mostly because of your parents."

"But not to *please* them. Just to keep them off my back."

"Oh. What about your classmates? Is it important what they think of you?"

"Most of them think I'm antisocial, but it doesn't bother me. I wish they liked me more, but what can I do?"

"Is there anybody you *are* trying to please?"

Embarrassed, Erin shrugged and said, "I don't know. I guess not."

"We've talked eight or ten times in the last few weeks, right?"

"Right. I like talking to you because you let me be myself. You care about what *I* think."

"I do care. That's what I'm getting at. It sounds like your life is loaded down with trying to please different people, even if you don't think of it that way. You keep compromising what you want in order to keep the pressure off. You feel like everyone's making demands—Matt, Jess, school, and your parents. Even your friends. I think it really bothers you that they think you're antisocial. You have to make an effort to ignore what they think."

Erin shrugged again.

"What's wrong with pleasing other people?" she asked.

"Nothing. But what about Erin Delaney? Who's pleasing her?"

"Nobody. Except you, I guess."

"Thanks. You see what I'm saying?"

"That I should go to Nate?"

"No, no, no. Maybe you should and maybe you shouldn't. I don't know about that. But I *do* know that you're so busy trying to keep everyone else satisfied that you're not pleasing yourself. Really you're just *cheating* yourself, taking a shortcut."

"What? How?"

"It's easy to give in to everyone else. It's not easy to face your fears about letting other people down, but you have to live your own life. You can't keep trying to be somebody you're not. So ... do something for your*self* once in a while. Tell Matt to take a hike if that's what you want. Tell your mom and dad what you think about college. There's no use hiding the truth—it's going to come to the surface sooner or later."

The warning bell sounded—five minutes until the first afternoon period.

"The truth is, I just want to get good grades so I can get out of my house and into college, hopefully Riverside."

Mrs. Hillis spread her napkin over the uneaten part of her meat.

"Erin, if that's all you want, there's nothing to worry about."

"No?"

"No. You know what it takes to get good grades at Brookstone High."

Briefly their eyes met, and Mrs. Hillis winked.

Erin's heart sank. That wink—what did it mean? Mrs. Hillis had exhorted her several times not to give in to the temptations to cheat, but ...

At the conveyor belt they deposited their trays and split off in different directions. Erin wanted to cry. She felt like a ping pong ball, emotionally. After the tense meeting with Mr. Myers, she had felt discouraged. Talking to Mrs. Hillis had refreshed her. But under the weight of Mrs. Hillis's foreboding final words, hope dropped away again. Oh! The pressure! She imagined herself being squeezed to thinness, to nothingness, almost like one of her pretty autumn leaves pressed between sheets of wax paper, stifled and silenced forever.

What would it take to gain Mr. McCauley's favor?

22

WITH A SPLENDID crackle of autumn glory, Robin's teeth cut through the polished red skin of the apple, squirting juice onto Brad's hovering face. Sweetness spreading along her tongue, she watched the familiar smile form under his mustache as his hand reached up to wipe his cheek. What a perfect November day—made for a picnic! The warm breath of Indian summer had wafted across the Midwest for Thanksgiving, hanging on for the whole weekend.

A word kept popping into Robin's mind—*surfeit*—a word that appeared in a poem she taught every fall and that students never could grasp. She always wanted to explain it by the synonym of *orgy*, which they might understand, but out of experience and decency she never went so far as to suggest that alternative.

She brushed a ladybug off the checkered quilt. When a ray of sunshine caught the diamond in her wedding ring, she withdrew her hand into the shade in her lap. No matter how far she went from Brookstone, she could not escape reminders of her husband. Zeb, who had promised that they would enjoy a four-day weekend. Zeb, who on Wednesday had modified his pledge to two days. Zeb, who after a flurry of Thanksgiving Day phone calls, glumly announced that he must fly to Seattle on Friday to "put out a three-million-dollar fire." Zeb, who went to bed so tired both nights of the "vacation" that he didn't even touch her. Zeb, whose final words before climbing aboard the plane were horribly hollow: "Honey, I love you, and I pray and I promise that this traveling won't go on past Christmas."

Maybe his prayer would find its way into God's ears. Every one of hers were plunging into a vast void of silence lately.

Brad pulled a cluster of grapes from the wicker cornucopia covered with a coat of brown spray paint, which they had purchased at a mini-mart somewhere north of Corbin Creek. Its contents were surprisingly fresh considering its orange-tinted wrap had been punctured and repaired with a patch of cellophane tape.

"Have you ever been here before?" she asked. "Or did we just take random highways and byways until we chanced upon a nice valley?"

"It's my first time here."

Robin took off her sunglasses to clean the large, round lenses. Her kids said they made her look "spunky." So far, Brad hadn't offered any comment about them.

"Where are we, exactly?" she asked.

"I don't know. Fifty-three is over there somewhere." He waved vaguely.

"We went through Corbin Creek five miles back. That was the last place I'm familiar with. It's right on the boundary of the school district."

"I'd say we're way out of bounds."

She regarded him through the lenses, which drenched his image in amber. *Out of bounds?* Was that an insinuation?

"But we don't have any choice in the matter, right? Fate just brought us here."

"Right. Why do you keep dwelling on that?"

"It's so meaningless," she stated matter-of-factly, wondering whether she could coax him into an argument. "Somebody of your intelligence ought to see that."

"I don't think it's meaningless."

"I do. How can we enjoy anything if even our emotions are pre-programmed?"

"I enjoy plenty of things."

"Like me?"

"Of course."

"I enjoy you too."

Brad lay back, using his rolled up jacket for a pillow. With the sun bathing his face in the season's last warmth, he closed his eyes. Robin began breaking small pieces off the end of a twig and tossing them onto his chest.

"Do you enjoy the fact that I enjoy you?" she asked.

"What's with all the semantics, English teacher?"

"*Do you?*"

"Yes. In plain English, I'm glad you like me."

"I'm glad you like me too, but what if you have no choice but to like me? Then why should it please me? Do you see what I'm saying?"

"I think you're making a mountain out of a molehill."

She flipped the rest of the stick playfully against his face.

Maybe she was asking too much. Wasn't it enough that Brad was willing to listen to her and spend so much time with her? Did he also have to bring to their relationship an identical or even compatible overall view of life? She and Zeb were both rather conservative, yet look where that consistency had landed them! What did it matter if Brad understood their mutual affection and joy differently than she did—it was still real, wasn't it?

"Beggars can't be choosers," she said.

Just words, lifeless words. She was begging *and* choosing. She was a choosy beggar. If Brad was involving himself with her only because of some all-powerful, all-pervasive, universal impulse that he was powerless to resist, then there was no pleasure for her. Robin's soul was panting for more than mechanical attraction that was no different from the kind of magnetism that operated on iron shavings. She yearned for true relationship, for—she had to admit to herself—real love. She wanted to walk proudly, confident of her worth. That wasn't asking too much, was it?

As they finished their cheese-and-lunchmeat sandwiches, their conversation slid into small talk about the end of the semester, grading final tests and papers, and plans for the spring. Brad mentioned that he would not be teaching a class at Riverside.

"When you're dissertating, you only have to teach one class every two semesters," he explained.

"That will give you more time," Robin said. "You need more time. You're way too busy. You're pulled in too many directions. You have too many commitments."

"That's for sure."

"Just be happy you're not married."

"Oh? Is it that bad?" he chuckled.

She herself was starting to wonder why she so habitually and unconsciously dropped hints about marriage or references to Zeb, subtle or otherwise, into conversations with Brad.

"I just meant it would be one more commitment," she explained.

"You're probably right." She watched his eyes follow a late flock of migrating birds. "Tell me," he went on and then, after a pregnant pause, "are you committed to your husband?"

"Zeb?" she asked, then felt silly at her own reply. "Of course I am."

"Then," he sat up, "are we having an affair, or what?"

"No. We're not having an affair. Not technically. Not yet."

"Not yet? What does that mean?"

"More semantics, I suppose," she said cautiously. "It means we haven't reached that stage yet."

"How will we know when we have?"

Was he *serious*?

"When it becomes *sexual*," she said bluntly, thoughts of Zeb intruding again. "I mean, that's really what *affair* means. It's just a euphemism."

"Right, but ..."

"But what?"

"I don't know. I'm just wondering out loud, I suppose."

"You're wondering about the emotional side of it, aren't you?"

In reply he merely shrugged and sighed.

"You wonder whether we've reached that stage yet, emotionally," she went on, aware that what sometimes seemed clear as a crystal lake to her—possibly because she had spent so many late, lonely hours exploring her own heart—was a muddy puddle to him.

"Don't worry," she said, "We'll just know." She laughed uneasily and added, "Trust me."

"*Trust* you? Why, do you have experience?"

"No. Do you?"

"Robin," he said in his earnest voice, "I'm enjoying every minute I spend with you. But it's, it's ..."

"It's what?"

"It's confusing."

"It's fated."

He pulled some grass and flung it at her laughing face. She was intoxicated with delight—despite her earlier focus on his philosophy, she wanted to avoid analyzing too closely what was happening between them. She feared just one thing: rousing her conscience.

"Seriously," he pleaded. "It's like a giant ... maze."

She opened her mouth to repeat her jibe that everything was fated—but his words, or rather that last word, checked her abruptly, its coincidence too great to ignore. Like a *maze*! That was the same analogy that had occurred to her in the hours after she had traded back rubs with Brad in his apartment a week earlier, those distressing hours when her scruples would not let her rest but kept grating against her complacency, forcing her to concede that she could not keep tiptoeing along the tightrope between flirtation with Brad and marriage to Zeb. She struggled to evade the self-assessment with its razor-sharp insight, but she could not. And so she surrendered—sort of. She accepted that she must back out of the fun but fuzzy relationship with Brad and work to love Zeb, even if loving him just meant waiting for him. She must back away from Brad, though exactly how to do that mystified her, and trying to envision a way to jump from the tightrope and land safely back in the land of her marriage made her dizzy and frustrated and ultimately angry that she had gotten lost in such a *maze* of self-deception. Yes, she had fallen for the deceitful lies of Brad McCauley! But no, even that was wrong, another lie, more deception. She could not blame *him* ...

And now his chance use of that word had immersed her once more in a torrent of incrimination. The day was tarnished, if not ruined. Yet still she fought.

Riding home, Robin ignored Brad's pleading and chose to not wear the motorcycle helmet. She wanted to feel the wind caress her face and neck, but she was disappointed when it whipped her with ruthless fury. By now she was used to the streak of scofflaw that emerged in Brad aboard his bike. He flouted every DO NOT PASS sign he saw. At first she had been afraid for her safety and angry at his contempt for sensible laws, but no harm had ever come, no siren and flashing light had ever called them to a reckoning, and over time she had fully accustomed herself to his cavalier attitude on the road.

They rumbled into the north end of Brookstone, still in broad daylight, the idea that she might be seen and recognized no longer frightening her.

At her back door, she trespassed over another threshold when she asked, with precarious feigned indifference, "Why don't you stay for dinner?"

She tried not to notice him surveying the interior of the house, but even when she was not watching him, she was aware of his roaming eyes. He asked a quaint question, whether he might lay his jacket over the back of a dining room chair. He must know we have special closets for coats, she thought, but he doesn't want to impose.

In the kitchen he asked for a glass of water and stood behind her as she poured it from the pitcher in the fridge. She heard him chuckle, and when she pressed him to explain, he pointed to a Bible verse, engraved and set in rose-tinted glass, hanging in the window above the sink:

> *Though outwardly we are wasting away,*
> *yet inwardly we are being renewed, day by day.*
> *—2 Corinthians 4:16*

"That's me," he said. "Outwardly wasting away."

"What about inwardly?"

He shrugged.

"No 'new creation' for you, huh?" she asked, making light of what was weighing heavily on her heart yet realizing he probably had no idea what she was referring to, locked up by his clockwork view of reality. Tick-tock, tick-tock. On top of offering no hope, how boring!

"Are you hungry, Brad? We ate only two hours ago."

"I can hold off a while longer. Are you going to make something?"

"Are you going to make something?" she mimicked him. "Don't act so surprised. I am a housewife, you know."

"We could order out."

"Not in Brookstone, Indiana, we can't order out. Unless you want to go all the way to Bridgebury or Lake Pritchard."

Robin gave him a superficial tour of the house, thankful that the door to the master bedroom was closed and avoiding that room. Brad was impressed with the stained woodwork—the stairway banisters, the trim framing windows and doorways, the baseboard.

"That must be worth a pretty penny," he remarked.

"It came with the house. But we restored it ourselves, with help from a neighbor across the street. He built the fireplace mantel too, and the corner cabinet in the dining room."

"That's a good kind of neighbor to have."

"He's a family and marriage counselor." As soon as she relayed this tidbit of information, Robin wondered why. It had nothing to do with them. "And a woodworker."

She guided him to the living room and the fireplace.

"Too bad it's so warm," she commented. "It would be nice to have a fire. We had one Wednesday night. The last couple of years we hardly used it. Zeb's too busy to cut wood. The only reason we have any now is that Howard—he's the man who did the mantel—cut down a walnut tree in my next-door neighbor's yard. The wood's probably still too green."

Why couldn't she just shut up?

Brad stood in front of the fireplace and looked at the Hillis family portrait.

"Your daughter looks like you," he said, as awkward speaking as she was listening. What do you do when you step into situations like this? In the contemporary teenage lexicon, she was clueless. Stuck in a maze …

"Sit down," she said. "There's probably a football game on, if you want to watch something. Or I could put on some music."

Glancing toward the stereo rack, she saw the cassette tape he had lent her. She had listened to it several times now, trying to make sense of its turgid emotion. Springsteen had turned a simple teenage joy ride into epic parody. The songs were populated with colorful figures like the Magic Rat, Spanish Johnny, Diamond Jackie, Fish Lady, Jack the Rabbit, and Weak-kneed Willie. She tried to imagine the two of *them* in one of those songs: Bookworm Brad and … Runaway Robin? Hapless Hillis? *Runaway* was the first thing that came to mind.

With nothing else to do, they rented a movie from the convenience store at the Amoco station. Brad volunteered to go for it, and he chose the safest title he could find from among the dozens of fifty-cent oldies—*Teachers*, a mediocre show about a high school teacher who tried to uphold the honor of the profession in the face of profound problems of every kind. In the end he got fired for helping a pregnant girl get an abortion. By the time the credits began to roll, evening had descended outside the living room. Brad returned the DVD while Robin fixed dinner.

Afterward, they sat in the living room and talked under the soft hum of the ceiling fan.

Brad ran down a list of his physical ailments from head to toe. Headaches, arthritic fingers, lower back pain, a knee that tightened up whenever it remained bent for a long time (such as when he sat at his computer), an Achilles tendon that was permanently sore.

"Every year I get two or three colds," he complained. "My immune system must be shot."

"At least your hair's not turning gray," Robin countered. "Mine is."

"No!"

"Yes it is. Only a few, so far."

"But that's not major. And it doesn't necessarily look bad, either." She blushed as she realized he was trying to visualize her with a full head of gray hair.

Somehow or other the talk about physical decay segued into talk about death.

"Your life span is programmed into your genes," Brad said authoritatively. Robin dreaded what came next: Brad twisted this biological research discovery into evidence for his Universal Clock and his tick-tock god.

But Brad's picture seemed too painfully real just now. God was nowhere near her life. Her prayers about Zeb might as well have been shouted into a pillow. If He were a student in her class, she would have turned in His Holy Name to the office for truancy.

"You're not old," she insisted when Brad described the early demise he felt the Universal Clock had ordained for him. "You can always turn back the clock. Exercise more, and eat better. Frankly, you eat like a ... college student."

"Exactly."

"Despite what I said this afternoon, you need a wife."

"How sexist. What would Ms. Priscilla Verhoven say?"

"Who? Oh, yes. The lady you had the argument with."

"It was not an argument."

"I still don't understand why you let her upset you so much."

"I didn't like her hair. Not enough gray."

"Don't change the subject."

"It was nothing."

Tick-tock. The clock on the mantel chimed at every quarter hour, and they were still talking at 10:30. Robin yawned as Brad described all his neighbors, finishing with the (he believed) lesbians living directly above his apartment.

"Things aren't that exciting around here," Robin grumbled. "We're so far from the civilization of Riverside. Mr. Floyd next door is the most colorful person around. He's ninety-five years old. He was teaching at Brookstone when there was a one-room schoolhouse in the 1940s. Later when it turned into a bigger school, he was a shop teacher, but he's been retired so long.

"He still mows his own lawn in the summer. He uses an electric mower, and someday he's going to mow over the cord and electrocute himself. It takes him all week to mow the whole lawn. He does ten or twelve strips each day, and by the time he finishes, it's time to start again!"

Brad laughed.

"He quit gardening two years ago," she went on, "because he can hardly walk anymore. That last year I remember him waddling out to his garden, bowlegged, dragging an aluminum lawn chair behind him and sitting in it and picking the ripe tomatoes off the plants. He would just leave them on the ground. Hours later his wife would come out and pick them up. Then she died. She was over ninety years old, too. She made the best popcorn balls for Halloween every year."

"You don't get the flavor of older people when you live near campus," Brad said.

"There's an elderly blind woman across the street," Robin continued. "In the family of the man who did the mantel. She's very nice and talkative. She loves marzipan at Christmas, and she listens to baseball games on the radio all summer long."

While the clock struck eleven, Robin paused.

"I wonder if when we're old," she mused, "younger people will remember us only for a few odd details. 'Oh, yes, Robin was the old lady with all that gray hair who rode the motorcycle.'"

It occurred to her that Brad was hoping to stay even later—till morning—and Robin felt her fatigue and loneliness urging her to invite him to stay. Zeb would never know. Was that what bothered her? She was too tired to think straight. Deceived, disoriented, missing somewhere in a maze of her own making …

Brad complimented her on a painting on the wall, and Robin couldn't resist saying, "It's better than a ripped up shirt."

"That shirt is the tip of the iceberg," he said. "Let me tell you about my sleeping adventures." And a half hour's stories followed—hilarious stories, but stories that wafted Robin further toward sleep of her own. Brad talked of an episode in which he woke naked on the front porch of a neighbor, and another when he woke fully clothed in the shower, with cold water reviving him. Once he had actually started his car in his sleep, also with no clothes on. And most recently, he had pounded a hole through the soft drywall of his apartment.

"I had the couch next to the wall then," he said. "One night I woke up and my hand was killing me. I wanted to see why it was hurting. But I couldn't find the light switch on the wall. So I got up and found another light, and turned it on. My hand was red as an apple, swelling. And there was the hole where the light switch had been. I had pounded it clear through the drywall, in my sleep."

"I guess it's good you're *not* married," Robin said. "It wouldn't be safe for the poor woman."

"I've never hurt anybody," Brad said.

"You've probably scared away every girlfriend you ever had."

He acted hurt.

"No."

Finally she felt she could ask a question without seeming too obvious.

"Oh? Do you have a girlfriend now?"

His delay in responding actually frightened her.

"No. I haven't had a girlfriend in …" He shrugged his shoulders.

A rush of excitement swept through Robin, a rush that surprised her. To hide it, she said, "Must be your fate. Tick-tock." She nestled into his arms on the couch.

"Tick-tock," he repeated, and his smile widened.

Robin took his face in her hands and drew it toward hers. Brad's lips were dry but they moistened quickly, and she felt his arms caress her back, sliding up and down, holding her in place. They parted with deep breaths and looked into each other's eyes.

"Wow," Brad said. "Happy Thanksgiving."

"Tick-tock," she said. He leaned forward into another kiss, more ardent and longer. At last, gently, she pushed him away. He rose with a hand around her arm.

"No, no," she said. "That's all, Brad."

His grip relaxed.

"Tick-tock. It's your fate to leave, too. I'm about to fall asleep."

"I was hoping for a different fate," he said.

"I'm sorry," she said, wrapping her arms around him. "You know the rules. Tick-tock." For a change she was actually glad his philosophy was so rigid. She couldn't help but send him home.

At the door, Brad's hand burrowed into hers, pressing into her palm something cool and metallic. A key to his apartment.

"Use it any time," he said. "The more the better."

When she shut the door behind him, she exploded into tears that continued until the phone rang, and she ran to answer, expecting Zeb, longing for Zeb, but it was only Jerri Roost, surprised and apologetic. She had dialed the wrong number off the memory pad of her phone.

December

⁂

23

MATT RADEMACHER'S THICK fingers curled tightly around the dice, suggesting that his sheer strength might squeeze out double sixes. When the red-spotted cubes tumbled onto the table and came to rest next to Cody's, Matt shouted "Yes!" and pounded his fist into his other palm. His five and four beat Cody's best pair, a four and a three. Cody studied the game board from behind the lenses of his horn-rimmed glasses, his gifted brain silently firing, figuring the odds. Because Cody was the most intelligent student at Brookstone High School, Erin could almost feel Matt's joy at rebuffing his attack—although intelligence had played no part in Matt's victory in the battle to defend the Middle East from Egypt.

She was the only girl present, but with everyone's attention fastened to the board, she did not feel awkward. During the weeks she and Matt had been dating, if you called it that, she had noticed a protective streak that emerged in him whenever they were with his friends, a streak that made her feel most comfortable with him in the company of others, even when the others were all boys.

Nevertheless, she had decided to follow Mrs. Hillis's advice and follow her own heart. Today she would break up with Matt. Unlike the future of the silly board game she was watching, the outcome of her improbable relationship with Matt was not in question.

Cody set down the three attacker's dice, and the hairy hand of Lance Tracer, his fingers still wet from the condensation on his beer bottle, scooped them up. He announced, "From Madagascar to South Africa," and Matt said, "Step right up and have your butt whipped, Lancer."

Lance said, "I'll attack with two armies. It will only take two."

The arrogance of Matt and his friends—of all boys, really—amused Erin. She bit her lip to keep from laughing as Matt rolled a four and a three against Lance's five and two. Each player lost an army. Now Matt could defend with just one army, however, and Lance attacked again with two. He rolled a six and a three; Matt's defensive throw was a four. Lance flicked Matt's last yellow token from the board. As it skittered across the concrete basement floor, Lance moved in five armies to occupy South Africa, set down the dice, and drew a card.

He breathed in with affected pride that made Cody laugh.

"Nice butt-whipping," he said to Matt.

"Take a continent, then pop off," retorted Matt, uncapping a can of bacon ranch Pringles. He added sarcastically, "What do you have there, a grand total of five territories? Wow, am I worried!"

Cody took a step backward.

"Cool down, Matt," he said. "It's just a game."

Matt mumbled something incoherent. Erin looked from Cody to Matt and back to Cody.

That week the school had updated the CUPP Scholarship standings, and to nobody's surprise, Cody Summers was leading in the race for the Gold CUPP. Whichever student won that honor would get half the money collected for CUPP from area business donors through the year—money contributed in the form of cash or checks literally dropped into the physical CUPP cups on display in the Main Office and presented to the winners at the end of the year. The second- and third-place students would win smaller pro-rated shares for the Silver CUPP and Bronze CUPP. According to a rumor Erin had read in the *Independent Clause*, the Gold CUPP total was approaching $8,000, a staggering amount since the majority of the money usually wasn't contributed until closer to tax time or graduation. Cody, on track to be the Brookstone valedictorian, stood to benefit most. Erin was pleased about that. He always treated her well. He deserved the scholarship.

As for the game of Risk, Erin had never seen it before, but it seemed pretty straightforward. You just tried to take over the world by rolling dice better than the other players. There was some strategy involved—you needed to build up your armies by winning battles and keeping control of conquered territories—but there didn't seem to be much of a point. It was definitely a guy game.

The board depicted a distorted world map, divided into regions such as Japan, Afghanistan, Egypt, Ontario, and India. Some of the territories bore unfamiliar names like Irkutsk, Ukraine, or Ural, while others were saddled with dull labels like Eastern Australia, Western U.S., or North Africa. Right now the board was covered with colored plastic tokens that represented individual armies. Matt, with yellow, had conquered the entire continent of South America, parts of Africa and North America, and Japan. Lance, with green, was mired in South Africa, tottering on the brink of elimination, controlling only a few territories. Cody's blue armies had seized the continent of Australia in his first turn and by degrees gobbled up the lion's share of Asia, the most valuable possession on the board. The fourth player was Tory Johnson, whose white tokens were scattered thinly over most of Europe and North America.

On Matt's next turn, he redeemed three cards to earn twenty new armies, which he massed in the Western U.S. for a drive to occupy the North American continent.

"You don't have a prayer," Tory said. "There's too many countries to take." He tipped his bottle of Bud Light and drained it.

"Observe," Matt said, jiggling the dice.

"He's right, mate," Cody said. "You'd be smarter to put every army on West Africa and try to finish off Lance. Then you'd get his three cards, too."

"Shut up," Lance blurted, slapping Cody's chest. "He knows what he's doing."

"No he doesn't," Tory repeated.

"Observe," Matt said. "From Western U.S. to Alaska." Lance rolled three sixes in two battles, inflicting heavy casualties on Matt's invaders, but simple numbers finally prevailed, and Matt took the territory. Moving fifteen armies into Alaska, he swept eastward, capturing Alberta and Ontario before bogging down against Quebec.

"What's the French word for *stupid*?" Lance asked. "Erin, you take French, don't you?"

"It's *stupide*," she said. "Or *imbécile*."

"Matt, that was *imbécile*," Lance said. On his next turn he recaptured the whole northern tier of territories, and for good measure, spread across the Bering Strait into Asia and sacrificed several armies needlessly just to erase Matt from Japan.

"That was *imbécile* too," Erin said. "Why did you do that?"

"To teach him a lesson," Lance replied.

"You could have taken the rest of North America and taught him the same lesson and not lost so many armies," Erin protested. "*Imbécile*."

"That's right," Lance said. "Stand up for your man."

Tory got up.

"I thought Tyler was going to be here," he said. "He would have his hands full, broadcasting this."

Lance grunted.

"Want another beer, anybody? Erin?"

Everyone laughed, except Erin. She was the only one not drinking. Matt's parents were gone for the afternoon, so Cody had brought a twelve-pack of beer along with the game, which was set up on a ping-pong table in Matt's basement. A fluorescent light dangled drunkenly from unfinished ceiling joists over their heads. The walls were rough gray cinder blocks, the floor cold concrete, smooth, polished by socks and slippers over many winters, not a comfortable place, to Erin's thinking, yet infinitely preferable to home with Mom and Dad there. By the logic of her personal calculus, Matt's pressure represented the lesser of two evils.

That was something she hadn't thought of when she determined to break up with Matt.

Erin dipped her hand into the bowl of pretzels. In a conscientious effort at better time management, she had set aside a couple of hours that evening to work on her history paper. As the time approached, however, she searched for excuses to nullify her prior plan. She grew sick at the thought of actually writing the paper. Her research so far had only skimmed the surface. An administrator at Grandpa Dee's retirement home had lent her a few ancient textbooks and more recent articles, but she preferred visiting with Grandpa Dee and the old folks rather than reading about their care.

In the Risk game, Matt stared at the board, perplexed at what had become of the numerous armies he had deployed on his previous turn. He is a true gambler, Erin thought. He's not afraid to lose, but he doesn't think very well. She cupped her hand to her mouth, leaned toward him, and whispered advice.

"Yeah," he said. Then he announced to Tory that he would wipe him from the board once and for all.

"No way," Tory said. "You won't get through two countries."

Erin said, "That's not what I told you to do, Matt."

"I don't care," Matt said. "Let's get it over with."

"It" was "over with" after six rolls, Matt losing decisively.

Cody locked eyes with Erin and then said, "Are you okay, Matt?"

"Yeah. I'm just tired of this. Don't take it personally."

"You sure? You've been acting this way for days now."

"You guys go ahead and play. I want to go out. Just make sure if I'm not back that your beer bottles are all gone by 5:30. Gone, as in *off the property*. Come on, Erin."

His strong hand devoured her slim fingers and pulled her to her feet.

"Bye," she said over her shoulder to the other three.

"G'day, Erin," Cody called. "Take care of that bloke, okay?"

In the van, Matt said, "I want to show you something at school."

"At school? It's Saturday."

"I have a key. If we can get in the building, I have a key to the art room. Mrs. Knowles gave me one so I could work on my project if I wanted."

"What if we can't get in the building? It'll be a wasted trip."

"*We'll take our chances*," he sung off-key to the tune of the senior theme song.

Erin felt butterflies in her chest. Would it be best to give him the bad news now or at school? Wait, she decided. Wait till he takes you home.

A few miles later, Matt said, "How's your paper for McCauley?"

"Don't remind me. It's not coming along very well. I was going to work on it tonight, but I don't want to. I never do."

"Do you have a hundred dollars?"

"No. You mean *with* me?"

"No, I mean at home, or in the bank."

"Yeah. I have it."

"Cody will do your paper for a hundred bucks."

"Come on. I can't do that. Is he doing yours?"

"I thought about it. I have the money! But seriously, I'm having more fun doing my own paper. If I get in a jam, I can always go to Cody."

Matt's flippant attitude started anger bubbling in Erin's blood. She wanted to talk some sense into Matt's thick head, but whenever she thought about what to say, how to argue with him, she grew confused and then hopeless, knowing that he would answer her by saying, "Everybody does it"—which was all too true, and she had no reply to that. She couldn't tell him *why* he was wrong. She just knew that he *was*.

"I can't," she said.

"I'll *give* you the money."

"It's not the money, Matt."

"Okay. I'm just trying to save you some trouble. Do it your way. You know what's best for you."

I don't think I do, she thought ruefully. I wish I did.

By the time they reached the school, the sun, its color distorted to maroon by the line of clouds along the horizon, was slanting low in the west, sending long cold rays across the campus. The sky overhead, clear and pale blue, draped the landscape in bleakness. The grass was brown, the trees bare, the parking lot empty. A young boy in a red stocking cap and blue sweatshirt was shooting baskets at the goal on the playground, sending out reverberations of dribbles and clangs.

"We're the only ones here," Matt said. "But we can get in. I know where Bragley keeps a key." He guided her to a service door behind the athletic wing and found the key on top of a section of ductwork hugging the brick wall.

"It's weird with no one else here," Matt mentioned offhandedly in the corridor that led to the Fine Arts wing. "Everything echoes." Later, in a hallway near the Art Department, he went from locker to locker, testing them. About every fourth locker opened.

"Are you just going to leave them like that?" Erin asked.

"Why not?"

Again, she felt stymied.

"Don't worry," he said. "Bragley will shut them. Did Jess ever tell you about the time we stayed in the building all night?"

"You did *what*?"

"Really. We used the key to get in the building, and we taped the custodian's room door so it didn't lock when Bragley left, so we could get at all the keys."

Erin had heard rumors of such antics but never believed them.

"It was a Friday night," Matt went on. "Once we figured out the keys, we spent all night going wherever we wanted. Free ice cream bars! It was cool. You should see LaGrange and Myers's offices! We even hid in that media resource room, where they keep all the music and DVDs, while there was some kind of booster club meeting going on out in the library. They never had a clue!"

At the art room door, Matt made her close her eyes. She heard the key slide into the lock and soon smelled musty air. Inside, Matt led her along and said, "Keep your eyes closed until I get the light."

Through her eyelids she knew when he had found it.

"Wait!" he called. "Not yet! Okay, now you can look."

Erin's eyes opened to a sickening sight—a sinewy human form, made of clay, two feet tall, pasty white, suspended by a wire about its neck.

"This is your art project? Matt, this is ..."

Choked by revulsion, she started to complain—but a glance at his face overwhelmed her with pity.

"Oh," she said, punctured with understanding. "Oh, I see. It's Steve."

For the first time in their relationship she reached for him, stepped over and set her head on his shoulder. She almost began to weep, torn by her sorrow for him and her hatred for the way he was manipulating her. His huge hand rested on her hip, and she did not push it away, frozen by the thought that his powerful hands—which heaved concrete blocks twenty feet into the river at the Junction, pulled down 220-pound running backs by their jerseys, and once karate-chopped a watermelon in half to win a bet—had produced such a delicate work of sculpture.

The figure's head slumped forward, submitting to death. Every muscle was relaxed, almost peaceful. But the texture of the surface, ridged and raggedy, invested the work with an aura of anger.

"It's not quite done," Matt said. "I still have to put the final outside coat on. Dollar bills. A hundred and fifty one-dollar bills."

"Are you serious? Just because you have money to throw around …"

"That's not why," he said. A different tone settled into his voice, a tone of confidence, command, and control. "It's the right thing to do, cover it with money, with the money I owed him, because that's why Steve died."

"Matt, you've said that so many times. If you know that, why don't you tell somebody who can do something about it?"

"Like who? That bastard Myers controls everybody, Erin."

"It can't be that bad."

"I can't believe how naive you are. I'm telling you, Myers doesn't do favors for people. There's always a payment. Believe me. I know."

"You make it sound like organized crime or something."

"I'm not complaining. If he can get me into a good college that helps me in my career, it's worth paying for. There's nothing wrong with it. So I'm not complaining, except for Steve."

"This is too morbid for me," she said. "Can we please go?"

As she suspected, Matt wanted to visit the cemetery again. Darkness had fallen, and the temperature lingered in the twenty-degree range. They stood before Steve Gutierrez's tombstone, side by side, Matt bowing his head. Erin sneaked a sideways glance at him and wondered what he was thinking.

"It's hard to believe we all end up here, isn't it?" Matt said. "Just like in *Hamlet*, with the grave-digger and the skulls and all that. Let's go. It's getting too cold."

Back in the van, he started the engine, turned on the heater, and set the stereo volume on low.

"Come back here," he said, and his enormous bulk squeezed between the front seats into the back of the van, which he had recently carpeted.

"Why?" Erin asked, uneasy again.

"Erin, there's so much pressure. I just need to hold you. That's all."

"What pressure?" *He* was talking about pressure?

"I'm just so upset still about Steve. I thought I would get over it, but I can't. I have all this energy bottled up inside. Rage, and sadness."

The words of Mrs. Hillis came to her rescue.

"I'm sorry for how you feel, Matt. Really I am. Steve was your friend. I wish I could do something to make you feel better. But I don't want to do what you want to do."

He sighed.

"Erin, everybody does it. Why won't you?"

She didn't want to reason with him.

"I just don't want to."

"Don't you know how pretty you are?"

What was that? A different approach? As a matter of fact, she *did* know about her beauty—or rather, about what everyone else considered her beauty. Her thick lips, the lower one protruding a tad more than the upper. Her eager eyes, infinitesimally crossed. The freckles around her nose. The one crooked tooth making her smile distinctive. Once, showering after a P.E. class, another girl had complimented her long legs and asked why she didn't show them off more ...

"I don't want to," she insisted to Matt, aiming for firmness.

"Why not?"

"I don't know," she whined. "It's just too risky."

"No it's not," he pleaded.

She forced herself to avert his gaze by directing hers toward the floor of the van, littered with empty Pringles cans. She said, "Take me home now, please."

Pressure, pressure, pressure! The only reason she wanted to go home was to be away from him, yet the only reason she had come with him was to be away from home! After a few hours at home, Mom and Dad would become unbearable with their questions and hints and expectations. Why couldn't she just go live with Grandpa Dee? And why did they let you visit him only on certain days?

If only Matt would stop pressuring her!

Suspended from the van's rearview mirror were a pair of dice on a string, a new addition that Erin had not seen before. While she watched them sway, a sudden, off-the-wall inspiration pricked her.

"You like to take chances, don't you?" she asked.

"You know I do."

"Okay. I have a challenge." She couldn't believe what she was saying. "We'll play a game of Risk, just you and me. If I win, you have to stop pressuring me."

"Yeah, and what's in it for me?"

"If you win, then I will."

"Will *what*?"

"You know what."

"I want to hear you say it."

"Why?"

"I just want to hear it from your own mouth."

When she balked, he said, "That's what I thought. You're just ... teasing."

"No, I'm not. I'll promise."

"Are you kidding me? A game of Risk? You don't have a chance." He started laughing. "You're kidding, right?"

His arrogance inflamed her with the same spirit of competition that drove him day to day. She exclaimed, "You're not so good, Matt! I saw you screw up against Tory today. You should have attacked Lance, but you wouldn't listen to me."

"But I was ready to quit anyway. I wanted to be alone with you. When I play you, the stakes will be higher, and I won't goof around."

That was true, she admitted, her shoulders sagging with new dejection.

"Can we play tonight?" Matt asked.

"No way! You at least have to give me a few weeks to learn how to play!"

"Okay, that's fair. You name the time and place."

"How about the first week of school after Christmas?"

"That's more than a *few* weeks. I don't know if I can wait that long."

"You're sick."

"Just kidding."

Six weeks was plenty of time for her to escape him, she figured. If we break up today, he will be chasing someone new by then.

When they turned onto her street, however, the van crunched through a range of potholes, which set the dice bouncing and swaying above the dashboard. Watching them, Erin thought of Matt's art project and recalled the horrible real-life spectacle of Steve Gutierrez dangling dead from the flagpole and the counselors pounding home the message that students must be alert for warning signs in each other's behavior.

Clearly, Steve's death was bothering Matt deeply. His sculpture— nothing had touched her so profoundly since the waterspout. That sculpture was a peephole into Matt's troubled soul. She didn't know what she should do, but she knew that she could not abandon him.

Not tonight.

24

"OH, MY," ROBIN Hillis said. "And Christmas still two weeks off!"

"It will be even worse next week," said Jerri Roost.

The scene was the food court of the Bridgebury Mall, so overrun by hungry shoppers that dozens of customers were sitting on the floor amid their bags to gobble down greasy slices of pizza, scoop Chinese food from waxy cardboard cartons, and untwist steaming pretzels into salty segments. The crowded court and the equally crowded stores throughout the mall made up the pre-Christmas frenzy that retailers loved so dearly and shoppers cursed so severely, cursed even as they plunked down plastic cards and paper currency.

"Well, I'm glad you invited me, anyway," Robin went on. "I don't know when I would have gotten around to shopping."

She could not remember her last visit to the mall sprawling along the southeast edge of Bridgebury. Thanks to the reluctance of the growing college town to invest in its infrastructure, in particular to restoring the crumbling U.S. highway that encircled the two cities, reaching the mall from Brookstone meant a good half-hour drive. Once their children were gone, Zeb and Robin had less reason than ever to shop there, so gradually the mall fell between the cracks of the present and into their family history. Robin spent a moment in front of a fancy kiosk deciphering the color-coded map of the mall's layout. There were a dozen new stores with names she had not heard before! One of her students had recently written a paper about the rapid turnover of merchants in the mall and its impact on student employees. Lots of her students worked here.

"I don't know if it was a good idea to bring Mother," Jerri Roost said.

Lena Roost, licking her fingers after handing Philip a cinnamon roll slathered with white icing, said, "Don't worry, Mom. She'll be fine."

"She might be overwhelmed," Jerri suggested, then commented to Robin, "While we shop, she likes to sit on the benches and listen to people talk."

"And," Lena added playfully, "critique their pron*ounc*iations."

Jerri recounted a story from their last trip to the mall, when Jane had complained that a girl kept calling jewelry *jool-er-y*, mangling the poor word by clipping one syllable and adding another.

Five minutes later, Howard Roost and Grandma Jane came through the glass doors. Jane's rubber-tipped cane hardly seemed necessary, she moved so slowly. Kids were darting back and forth from the arcade to the popcorn outlet, so Robin understood Jerri's concern about Grandma's safety.

"Don't let me slow you down," Grandma said to the group when she arrived on Howard's arm. "Just find me a place to sit, and I'll be happy watching the world go by." Robin smiled at the sparkle of humor in the old woman's blind eyes.

Howard said, "I'll check on Grandma Jane every fifteen minutes. Let's all agree to meet back here at a certain time."

"How's six o'clock?"

Everyone agreed. Lena and Philip struck out toward the east branch of the mall, Howard said he would visit the bookstore first, and Jerri and Robin were left with Grandma Jane.

"Are you sure it's okay to leave you here?" Jerri asked once more.

"Just bring me a cookie," Jane answered. Her aged voice cracked— Robin marveled to think that it had spoken its first soft words when Teddy Roosevelt was president, carrying a stick bigger but not shinier than Grandma's aluminum cane.

By unconscious mutual consent, the women headed toward the west wing with its heavy concentration of clothing stores.

"I'm so glad you came," Jerri said. "I feel like we haven't visited in years."

"I know. I wish Zeb was home more." Hearing herself, she immediately wished she could retrieve the words. The last thing she wanted was to open the door to a conversation about her marriage or her ongoing inner turmoil, especially with Jerri.

"So how are things with him?"

She resented the question, the prying. Weeks before, she had cried on Jerri's shoulder and confessed that Zeb's absence was killing her. But her attitude had changed, shifting 180 degrees for a time, oscillating ever since with the ebb and flow of her conscience. Whenever Jerri had tried to follow up, Robin had talked as if things weren't really so bad. And now they truly weren't—because Brad was filling the emotional void left by Zeb. Her marriage was no one's business but hers.

"He's still gone too much," Robin said judiciously. "But I can live with it. After Christmas he'll either get his promotion or he won't. Either way, he'll be home."

Just how would she feel about that? Up to now she hadn't considered how tangled her life might become. Plainly, her relationship with Brad had passed the boundary where she might cut it off with no emotional fallout. Even if out of respect for her marriage she would not sleep with Brad, he still held sway over her affections, so much so that when Jerri had asked her to come shopping, her imagination had at once begun sifting through ideas about gifts for Brad. A tie? A pair of shoes? A set of mugs?

A fair-skinned employee was cleaning the glass over a display case, using way too much Windex, which made Robin think about that smudge on her classroom whiteboard that would not come off despite the array of cleansers she had tried. She still had not asked Bragley for help.

"Do you mind if I ask you a personal question?" asked Jerri.

Robin's frightened heart fluttered.

"That depends."

"There was a motorcycle at your house the other night."

That was no question, Robin thought.

"A motor—oh! That would have been Brad McCauley's. A part-time teacher at Brookstone." Did she need to explain further? "Dropping off some mail from school." How transparent!

"Oh. The postman."

What was *that* supposed to mean? Did she detect a flicker of suspicion in Jerri's sly smile?

Mercifully, the subject was dropped when they stepped into Julie's Casuals, where Jerri bought a sweater for Lena. In the next store, Thompson's, Jerri sorted through the bin of hats, saying, "I think Howard would look good in a hat. He's never worn one, but I think a hat would make him look distinguished."

Robin stifled a giggle. Sometimes Jerri seemed oblivious to how lucky a woman she was. Whatever he looked like, Howard Roost was the most respected man in Brookstone. His judgment held a premium value among the town's decision-makers when the time came for community political and business decisions. Even though he and Jerri had homeschooled their children through the lower grades, he was regarded as a bit of a public education expert. He was known for volunteering his time on community projects. Most of all, though, he had helped rescue numerous families from a gamut of social ills. Drugs, child abuse, emotional neglect, teen pregnancies—Howard had dealt with most modern-day problems. Sometimes they hit close to home: Philip had been born out of wedlock when Lena was only fifteen.

While Jerri compared hats, Robin went to the tie rack. She found a basic blue one with white polka dots that Brad would be able to wear with a number of different shirt-and-slacks combinations. There was a red one also that might be a versatile addition to his wardrobe. Then she spotted a tie that almost made her explode with laughter—it was covered with little clocks! Each one had a different time. What a personal statement that would make! It would be a great gift, though probably too loud for Brad.

"Find a good one?" Jerri's voice asked.

"Yes. I think this will look good on Zeb, don't you?" She held it up in the air to facilitate Jerri's judgment, as though an image of Zeb also floated there. At last she selected the blue-and-white one. When she bought it she asked for a box to take home.

Half an hour later they stopped for a snack at the Pizza Bar. As Jerri sipped a cherry Coke through a split straw that hissed, Robin's discomfort grew. Jerri's silence scared her. Suppose she had seen Brad's bike behind her house more than once? Thank God she couldn't see through drawn curtains, or around corners to the back door and porch.

"You know," Jerri said pensively, "the mall is for kids. Every time I come here I feel more out of place."

Santa Claus was taking orders and posing for pictures in front of a glittering fountain decorated with ersatz icicles and snow drifts. The line of children waiting to whisper their wishes into his cotton-covered ears wrapped around the display twice and tailed off toward the jewelry center.

Jerri went to check on her mother, and Robin used the opportunity to get away, promising to rendezvous again outside JCPenney.

Another idea came to her. She could give Brad a clock for Christmas! It was the last thing he needed, true, but it would be better than an article of clothing or dishes. A clock would tell him that she accepted who he was and what he believed, even if she disagreed with the latter.

She squeezed into a spot at the end of a crowded wooden bench to think it over, the arcade less than twenty feet away, flamboyant and loud with the ranting and raving of screaming kids disappearing into and emerging from its lurid, lighted vaults. Their noise plus the monotone of the bells nearly drove her insane.

Yes, the mall was a place for children, she thought. Jerri was right on target, about that.

She heard a chubby-faced, freckled boy wearing a backwards baseball cap describe to his buddy how to "trip" one machine so that it spat out unearned tickets, which could be redeemed for tokens. They discussed the procedure in straightforward, amoral terms, like adults talking about directions to a restaurant. Afterward, they rushed into the arcade to try the technique.

Robin shook her head. The kids were not even teenagers yet, too young to adore the opposite sex. Listening to them worshiping at the bright altars of the arcade, she winced under the embarrassment of a sharp insight—when she had made her vows at a different altar to love Zeb forever, Brad McCauley had been only ten years old.

Full of fussy kids and frustrated parents, the Santa Claus line crept forward with fitful lurches. An argument arose about someone cutting in line, and tempers didn't cool until a mall security worker helped settle the controversy. The alleged cutters, as far as Robin could tell, got to keep their place.

She tried to think about Zeb and what to get him. Even when they were communicating, he was hard to buy for. He never asked for anything particular, but, to his credit, he always seemed pleased with whatever surprises she set under the tree. Maybe that meant he was *easy* to buy for. But she found it impossible to think about him for long. While the fountain behind the Santa display rose and fell in its pleasant, programmed rhythm, Robin daydreamed about the splendid engineering fountain at Riverside University, a landmark where students flocked to study or socialize almost year-round. She imagined herself waiting to meet Brad, sitting among the sunbathing coeds in the grass, reading a paperback novel, her pants rolled up above her knees, her sandals kicked off, her eyes shaded by her orange sunglasses. A young man tapped her on the shoulder from behind—she had been mistaken for one of the twenty-year-olds. He apologized repeatedly and glided away on rollerblades....

Muted music floated into her ears. She opened her eyes to see a couple of teens, holding hands, fingers interlocked, floating past. They both had earphones around their heads, connected to music players hooked into their jeans, oblivious to the world. Should weather warning sirens began to scream, the kids would never know.

She fought to concentrate on Zeb. Even after buying a gift for Brad, her concentration kept returning to him. Every store yielded up new possibilities. MusicLand was hyping unabridged collections of various rock-and-roll artists—older stars like Elvis and the Rolling Stones and Rod Stewart as well as newcomers whose names were familiar to Robin through her life with students—and among the displays she found the complete works of Bruce Springsteen at the base of a life-size cardboard cutout of "the Boss." He had a strained, almost constipated smile (as though singing were a great pain that he wanted to hide), and he held his guitar low against his hip (as if it weighed fifty pounds). Robin recalled dimly a line from one of the songs on Brad's tape, something about a singer getting a guitar and learning how to make it talk.

In another store she found motorcycle equipment and accessories, including helmets, too expensive to buy, but she spent a moment looking at them. What mad variety. One helmet was white and sleek with a dark visor like the helmets worn by the Imperial Storm Troopers in *Star Wars*, the galaxy's finest soldiers, who even with their high-tech laser guns could not hit Luke Skywalker from ten feet away.

Brad was scheduled to attend a conference at the University of Chicago the second weekend in January, where he would present a paper (one chapter from his dissertation) to hundreds of fellow history scholars from across the country. He planned to drive up and room with another Ph.D. candidate in his department, a woman named Kelly who owned a car. The idea that they would share a hotel room alarmed Robin, although Brad acted as though that kind of arrangement was not unusual among contemporary graduate students. She didn't delve any deeper into their plans.

As she dallied in the aisles of a Buck Stops Here store, where every item cost less than a dollar, Robin began to form a humorous plan to assemble a care package for Brad's trip. Names began to run through her brain, and finally she chose one: *Super Scholar Survival Pak*. It would include a new razor and blades, a travel-size can of shaving cream, toothpaste and a brush, a Riverside coffee mug. Her imagination ranged freely across the fields of potential. She could include the tie, and use the clock as a Christmas gift. There ought to be a clipboard and paper pad and pen; after all, he was going as a researcher. For a gag she could include a pair of briefs, because he said he slept in the nude but he wouldn't have that luxury (she hoped) with this "Kelly." She should of course write an intimate message on the waistband of the briefs ... In a torrid spate of spending, she bought it all, everything she could think of.

Later she joined Lena and Philip when they appeared among a stream of shoppers heading to the north wing.

"Philip wants to go to The Athlete," Lena said. "He's into LeBron James. He wants a number 23 jersey."

"Philip, I thought you liked baseball," Robin remarked.

He looked at his mom.

"Well," Lena said. "Are you going to answer Mrs. Hillis?"

Call me Robin, she thought. You're not my student any longer, but you're still my neighbor.

"I like Kevin Durant, too," he explained.

Howard Roost joined them in The Athlete. Philip was standing before a display titled SUPERSTARS, awestruck, staring up at the photographs of famous athletes, past and present, from many sports.

Howard shook his head.

"These days everyone is a superstar," he said cantankerously.

"What's a superstar?" Philip asked.

"It's one of the best players. But when I was your age, there were only a couple of players we called superstars. Today everybody is called a superstar. What a shame." He pointed to a photo in the display. "See this guy? His batting average last year was about .225. How can he be a superstar?"

Philip said, "I don't know."

Howard laughed. Robin was wary of his philosophy of talking to young children as if they were adults. He and Jerri had achieved great success with homeschooling, academically at least. Their son Scotty was starting a business in Chicago. But what about Lena's teen pregnancy? Robin always wondered whether this reflected the major shortcoming of homeschooling, its inability to socially integrate kids. Lena's trouble had come when she entered public school.

"You know who the real superstars are, Philip?" Howard asked, his eyes shining keenly from their deep, winsome sockets.

The boy shook his head.

"It's people who love God with all their heart and soul and mind and strength. And little boys who love their Mom and Grandpa and Mrs. Hillis. Are you a superstar?"

A gap-toothed grin spread across Philip's face.

"I love Mom," he said. Howard patted him on the back and said, "So do I."

At Radio Shack, Robin pondered telephone answering machines. She feared spending too much money on a gift that might soon be obsolete. Their son Trevor had hinted that he would like to get one, yet he had also talked of shutting off his land line altogether to "go cellular." Trevor was easy to buy for: Whenever you asked him what he wanted for a birthday or for Christmas, he pulled out a list of things he needed. Robin decided to wait and talk to Trevor's wife, Katie, before buying him a gift.

As for Anyssa, well, the mall had nothing for her. She was waist-deep in her business studies. Everything in her life was oriented toward becoming a business director for a church or missionary organization, so the best Zeb and Robin could do was support her single-mindedness. Zeb had suggested they simply give her a big gift certificate to the school's bookstore, and Robin had not thought of anything more suitable.

Around 5:30 Robin sat down on a bench near JCPenney to wait for Jerri. During their two hours apart, Robin's wavering heart had softened toward her friend, recognizing that her irritation at Jerri's undue curiosity sprang not from any genuine injustice but from her own envy—envy for Jerri. Howard was always there for Jerri, she reasoned, so how could she understand my problems?

Next to the Penney store was a First Fidelity Bank branch, closed since three o'clock, protected by a metal fence extending from ceiling to floor. There was an automated teller machine outside, though, and every few minutes someone stopped to remove cash. Robin wondered how much money they put in the machines.

Jerri returned and sat down.

"My feet are killing me," she said. "I should have worn tennis shoes like you."

She rustled through her plastic bags and pulled out a box.

"Look, I found Howard a hat."

Robin nodded listlessly.

She really *was* jealous of her neighbor! It truly bothered her that Howard was here and Zeb was off in Chicago. She wanted her husband to shop with her, clean the house with her, watch TV with her, eat with her, and sleep with her. Why should she have to give it up? Worst of all, why should she have to give it up and then have her neighbor flaunt her misfortune in her face?

But her conscience refused to give ground against every assault from her selfish soul. Some of her reasons or excuses were silly, some simply sorry, none of them serious. As much as she resented Jerri's interference, she knew in her heart that whenever she was near Jerri, she saw her own predicament more clearly. And who could say? Maybe her jealousy of Jerri and Howard ought to prod her toward fighting all the harder for Zeb and her marriage rather than surrendering lamely to the passion of the moment and chasing after Brad McCauley. Maybe. She knew what she ought to do, yet the choice was hers. She threw up a feeble prayer, asking for a sign, all the while knowing that she needed no sign—she just needed to choose.

On their way back to the pre-arranged meeting place, Jerri said, "Robin, maybe you don't think it's my place to intrude. But if you're having trouble with Zeb, you know Howard and I will do all we can to help."

"Thanks, Jerri. But I really think you're blowing it all out of proportion."

Why had she said that? Why had she so cavalierly tossed out that pronoun *it*, as if to suggest that there was something to *it* after all! She had stumbled right into the trap!

They walked along in silence.

Then Jerri said gently, "That motorcycle was there a long time."

Robin sighed inwardly.

"He's a colleague and a good friend, Jerri. You don't expect me to not even invite him in, do you?"

"It doesn't matter what *I* expect, does it?"

"No, you're absolutely right," Robin answered curtly. Then she wondered whether she had even understood Jerri's question. "For God's sake, Jerri, you're making me feel like a ... like a *slut*. There's nothing romantic between us. Nothing sexual. And I'll make sure there never is."

"Robin, be careful," Jerri pleaded softly. "It's adultery long before it's ever sexual."

25

YOU BECOME THE same kind of person as the god you worship, or so claimed a campus ministry speaker that J. Bradford McCauley overheard one sunny day at the Engineering Mall his first year at Riverside. The crispness of the philosophy stuck with him. The message was neat and clean. There were no loose ends.

On a brisk, high-skied afternoon in mid-December, remarkable for the pungent smell of late-burning leaves in the air, he kick-started his motorcycle, its engine heating up as he thrust his fingers further into his gloves. Just three weeks earlier the temperatures had soared magnificently into the seventies in what seemed like a natural benediction on his budding liaison with Robin Hillis. The pendulum of the Universal Clock was sweeping him through a period of pleasure, at least on that interpersonal level, and he had greeted the change with open arms—three weeks earlier.

For the past three days, the pendulum was reversing direction, perhaps. Who could tell? Clocks, watches, all timepieces were complicated machines inside, behind the deceptively simple outward face with its two or three friendly hands and the manageable mathematics of twelve numbers in a circle. Regardless of the pendulum or the clock, Robin was changing directions, or changing speeds, if he was reading her moods accurately. Nothing had happened after that Thanksgiving afternoon-turned-evening with its promising good-night. She had not used her key to his apartment; neither had she explained why not. At school, she did not avoid him but did seem hesitant, guarded. Why? Every time he replayed that glorious day in the cinema of his mind, the only scene of conflict he could recall was her usual playful annoyance with his philosophy.

Even as the motorcycle engine warmed, however, he suspected that something more serious might be coming between them. Twice, on the verge of their spending a night together, she had stopped short and backed away, apologetically but abruptly, as if remembering at the last possible moment that she was supposed to be elsewhere, that she had a prior commitment. That was how he interpreted her change of mind.

She was concealing something from him.

And the knowledge that he was concealing important parts of his life from Robin undercut his hope, too. He longed to tell her about the awful "incident" that had crowned with agony his single year of teaching high school in Ohio. If just one person believed in his innocence, that encouragement would pulverize the huge obstacle that had kept him from flourishing. The truth was, he had never propositioned Mary Ann Childress, no matter what she and her parents and the settlement document legally maintained. He had been a coward—and fool—to give in.

The sun's weak winter rays gathered comfortably behind his helmet visor, though as soon as he accelerated on the roads the chilly air creeping around his face would chase that warmth away.

Of course, there was another secret that Robin seemed destined to know. The last time she had come to his apartment, he had allowed her to skim through some dissertation documents on his computer. Looking at the folder contents, she had asked about a locked file whose name was BM.

"It must be a personal file," she said. "BM for your initials, right?"

"Right," he lied, thankful for the ironic coincidence. In fact, whenever he made a payment to Travis or sent him a note regarding their *blackmail* transactions, he kept a record, a written record in his safe that he duplicated electronically in the password-protected file. Robin's snooping ended with her question. But McCauley wondered, was the Universal Clock bringing him and Robin together for this secret to be revealed? Just as he yearned to take someone into his confidence regarding the Childress fiasco, he felt he must tell someone else about his entanglement with Travis. Should he regard Robin's appearance in his life as God's provision—or providence, as the Founding Fathers called it?

Perhaps, perhaps. Trying to pry the inscrutable secrets of the divine logic from the give and take of daily living was like trying to track and eliminate a mole from a garden, futile unless the mole made a mistake, or gave in.

And even if he was right about his relationship with Robin, what could he say about the latest twist, the latest secret he was guarding? As the quarter had progressed at Brookstone High School, Tolan Myers had tightened the screws on him. When he refused to change Tory Johnson's grade, Myers raised it anyway. When he complained, Myers and LaGrange offered to pay him to not raise a ruckus and to cooperate with them in the future. They seemed surprised at his fastidious adherence to a code of academic ethics. And therein lay the supreme irony—or his greatest hypocrisy—that he, J. Bradford McCauley, would so tenaciously defend integrity on one battleground but so ruthlessly stomp it to death on another. His own inconsistency halfway convinced him that the Universal Clock had a sense of humor.

With the cold gravel of the apartment parking lot crunching under his tires, he roared onto Highway 53 to meet Robin at Dairy Queen. His god was a hidden god, McCauley thought, and now he was a man hiding many things. Yet he longed for freedom and openness, for unstrained and unsuspecting relationships with people, for trust and understanding and acceptance. Did that mean God wanted something different, too? Was it fair to talk of God inductively?

No, that was not fair. He could be sure of himself but not of God. What he was sure of was how small his world had become. Only in the arena of scholarship did he feel alive and confident, but even there his own stupidity and the blind chance of Gregory Travis's discovery were marring his luster. His attraction for Robin kept growing, however, so maybe she would be his path to … to what? He was heading somewhere, but where? If not into the luminous sphere of academic superstardom, then where?

Mulling over his secrets, longing to lighten his burdens, he decided on a conservative course of action. When he met Robin today, rather than spilling everything, he would start with the simplest secret, the least harmful and the closest to home for her. He would tell her everything about Myers and LaGrange. Then, if she supported him on that point, he might crack open the door to the darker history he was hiding.

Highway 53 was virtually empty, so he gunned his machine to 65, 70, and 75 miles per hour. The only state cop he had ever seen on this stretch of road had been parked at Hap's Corner shooting the breeze with farmers during planting season. Flat fields spread out on either side of him today, fields that a few months before had been green with corn and soybeans in flashing rows stretching to horizons east and west. For an exhilarating moment McCauley felt eighteen years old again, standing tall on the border of boundless promise. Snatches of magical Springsteen lyrics fired his blood with triumph, lyrics about roads taking him wherever he wanted and wheels turning into wings and flying him to a promised land of reputation and maybe even romance ... Whenever he thought about such adrenaline-crazed lyrics now, he interpreted them in terms of himself and Robin. The pedestal of scholarly fame would be cold and lonely if he had no one to share it with.

When he reached the flat cylinders of the Amoco terminal south of Brookstone, painted brilliant white by the late-day sun, McCauley slowed his bike to the legal speed limit. A truck was dumping a load of crushed stone in a long driveway off the highway, and in one of the spacious backyards nearby, several kids were playing football, their breaths rapid and steamy. A gray-and-white cat sniffing at debris in a culvert looked up alertly as McCauley thundered past.

From a hundred yards away he saw the gibberish on the Dairy Queen sign:

F Z

O   A   IE

56   3

At some point in the remote past, those letters and numbers had formed part of an intelligible message that he often tried to reconstruct. The **F** and **Z** made him think of FROZEN, but his detective work always got mired in the mud of vowels on the second line. The sign had not changed since the first day he noticed it at the beginning of the fall quarter.

Going through the door of Dairy Queen, he came upon another situation all too typical of the restaurant. A teenage boy, probably a Brookstone student, was crouching inside the cramped vestibule, dabbing at a pool of spilled chocolate milkshake with a small napkin. In his other hand was a stack of perhaps fifty more napkins. Another boy was standing over him.

"Okay, don't help then," the first boy said.

"Why don't you just ask them for their mop?"

"They gave me the *napkins*, that's why!"

"Don't they *have* a mop?"

"How do *I* know?"

"Every store has a mop. Just ask. Besides, it's their job to clean up if somebody spills."

"Are you gonna help me or not?"

"Here. I'll throw away the wet ones."

"Thanks a lot."

"It's a good thing it was free, huh? Can you get another one? If you ask Kyle?"

"How do *I* know?"

Brad excused himself and stepped over the spill.

He went straight to the counter and asked, "Do you have a mop? There's a spill over by the door."

"I know," said the girl, DORIE according to her badge. "But they almost have it all clean now."

Kyle came around the corner shaking his head. He called to the boys sarcastically, "Good job, Jeremy. Real good job."

Jeremy looked up with an expression that said Kyle could finish the cleanup himself.

His perceived civic obligation met, McCauley turned around to see whether Robin had already arrived and was waiting for him.

He saw her from behind—her short blond hair above the fluffy white collar of a blue coat—but she was not alone.

Seated across from her, nodding with evident interest, his attention fixed on her hidden face, his brow crinkled gravely, was her husband.

Zeb.

McCauley's heart plunged into the pit of his hungry stomach. His first thought was that the portrait above the Hillis fireplace pictured the man perfectly. He was fair-skinned, rather short—did small people always marry each other?—with light auburn hair, thinning on top. Reflexively, McCauley compared himself to Zeb, and hair emerged as one area where he was clearly superior. Where was Zeb's briefcase? But there was no briefcase. Zeb did not appear to be in any hurry whatsoever. His gray overcoat was drooped casually over the back of his seat.

Hearing Kyle ask for his order, McCauley glanced at the menu board and blurted out the first item he saw under the red banner that proclaimed: PROUDLY OPERATED BY THE FINEST STUDENTS OF BROOKSTONE HIGH SCHOOL.

"Foot-long hot dog and ice water."

"You want anything on the hot dog?"

"Whatever is regular."

"Stay or go?"

"Go," he said with no hesitation.

Considering all they had to do was steam the hot dog and stuff it inside a bun, the kids took forever to prepare his order. McCauley felt embarrassed, almost ashamed, witnessing their ineptness; still, he didn't dare turn toward the dining area. Robin did not expect Zeb to be home—or did she? He racked his memory to recall whether she had said anything at school that day. Maybe this was her way of telling Brad to leave her alone. Or maybe she couldn't get away from Zeb, and this was the best way she could let Brad know she hadn't forgotten him. If only she had sat facing the door, he might have been able to search her face for an answer, an averted glance, a twitch of a smile, a subtle nod in his direction, anything.

Rather than wait, he made a trip to the restroom, excusing himself past the kids still sopping up their milky mess. When he came out, Zeb himself was stepping over the shrinking puddle of chocolate. Two steps later, he stopped to wipe milkshake off the bottom of his wingtip shoe. McCauley saw him shaking his head, so he said, "Can you believe this place?"

"Oh, it's all right," Zeb said languidly. "Everybody screws up."

The word choice made McCauley cringe. You should know, he thought accusingly. But he also remembered Mary Ann Childress, his own worst screw-up.

"In this place, it's a way of life," McCauley offered, empowered by anonymity. Zeb did not know who he was.

"They're young," Zeb said. "They'll do better someday."

Outside, McCauley sat on his bike and took two bites of the hot dog. Suddenly, his hunger was as far away as … Robin. He dumped the food and the drink in the nearest trash bin, started his motorcycle, settled the helmet over his head, and edged along the windows where Robin and Zeb sat. Then he revved the engine twice to draw her attention and let her know that he had come. Without looking in, he sped away. *Bye, bye, Birdie,* he thought.

A freight train was rumbling through town, so McCauley stopped behind a line of vehicles, the crossing bell clanging like clock chimes. He counted one, two, three, up to twelve, but the clanging continued, to twenty, to fifty, forever. He breathed in deeply and let out the air slowly, between pursed lips, fogging up his visor. His eyes were distracted by the flash of a woman's earring in the driver's mirror of the blue Skylark in front of him. Up and down it bobbed as she chattered or perhaps bounced her head to music. McCauley followed the line of her jaw in the mirror until his eye came to rest on the smooth pale skin of her cheek.

A knot formed in his stomach, a knot too tight for any acceleration in the southbound lane of the highway to untie. He missed Robin's arms around his stomach. The depth of his attachment to her was unmistakable now. There might be plenty of doubt about what would happen between them next, but there was no doubt about how he felt at this moment, no matter how much he tried to tell himself that the relationship had not progressed beyond the "casual" stage.

Hours later, he tried to focus on his computer screen, but its text failed to elicit one iota of his interest. From Jefferson and Locke his thoughts kept flying to Robin—in nice weather she walked to school, wearing tennis shoes and white socks over her stockings, carrying her dress shoes in a paper sack or her purse. The longer he sat before his monitor, unproductive, the further into his affections stepped Robin's small white-shod feet. He imagined those pretty shoes striding confidently along the sidewalk, balancing like a child on a rail, hopping spunkily up stairs, tiptoeing to reach something on a high shelf. At Dairy Queen she had been physically unapproachable. Now he could not separate his heart from her images.

He stretched, wincing at pains in his knees and shoulders, the ticking of the clock next to his computer growing louder, mocking him. His body was deteriorating, "wasting away" as the trinket in Robin's kitchen phrased it. He had told her it described him perfectly, yet he also had taken solace in words from a motorcycling song he loved, words contrasting the assault of the outside world with the serene safety of romance and passion felt inside—words whose harsh opposition had eluded him before seeing the Bible verse so quaintly wrenched out of context and turned into a bauble to hang in a window. Oh, he was certainly wasting away.

Tick-tock. He had deadlines. His dissertation might sit for weeks with no ill effects, but nearly fifty high school research papers were screaming for his attention. Maybe they would take his mind off Robin. Switching off the computer screen, he moved to the couch with a thick manila folder of papers. His red pen would not write, so he spent a few minutes looking for another. Then he turned the thermostat up a couple of degrees and made himself a double cup of microwave hot cocoa.

At last he felt ready to begin.

The first paper he pulled from the folder was titled "Leather and Lace: A History of Football Strings" by Matt Rademacher.

26

WAITING FOR GRANDPA Dee on the bare brown bank above Lake Pritchard, the ground cold and hard through her sweatpants, Erin Delaney followed the lazy progress of the bright white *Madam Harrison* as it floated along, engines barely audible, running year-round now, evidently. Some years the Brookstone High School graduating class held its Senior Party on that boat. She lay back and studied the clouds overhead. For some reason they made her think about God, clouds did, clouds and wind and nothing else, really. Maybe because they seemed so far away, so far above her, so uninterested in her life.

She was just not sure about God.

Mrs. Hillis, on the other hand, was showing great interest in her life, an interest both refreshing and threatening. Refreshing because it compensated for her parents' indifference to her feelings about her present and her immediate future, threatening because it emphasized her weak connections to her own flesh and blood, connections that ought to be stronger, sacred. Out of the blue two days earlier, Mrs. Hillis had returned those journal entries from way back in August, the ones where you had to give your senior-year goals, and now she added insult to that late-summer injury by forcing all her seniors to *review* their goals and *assess* their progress toward them. What torture! As if Erin had not already been beating herself up for her failure to grow a spine, take the reins to her life in her own hands, and put her parents and siblings and cousin and boyfriend in their proper places! She was practically addicted to stabbing herself daily with self-incrimination; now her English teacher had come along, grasped the handle, and twisted the knife even deeper. All Erin could do on this new paper was to admit, in a fit of honesty, that she was just as far away from taking control of her life today, a few weeks before Christmas, as she had been during those sweltering days of the new school year. Dashing off the truth so quickly and violently actually made her feel better. The very next day Mrs. Hillis had returned the assignment, unscored but bearing a comment—the last thing she expected—"Don't sell yourself short! Don't cheat yourself! From what I can see, you are marching marvelously toward your senior-year finish line." In purple ink, in Mrs. Hillis's trademark slanted penmanship. With *marvelously* underlined, plus a squiggly-lined arrow at the bottom of the page, indicating there was more on the back, where Erin found the following: "Haven't you ever heard that 'the heart is deceitful above all things'? Maybe you just can't see the truth with your own pretty eyes." Some obscure quote, the kind English teachers were always springing on you. As if Erin would know where it came from. Probably Shakespeare, or Dickens, or Dickinson.

Well, even if she couldn't see what Mrs. Hillis claimed to see, Erin still felt encouraged. Especially by the *marvelously*. The *marching*, though, made her think of herself as a soldier just taking orders from somebody else.

Across the lake rose the white skeleton and undulating loops of the tallest roller coaster of Pritchard Park, closed for the winter. The line of the roller coaster's top curves was gentle but pronounced, like the margin of the brittle white oak leaf she was twirling in her hand. Two summers ago she and Nathan Dyer had spent countless evenings at the park and shared hundreds of trips on that two-minute, fifty-cent ride. He had lost so many hats! Now, staring at the roller coaster, she saw in it the perfect emblem of her emotions.

In the days after proposing her bold wager with Matt, she had almost forgotten his pressure. Buying time was all she needed to do: She had no intention of carrying through with her promise. In fact, she doubted she would even play the game of Risk against him, although it might be fun to try to beat him. In his company now she felt almost buoyant, and she noticed a new attitude toward her from Matt's friends, which made her wonder whether he had told them about their bet and it had somehow, in the alien logic of boys, boosted her stature in their eyes.

However, on the heels of her peace with Matt, a discouraging counterbalance had fallen. Two nights later Dad had cornered her about college. She wanted to put off that discussion until spring, but he came to her room to confirm that she had filled out materials for several schools, including his beloved favorite, Princeton.

"We received this in the mail today," he explained, holding up a form from the admissions office, with a checklist of documents not yet submitted. One check mark was next to a financial aid form—"Don't bother about that one," he said—and the other was on a transcripts request.

"Mr. Myers sent that in last week," Erin said. "They just haven't got it yet."

"Okay, good. Now the letter says your admission is contingent on your grades for this year. Are you keeping your 3.5?"

Her heart leapt in fear.

"So far," she said. Even that tiny hedged answer was an outright lie, for she knew that the history paper she had turned in a week late would earn her at best a C in Mr. McCauley's class, more likely a D. There were days when such a prospect would have appalled her. One of the Delaney sisters getting a D? But the whole game of high school grades and college admissions had wearied her to the point where she just didn't care anymore.

"That's my girl," her father said. "I had a talk with Tolan Myers a few days ago. He said you were having a little trouble with a project in a history class. How's that coming?"

"I already handed it in."

"Good, good. I volunteered to call your teacher and talk with him, and Myers gave me his number, but I was too busy to call until yesterday."

Oh, no, Erin thought. That means he knows my paper was late. She braced herself for an axe to fall, but her father said, "Mr. McCauley, is that his name?"

She nodded.

"He sounded kind of defensive. He's one of those part-timers, isn't he?"

"Yes."

"I could tell he was afraid from his voice. As a doctor you get used to hearing people who are afraid. Maybe he's not used to hearing from parents. Anyway, he said you do a good job of participating in class discussions but you missed your deadline on the project. I asked him how I could help, and he said there wasn't anything I could do—he said you would have to earn your grade just the same as everyone else. He said you could do extra credit work if we weren't happy with your grade."

Erin wondered why her dad had said *we* instead of *you*.

"Most of the course grade comes from that paper," she explained. "I won't know what I got on it until after vacation." How adept she had grown at pushing pain back on the calendar! January now waited with two days of doom—the Risk game with Matt and the return of her history paper. It would not be a happy new year.

Erin decided this was as good a time as any to raise her objections to her whole life being scripted with next to no input from her.

"Dad," she began, "we need to talk more about college."

"Okay. Anytime you want."

"Would right now be okay?"

"You don't sound too enthusiastic right now."

"I'm not, Dad." She hemmed and hawed. "What if I told you I don't want to go to Princeton?"

"Oh. I see. Well, I've been assuming ... but any of the schools we've applied to are fine with me and your mom. You can choose. They're all excellent schools."

"But what if I wanted to go to some other school that I—we—haven't applied to?"

"What school did you have in mind?" A sternness invaded his tone, but there was no sense in her hiding the truth.

"What's wrong with Riverside?"

"*Riverside?* Riverside. You can't be serious, Erin. With your academic record, you're qualified to go to practically any school in the United States. Why would you choose Riverside? And for pre-med ..."

To mention Nate would earn a swift veto. So she said, "Because I've been thinking that my real interest is not medicine or biology but forestry, and Riverside has a great program."

"That's true, it does," her father said. She exulted—he was impressed that she had thought it through and done some research. "But let me do some checking. There are bound to be better programs. I'll find them."

He started to go, but she said, "Wait, Dad. There's something else."

"Yes?"

"About my grades. They may not be so good this semester. I think I might have really messed up that history project."

"Erin, don't give me that!" he thundered. "You do whatever you have to do to keep your grades up. I don't want you to blow it when you're this close to what for almost any eighteen-year-old girl in the country is a dream come true. Do you understand?"

"Yes, but—"

"But what?"

"It's too late now. The semester's over. It will just depend on how the teacher grades me."

"No! You still have a week! You contact him and arrange to do extra credit, whatever it takes, whatever he says."

"But it's too late." Mr. McCauley had reviewed his extra-credit policy. The best you could do was raise your grade one letter.

"Don't be silly, Erin. It's never too late. You've got nearly a whole month before grades actually come out, right? I don't have his number anymore, but do you know how to get hold of Mr. McCauley?"

"I suppose so."

"Then do it. Understand?"

"Yes, sir."

Again he started to leave her room but lingered at the door.

"We'll leave Riverside on the back burner for now. I'll find the best forestry program in the country. You just concentrate on keeping your grades high enough for Princeton. If you do that, then you'll be able to get in wherever we finally decide."

Wherever *we* decide, Erin thought glumly. She would be happy if even *that* were accurate, but it was not. Wherever *Dad* decided would be more like it.

Her discomfort under her own roof heightened when both her sisters came home to Orange Stone two weeks early for extended Christmas visits. Almost at once her father began bragging at the dinner table about the bright future of the "third Delaney," as he called Erin. He dropped every university name that he had discussed with her—Stanford, Berkeley, Harvard, Duke, and about ten more—but his emphasis mostly fell on Princeton, which delighted Sarah, who promised that she could fix up Erin with the best advisers, point her to the best housing, and warn her about which teachers and frat houses to avoid. You would think Sarah was still a high school sophomore, Erin thought. Wouldn't she ever grow up?

Convinced that nothing on God's green earth could persuade her to go to Princeton, Erin dreaded the imminent, ultimate confrontation with her parents over the issue. At least now her father had an inkling of her thinking. Even Patti and Sarah were pestering her about her plans. She didn't have the courage to tell them she would be most happy to study something as bland as forestry at a school as boring as Riverside.

One terrible possibility might still loom in her future. What if, when she finally made it clear to Mom and Dad that she had set her sights lower than they had, they absolutely refused to honor her wishes? Would she be able to afford to go to Riverside without their help? Probably not—she had no job, and every year the university fees and tuition went up about five percent. Grandpa Dee might help her, but going to him would strain the family relationships even more.

She couldn't do anything to hurt him.

So on this Saturday morning, partly to escape studying for her final exams just three days off, she had helped him rake the few late-falling leaves scattered across his tiny backyard and clumped in the corner of the fence. She had discovered and preserved two pretty oak leaves to press and mount in her scrapbook. Now, as she sat with her arms wrapped around her knees, she wondered where all the leaves were that had fallen on the hillside. Who raked or blew them all away? The landscape was dead but immaculate.

"Aw, the city does it," Grandpa Dee explained when he joined her for a walk around the lake. "They come out here with these gigantic trucks that vacuum up all the leaves. They rake 'em and blow 'em into piles first. They can do a whole area like this in one afternoon."

She smiled at his quaint awe of technology that she regarded as commonplace. Mr. McCauley sometimes spoke about the speed of modern changes leaving older people behind. Grandpa Dee was a case in point.

Erin also realized why her history project had floundered in the preliminary stages, forcing her to whip up a hurried, mediocre effort during the last week of school. Every time she had come to visit Grandpa Dee, she had intended to also talk to the administrators and slowly put together her paper. But once she arrived, her grandfather's personality always carried her away. It was just too interesting and too much fun to stay with him, talking or playing dominoes or watching stupid TV shows. He was a fountain of fascinating, fun-to-hear memories about old cars and farming and fishing and one-room schoolhouses and the towns around the lake. Her project was stale compared to his fresh stories and dynamic vitality. Whatever she wrote would seem insignificant, unjust.

"So how's that rich boyfriend?" he asked.

"Who, Matt?"

"The rich fella?"

"You mean Matt."

"The fella who won fifty million bucks."

"Fifty *thousand*."

"Yeah, Matt. Has he spent it all on you yet?"

"No. He bought a van, that's all."

"A van? Is it a nice van?"

"It's used. He's fixing it up."

"He gonna ask you to marry him?"

"*Marry* me? I don't think so."

"Bake him a cherry pie. That's what got me."

"Grandma Dee's pie is what made you marry her?" She remembered those delicious fruit pies from her girlhood.

"Pie had a lot to do with it."

"It's a lot different now, Grandpa." She tried to be gentle. "Boys look for other things in girls."

"Like how well they turn letters?"

"That's the idea. What time is Vanna on tonight?"

"We already missed her."

"I'm sorry. You should have said something."

"Aw, I don't mind. I spent ninety years without her; I can spend a day without her."

"I think I'm going to break up with Matt," Erin said. She wanted to get someone's reaction.

"Yeah. Fifty grand isn't enough."

"Not that!" She playfully slapped him on the arm, and he faked as though he were reeling from the blow.

"There's just too much pressure with him."

"You do whatever you think's best. You always said you liked Nathan better anyway. Where's *he* at these days?"

"Right now he's in Florida with his aunt. He's going to college at Riverside, though."

"You ought to pick up the phone and call him and tell him he's letting the best thing in his life get away."

"I could never do that. I haven't talked to him since summer."

"You know his number in Florida?"

"Why?"

"Let's call him. You can do all the talking."

"But it would cost too much."

"So what? Your mom and dad pay the phone bill."

"But they wouldn't want me to call him."

"I'll call, you just talk. They'll never know. If they ask questions, I'll say I was calling my girlfriend on one of those 900 numbers."

She and Nate talked for almost ninety minutes. Grandpa Dee watched reruns of cop shows in the living room, and Erin curled up with her back to a door and caught up with Nate—his semester, his classes, his teachers, his roommate, dorm food, parties. He knew that she had been going out with Matt.

"How'd you know?"

"Jess called me and told me."

"She *called* you? She never told me. I don't like Matt, but I sort of got pushed into it."

"That's the great thing about college. You really are on your own. Nobody can push you into anything. But that means you can't blame anything on anybody else, either."

She asked if he had a girlfriend and shut her eyes anticipating his answer.

"Not really. I've gone out a few times, but none of the girls I've met are my type. Know what I mean?"

"Well, if you weren't so picky," she joked. For an instant she felt happier than at any time since they had split up. But his next words put an end to that short-lived elation: "I guess I'm finding out I don't have to have a girl around to be happy. No offense."

She kept trying to tell him, indirectly, that she didn't like Matt and that she missed him. They had not talked in so long—did he understand what she was trying to say?

"I might come to Riverside next year," she said at last. "Mom and Dad are against it, but it's where I want to go."

"Instead of Princeton?"

"Princeton? How do you know about Princeton? Jess?"

"She said your Dad was going to get you into Princeton."

"I couldn't stand to be so far away. I know we're going to have a big argument when I tell them I won't go there."

"You just keep disappointing them. First it was me; now it's college."

"They didn't *hate* you. They just, just …"

"Hated me."

"Yeah, hated you." They laughed.

"*I* didn't," Erin said, and shut her eyes again. "Do you ever miss me?"

"Sure. Sometimes."

"Like when?"

"I don't know. Sometimes."

On the whole it wound up a disheartening talk, Nathan not giving her even a wisp of the encouragement she longed to hear, she too afraid to explicitly ask for it. She felt too vulnerable. What if he said they had no future? What would she do? It was better to keep hope alive, at least.

And yet, after she hung up and rejoined Grandpa Dee for the end of his TV show, regret gnawed at her soul. Regret for not being more direct, regret for procrastinating on her research paper and precipitating even more conflict with Dad, regret for being so scared of saying what she really believed and doing what she really wanted.

That night after dinner, Sarah nudged her in the hallway and said, "Are you and Matt doing anything tonight?"

"No."

"Come to my room, then. I haven't talked to you in ages."

Everyone except Dad went to bed during or after the late television news, at which time the sisters retreated to Sarah's room. Erin hadn't set foot inside it for months, and when she collapsed into a bean-bag chair, she realized why: There were too many reminders of her inferiority. The walls were decked with awards, certificates, prizes, and letters of commendation. A string of sixteen blue ribbons looped beneath a bookshelf, representing Sarah's sixteen consecutive quarters on Brookstone's all-A honor roll. There were letters from four jealous university presidents and one governor congratulating her on her academic accomplishments. There were awards for CUPP achievements and for scholarship essays. There were photos of her with other Indiana valedictorians.

Truly, Sarah's success made Erin's adequacy seem pitiful.

As Erin expected, the purpose for Sarah's invitation was twofold. First, she wanted to get her reading on Douglas Kraftmeyer, Patti's boyfriend.

"I wish he'd relax," Erin said. In the hour or so that she had been in his presence, he seemed uptight.

"I know why he's nervous," said Sarah. "Don't you?"

"Yeah. It's his first time meeting Mom and Dad."

Sarah shook her head with animation.

"That's not all. I just know he's going to propose to Patti. She thinks so too. I talked to her for four hours last night!"

Soon Erin learned why Sarah was so thrilled by the prospect of Patti's marriage. Douglas was a stock broker, so Sarah was seeing a dollar sign on the end of his name. No wonder he had said, "Please don't call me Doug."

"Did you know Matt won $50,000?" Erin asked.

"Douglas will make ten times as much every year," Sarah said.

Then she directed the conversation toward her own boyfriend, George the painter. Curious George, Erin liked to think of him, certain he must have been peeping at Sarah when she discovered him painting—*panting*, more likely—outside the apartment window, hanging onto the ladder like a monkey.

"If you come to Princeton, we'll find you an apartment that needs painting," Sarah said. Always *we*. *We* this and *we* that.

Sarah then set sail on a monotonous tale of everything she and George had done since Thanksgiving. Erin nodded occasionally as her mind wandered around the room. Her eyes kept returning to the beacon of the sixteen honor-roll ribbons. Finally, as Sarah returned to the harbor of the here and now, Erin asked, "In high school, did you ever cheat?"

"Who doesn't?"

"Did you have to?"

"Probably not. But everybody else was, and you couldn't take a chance that they'd cheat their way past you."

"You used to do homework for people, didn't you?"

"You mean I *tutored* them," Sarah corrected her. And suddenly the curtains over one of the dark mysteries of Erin's high school career parted. She had always wondered about the flyers stuck into the locker door vents and stapled to bulletin boards offering personal tutoring to underclassmen from juniors and seniors on the honor roll. She had never availed herself of the help because she never needed it. Now she knew the truth.

"Did you make very much money?" Erin asked.

"Hundreds of dollars. Maybe thousands. How do you think I paid for my prom dress?" Erin recalled how that dress had raised eyebrows in the family—it cost $550.

"Did you ever do things to get a grade raised?"

"*Things?* Do what things?"

"Like I heard Jess say that she babysat for a teacher once and got a grade changed to a letter higher. And Matt said he did a lot of yard work for Coach Batta and got a grade raised two letters."

"Whatever it takes," Sarah said. "It's a jungle. Why?"

She explained her dilemma in history class.

"Dad wants me to call Mr. McCauley, but I know what he'll say: His policy is that extra credit can only raise your grade one letter. So I wonder what I can do."

"Send him a gift. Buy him a pizza. You'll think of something." But Erin's difficulty had triggered Sarah's problem-solving temperament, which refused to merely suggest. "There are exceptions to every teacher's rule. Tell me more about him."

Erin didn't know much about Mr. McCauley beyond the hearsay and gossip. He was thirty-five years old and very handsome but sort of shy except when it came to talking about history. His first love was the period of the U.S. Revolutionary War. He was poor but comfortable that way. He rode a motorcycle. Oh, and he was supposedly fooling around with Mrs. Hillis, but nobody knew how seriously. He was not married.

"Well, there you have it," Sarah said. "It's pretty obvious what you can do. He's thirty-five, handsome, and single. You figure it out."

"What?"

"Jeez, Erin, you're not stupid. Use your imagination."

Erin's lips and throat went dry. She cringed as she recalled Mr. McCauley's words from the first day of class, spoken directly to her: "Your future is in my hands." He could not have known how prophetically he was speaking.

There was a tap on the door, and Sarah called, "Yes?"

Dad stuck his head around the corner and said, "Good night, girls. Is everything all right?"

Sarah told him everything was fine.

"You seem kind of serious."

"It's just girl talk," she assured him. Averting his gaze, Erin focused on a stack of magazines sitting on Sarah's suitcase. On top was a lingerie catalog, its blond cover girl, half-naked, her eyes lost in back of dark sunglasses, leaning provocatively against the fluted white post on a rustic front porch—a setting almost identical to one she and Nathan, dressed tastefully, had chosen for senior photographs back in June, before their break-up. Even here in her sister's lair lurked reminders of him …

"Okay," she heard her dad say. Then she felt his eyes boring toward her heart as he added, "I hope you're talking some sense into your sister. See you in the morning."

When he was safely gone, Sarah said, "Dad said he's upset that you don't want to go to Princeton. I wasn't supposed to tell you. He said he thought you'd see that it's the best thing before it's too late."

"Thanks for telling me," Erin said, her dejection deepening. "Whose side are you on?"

"It's not sides. It's reality. That's your problem, Erin. I don't mean to be critical, but you just don't want to see the world as it really is."

Erin's thoughts zig-zagged to Mrs. Hillis's similar observation—Mrs. Hillis, whose comment that Erin knew how to get good grades sort of echoed her father's and even Sarah's exhortation to do whatever was needed to get that history grade raised. *Pressure, pressure, pressure!*

"No, you're right," she said, repressing her urge to lash out at Sarah. "Maybe I need a good night's sleep." That was the most graceful exit she could muster.

Back in her own room, she wrestled with her troubles. She could not endure the constant stress any longer. It was driving her crazy. For weeks it had been poisoning her peace, stealing her sanity and even her sleep. Only one possible solution presented itself, and the longer she considered it, the more inevitable and inviting it seemed. As risky as it would be—personally, in the here and now—she knew that long-term it would be the best decision. She simply had to take matters into her own hands and stop waiting for blind chance or relying on other people like her parents or even Nathan to come around to her way of thinking. She saw that Mrs. Hillis was right, that waiting for something that would never come was just another kind of cheating—cheating herself.

It was settled, then. For the rest of the school year, she would do whatever she needed in order to get good grades—not for the sake of Princeton, but just to keep Mom and Dad satisfied. Once she went away to college, even if she was sent kicking and screaming to Princeton, she would be outside their suffocating influence and could follow her own heart in a U-turn back to Riverside, if she chose. She hated to wait that long, but what else could she do?

For now, then, she had to boost her history grade.

She shut her blinds, turned on piano music, and dressed for bed. Then she crawled under the comforter, her thoughts dallying on Nathan, and by the light of the bedside lamp began to flip through the catalog of intimate lingerie she had taken from Sarah's room.

27

THE LOW BUZZ of Zeb's electric razor nudged Robin awake. Through the vertical slit of the half-opened door to the bathroom she saw his reflection in the mirror, his face turned obliquely, his free hand checking his chin for spots of stubble. Why was he shaving? Maybe he had to go into his Bridgebury office.

She felt dull, utterly dull.

Why? Her emotional torpor mystified her, especially coming after the previous day, which had ballooned so pregnant with hope once Zeb's business trip was cancelled. She had nearly burst with anticipation that his insane travel routine was breaking up, until the usual prick of disappointment deflated her once more. So she fell into a fit of melancholy. Perhaps she was fooling herself, trying to rev up feelings of love for her husband that were only illusion. Was that it? Was she just trying to be faithful to a marriage that had already ridden off into the sunset, an idea that had faded into the mists of memory, receded into history? Was she just playing the part of the dutiful wife, trying to look good and faithful and obedient, to keep her promises? Yesterday, buoyed by the circumstance of his unexpected presence, she would have shouted *no!* at the top of her lungs. But then … last night with Zeb she had tried to fan sparks into flames but failed, their mutual fatigue descending and dominating, the sparks just … *flying upward*, she had to admit, morosely.

And this morning she felt thoroughly, utterly, oppressively, depressingly dull. There was no other word for it. Even the sound of the razor, after waking her, now threatened to put her back to sleep.

The fact that she could regard Zeb's proximity with such cool, objective distance troubled her—or at least it *should* be troubling her. She knew it should be. She ought to be head-over-heels happy that he was in the next room, awake, and that she was alone with him. Yet *his* distance for so long was responsible for *her* distance now. And still, she was not angry, not really. She was … indifferent. That was scary. There was no question of holding a grudge, either. Why not? It made sense that she should be resentful for her mistreatment the past many months. Yet she just couldn't muster up any strong feelings one way or the other.

The hum of the razor continued, rising and dropping in pitch as Zeb's hand moved around his face.

Her introspection deepened. She was surprised at her comfort in justifying the anger she *should* be feeling, and at the absence of any guilt for thinking of Brad McCauley while she considered Zeb's mirrored image. Something was definitely out of kilter in her thinking or feeling or judgment. Something wasn't right, something even bigger than the naked fact that she and her husband were struggling.

Her pillow felt fluffy and warm, and the ice on the windows whispered that it was okay to laze away as long as she wanted. She turned on her side and kept watching Zeb, who stepped silently into the bedroom and gingerly worked open a dresser drawer in search of socks. Next he took a pair of slacks from a hanger in the closet and pulled them on, his attempt to keep quiet only magnifying the whoosh of the fabric sliding against his skin. Robin wondered whether he had showered. Had she slept through that noise?

"Hello," she mumbled groggily, carefully electing not to say, "Good morning." The shorter greeting seemed more appropriate for a stranger or an acquaintance than for her husband. She was truly torn regarding how to treat him.

"Hi, honey," he whispered, as though a third person were sleeping in the room.

Duty nudging her, she tried once more for the passion that had eluded them the night before. She patted the comforter beside her and said, "Come here."

Zeb slithered partway under the covers, his clothing cool and rough next to her warm, smooth skin. He reached over to his pillow and bunched it behind his head; then he put his arm around her shoulder and drew her against him, awkwardly but solidly. She rested her head on his breast and strove to decipher the distant code of his heartbeat.

"Still tired?" she asked. Her fingers unbuttoned part of his shirt and stroked his chest, not out of any passion but out of habit, out of obligation—she was genuinely curious whether her gesture might rekindle the promise unfulfilled six hours earlier.

Zeb's hand arrested hers and he said, "No. But I need to go to work for a few hours. I thought I would get business out of the way first today, okay?"

"When will you be home?"

"Don't make me promise," he pleaded. "If I say noon and don't make it home by then, I'll feel terrible. So don't make me promise. Don't even ask me to guess."

Robin sat up quickly, her face bright with a new idea.

"Can I go with you?"

"You'll just be bored, honey."

"I know, but—"

"It'll be harder for me to get anything done with you there," he complained. "I'll be thinking about you and how bored you are and it will take me even longer to finish."

He got up.

"Want me to fix you some breakfast?" he asked, offering an olive branch when she was in no mood for peace.

The night before, while he had powered down with *CNN Headline News*, she had gone to the bedroom to prepare for him, showering, shaving her legs, powdering and perfuming, slipping into the nightgown he always called his favorite, lighting aromatic candles, and putting on tender instrumental music. Yet when he dragged into bed he was too tired to touch her. They lay beside each other in complementary embarrassment, Zeb guilt-ridden for his fatigue but Robin feeling ironically and equally guilty for bringing his guilt to the surface. With an apologetic kiss, he turned away from her, and he began to snore long before she blew out the candles and heard the music automatically shut off. At half past one she woke and fought to focus on Zeb rather than Brad—in the morning, she told herself, he will be rested, and except for the candles being shorter and unnecessary, everything would be the same. Sometimes you had to wait for good things.

Now that daybreak had come, though, her heart was a maze, a surging maelstrom of contradictions. At last, bitterness broke the surface. "No," she answered him. "I'm not hungry for food."

He huffed out of the room. Her implication had struck its target.

Fifteen minutes later she heard the front door creak open and close and his car start up. Once again Zeb was gone and she was alone.

My heart aches, she thought, remembering the poignant introduction to the ode by Keats she had taught her senior literature students that week. A lively discussion ensued when she asked the class what the poet meant by *heart*. One boy said convincingly, "It's a synonym for soul," as if his pronouncement was the final word, but another student asked, "What's a *soul*?" On the whole, the kids had no notion of what the *soul* was.

> *My heart aches, and a drowsy numbness pains*
> *My sense, as though of hemlock I had drunk,*
> *Or emptied some dull opiate to the drains*
> *One moment past, and Lethe-wards had sunk ...*

Like the poet's heart, her marriage was falling into oblivion. Yet *hope springs eternal*, she remembered from another poet, the one whom Brad respected—Brad, who had become her new hope, her lifeline as she sank into a widening whirlpool of conjugal despair.

Thinking of him finally gave her the impetus she needed to climb out of bed. All the ingredients she planned to include in his *Scholar's Pak* were jumbled in a shopping bag squirreled away in a utility closet, and she needed to wrap them before Zeb found them. During every hiatus in his travel schedule, he fell under a house-cleaning spell—fueled by his shame, she had no doubt—and he would eventually stumble upon her secret cache. Robin, simmering with anger, humiliated, rejected by his morning departure, felt vindicated in shifting her attention toward someone else.

Still, her earlier self-critique had not entirely abated, and she recognized ruefully that her soul was, more than anything else, *wavering*. Or, to apply a sophomore-level vocabulary word, she was adrift in *equivocation*. Soon she would need to come ashore to either Zeb or Brad, to choose between hope and hopelessness, between making a new promise and breaking an old one. She couldn't live forever in this limbo. It was time to choose. Oh, she had told herself the same thing many times already—yet still she kept the moment of decision at arms' length.

She waited, and waited. For what?

Beneath her mattress she had stowed a card for Brad some nights before, having started a note, struggling for the best words. Now she retrieved the card, propped both pillows behind her, and continued to craft her composition. Like many of her students, Robin tilted her head while engrossed in deep thought, and when she felt a crick in her neck, a new item for inclusion in her care package occurred to her—a gift certificate for Brad to visit her chiropractor! She smiled to herself. The package was already bloating, though. Maybe she should hold back certain items for later.

After finishing the card, she got dressed and ate a bowl of Special K cereal livened up with quarter-sized banana slices. The front of the cereal box was dominated by a smiling, scarlet-jerseyed LeBron James—little Philip Roost's current idol—which catapulted Robin's thoughts across the street to her neighbors. Since the day of their Christmas shopping together, Brad's motorcycle had not been on Dogwood Street or in the alley behind her house. Hopefully Jerri wasn't keeping a daily and nightly vigil, but you never knew what your neighbors, even your best neighbors, were capable of.

Zeb had set up an artificial Christmas tree, decorated mostly with ornaments the kids had made during their childhood years. Catching a glimpse of it, Robin felt her resolution falter again. Maybe Zeb will take me to dinner tonight, she thought. Or a movie. Or we could go shopping in Indianapolis. The options were unlimited, but even though she labored to put a positive spin on the day, images of Brad kept interfering. As soon as she envisioned a dinner with Zeb, she looked across the table and (as her guilt wrestled with self-justification) found Brad smiling back at her. Whether she imagined watching a dreamy romantic chick-flick or a fast-paced adventure movie for guys, she felt more excitement at the idea of sitting in the dark next to Brad than next to Zeb.

Friday was not her scheduled day for housecleaning. Nevertheless, her routine always went haywire during vacations, and because the living room at least needed dusting, she went to work with furniture polish and a rag. To chase away the maddening stillness of the house, she turned on the Bruce Springsteen tape. She had held on to it far too long and every few days made a mental note to return it to Brad. By now, having listened to it eight or ten times, she had softened her first uncharitable judgments of its merits. Several of the songs had grown on her until she hummed along and mouthed the intermittent words and lines she had memorized.

Certain lyrics seized her, charging her blood with a fervor both strange and familiar—strange in that she saw it in her teenage students, familiar in that it echoed down from the passion of her own remote adolescence. As she listened, she often caught herself wondering what Brad felt whenever he heard the words about wild abandon and the wind and the road and the future alive with infinite possibility. Did he understand the symbolism, or was that just her English teacher side intruding? To him, was the music only a snappy beat and melody giving voice to the lusty urges of testosterone? The last time she had gone riding with Brad on his motorcycle, the words of the songs had taken on new life as she realized how true they were, not just as a barometer of personal emotion but also as a reflection of the culture that generated them. As the music proclaimed, the night really *did* have a life of its own that she had either long forgotten or never intimately known.

Robin's hand absently ran the dust cloth along the varnished tabletops, mantel, and baseboard. Her voice and her heart hummed her own accompaniment to the music. Today she caught herself paying particular attention to a different song, whose title she did not know, a song about the perils of uncommitted love, and with a twinge of identification with the fictional girl in the lyrics, Robin wondered whether she could trust Brad more deeply.

The song accused a boy named Johnny of being a cheater and a liar, and she thought of herself and Brad: Was his heart cheap? Was hers? Every scrap of her upbringing and faith cried out against this blasphemy—*No! She was not cheap!* She was infinitely valuable in the eyes of God! But as soon as she built herself up, her conscience denounced her for her mammoth hypocrisy: She was crying to God as she turned away from the husband God had given her. She mumbled the lyrics of the song, which suggested that the boy would be unfaithful but the girl would not care ... But Robin *would* care! She abruptly came to her senses, the muscles of her arm aching from the pressure she was applying to the oak banister of the staircase. Above the song she heard the doorbell ringing. She turned the volume to low and hurried to answer.

Through the peephole she saw the Roosts.

Philip had been designated as the family gift-bearer, straining under a box about eighteen inches square, smartly wrapped in a green patterned paper, tied with a white ribbon, topped with a multi-colored bow. It was not heavy, Robin discovered when she took it from him, only unwieldy for a six-year-old.

"We wanted to catch you when Zeb was home," Jerri said, "but we saw he motored off already."

"He just had to go to his office for a couple of hours," Robin said uncomfortably. Why *motored*? "I'm so excited to have him for the whole day—almost." Saying it, she actually felt her heart rise in expectancy.

Jerri and Howard joined her in laughing. Lena watched Philip, whose eyes had frozen on the stairway.

"I think Philip wants to explore again," she said. "Do you mind?"

"Oh, of course not!" Robin said. "You know your way around, Philip. Go on!"

Philip waited until Lena nodded her permission before he headed up the stairs.

Robin ushered them to the dining room and served the last of Zeb's coffee. Their small talk centered on her vacation, their unfinished shopping, the weather, and an idea they floated every winter but had never executed—throwing a special Christmas party for the "senior, senior citizens" on the block. There were five people older than ninety, including Jerri's mother and the Hillises' next door neighbor Wayne Floyd. Lena excused herself to track down Philip.

"Also," Howard said, "Jerri and I wanted to ask you and Zeb to church with us Christmas Eve."

Their families had gone to such candlelight services several times. Somehow, though, this invitation sounded off-key, strained.

"I'll mention it to Zeb," she replied defensively. She felt cornered, violated almost. Did Howard share Jerri's suspicions about her and Brad? Did he even know? Of course he must, she told herself, because he and his wife actually *talk* to each other. Once more she was aware of vacillating, being tugged in two directions, both accusing and protecting her husband.

Lena reappeared with Philip in reluctant tow, and they all headed for the front door. Howard paused to look around the living room.

"This is some of the best work I've ever done," he said, his hand resting on top of a freestanding bookcase. "If I ever went into private business, I would want to use your house as a demo!"

His attractive eyes always looked like they were smiling. Even if you hid the bottom half of his face, you would always think he was smiling. The circles around his deep sockets had the hilarious effect of multiplying the happiness; the crow's feet creeping from the corners of his eyes branched out in a wordless joy. Robin imagined that a careful sculptor had spent a lifetime refining Howard's eyes, forming each line and wrinkle to maximize the delight they would fling forth.

When the door closed behind them, Robin sighed with relief. But as the clock's minute and hour hands swept forward, past eleven o'clock, past noon, toward one o'clock, the cold grip of loneliness enveloped her once more. She would almost rather be with Howard and Jerri and risk their snooping than sit alone wishing for Zeb to come home.

Fifteen minutes later she called Zeb's office and got a busy signal. Every five minutes she tried again, with identical results.

So she dialed Brad's apartment. The phone rang and rang; he had said he would be spending long hours in the libraries during vacation.

At precisely 2:37 she decided she had throttled her expanding rage long enough. Zeb had evidently removed his office phone from the hook. Very well, then, she would drive to Bridgebury and find him.

But even that plan was doomed to many amendments. Before she ever got out of town, she stopped for a quick lunch at Dairy Queen, thinking of Brad through every inch of her chili dog and every sip of her coffee. Then, passing his apartment north of West Bridgebury, she stopped, let herself in for the first time ever with his key, and taped a note to his computer screen:

HAPPY HOLIDAYS FROM SOMEONE WHO IS BORED TO DEATH. LOOKING FORWARD TO THE END OF VACATION, IF YOU CAN BELIEVE THAT. CAN'T WAIT TO SEE YOU AGAIN. —R

It took every ounce of restraint to avoid scrawling LOVE before her initial.

Zeb's car was not in the Key-Comm employee parking lot when Robin drove in, so she swerved into his designated spot. The front doors were not locked, even though most of the salaried staff had already begun long weekends before Christmas, which fell on a Tuesday. In the stairwell leading to the sales floor, she ran into Zeb's friend Jake Morris, whose face registered surprise at seeing her.

"You just missed Zee," he said. "He was pretty upset when he left, too."

"He ought to be," Robin groused. "He said he would be home by noon."

"Kline asked him to fly to Baltimore tonight," Jake said.

Robin's heart fell and her shoulders slumped.

"Sorry to be the bearer of sad tidings," Jake added.

"Please tell me you're joking."

"I wish I could. I'm sorry. Zee's been trying to call you for the last hour."

"But Jake, doesn't Kline realize that Zeb Hillis has a wife? Does Kline expect me to just sit at home and grow old gracefully while he sends Zeb all over the civilized world? What am I supposed to do—learn to knit by the fireplace? This is really getting old! First Zeb said he thought it would be over by the end of the summer. Then it was Halloween, then Thanksgiving. Now it's not until the new year? Where will my husband be on Christmas Day?"

Jake's face signaled that he had not intended to open a can of worms.

"Oh, I'm sorry, Jake. But what am I going to do? I know my TV better than I know my husband anymore."

"Listen," said Jake. "Zee did *not* want to go to Baltimore. That's why he was upset. He spent ninety minutes on the phone trying to take care of the business from here. But you know the way it is—sometimes it just takes face-to-face contact."

"*Face-to-face contact!?*" she shouted. "I can't believe I'm hearing this! What about face-to-face contact *with me*? Where does it say that to climb up the company ladder you have to trample all over your wife? Is Kline even here today? I'd like to talk to him."

"He's not here. He's in Boston, I think. Listen, Robin, it's not Kline's fault either. It's nobody's fault. Kline isn't making Zeb go—he just asked him. It's up to Zeb, not Kline."

"Oh, *Zeb* gets to choose. That makes me feel a *lot* better," she fumed. "Hmm. I wonder what he'll do?"

Jake started down the steps toward her until Robin, still seething, left the building.

A crazy idea came to her, an ultimatum. To demonstrate to Zeb once and for all that she could not endure his absences any longer, she would *drive* to Baltimore, track him down at his hotel, and bring him home. The company could save his airfare. How far was Baltimore? What routes did you take? Even as she pondered her plan, her irrepressible self-scrutiny kicked in again, pummeling her under ruthless inner interrogation. What did she really hope to accomplish? To look like the faithful and long-suffering wife? To back Zeb into a corner and force the issue? Or to give her grounds for leaving Zeb and choosing Brad? She could not believe the things she was turning over in her heart!

Back in her car, she actually took a simpler route. North on 53 to Brad's place.

Without knocking, she slipped her key into his lock—it took less raspy effort this time—and went inside. Nobody was home. Her note still hung on his computer monitor. It was four o'clock.

For half an hour she read his manuscript, more alert to grammatical errors and stylistic inconsistencies than to content; eventually, she knew, he would ask her to proofread and edit the whole thing, so she might as well get a feel for it. After ten pages she paused, having discovered that he had the same weakness for dangling modifiers and passive constructions that marred most academic writing.

She sat on his unmade bed and toyed with the comically small television. There was a football game on one of the networks, but when the score flashed leading into a commercial, she had to squint to read the tiny letters and numbers. Perhaps she ought to add a TV set to her care package. A real TV set.

At six o'clock the first new pangs of hunger struck. Yippy's Pizza Parlor, the hole-in-the-wall joint that Brad liked so much, was ten minutes away. She bought a large deluxe and brought it back to the apartment in hopes that he would return, but no. She ate three pieces, picking off the onions, then crammed the remainder into the fridge.

Collapsing again on his bed, Robin sighed under the weight of her wavering, the burden of the day's contrast. As she had waited for Zeb in the living room of the house they had purchased and labored to improve, where they had raised two children over the lovely arc of twenty years, she had grown progressively vexed with boredom and anger; yet here and now, waiting secretly for a younger man who had been a total stranger a few months earlier, waiting in an apartment that should seem foreign and unwholesome and sinful—lying in his own bed, no less—her anticipation was soaring. She knew Zeb was coming home (if only to pack for another trip) but she did not know whether Brad was even in town. He might be a million miles away—in Baltimore, even—but waiting for him was exhilarating.

Robin searched for his boom box, finding it under a damp towel on the bathroom floor; however, her search for any Springsteen music proved fruitless. Around seven o'clock, she rewrote the message on his computer, lowercasing the words to make them appear more personal and adding Love, Robin. That sounded too bold. Yours, Robin. That carried implications of throwing herself at him. Sincerely, Robin was far too formal for a two-line note. At last she came full circle and settled on a curvy dash followed by her initial, more ornate this time, its descending stroke trailing off in a flourish.

She picked up trash, cleaned the kitchen counter, dusted his windowsills and bookshelves with a moist napkin. Twice, footsteps outside set her heart racing, but the noise was only the neighbors. She spun the lock on Brad's safe a few times and tried random sets of three numbers. Of all the curious things about him, his safe was the strangest. Did she know anyone else in her life who had a safe?

At eight o'clock her audacity leapt to a new level. She turned out the light, took off her shoes, and climbed under Brad's covers. Every sound seemed like a scream—voices of other tenants coming and going, vehicles on the highway, footsteps, doors opening and closing in other apartments, and her own heartbeat. She wondered what it was like to sleep in the nude. He must have a high body temperature.

Would he ever come home? What else could she do to tempt fate? Undress? Take a shower?

Did she really *want* him to find her here?

At nine o'clock she imposed a deadline of fifteen minutes. She nuked another piece of pizza, shorn of its onions, and looking for a soft drink, discovered a bottle of wine. At least *he* was thinking of her. She found a corkscrew, intending to open the wine, when a line from a W. H. Auden poem teased her from the margin of her memory, giving her pause till she recalled it—*the desires of the heart are as crooked as corkscrews*—and abandoned her plan.

She gave up and drove back to Brookstone.

Brookstone, boring Brookstone, where one final surprise awaited her before the day would wind down: Zeb's car parked in the driveway, and Zeb himself parked in the recliner watching a movie when she walked in.

"Where have you been?" he asked, not masking his irritation, but before the words had finished falling from his tongue she was answering in a tone of affected offense, "What are *you* doing here? I thought you were in Baltimore!"

Pain washed over his countenance. Still, Robin's sympathy had dried up long ago, sometime during her short, hot talk with Jake Morris.

"No," Zeb said. "I told them I wouldn't go. How did you know about that?"

"I talked to Jake." She was about to continue "at your office" but held back. What was the use? As upset as she was now, she didn't want to give him the pleasure of knowing she had been looking for him. So she added, "On the phone."

"Robin," he went on accusingly, "I've been here since about three this afternoon! You could at least have left me a note. Where were you?"

"All over. I went shopping."

"Oh, okay. You need help bringing in your bags?"

What? Was he trying to catch her in a lie? She said, "No, I didn't buy anything." She felt herself dipping deeper into her deceit. "I found some things. But then I realized I didn't have my purse. So I just kept looking and not buying. Besides," she said triumphantly, "I just wanted to be out among *people*. I was so tired of being *alone*."

"Did you have any dinner?"

"I stopped for pizza." Finally, a truth. "I had this old coupon in the car so I could eat for free."

Robin took off her coat and left the room—*fled* the room. With all his questions he was worse than Jerri Roost!

"Honey," he called a few minutes later. "What's this music you're listening to?"

"Oh, that!" She came and took it from him. "A student asked me to listen to it." Another truth, sort of. She was getting good at this! "Just some kids' music."

An hour later, in bed, Zeb said soothingly, "I said *no* to the trip because I wanted to say *yes* to you."

"How poetic," she replied brusquely. A visible chill swept through the room. Zeb lay back with a sigh.

Robin did not feel even a slight prick of pity as she turned her back to Zeb, curled up in the warmth of the bed, and with every conscious thought embraced Brad McCauley—knowing all the while that her withering, wavering soul might loiter there but would never settle there. She had thrown herself into a battle she could not win. She had engaged the truth as an enemy, and the truth would prevail.

The day's long tug-of-war in her heart proved that.

Decisively.

Her equivocating might endure for the night, for a very long night, as long as she clung to it with her selfishness. Yet eventually a morning would dawn, a glorious morning awash in the sunny golden rays of renewed purpose and joy.

Her dalliance with Brad might outlast her anger with Zeb, but neither would ever outlive something more permanent, something eternal—her love for her husband.

28

HOUR BY HOUR, the calendar's last day ticked away, minute by minute, second by second.

And as though aligned by some secret sympathy with the vanishing year, the tiny, tightly circumscribed world of J. Bradford McCauley continued to erode, to crumble at its shrinking edges, with startling visibility. First, two of his clocks quit running. Next, he chipped a molar while munching on—of all the improbable culprits—french fries. His ever-suspicious mind coupled the events in an augury of conspiracy, behind which stood the great, impassive Universal Clock, whose cosmic battery ran forever, and whose intelligence, implacable and inscrutable, seemed bent on his destruction.

The worst part of the broken tooth was its timing. Finding a dentist on New Year's Eve would be futile. Fortunately there was no pain, although his tongue was already scraping itself raw against the jagged surface of the filling still anchored in the middle of the crack. Also fortunately, he verified from a classmate stranded on campus that his emergency was covered by his graduate teaching assistantship's meager insurance plan, meaning he could afford to fork over a few dollars to get new clock batteries, which he found, overpriced, at the Seven-11 across the street from ¿Que Pasa? Paying the cashier, he watched the early revelry building at the campus's number one bar and made a pact with himself: If he wrapped up the current chapter of his dissertation before eleven o'clock, he would reward himself with a beer and help the rowdies ring in the new year.

Once his clocks were running and synchronized, he felt energized to write, but en route to resuming his work he stumbled over the file named CHEAT, which sent his attention down a side track. With Robin unavailable during the week after Christmas, McCauley had managed to grade every last high school history project—and among them he had identified half a dozen indisputable cases of pure plagiarism.

First and funniest was a wonderfully executed pile of balderdash from Matt Rademacher. The paper's form was almost flawless in terms of in-text citations, works cited, outline, spelling, punctuation, and indentation, but its content was cleverly disguised claptrap cobbled together not from unreliable online sources but instead from Matt's own daring, arrogant imagination. Apparently his sole intention was to see how huge a prank he could pull. This was the same student who had won $50,000, McCauley remembered, and who regularly trumpeted his reputation for taking chances. Fine. But now he had gambled big-time and lost. McCauley could not understand the kid's motivation. Why spend so much time dressing up a paper that was nothing but hogwash? He recalled a quip from Professor Travis and considered including it on his closing comments to Matt: "You can't polish a turd." That would be an appropriate academic assessment, perhaps, yet it might backfire on him professionally, so he checked his impulse and merely played tit-for-tat with Matt by heaping extravagant handwritten praise on the paper before waxing realistic in the final sentence and assigning a grade of F.

A second paper, chock full of plagiarism of the most transparent and least artful sort, was easy to catch because it basically copied a paper McCauley had graded the previous year! Its original form had earned the writer an A. The plagiarist had not even bothered to alter the title: "The History of the Automobile in Rock and Roll Lyrics." One reason McCauley recognized the paper was that it had lavishly cited Bruce Springsteen. With minimal effort McCauley learned that the original writer, now graduated and probably enrolled at a big-name college in another state, had uploaded his research essay to a web site—probably for payment—which in turn offered it for sale to anyone in the world.

In two other cases, McCauley strongly suspected that students had turned in papers actually written by Lance Tracer. McCauley knew from essay test responses that Lance was a gifted writer with a fluid graceful style and a knack for rigid organization. However, Robin's expert English teacher's eye had helped him see Lance's stylistic quirks. He tended to start sentences with prepositional phrases far more than most student writers, for example, certainly more than the students who claimed to have written the papers in question. In addition, Lance had mastered constructions using semicolons, which Robin claimed few high school writers knew when or how to properly use. These cases were more problematic for McCauley since he could not prove Lance's complicity. He might confront Lance or the other two with his circumstantial evidence, but he opted to do nothing. Unless Lance had done the *thinking* for the papers, he might not technically be in the wrong.

Finally, a couple of other papers lifted substantial passages from periodicals. Those violations were easy to spot because the writing styles of the "collaborating" authors were so markedly distinct. For fun, and to share the evidence with Robin, McCauley calculated the average word length of paragraphs he believed were copied and compared it with the students' own paragraphs. The plagiarized material averaged 128 percent longer! He confirmed his suspicions by finding the sources in a Riverside library, photocopying the pilfered passages, and stapling them to the back of the papers along with his comments and the F grades.

Midway through this assiduous pursuit of documentation, echoing along an otherwise deserted underground tunnel linking two campus buildings, he paused to pose a sensible question. *What was he doing?* Why was he expending so much time and energy chasing a few teenage cheaters, clueless kids who in another six months would recede to insignificance in the rearview mirror of his career as he sped away forever from Brookstone High School, from Riverside University, from central Indiana? His motivation was tough to figure. His first thought was that he was simply avoiding the task of working on his thesis—an explanation that was too simple. No, something more than mere procrastination was driving him.

Done grading, McCauley entered his notes about the cheating into the computer file devoted to that purpose, inflating it to 8,800 words. Then he got a glass of water, flexed his fingers, and opened the file for Chapter 10 of his dissertation, in which he read between the lines of correspondence among several of the nation's founders during the time of the Constitutional Convention.

His current chapter argued that a reference to "our fate" in a letter from James Madison to Thomas Paine was more than casual. In many of Madison's preserved speeches, as well as in his letters to Christians, Madison used the term *destiny* almost exclusively when referring to the political future of the nation. Yet in correspondence with deists, he chose the word *fate*. This discrepancy was no coincidence, McCauley contended. The terms were not interchangeable. *Fate* was less personal, so Madison preferred it in private communications because it better reflected his true position.

Something about the analysis hung incomplete, though, something unreasonable. Something wasn't tracking along his line of logic. This general suspicion had nagged him for weeks without becoming specific enough to deal with. McCauley wished Robin were on hand to help.

He had heard from her just once during the week, two days after Christmas, when he bucked his better judgment and called her under the pretense of thanking her for her gift, which now sat ticking on the kitchen counter, newer and nicer than any of his other clocks.

"Zeb's not giving me much time to myself," she had said, her tone of voice impossible to decipher. "It's strange. Different. I didn't expect this."

"You don't sound very happy about it, if you don't mind my saying so."

After a troubling pause, her voice answered, "It's strange, that's all. I can't figure it out. We're together almost every hour of the day, but we never *communicate*. He works for a telecommunications company and I teach English and speech, but we can't even talk to each other. And still ..."

Thankfully, she changed the subject, but their conversation had lasted less than two minutes. McCauley imagined Robin whispering into the phone in a closet, fearful that Zeb would hear her voice, jerk open the door, and catch her red-handed.

Although they had made no plans for their next get-together, Robin promised to send him something special before his trip to the Chicago conference, toward which her attitude had softened once she learned the "Kelly" he would go with was a male and not a female grad student.

"I hope you come with it," he said. A more prolonged pause fell over the line, ending when she replied, "Oh, Brad, I wish we … gotta go now. We'll talk soon!" Had Zeb come into the room? Or did Robin want him to think so? More likely, McCauley thought, he was just making up everything. But still he wondered: What did Robin *wish*?

Without having asked her, he knew she had been in his bed a few nights earlier when he had staggered home mentally exhausted after midnight—the smell of her musky perfume hovered like a hint above his sheets. He had wishes too, he thought now. And glancing at his computer screen, he had needs. The ticking of the clocks propelled him back to his dissertation, but not long afterward he returned to imagining Robin.

He decided to risk calling her.

When she answered, he said, "It's me. Just say yes or no—are you alone? Are you able to talk?"

"No. Just a minute." After thirty seconds of rustling—moving to a safe place, he imagined—her voice returned, "I need to talk to you. Are you at your place?"

"Yes."

"Stay put. I'll be there as soon as I can."

Fifteen minutes later she knocked and let herself in. He greeted her with a hug but she hurried past him, taking off her coat and draping it over the back of a chair at the kitchen table, where he had set the wine bottle and two glasses in plain sight. Her back toward him, she picked up the corkscrew, shook her head, and said, "I told Zeb I needed to get out. I hadn't been out all day. I can't stay long."

When she turned around, her face wore a troubled expression that drew him toward her, but she raised her palms, and her next words were firm and measured: "This can't go on."

"Oh," he said. "Oh."

His heart dropped,

"Do you want to sit down?" That seemed like the right question to ask. Equally uncomfortable, she nodded but stayed where she was.

"Would you like a drink?" Gestures suddenly assumed tremendous importance to him. Making that offer also seemed like the gentlemanly thing to do. But not the wine, clearly not the wine. "Some coffee?"

She waved away the small talk and moved toward him, arms wide for another embrace.

"I'm so sorry, Brad," she mumbled into his sweatshirt, not crying but not far off, either. His arms went around her small shoulders, automatically, mechanically.

"Say *something*," she said finally.

"Okay," he answered, guiding her to the couch and ensuring there was a foot of space between them. "Okay. I guess I'm not surprised. I mean, when you take a step back and look at us, I really don't belong, do I?"

"Oh, it's *me*," she said, avoiding his gaze. "I'm the one who never should have ..." She gestured around the room as if to encompass everything.

The atmosphere thickened with quiet reproach. He had to say something to chase away the awkward silence.

"Okay, but ... it's no secret, is it? I don't fit into your world, and you don't fit into mine. I wish we did fit, but we don't, do we? I guess I knew that eventually you would see that, too. Not wanting it, but expecting it." He hoped she would disagree, but no, she did not open her pretty mouth. He explained, "At this point in my life I'm caught between worlds. I don't fit into the academic world at Riverside, not entirely, not with my part-time job away from campus, and not with my history—and you don't even *know* my whole history, my *personal* history, I mean. And I don't belong at Brookstone High School either, where I'm just a part-timer from another town, another state, just passing through. I'm a drifter. No family—"

Then Robin spoke with a strange insistence: "You ought to give the family world a try."

The idea seemed so out-of-the-blue that he didn't know how to respond.

"It may not be for everybody," Robin went on, "but it's for a lot more people than ever realize it."

"I don't think it's for me."

She nodded, still eluding his gaze.

"I know there are things about your life you have wanted to tell me," she said, "and that's up to you, from this point on, but from this point on, our relationship needs to change. It's just not right, what we're doing. What *I'm* doing, anyway. I know you don't believe about right and wrong the same way I do, but—"

"That's not the issue," he interrupted, irritated. Sooner or later he knew that her reasons would converge on his beliefs. "What matters between us is how we *feel*. Isn't it?"

"Ultimately, in the big scheme of things, maybe. I don't know. What I *do* know is how I feel right now, and this can't go on. And ..."

"And what?"

"It's not my place to tell you how to live your life. But if you're running from something, from who you really are, you can't go on doing that, either. You were not *born to run*, no matter what that stupid song says. And I have to get you that tape back. Oh! I probably sound like a mom, saying all this, don't I?" She reached across and squeezed his wrist. "Forgive me for that. Please forgive me, please, but I had to say it."

Did *he* have anything he *had* to say? Nothing urgent came to mind. If anything ever did, well, they would still see each other every day at Brookstone, unless she avoided him there, which would be easy enough. It would be a teenage thing to do, but it would be easy enough.

"Please?" she insisted, squeezing again.

"Hmm?"

"Please *forgive* me. I asked."

"Sure. No harm done." He grasped her hand, raised it to his lips, and kissed it gently. Her fingers brushed his cheek.

"Brad, I've been going back and forth on this in my heart for a long time. I think you're great, but—"

He interrupted again, "You don't need to explain. I just told you how I know I don't fit with you. I've loved every minute with you, but even in my wildest imagination I didn't think anything would happen, not beyond the spring."

"But there's something else I need to say. Then I have to go."

"Okay."

"This is going to sound like I'm crazy."

He waited.

"I know I'm doing the right thing here," she went on, faltering, "but I don't know how *well* I'm doing it, and I'm just not sure …"

"Not sure about what?"

"About how well I can carry through. I guess I'm afraid I may have already gone too far with you."

"What?" He had no idea what she meant.

"I know what I really need to do," she said. "I just don't know if I *can*. I have to be honest about that."

What did that mean? Was she sending him a hint? Teasing him? Tormenting him?

"Robin, I don't know what you're trying to say."

"I don't know, either. I'm just scared for what will happen in the spring."

"Scared? Why?"

"I just don't know if I can do what I have to do."

His restraint dissolved in a sarcastic laugh.

"Meaning what?" he asked.

"That's all I can say. I don't know how else to put it."

She sounded as confused and divided in her commitment as so many of the Revolutionary War settlers with their loyalties split between Crown and colonies …

She faced him and got up, saying, "I have to get back now."

"Really?" Now *he* was teasing, sort of, fishing for the truth behind her insinuation, her ambivalence.

"Yes, really. I have to go home."

He enfolded her in a final, wordless hug.

His night now ruined, McCauley retreated to the only place he felt comfortable and competent, the world of his dissertation, aware that even its stability might disintegrate at the whim of Gregory Travis. He tapped out a word, a phrase, a fragment, then deleted it all, repeating the same cycle several times, till around nine o'clock he surrendered and headed to ¿Que Pasa?

The bar, not yet crowded, was still terribly noisy. A football bowl game was on TV so he sat at the counter and sipped a Budweiser. He missed ¿Que Pasa? Before starting to spend his free time with Robin, this had been his favorite hangout. It was impossible to think about U.S. history here, where everybody was living in the present, living for the moment. His mind could relax.

Sitting beside him was a young man with tinted glasses and a plaid flannel shirt, talking to his girlfriend on the next stool, her hair a rainbow of dyed colors, her leather skirt tightly hugging her hips, her wrists flashing with many bracelets. They were probably headed for a dance floor closer to midnight, McCauley surmised. The girl whispered something into the guy's ear, and he ran a finger down the top of her chest until it met the fabric of her leopard skin top. McCauley watched a series of plays of the football game, unable to avoid thinking of Robin's hard sternum.

He wondered where she and Zeb would be at midnight.

By 10:45 he was partied out. The crowds at ¿Que Pasa? always sapped him unless he had a companion. As he walked to his motorcycle, he noticed many lit windows in the apartments above businesses that fronted the streets, and he had to dodge a fair number of merry-makers on the sidewalk, but on the whole it was a bleak evening. Snow had yet to fall this winter. The only precipitation had been rain, and tonight curtains of icicles hung from gutters and downspouts. The cityscape seemed hard and unforgiving, a pallid tableau of intersecting and overlapping darknesses. McCauley decided to walk around campus before going home. He passed the Gearhart Management Building, home to the office of Ms. Priscilla Verhoven. What did embittered feminists do to celebrate holidays? Probably got together to invent new ways to threaten and torment men, the world's only real evil.

McCauley looked up at the granite face of the Gearhart Building with its large, austere clock, whose long metal hands swept their time around a circle marked with dots instead of numbers. The hands were almost together near the eleven o'clock mark, as though applauding in stop-action, or praying with a sleepy tilt. The minute hand was about five feet long, strong enough to support his weight—in a fleeting burst of fancy he imagined himself hanging onto it, holding on for dear life, like the hero in a Hitchcock movie whose name eluded him. Once he had met a movie fanatic at ¿Que Pasa? who mentioned about fifty movie titles in the space of their half-hour shared drink. He struggled to remember her name—Betsy? Betty? Becky? The Gearhart clock had a second hand, too, the diameter of a baseball, racing around the dotted circumference. Absorbed with that hand, McCauley found it impossible to think of hanging on but easy to imagine being pushed along, or poked along, or dragged along, through life. The new year was peeping over the threshold. What surprises did the Universal Clock have in store for him?

Robin's decision to split up with him spread fog over his expectations for the spring semester. Mentally mapping his future, he had envisioned marching toward his Ph.D. with her support at least in the form of secret cheering from the sidelines, and concluding his high school teaching bolstered by her friendship. Moreover, until Zeb had reappeared, he was on the brink of trusting her enough to share with her his burdensome personal and professional secrets. Plus, in the wake of his research-paper grading, he was definitely interested in taking action against the cheating students and exploring the shady system orbiting LaGrange and Myers. Their arrogance had stirred him from lethargy to belligerence. He was actually itching for a fight—what did he have to lose? Only the precariously guarded secret of Gregory Travis ...

At his apartment, long before midnight, an especially deep yawn pushed him to abandon his hopes of watching the giant ball come to earth in Times Square on TV. He flipped off the set and closed his eyes. His clocks were synchronized only in the time they displayed—their ticking was misaligned. McCauley made an effort to isolate each clock's signature pattern in the blended ticking.

Drowsed by this exercise, dozing, he thought he heard a soft knock on his door. It was difficult to be certain, but he strained to catch it again. There it was! A light tap in rhythm with the clocks! His heart raced with the hope that it was Robin escaping Zeb and coming back with second thoughts, or at least to wish him a happy new year in person.

He threw on a bathrobe and slippers as the quiet tapping continued. Through the peephole he could make out the shape of a woman's shadowed face, dark because the outside light had never worked. Whoever was tapping was not Robin, though. This woman was too tall.

McCauley turned on the foyer light and opened the door. The woman must have been lost, perhaps looking for a different apartment. She was wearing high-heeled shoes and an ankle-length fur coat whose front was opened just enough to let him see the top of a lacy outfit.

"Yes?" McCauley asked.

She stepped forward to the threshold, and the foyer light fell fully on her face. He hazily recognized something about her features but could not place her.

"Mr. McCauley?" her voice quivered.

"Yes?" He felt foolish—was she one of his university students?

"I came to talk about my grade."

Puzzled and paralyzed on the spot, he stepped back and the woman stepped inside, awkwardly, unbalanced, perhaps tipsy. His stomach began to tighten. Without any clear reason, he sensed he had already committed a terrible error and opened himself to a terrible danger. Now he could see the woman's face. He still couldn't tell who she was, but he knew why. She was smothered in makeup—thick eyeliner, false lashes, too-red lipstick, and generous clouds of rouge on her cheekbones—and drowned in a floral perfume. Everything about her appearance was so overdone in an amateurish way that he wanted to laugh. She was obviously not here to talk about her grade.

Suddenly her identity clicked: Erin Delaney.

No wonder he had not recognized her sooner. He had never seen Erin wearing makeup, and her hair, which usually hung straight and loose, was now piled gloriously on top of her head, except for one enticing strand that fell in a bouncy spiral in front of her left shoulder.

"What do you mean?" McCauley asked. He knew he was not thinking clearly. Taunting, haunting phantoms from his past flitted before him—Erin's presence scared him as much as a reincarnation of Mary Ann Childress.

"I thought we could work something out." Her voice was nearly cracking. "For extra credit."

"Whatever you say," he answered evenly, moving backward.

Erin let the fur coat slide off her shoulders.

McCauley's head and heart swirled. Even as he realized that she must have rehearsed this move, he quenched a gasp and swallowed. Her overdone makeup could not mar the truth that she was lovely, even alluring in a comic way. He scrambled to remember what grade he had given her on her semester project, but he could not think. His eyes were trapped. She was wearing almost nothing, a loose camisole on top, and panties, tight at her waist but loose over her narrow hips, all fringed with lace, all selected to give another person—himself, evidently—easy access to everything it hid.

She reached up and unpinned her hair, and when she shook her head all her gorgeous, newly permed hair tumbled down silently like a seductive cascade of free sex.

"I *have* to get a good grade on my project," she said. Her voice sounded louder, more sure of itself, and he discerned a tone that was almost threatening. Her eyes were dark from the makeup and the meager light above her, but McCauley tried to see into them, certain they were close to crying. He did not smell any alcohol.

"Erin," he said. "What in God's name are you doing?"

"You know."

Her hands reached behind her neck, and her bust rose under the sheer fabric, and McCauley said quickly and sternly, "No, I don't! Stop this!"

She hesitated—and McCauley sensed himself gaining the upper hand.

Yes, he *did* know what she was doing. But *she* didn't, not really, did she? How could she? How old was Erin Delaney? Seventeen? Eighteen? Maybe only sixteen?

Her hands came back down and looked uneasily for a comfortable position, but there was none to be found.

"I'll do anything you want," she said, pleading, nervous, more frightened than he was.

"I want you to go away," he said decisively.

Inside his bathrobe he was sweating profusely. Never had he known how deeply Mary Ann Childress—who had never gone this far—still affected him. His stomach churned with near panic.

Erin crossed her arms over her chest. A spell broke. McCauley felt tension draining away, and Erin's next words poured from a wholly different girl: "But Mr. McCauley, if I don't raise my grade, my parents will kill me!"

That was familiar teenage whining.

Her shoulders rose and fell convulsively with her first sobs. McCauley bent down and picked up the coat, a soft fur that was probably real. As he wrapped it around her shoulders, her tears came copiously.

"Sit down, sit down," he said, and she followed him submissively and settled awkwardly on the couch. He handed her the box of tissues that sat on the coffee table, real Kleenex—a gift from Robin to help him battle his recent cold.

"How did you get here?" he asked.

"Matt's van," she blurted.

"Matt? Rademacher? He brought you?"

She shook her head no.

That's good, he thought.

"Does he know you came here?"

Again she shook her head. But surely, he thought, the two of them had plans for the evening.

"I'm supposed to meet him in front of ¿Que Pasa? before midnight," she explained through sniffles. "He went earlier with some friends from Riverside. He said he could get me in."

This struck him as reasonable; the bar was notorious for its lax scrutiny of underage customers.

"Erin, what were you thinking? You're a bright girl. Why did you do this?"

"I *had* to."

He went into the kitchen and poured her a glass of generic diet cola. From the stack of graded papers on the table he found hers—she had passed, but barely. D-minus. Two letter grades deducted for two days late. She had not cheated, though. He decided not to tell her the grade, at least not right away. He gave her the drink, excused himself, and changed into blue jeans and a Riverside sweatshirt. When he came back she was holding the glass with both hands in her lap, the flowery scent—lilac, he guessed—rolling off her trembling form in thick waves.

"Did somebody put you up to this?" he asked.

"Mom and Dad."

"*What?* Your parents know you came here?" Like the carbonation fizzing in the soda, his fear bubbled up again.

"No, I just mean it's their fault. They always put so much pressure on me and I know I can't live up to their expectations because I'm not a brain like my sisters but they all expect me to be but I can't. So …" She paused, catching her breath. Then she seemed to gather and tie up all her confusion and toss it aside. With a surge of resolution she declared: "I decided I had to do something to take control of my life."

As she spoke, Erin stared down at her high-heeled feet. Her tear-soaked eyelashes looked like arcs of tiny spikes, like the year's last icicles, like the jaws of a Venus fly-trap. Mascara had trickled down her cheeks, and her dabbing at her eyes with the tissue was leaving black blotches. She looked like a battered woman. If Priscilla Verhoven were here, she would make Erin a prize exhibit not of harassment but of abuse. How would Ms. Verhoven have critiqued the way he was handling this "situation"?

"I haven't talked to *my* parents in many years," McCauley said.

Erin looked up. "Why not?"

"I didn't live up to their expectations."

"You didn't?" She sipped her cola and asked, "Do you have a coaster or something?"

"Just put it on the table. It's okay." McCauley chuckled. "Something happened to me. I can't tell you any details; legally I'm not supposed to talk about it. But I was accused of doing something I didn't do. It was never proved, but to avoid a trial or any other kind of trouble I accepted a settlement. It didn't mean I was guilty, but my parents treated me as if I was."

"I don't get it. If you were innocent, why didn't you stick up for yourself?"

McCauley sighed and nodded.

"That's exactly what I say today. But back then I was young, and stupid, and afraid. Really afraid. The lawyers were circling around me like sharks. The easiest way out was to do what they wanted, because I was afraid to go to a trial and lose."

"But what did you do? *Hurt* somebody?"

"I can't tell you any details. But I hurt my*self.* I cheated myself out of one whole career that I loved."

"I don't get it. Why are you telling me all this—because I bad-mouthed my mom and dad?"

McCauley nodded, and Erin smiled feebly.

"I wanted you to know that I understand how much parents can hurt you."

"They're good parents, but ..."

"You don't need to defend them. I'm sure they're doing their best, just like we all are."

She sniffled and fell into another paroxysm of weeping.

"What? What is it?" McCauley asked, wondering what he had said to trigger the new tears.

"I didn't do *my* best. On that history project."

"No, I didn't think so."

"I was trying my best, but ..." More crying followed.

Eventually McCauley pried from Erin her explanation. She had paid her grandfather several visits, hoping to gather information from the nursing home officials about the history of that industry and service. But her good intentions always evaporated in the warm companionship of Grandpa Dee and his friends in the village. The last two times she had gone there, she had spent all her time just talking to the old folks.

"That's the part I liked best," she said, her face brightening. "I could sit with those people all day and watch their game shows on TV and play dominoes and backgammon and cribbage and cards and listen to them talk about the way things were back when they were kids."

Whatever the excuse, she had fallen so far behind that finally she had to dash off an inferior product that was two days late.

"I understand all that, Erin. But that doesn't explain, or excuse ... this." He indicated her coat and everything beneath it and behind her teary visit. "Why would you think you could come here and ... what? Work out a better grade?"

"Because everyone else cheats," she said with another swell of conviction. "Even Mrs. Hillis told me I knew what it takes to get good grades. And Mr. Myers. And I remembered what *you* said the first day of class." Her wet eyes, angry, almost vengeful, rose to confront him.

"What *I* said? What did *I* say?"

"You said my future was in your hands. You were saying it to the whole class, but you were looking right at me. I remember it."

"What are you talking about? I said that? I never said anything like that!" Suddenly he was fighting a fierce panic. If Erin spread that rumor, she *would* turn into a new Mary Ann Childress. He almost expected her to reach inside her fur coat, produce a list of witnesses, and calmly name her price for silence. Maybe the family lawyers were outside waiting.

"I remember you said it," she insisted. "That's why I came."

"Whatever I said," he tried to clarify, "you misunderstood. I would never say anything like that—not to mean what you thought it meant."

"Well, I'm sorry."

McCauley was not trying to extract an apology. He didn't expect one or need one, but hearing it was like escaping from a violent storm, stepping underneath the safe serenity of a dry canopy. His despair dissipated.

"Thank you," he said. "I'm sorry, too."

"But what about my grade?"

"Well, you're right about that. You didn't turn in a very good paper. But there is a way we can work it out. We'll let you borrow from your next-quarter grade."

"Borrow? What does that mean?"

He explained Tolan Myers's arcane, dubious method as though it were standard operating procedure. Erin was too clever to not notice the downside, though.

"What happens if I don't make it up third quarter?"

"Well, there's always fourth quarter."

"Then what?"

"Don't get too worried, okay? I've never had any trouble with this before."

"Okay."

"Now, what do you know about oral history? Have you ever heard of it?"

She shook her head.

"From what you were telling me about your grandfather and the other people in his retirement village, I think you would love to do an oral history project. We'll set something up when school starts again. I think you'll like it."

"Okay."

"Can I ask you a question, Erin? When you said that everyone cheated, what did you mean, exactly? Were you just exaggerating?"

"Well, not *everyone*. But more kids than you would ever think."

"Like, say in your class. How many cheat?"

"In history class?"

"Right."

"At least half."

"Really?"

"I hope you don't ask me to give you any names."

"No. Unless you want to."

"I'd rather not."

"Okay. I understand that."

"Nice Christmas tree," she said with more energy, pointing to the eighteen-inch artificial tree in the corner, a half-price special from Target that he had bought three years earlier but never put up until this year, spurred by the incentive of a gift from Robin to set under it.

Sometime during their talk the clocks and calendar pushed past midnight and nestled into January. Funny, he had not heard the chimes or any firecrackers or car horns or other noise from outside.

"I should get going," Erin said. "Matt will wonder where I am."

She stood up, holding her coat closed tightly.

"Here," McCauley said, picking up a barrette from the floor. "Don't forget this."

She laughed uneasily.

"I'd better walk you back to your car," he said.

"You don't have to—"

"I'd better. This is New Year's Eve, and … Come on." Erin had no clue how attractive she was, or how vulnerable she looked with her tear-streaked face, or how those factors might converge in the drunken vision of revelers she might meet outside. Still innocent, she would be a prime target on a college campus this night, with spirits flowing freely and inhibitions running low.

He escorted her to Matt's van.

"You're not planning on wearing this to ¿Que Pasa?, are you?"

"No, I have something else to put on in here."

"That's good. Well, I don't want to sound just like all adults, but the best thing you can do is put the pretty outfit away and save it for someone later in your life. Okay? Or do I sound like your parents?"

"My parents … I hope they never find out about this."

"I hope not, too. Happy New Year. I'll see you in a couple of weeks."

"Happy New Year."

Once she had disappeared around the corner, he trudged up the steps back to his apartment, worn out from the last hour, the sorry day, the departed year. All he could think about now was whether he would ever get a chance to tell Robin about Erin, and, if so, how to tell her. What would he say? *Nothing happened, but something happened.*

Shutting his front door and bolting the lock, he remembered how his heart had jumped at hearing the first faint taps. He placed his hand on his side of the door, cold through the fiberglass. Now that Erin was gone, he wished all the more fervently that his surprise visitor, bedecked in silky lingerie and willing to grant any favor, had been Robin Hillis.

That would never happen now.

The chorus of clocks tolled their intermingling 12:30 chimes while he flipped off the lights. He stripped off his clothes and slid into bed, where, as he drifted to sleep on the gentle ticking that ran together into a dreamy stream, he marveled at the palpable irony taking hold in the infancy of his new year. For all his professional over-the-shoulder focus, for all his emphasis on looking backward, he felt a kick of adrenaline as he looked forward to what lay ahead, to what the next six months of his life, professional or otherwise, held in store.

Contact Information

To order additional copies of this book, please visit
www.redemption-press.com.
Also available on Amazon.com and BarnesandNoble.com
Or by calling toll free 1-844-2REDEEM.

CPSIA information can be obtained
at www.ICGtesting.com
Printed in the USA
BVOW08s1134220118
505965BV00005B/589/P

9 781683 140153